STEALING FACES

ALSO BY MICHAEL PRESCOTT

Comes the Dark

Michael Prescott

STEALING FACES

A SIGNET BOOK

SIGNET
Published by New American Library, a division of
Penguin Putnam Inc., 375 Hudson Street, New York, New York 10014, U.S.A.
Penguin Books Ltd, 27 Wrights Lane, London W8 5TZ, England
Penguin Books Australia Ltd, Ringwood, Victoria, Australia
Penguin Books Canada Ltd, 10 Alcorn Avenue, Toronto, Ontario, Canada
M4V 3B2
Penguin Books (N.Z.) Ltd, 182–190 Wairau Road, Auckland 10, New Zealand

Penguin Books Ltd, Registered Offices:
Harmondsworth, Middlesex, England

First published by Signet, an imprint of New American Library,
a division of Penguin Putnam Inc.

Printed in the United States of America

ISBN: 0-7394-0610-8

ACKNOWLEDGMENTS

My thanks to all the people who helped in the preparation and production of this novel, including Joseph Pittman, senior editor at NAL; Michaela Hamilton, associate publisher; Laurie Parkin, sales manager; Carolyn Nichols, executive director; Louise Burke, publisher; and my literary agent, Jane Dystel. Their support, feedback, and energetic assistance were invaluable in making the book a reality. Writing is a solitary activity only in part; to an equal extent, it's a team effort—and I've got a good team behind me.

Readers are invited to visit my website at http://michaelprescott.freeservers.com/ where you'll find information on my previous book, *Comes the Dark*, as well as my E-mail address, book reviews, and other stuff. If for any reason the site has been moved by the time you read this, simply search for my name and this book's title in any major search engine.

—Michael Prescott

Light thickens,
And the crow makes wing to th' rooky wood;
Good things of day begin to droop and drowse,
Whiles night's black agents to their preys do rouse.

—Shakespeare, *Macbeth*

Prologue

She had been a person once.

Hours earlier, when she started her long run through the hills under the moonless sky, she'd had a name and a job and a son to live for.

All of that was gone now, and she was only a scratched and muddy animal crawling through tall stands of reeds along a stream bank.

She was instinct and reflex. Her world was a flow of sensation—the movement of her body, the rack of pain, the press of fear.

The chase had taken her dignity and her freedom of will, and the shock of the bullet in her leg had taken her memories and hopes. Blood loss and rising panic had done the rest.

Somewhere, not inside her but out there, apart from her and distant, a presence named Sharon Andrews hovered like a ghost. Sharon Andrews, thirty-four, divorced mother raising a seven-year-old boy named Todd, working five days a week as a receptionist in the showroom of Edison Auto Mart on East Speedway Boulevard in Tucson, Arizona.

This woman, this Sharon Andrews, had read dinosaur books to her son in the evenings. She had worried about the rent on their two-bedroom apartment when the alimony check was late. She had stopped at the local video store once a week to raid the bargain bin for Disney movies on sale, used, for $9.99. When she smiled, her mouth turned downward, and when she sneezed she said, *Excuse me,* even if she was alone.

This woman, this Sharon Andrews, had been all quirks and opinions and worries and loves and disappointments and ideas picked up from magazines and strange, lonely moods when she wondered about the infinite.

This woman did not exist anymore, and would never exist again.

Where she had been, there was the bloodied, wounded, tattered, desperate thing now splashing into the shallow stream, drawn there by an agonizing thirst and a need to soothe the burn of the bullet hole.

The streambed was slick, and her bare feet slipped in a groove of ooze. She fell in the water, inhaling some of it, gasping and retching, then struggled on.

She had no conscious reason to continue. She did not lash herself with *what-if* and *if-only*. She was aware of no plan, no strategy for survival, and nothing but fear had impelled her down the steep hillside to the stream.

A person might have imagined that the stream would erase her trail and throw off her pursuer, but there was no person now.

Sometimes limping, sometimes crawling, she splashed through ten inches of water, traveling with the current because she was too tired to resist it, covering distance she couldn't measure, running a race with an adversary she no longer clearly remembered.

The stream curved, narrowing. Somewhere a coyote sang to the night, its cry high-pitched and sad.

She'd heard it before, when she was Sharon Andrews. Then, she had ignored it, knowing coyotes were no threat to her, but now she knew nothing but direct perception and intuitive response, and the predator's song chilled her.

She ran faster and lost her footing again, coming down hard on the soft bank, spattered with muck, and abruptly all motion fled her, and she lay utterly still.

The night was large and silent, heavy with darkness. She looked at the sky. The stars had dimmed.

She did not understand that the leakage of blood from the hole in her leg had impaired her thinking and now even her vision.

She was aware of pain and weakness, hunger, and the fast feathery beating of her frightened heart.

This was all there was for her, this and the great stillness all around, the silence that stretched and stretched as if it might last forever.

The second bullet caught her in the hip.

She jerked with the impact, her eyes watering in surprise and pain.

Her hands found the bullet hole and felt the rush of sticky warmth suffusing her skirt. Blindly she tried to plug the hole with her fingers, but the effort was hopeless and she was much too tired.

She'd never even heard the gunshot—perhaps her startled yelp had covered the noise—but she heard the coyote again, keening a ululant song.

It was not a coyote, of course. It never had been.

It was him.

Some part of her registered this fact. She looked behind her and saw him striding along the bank of the stream, the pistol in his gloved hand.

If she had been Sharon Andrews, she would have known she was finished. Somehow she knew anyway, though her body fought against the knowledge, insisting on survival.

When he reached her, she was clawing feebly at the mud, straining to rise, but she would never rise. The second shot had shattered her hip and damaged the base of her spine, leaving her legs limp and unresponsive even as her upper body thrashed and flailed.

Crouching beside her, he touched the carotid artery at the side of her neck. She moaned.

"Quiet now," he said. "Quiet."

Roughly he turned her on her back.

A light snapped on, dim and red, a low-power flashlight with a red filter.

Swimming in the red haze was the blur of his face. He leaned close, studying her, his eyes narrowed and intense.

"Now I see you," he whispered. "Now I see you as you really are. I see the essence of you."

She heard words, but they meant nothing, they were only sounds, dull sounds. She was sleepy.

Her eyes were closing when she saw the knife.

He'd slipped it from a sheath at his waist. A long knife with a double-edged blade.

A last reflex of fear stiffened her.

"There, there." He set down the flashlight. "Be calm. This won't take long."

Then he was bending nearer, one hand on her chin, the other holding the knife against the tender hollow of her jaw.

"You wear a mask," he said. "All your life you've worn it."

His tone soothed her, a steady tone that stroked her in a calm caress.

"But not tonight. Tonight you've been unmasked. Tonight you're pretending no longer. Isn't it good, not to pretend? Isn't it right, to be real for once? To be only what you are?"

She didn't understand, but she knew there was only a little more to go, and she relaxed, waiting for it to be over.

"The process is almost complete. Just this last step, to make it official. The final stage of liberation from your stale disguise."

The knife point pricked her, but the pain was someone else's. Past his face, the night was growing darker.

"Are you ready? Ready to remove the mask?"

He knew there would be no answer. But she was indeed ready. He could tell.

And so was he.

The knife moved, slicing the soft flesh under her chin, and before she could resist or even scream, he took the loose skin flap in both hands and in a single practiced motion he peeled off her face.

PART ONE

NIGHT'S BLACK AGENT

1

On a Monday evening in September, five months after he had hunted Sharon Andrews in the southern foothills of the White Mountains, John Cray drove into Tucson in search of a fresh kill.

It was a long drive, one he enjoyed, especially when the sun was westering, its light golden on the hills and desert flats. He headed south on Route 191 toward Interstate 10. The highway was uncrowded. A few pickup trucks shot past in the northbound lane, and far behind him sparkled a glimmer of sun on a chrome fender, but otherwise he was alone.

Solitude suited him. Cray was hemmed in by people throughout the day, even on weekends. The work never stopped, it was frustrating and demoralizing, and there was so rarely any relief.

But he would find relief tonight.

The road passed lightly under him. Ruts and potholes were smoothed away by a precision suspension system, and the engine's soft hum disappeared behind the controlled violence of Mahler's Eighth on the CD player. Cray settled deeper into the leather seat and felt care leave him.

He had paid more than $50,000 for these niceties,

without regret. The salesman at the Lexus dealership had assured him that the LX 470 was the finest sport-utility vehicle on the market, exceeding even the rival Mercedes model. It was, he'd said, the perfect choice for the driver who would not sacrifice comfort, yet required the capability to travel off-road.

Cray required that capability. He had not told the salesman why.

As he approached the interstate, he noticed that the car with the chrome fender was still behind him, a mile in the distance, maintaining a steady rate of speed.

The freeway took him southwest, then curved north into Tucson. Downtown's modest skyline passed on his right, a few medium-high office towers, tiers of windows glazed red with the sunset. Around the city lay the mountains, range upon range, pasted against the deepening cobalt of the sky.

Just north of the city limits, Cray turned off the interstate and traveled through the Catalina foothills on Ina Road.

The sun was in his rearview mirror now, and only night lay ahead.

Resort hotels were scattered among the steep canyons and high ridges of the foothills. He chose an older one, recently renovated, a place unlikely to be too crowded in September. The tourist season did not start until the heat abated, and in the desert, summer lingered an extra month or two.

The parking lot near the lobby was largely empty. Cray parked the Lexus in a corner spot, away from the light poles. He did not want the vehicle to be noticed and perhaps remembered.

He was careful. Experience had made him wise. In twelve years of nocturnal adventures, he had slipped up only once.

Still, his one mistake had been recent enough to make him doubly cautious now.

From his studies of criminal psychopathology, he understood that self-control was critical to his continued success. The ones who got caught, the ones whose names the public knew, almost invariably were betrayed by their own spiraling appetites. They went faster, abandoned caution, pushed the envelope of risk, and lost everything.

Whenever one of them was apprehended, the fool was always stupidly surprised to discover he had covered his tracks less carefully than he'd imagined. It was apparent in the suspect's face, captured in shaky close-up by a handheld news camera: the dull astonishment at having been arrested, the incredulity at finding himself no better or no smarter than those who'd come before.

Cray knew he could fall victim to the same hubris. Still, he *was* better.

He was more intelligent than most others who enjoyed similar pastimes, and his needs, though intense, had not ossified into obsessions. He could avoid the obvious, costly mistakes that recklessness would breed.

But even he could not hold out indefinitely against the urgings of his deepest nature. Months might pass, or even a year or two, and then one day he would feel it again, too strong to resist: the itch in his fingers, the insomnia, the sexual arousal that kept him hot and agitated.

He had felt it for the past three weeks, stronger with

every passing day. So here he was, a wolf in a sheep's mask, stalking the witless flock.

Before leaving home, he'd shed his business suit in favor of his standard nighttime ensemble. He was dressed entirely in black. Black boots, black denim slacks, black long-sleeve shirt.

His shirt collar was buttoned, though he wore no tie, and his dark hair was slicked back. Lately his hair was sparser than it had been, and his hairline had begun to recede. His forehead was pale and smooth, like a skull.

The black ensemble gave him a mildly dangerous edge, but his face was that of any other man in middle age who worked hard and bore up patiently under life's load. A nice face, people would say: a kind and thoughtful face. And they would wonder why he had never married, what private heartache kept him solitary at the age of forty-six.

Sometimes, gazing in a mirror, he glimpsed the reality behind the persona, his living soul behind the public mask. It glimmered in his eyes, gray-green eyes, amber-flecked, which had looked deeply into the essence of things, eyes that did not flinch from horror.

His eyes were not nice or kind or thoughtful. Anyone who had seen those eyes, really seen them, would no longer wonder why he was unmarried.

As he crossed the parking lot in the sunset's afterglow, the air, desert-dry, brushed the nape of his neck like a caress of velvet.

Adjacent to the lobby was a bar and grill, a place of soft music and glimmering candles, uncrowded at this hour. Cray took a window table and ordered a margarita, then watched the fading sunset and the growing dark.

The mountains vanished into the night. But the city remained, a spread of twinkling color, large and misty.

Cray looked at the lights for a long time, lifting his glass now and then to taste the tequila's soothing burn. It was not the lights that fascinated him. It was his awareness of the people represented by those lights, a half million people or more, with different names and different backgrounds, strangers to one another, living, struggling, dying, each one an individual.

Yet how easily their individuality could be discarded. And if it could be stripped away, then was it even real?

Or was it only a disguise, a persona—complex and subtle, yes, rich with nuance, elaborately refined, but nonetheless a mere facade?

Cray looked toward the long mahogany bar at the front of the room. A man in tapered jeans and a big-buckled Western belt had just mounted a bar stool beside an unescorted woman in an invitingly short skirt.

The man would say something, and the woman would respond. Perhaps he would offer to buy her a drink; perhaps she would agree. He would compliment her dress or her hair or her eyes, and she would ask what he did for a living.

The two of them operated purely on instinct and reflex. Every move, every word, every detail of their grooming had been prompted by the unconscious emulation of others or the irresistible pull of instinctual drives.

The man wore those jeans and that belt because he had seen other men wearing them; imitative as a monkey, he had bought them for himself.

He had come to a bar because it was where other

people would come. He had taken the empty seat beside the woman because this too was the action that was expected of him.

His conversational gambits had been picked up from movies or TV shows or from dialogue he'd overheard in other bars—nothing original, lines spoken by strangers, who in turn copied behavior they had witnessed elsewhere.

The ritual of offering to buy a drink, of making some cheap and obvious toast, of clinking glasses, all of it was a show played out countless times by countless others.

And if the woman allowed him to take her home, she would do so only because it was expected of her, because she had been raised in a culture that permitted and slyly approved of such behavior; she would be fitting herself seamlessly into the social framework that had shaped her.

The only honest part of what either of them did was their instinctive need for sexual relief, and this was a need they shared with every animal.

Cray had heard much about the dignity of man, but what he had seen was only the vacant thoughtlessness of a herd. The mind was largely an illusion; the great majority of people were, for all practical purposes, unconscious most of the time. Their conscious minds, if functional at all, served only to provide a veneer of rationalization for behavior patterns already prompted by social conditioning and instinct.

Cray considered the woman in the short skirt, and saw a mandrill, her buttocks flaming red in sexual heat. He studied the man dutifully attempting to seduce her, and saw a rutting gorilla driven by the need to establish himself as the alpha male.

Those two were random examples. He could have focused on anyone around him and seen the same. There were exceptions, but they were rare. In his life he had found only one person able to understand, really understand.

One person besides himself.

"Sir? Would you like to see our dinner menu?"

A waitress had paused by the table, smiling at him from under a raft of loose auburn hair. Her name tag read DEBBI.

"Not quite yet," Cray said. "Perhaps you could bring me another drink."

"Right away." Her smile brightened, and she shook her ringlets of red hair as she walked away.

Cray watched her go. She was most cheerful, a healthy and vital young animal, but he wondered how long her high spirits would last if he took her into the mountains tonight and used her for sport.

The prospect did not entice him. He could do better. Debbi the waitress was too youthful and unformed to be really interesting. It was preferable to select a mature specimen, ripe for harvest.

He needed to find a woman who was alone, or who could be separated from her party. He would target his victim, trail her to her home or hotel room, then carry out the abduction. He would find a way to do it quietly.

Cray let his gaze travel around the room. A fair number of the tables had filled up since his arrival.

In a general sense he knew what he was looking for, but he had no precise image in mind. She might be tall or short, blonde or brunette or red-haired. She might be of any race. He liked them slender, never younger than sixteen or older than forty-five, but those were his only criteria.

Most of the patrons around him were couples, but a pair of unattached women sat at the bar, talking to the bartender and watching *Monday Night Football* on a large, muted TV.

There were no other solitary women in sight . . . except one, seated in a far corner.

Cray glimpsed her face, half-concealed behind a wide-brimmed straw hat. For an instant she seemed to meet his gaze, and then she averted her head slightly, a movement so subtle as to be almost natural.

"Here you go." Debbi the waitress, returning with Cray's second margarita.

He accepted it with thanks, then held the cold glass in his hand.

It was a hand that trembled now, only a little, and not so obviously that anyone would notice. He sat motionless, afraid to lift the drink and perhaps spill it. He studied the distant city in the window.

To the southwest he could see the lighted towers of downtown Tucson. Downtown, yes, where he'd gone on Saturday night, only forty-eight hours ago.

A street fair had drawn him there, a monthly bacchanal that attracted throngs of students from the university and other locals in search of fun and distraction. The scene had been crowded and noisy. Bands played on street corners, a blare of drums and amplified guitars and caterwauling voices. People threw money into open guitar cases at the musicians' feet, because it was expected of them.

University students, back for the fall semester, yelled primal challenges at the night sky. Here and there a juggler or a magician would attract an audience, as their counterparts had done in medieval markets and Roman festivals.

Human nature never changed, because at its root it was not human at all. It was something older.

Cray had been musing on this as he wended, supple as smoke, through the noise and shadow-flicker of the crowd. The subject often occupied him. He had written a book, well received, to explore part of it—the less dangerous part. The title had been *The Mask of Self*.

He'd thought of masks as his eyes, narrowed and alert, scanned the swirl of faces around him. What part of these people was unique? Not their attire or grooming, their mores and tastes, not even their thoughts. What, then? Their souls? And what was the soul, if not the primordial part of them, predating words and ego? What was the soul, if not the beast within?

Yet they did not release the beast. They kept it caged and hidden. They hid it even from themselves. They wore masks, all of them, masks of flesh—smiling or frowning masks, as unreal as the stylized faces worn by Roman actors in the last decadent days of Empire.

He saw those masks and yearned to strip them off and see the bare truth beneath, the truth that was blood and fear and a racing heartbeat.

And then he had seen her.

Only fleetingly, a pale face in the swarm.

Blonde hair, a slim neck, white arms.

She was gone almost before he registered her existence. But in the instant of eye contact between them, he had sensed something, a frisson of mutual excitement.

He wanted her.

She was the one.

But she'd vanished. Though he looked for hours, elbowing his way through the masses of strangers, he had not spotted her again.

Until tonight.

The woman in the corner, with the straw hat that almost hid her face . . .

A pale face. And beneath the hat, a wisp of blonde hair.

It was the same woman.

He was certain.

He wanted to believe that this second sighting was a coincidence. But to believe in coincidence required faith.

Cray had no faith. He did not believe.

There was, then, no explanation for her presence except the obvious one.

He remembered the glint of chrome behind him on Route 191. The car that had maintained a steady distance from his Lexus, mile after mile.

Her car. It must have been.

She had followed him to the street fair. She had followed him to this resort.

She must be staking out his home and tailing him whenever he left.

She was . . . *stalking* him.

Cray peered into the salt-rimmed margarita glass, turning the thought over and over, marveling at it, fascinated and afraid. It made no sense. The very idea was preposterous, an inversion of the normal order of things.

He knew who and what he was. He was a predator. More than that—the essence of all predators. He was cruelty and stealth, he was hunger, he was quickness in the night. He was rapacity personified, the universal wolf. He hunted and he killed, and to him screams were music.

No one hunted him.

He was not prey. That role was left to others who could play it better. Who had played it again and again on many secret nights, year after year.

Others, like the woman across the room.

He watched her without turning his head, using peripheral vision. At a distance of thirty feet her profile was hard to discern clearly. She had a round, childish face, and her blonde hair was tied back in a ponytail. Her small, pale hands fidgeted on the table. She crossed and uncrossed her legs, reached tentatively for her drink and then pulled away.

Nervous. Vulnerable.

A deer at a water hole.

And he—he was the lion in the tall grass.

Yet tonight the deer stalked the lion.

He could almost understand it if she were a cop. But an undercover cop was a professional, trained to shadow a suspect without being noticed. This woman's technique was clumsy. Twice, on two separate nights, she had looked directly at him and caught his gaze.

She was no cop. She was an amateur.

If she knew or even suspected who he was, then why not call the police, tip them off, let them handle it?

Well.

He would have to ask her, that's all.

Cray relaxed, his frown of concentration easing into a smooth, unreadable expression again.

Things were fine. No problem. He had needed a victim, hadn't he? Now he had one.

Before he played with her, he would make her talk. She would tell him everything. Then he would start her running, and he would follow, predator and prey in their proper roles again.

He had not yet touched his second margarita. Calm now, he lifted the glass and licked salt from the rim, then settled back in his chair and mouthed a silent toast to the mystery woman.

To your health.

2

Elizabeth Palmer watched the man at the window table as he finished his second drink. She was relieved to note that he'd looked in her direction only once. If he had noticed her, if he'd recognized her from one of the previous nights, then surely he would have sneaked another glance her way.

Her fingers tapped nervously on the tabletop until she became aware of their senseless drumming and made herself stop.

She was probably safe. Wearing different clothes, her face shielded by a hat, her corner table in shadow, she must look like a different woman to him.

Or maybe she was just kidding herself.

She'd known there was a good chance she would be spotted eventually. She could beat the odds for a while, but not forever. And if Cray was on to her . . .

She didn't like to think about that possibility. If Cray was the man she feared he was, then her fate would be the same as that of the other women.

Elizabeth couldn't guess exactly what he did with them, what sort of mental or physical torture he inflicted before the kill, but it would be bad, and there would be no escape.

And at the end, of course, he would take his victim's face.

The thought chilled her. She hugged herself. She had thin, pale, lightly freckled arms prone to goose bumps, and she held them tight against her body, her wrists crossed over her small, shy breasts.

Being in the same room with him was hard. She wanted to get up and run, as she had run from him once before.

Was she crazy to have run so far, and for so long, and now to seek him out and risk everything, merely to confirm a suspicion that might be groundless?

You must be really brave, Elizabeth, she told herself. Or really, really stupid.

Maybe it would have been better not to enter the bar at all. She could have waited outside, hoping to catch Cray when he left.

But she'd tried that strategy a week ago, after tailing him to a bikers' bar on Tucson's dangerous south side, and when he departed, she'd nearly missed him.

She couldn't afford to take that risk. Didn't dare let him out of her sight.

Because, if her suspicion was correct, he was getting ready to try something.

She could almost feel it, sense it, as surely as she could sometimes sense the gathering electricity in the air before a summer thunderstorm.

She touched the purse in her lap, feeling the small hard shape of the most important item inside, simply to reassure herself that it was there.

Surreptitiously she studied Cray. She had not been this close to her quarry at any time since her return to Tucson.

He had been thirty-four when she'd first known him. He was forty-six now. His profile was sharper, more angular, than she recalled. He'd lost weight, but although lean, he was far from scrawny. His long shirt-sleeves did not quite conceal the sinewy muscles of his arms, and his tapered slacks wrapped his strong thighs and calves like a second skin.

Black shirt, black pants. He'd worn the same outfit every time she'd followed him. He was a man in silhouette, a living cutout of the night.

Last Saturday, shadowing Cray in the hectic downtown streets, catching glimpses of him in the crush of people, she'd seen the way he carried himself—the long, liquid strides, the loose swing of his wide shoulders, and always his head turning slowly from side to side as he scanned the crowd.

He had reminded her of a panther, sleek and black and lethal, a hungry animal on the hunt. She'd imagined he was sniffing the air, picking up the scent of prey.

But of course she could be all wrong about him. That was the thing to keep in mind. John Bainbridge Cray might never have killed anyone.

In the whole time she had watched him, he'd done nothing worse than make a few forays to Tucson nightspots. On such outings he was always alone, which was unusual, and he kept to himself in crowded places, never seeking company.

But aloofness was no crime. Eccentricity was no crime.

Even what he'd done to her, so many years ago . . .

No, even that was not a crime. Or, if it was, it was a crime for which there was no name, a crime that could never be proved.

Her fingers were drumming the table again. She stopped herself. Her hands were always doing that, fidgeting and worrying at things. Restless, undisciplined hands.

She supposed they suited her. She was always on the move too, wasn't she? And always nervous, always on edge.

She felt someone looking at her and glanced up, afraid that it was Cray, but it was only the bartender, yards away, polishing a glass. He'd smiled at her when she entered, inviting conversation. She had ignored him, anxious to take her seat before Cray saw her. Apparently her indifference had left him undeterred.

She couldn't imagine why he was interested in her. She had never thought of herself as particularly attractive. Her eyes were pretty—men liked blue eyes—but her mouth was too small, and her cheeks were too round, and she had too many freckles.

At nineteen she'd been cute, she supposed. Justin had thought so when he married her. Still, nineteen had been long ago. She was thirty-one now and felt older, and whenever she looked in a mirror, she wondered just who it was she saw.

Her gaze shifted away from the bartender. She glanced at Cray again.

He had half-turned in his chair, reaching behind him, his hand in his back pocket, and she realized he was taking out his wallet. Apparently he wasn't staying for dinner. He meant to pay for his drinks and leave.

To follow him would be too obvious. She had to exit first.

Elizabeth fumbled in her purse, found a bill that was

either a five or a ten, dropped it on the table. If it was a ten, she was overpaying by a rather serious margin for her glass of ginger ale, but there was no time to worry about it. No time, even though ordinarily she would almost rather die than throw away money, having so little to spare.

She eased her chair away from the table, afraid to scrape the legs on the bare floor and draw Cray's attention. Then swiftly she crossed the room to the exit, merely nodding at the bartender when he waved good-bye.

On the TV behind him, the football game continued. The Panthers were slaughtering the Saints. Not a good sign.

Elizabeth entered the lobby, then paused, pretending to adjust her purse while she glanced over her shoulder. Through the glass door she saw Cray rising from his chair, scattering bills on the table.

He would be out here in a moment.

Once in the lobby, he might leave via the front door, which led to the driveway, or via the rear door, which opened onto the terrace. There were other possibilities. He might go to the gift shop or find a rest room. She had to wait and see, but she would be too conspicuous just standing here.

"Help you, ma'am?"

The question startled her. She glanced at the front desk and saw the clerk watching her with a courteously unreadable expression.

Cray must be approaching the exit. He would be right on top of her in seconds.

She had to do something.

"Yes," she answered. "At least I hope you can."

She walked quickly to the desk, having no idea what she was about to say.

The clerk smiled. "We're here to serve. What can I do for you?"

"Well, I was just wondering . . . Does the hotel have a tennis club? I mean, a private club for local residents to join?"

She wondered where that inquiry had come from. She'd never played tennis in her life, and there was no private club of any kind that she could possibly afford to join.

The clerk nodded. "As a matter of fact, we do. I may have a brochure here someplace."

He shuffled through some documents, and she leaned close, averting her face from the door to the bar.

When she heard a rustle of displaced air, she knew the door had opened.

Cray was in the lobby with her. She forced herself not to look up, not to betray the slightest concern.

"Sorry," the clerk said. "I seem to have mislaid it. But you can get the information at the tennis center. They're open until nine."

"I'll do that."

At the edge of her vision, the door to the rear terrace opened, and a figure in black passed through.

He'd gone outside.

Once he left the immediate area, he could go anywhere on the resort's spacious grounds, and she might never track him down.

She stepped away from the desk, saying a quick thank-you.

"Do you need directions?" the clerk asked.

"I think I know where to find it." Hurrying for the terrace.

"That's the wrong way, ma'am."

"I can find it." Move, move.

"But that's the wrong—"

She pushed open the door and emerged onto the terrace, and at the desk, the clerk shook his head slowly.

He was not actually a clerk. His proper title was night manager. He saw all sorts of people come and go. Sometimes he thought of writing a book about it. He had a degree in English literature from the University of Arizona, for all the good it had done him.

Most of the people who stopped at the desk could be sized up easily enough, but the woman in the straw hat intrigued him, and not just because she was pretty and her voice was the type he liked—hushed and shy and faintly smoky, a bedroom voice.

She had been lying, of course. She had no interest in the tennis club. He doubted she could afford it. She was wearing a yellow blouse and a white skirt, a summer outfit not quite appropriate for late September, even in the desert heat. The blouse was faded, and the skirt had begun to fray at the hem.

He was a writer, or at least he liked to think so, and he had been told that writers noticed such things.

But none of that was the reason she intrigued him.

It was some quality in her eyes, her face, something that lay behind her quick smile and bright demeanor. Something like . . . desperation.

And as he recalled from one of his many English classes, the root word of *desperation* was *despair*.

3

Elizabeth emerged from the lobby into the balmy night, sure that Cray would be moving fast, nearly out of sight.

But he surprised her. He stood at the railing, absorbed in the view of the city.

She stopped outside the door, once again at a loss for anything inconspicuous to do.

Damn. She just wasn't very good at this.

Sneaking around, hiding from sight, spying on a man like Cray—there were people who could do such things, but Elizabeth Palmer was not one of them.

At any moment Cray might turn, and then he would see her. He couldn't do anything to her, not in a public place, but once he knew she was after him, she would not be safe again, ever.

All right. Think.

There were two routes he could take when he was done admiring the view. He could return to the lobby or descend to the swimming pool.

Gambling on the second outcome, Elizabeth walked quickly to the steps and headed down, never looking back.

Two children splashed in the shallow end of the pool. A thirtyish couple, no doubt the kids' parents, shared drinks at a poolside table, laughing softly at some intimate joke. An older man lounged in a foaming spa nearby, a white cap tilted on his head. The moon was out, white and full, and woven around it was a vast wreath of stars.

Briefly Elizabeth wished she could just stop here, recline on a lounge chair and forget everything she knew and everything she suspected.

Let Cray go. Let the world fix its own problems; God knew, she had enough problems of her own. It would be so good to rest, and she'd had so little rest in the last twelve years.

She did, in fact, sit on a lounge chair, but only to rummage through her purse in an elaborate pretense of looking for some lost item.

The ruse was getting old, and she was beginning to worry that she had miscalculated about where Cray was likely to go, when she heard footsteps on the stairs.

His footsteps. She knew it, even without looking. Footsteps that were quick and light, preternaturally nimble.

A flicker of black, and he passed the spot where she was seated, heading down a pathway.

She got up and followed.

Part of her knew it was reckless to press her luck any further. In the crowded street fair the risk had been acceptable. Here at the resort there was too much open space. She was liable to be seen at any time.

But she had to do it. This was her responsibility, and hers alone. The whole city was afraid of the man who'd murdered Sharon Andrews, but only Elizabeth might know his name.

The path was lit by small lanterns at ground level, glowing like the luminaria set out at Christmas in many local neighborhoods. The ambient light blended with the pale radiance of the moon. She could see Cray easily, fifty feet ahead.

He passed between two buildings. Someone sat on a second-floor balcony smoking a cigarette. Through a ground-floor window a TV was visible, casting a blue flicker on a large bed with an ornate headboard.

Elizabeth thought of the motel where she was staying. The bed sagged, the TV didn't work, the toilet had a funny smell. In the afternoons she heard noises of frantic passion through the walls; the adjacent rooms seemed to be booked by the hour. For this opulence she was paying nineteen dollars a night.

She wondered what it cost to stay at this resort for just one day. As much as she could earn in a week, probably—if she had a job. Which, at the moment, she did not.

Cray seemed to know where he was going. Elizabeth kept her distance as he crossed from one path to another, skirting a second swimming pool, smaller and less busy than the first.

On the prowl. He hadn't found what he wanted in downtown Tucson's crowded streets, so he was looking here. Hunting prey.

She couldn't imagine how he meant to handle the abduction, but he would find a way. He had experience in such things.

Or perhaps he was just a lonely man taking a nighttime stroll on the landscaped grounds of a resort. Perhaps he had no sinister purpose.

She wanted to believe this. She wanted to leave Tucson and resume the life she'd led, and to feel no pang of conscience on sleepless nights.

Ahead, Cray went down a short flight of steps and disappeared amid the mesquite trees and weedy underbrush. A sign read FITNESS TRAIL.

Elizabeth hesitated at the top of the staircase. The trail seemed empty and dark. A good place for an ambush. Suppose he had seen her in the bar, after all. Suppose he was deliberately leading her here, to the edge of the resort, away from more public places.

Well, she was ready for that.

She opened her purse and reached inside for the Colt .22 she'd bought at a pawnshop after arriving in Tucson. It was a small gun, lightweight but fully loaded, and she knew how to use it.

She had used a gun once before.

The thought made her tremble, and for a moment she worried that she couldn't go forward, that the old memories might swamp and capsize her, as they sometimes did.

Not tonight. Tonight she had to be strong.

There might be a life at stake, the life of some woman who was a guest at this hotel, a woman who would be kidnapped and killed and buried in the wilderness, like Sharon Andrews.

She slung the purse over her shoulder to free her hands. Holding the Colt down at her side, out of sight, she descended the staircase and advanced along the trail.

Immediately she spotted him. He was not lying in wait for her. He was moving quickly, at a brisk walk, perhaps working off the effects of the two drinks. She followed, taking care not to make a sound.

Foliage hemmed in the trail on both sides. Moonlight glistened on cactus needles, pale as ice. A saguaro, its thick arms outspread against the sky, loomed like a monument in the night.

Cray increased his pace, almost jogging.

She hurried to catch up, but she couldn't run without being overheard.

The trail curved. Cray shrank and vanished, lost to sight behind stands of prickly-pear cactus and palo verde trees.

She risked a short sprint, hoping to close part of the distance between them, and then she rounded the curve and stopped.

Dead end.

The trail finished here.

And she was alone.

But she couldn't be. Cray had to be somewhere nearby.

Unless he'd left the trail and continued through the brush, and why would he do that?

He must be hiding.

This *was* an ambush. Had to be. He'd led her to this desolate spot, and he meant to strike.

Her gun came up, gripped in both hands, and she spun in a full circle, then back again, daring the darkness to attack her.

There was only silence and the strange, pensive stillness of the desert in moonlight.

If Cray was here, watching her, he had not chosen to show himself. Maybe the gun had scared him. Or did he have a gun of his own, a silenced pistol, and even now was he drawing a bead on her, ready to take her down with one shot . . . ?

She had to get away, get away now.

The gun was shaking in her hands. He must be laughing at her. Enjoying her stupid panic even as he lined her up in his sights.

She took a backward step, then turned to confront him if he was behind her, but he wasn't, and she ran three yards down the trail and turned again, certain she had heard him or heard something, but there was no noise, no movement, and finally she couldn't take it any longer and she broke into a reckless run, gasping as she retraced her route along the trail in a blur of moonlight.

Once or maybe twice she blundered off the path, and sharp teeth bit her, teeth that were cactus spines or the pointed tips of agave leaves. Pain surprised her but did not slow her down.

She was out of breath and shaking all over when she reached the staircase and climbed back to the path.

Amid the lights of buildings and pathways she remembered the gun in her hand. Clumsily she stuffed it in her purse, leaving the clasp unfastened so she could grab the .22 instantly if she needed it.

Voices floated to her—a family walking back to their room. The same family she'd seen earlier, the kids in the swimming pool and the parents drinking at a poolside table.

As they passed her, the father looked at her strangely, and the younger child, giggling, was shushed by his mom. Elizabeth didn't understand until she stopped at a fountain and caught her reflection in the water.

She was a mess. She'd lost her straw hat somewhere on the trail, and her hair was windblown and tangled and studded with broken bits of leaves, and her face was inflamed with a wild-eyed, panicky stare that almost scared her.

She looked like a street person or a drug addict—or perhaps just a girl who'd had a good roll in the hay.

The thought coaxed a smile from her. She relaxed a little, then stiffened again, superstitiously afraid that by lowering her guard she had invited an attack.

But there was nothing.

"Stop it," she whispered to herself. "You're driving yourself crazy."

These were not the right words to use. She regretted them as soon as they were spoken. They touched a part of her that was still tender, still too easily liable to be hurt.

She sat on the rim of the fountain and combed out her hair, allowing herself to be soothed by the simple, repetitive chore.

Then she set off once more, searching the hotel grounds.

Cray was here. Somewhere.

She would find him.

4

But she didn't.

She wandered up and down the network of paths for more than two hours, the purse clutched tight, the little Colt within instant reach. She found the tennis courts, lit up but deserted. She climbed the stairs to an observation deck and found it empty as well.

Cray was not loitering near any of the three swimming pools, he was not in the restaurant or in the bar, and the gift shop and the wellness center were closed.

She even dared to try the fitness trail again, venturing along its entire length. Cray was not there either.

At the trail's dead end, where she had panicked before, she forced herself to probe the brush. With a pocket flashlight she swept a cone of amber light over cholla cactus and wild purple sage. She found no shoe prints, no sign of human passage.

It was as if Cray had vanished into air. As if he had never existed at all.

She didn't like that thought.

Briskly she doubled back along the trail. She wasn't sure quite where she was headed until she found herself approaching the lobby.

Then she knew that she meant to check out the parking lot.

She wanted to see Cray's SUV, the fancy Lexus he drove, because the vehicle was something real and tangible, and it would prove that Cray was real also.

The Lexus was black, of course, like Cray's ensemble. Somehow he kept it spotless even in the desert, where dust and rainstorms competed to dull any automobile's finish. From the first time she'd seen it, she had thought the vehicle suited him. It suggested both civilized refinement and a dangerous addiction to thrills, and it seemed at home in the night.

And now it was gone.

A red Fiat was parked in the space the Lexus had formerly occupied.

Elizabeth looked at the Fiat, turned away, then looked again. A shiver ran through her, and for a dizzy moment she was sure she was losing her mind.

Cray wasn't here.

He'd never been here.

She had been pursuing a phantom all night long. A delusion, something conjured by her brain, not part of external reality at all, and suddenly she felt it again—the disorienting awareness of a gap between her mind and her environment, between consciousness and reality, and as she stood unmoving, the gap widened and became a chasm, and into it she was falling, falling. . . .

Head lowered, eyes squeezed shut, she forgot everything except the need for calm.

Time was suspended. She was not herself. She was only a stretch of blankness with no body, no mind.

Then finally the panic was gone, and she was all right, not crazy, and the world had not strayed from its orbit.

There was still no Lexus, only the red Fiat, but that was fine. Because, of course, there was an explanation. A very sensible explanation.

Cray had left.

That was all. So simple.

He had been here, she really had seen him and followed him, and he really had disappeared somehow in the dark, but there was nothing supernatural about it, nothing to upset the balance of her mind.

He had simply returned to the parking lot and driven away. He could be anywhere now. She would not find him again tonight.

And although she knew she ought to be sorry she had lost him, she was too tired to feel any regret. She wanted only to go back to her sordid little motel room and lie on the sagging bed and stare at the busted TV until sleep came.

Tomorrow night she would follow Cray again, from his home. Tomorrow, when she had the strength.

Nodding in assent to this plan, Elizabeth crossed the parking lot to the far corner, where she had left her car, a 1981 Chevrolet Chevette with 92,000 miles on an odometer that doubtless had passed the 100,000 mark at least twice. The four-cylinder engine was held together with spit and paper clips. Every part of the car rattled. The seat belts were broken and the ventilation ducts were clogged.

The hatchback had cost $350 when she bought it two years ago in a liquidation sale at a car lot in Flagstaff. The salesman had seemed ashamed to sell it to her, but she could afford nothing better. Remarkably, the Chevette had proven reliable enough.

She unlocked the door on the driver's side and sank

behind the wheel, then jerked upright with the sudden certainty that Cray was in the car with her, in the backseat, waiting to take her by surprise—

He was not in the backseat.

He was nowhere.

"Oh, quit it," she snapped, tired of herself. "Just cut it the hell out."

She keyed the ignition, and instantly the car began to shake like a washing machine on the spin cycle. With an unsteady hand Elizabeth rolled down the window to get some air.

Pulling out of the lot, she cast another look at the red Fiat, which was still a Fiat, not a Lexus SUV.

Cray really was gone.

She'd done her best, but he had slipped away. There was nothing more she could do. Nothing.

Except, of course, there was.

5

Elizabeth Palmer.

Cray repeated the name silently in the confines of his Lexus, over the low hum of the engine.

Elizabeth Palmer.

A reasonably mellifluous name. One he was likely to remember, if he had ever heard it before.

He tried it aloud: "Elizabeth Palmer."

The taste of the words in his mouth was sweet and subtle and forbidden. He liked it.

He was driving down Oracle Road, the highway that descended from the outskirts of the Catalina foothills into Tucson's downtown. Traffic had worsened in the city throughout the past decade, and tonight, at nearly eleven o'clock, his SUV was part of an endless flow of cars and pickup trucks, while the northbound lanes to his left were a thick mass of headlights.

Ordinarily he disliked city traffic. It made him grateful to live far from town, thirty miles to the east, where the roads at night were dark and quiet under the undimmed stars.

But tonight the congested streets were helpful to him. He would have found it difficult to follow Elizabeth Palmer on an empty road. She might have seen his headlights, as he'd seen the glint of her chrome.

She would never notice him now. He could follow her as far along Oracle as he pleased, keeping her red hatchback just within sight.

No doubt she was heading home—wherever home might be. He was curious about that. He would be able to tell a good deal about her simply from her residence. And once he had subdued her, he could search the place, comb through any file cabinets or desk drawers, learn who she was and what she was after.

His desire to see where she lived was one reason he had chosen not to attack her at the resort. The other was simple prudence. Though he might have surprised her on the fitness trail and rendered her unconscious, he would have had difficulty removing her from the hotel grounds without being seen.

And to kill her at the hotel and leave her there would be too great a risk. Someone might remember that she had left the bar soon after he had, that she had walked in the same direction he had taken.

No, it was better to abduct her from her home, interrogate her in solitude, and when the night's sport was done, leave her body in the desert for the turkey vultures to find.

After losing her on the fitness trail, he had quickly doubled back to the parking lot. Since obviously she had followed him, it seemed safe to surmise that her car was parked near his own.

He'd moved his Lexus to another part of the complex, and from a hill he had watched the lot until the woman returned, hatless now, and wary. She must have spent two hours looking for him. Good. He wanted her tired, frustrated, not thinking clearly.

She got into a Chevrolet Chevette, the oldest and most unprepossessing vehicle in the parking area. Irrationally he was disappointed. He'd expected her to drive something better.

Before she left, he trained a pair of collapsible binoculars on the car, and in the light of a sodium-vapor lamp, he read her license plate. An Arizona plate, battered and soiled like the car itself.

He departed from the resort when she did, and followed her at a safe distance, listening to a handheld radio he kept in his glove compartment. The cheap speaker crackled with police codes.

Cray had purchased the radio from a black-market dealer who advertised on the Internet. Commercially available scanners only received police frequencies, but this radio was a transceiver; it transmitted on police bands. Cray could talk to the police.

As the hatchback pulled onto Oracle, Cray had heard a Tucson PD traffic unit call in a ten-seven. The officer was going on a break. Cray had waited a minute or two, to be sure the cop was out of his car and safely preoccupied. Then he pushed the transmit button.

"Traffic five-six," he said in a neutral voice. "Can you, uh, ten-twenty-eight a stoplight?"

"Go ahead, five-six," the dispatcher said.

Cray recited the hatchback's license number. There was silence as the request was processed.

He was sure the dispatcher suspected nothing. His only worry was that the traffic cop might still be monitoring the frequency. If so, he would have heard his unit number, Traffic 5-6, and would alert Dispatch to the scam.

Most likely, however, the cop was using a public rest

room or ordering a Big Mac and fries, or engaged in some equivalent proletarian distraction, and paying no attention to his radio at all.

"Traffic five-six," the dispatcher said.

Cray smiled. "Five-six, go."

"Twenty-eight returning. December ninety-nine, Chevrolet Chevette, to Elizabeth Palmer."

They all talked that way, in shorthand. Cray knew the codes and phrases. The dispatcher meant that the requested information had come up on the computer: the vehicle registration was valid through December of this year, the car was a Chevette, and it was registered in the name of Elizabeth Palmer.

Cray had repeated the last name in a questioning tone, and the dispatcher had spelled it in code: "Paul Adam Lincoln Mary Edward Robert."

"Ten-four," Cray had said, switching the radio off.

Now, as the Chevette passed Grant Road, approaching downtown Tucson, Cray tried out the name one last time:

"Elizabeth Palmer."

He didn't know it. The name was new to him.

So this woman, this Elizabeth Palmer, was not someone from his past, not a piece of his life.

She was a stranger.

Very odd.

He would have many questions for her.

And she would answer them all. He would see to that.

Idly he wondered what she was thinking and feeling right now. Most likely she had not eaten dinner. Perhaps she was thinking of a meal she could fix for herself. Her last meal, but she wouldn't know it.

Or possibly her thoughts had wandered to some

current or former boyfriend in whose arms she had experienced the intimacy that passed for passion in this debased age.

She might be musing on love, or her future, or some pretty memory.

He enjoyed this game of speculation. It made her real to him, a person with a life.

Though not for long.

Traffic thinned as Oracle curved into the dark grid of downtown streets. Cray fell farther back.

She must live here. Not a good neighborhood.

He expected her to veer off toward one of the residential districts, but instead she kept going into the heart of downtown, where the street fair had been held on Saturday night.

Oracle Road was called Main Street here. At the corner of Main and Sixth, Elizabeth Palmer parked her car.

Cray cut down a side street, then circled around to Main, a block south of the parked car, and found a spot at the curb. He was in time to see Elizabeth Palmer emerge from the Chevette and jaywalk across the street.

There were no apartments nearby, no motels, only a bar with a neon sign.

He knew that bar. He'd stopped there last Saturday and tossed back two fingers of dark Caribbean rum before prowling the crowded streets.

And now Elizabeth Palmer was here, for only one imaginable reason.

She had not headed straight home, as he'd assumed. She was still hoping to find him, the persistent little bitch.

Having seen him in the bar two nights ago, she was revisiting it on the chance that he had returned.

Cray watched her hurry to the front door and step inside. She'd thrown on a jacket, he observed, some sort of cheap zippered thing that looked too big for her. Master of disguise, he thought with a slow shake of his head.

By the end of the night, all her disguises would be stripped away, even that most personal and intimate disguise known as the self.

Then she would not be Elizabeth Palmer at all. She would be the primal essence of the human animal—the bundled nerve cells of the brain stem, the autonomic functions of the body.

She would be pure, liberated, and absolutely honest for the first and only time since infancy.

It was a wondrous transformation. He'd written about it in his book. Not everything, of course. He'd omitted the more dangerous ideas. Still it was remarkable, the things a person could write from behind the cloak of disinterested scholarship.

Imagine if he were to approach a stranger and tell him that his life was worthless and meaningless, his most cherished virtues a lie, his aspirations and convictions a stupid joke. Cray would be lucky to escape a fistfight.

But write it in a book, and the world turned upside down. Tell people, as he had, that their personalities were an illusion, their every conscious thought only an irrelevant by-product of biological processes, and that they were apes, or lower than apes—automatons, robots—and they shook his hand, requesting his autograph and wanting more.

He spat in their faces, and they licked it up like candy. He had expected angry denials, defensive ridicule—anything but what he'd received.

Money.

Acclaim.

The Mask of Self was in its fourth printing. There was a trade paperback edition in the works, with a new foreword by the author. His book had not quite achieved bestseller status, but he had earned enough to pay for the Lexus and to fund a comfortable portfolio of diversified investments.

Yet in retrospect he saw that his amazement was misplaced. He had spoken the truth, and it had filtered through the layers of deception people wove around themselves. He should not have been surprised. In their instinctive, visceral responses—in the bodily wisdom that the ancient Greeks called *thumos*—people knew what they essentially were.

They knew and, hating the disease of consciousness, they instinctively sought a cure.

The door of the bar opened, and Elizabeth Palmer emerged. She'd spent only a couple of minutes inside, enough time for a quick look around, perhaps a question asked of the bartender—*Have you seen a man in here, all dressed in black?*

She hurried to her car, her steps nimble and fast.

When the Chevette pulled away, Cray followed.

She would keep looking, of course. Though she must be tired and hungry and scared, she would not give up.

That was all right. Cray had time.

He had all night.

And, like her, he could be persistent in the chase.

6

Cray stayed well behind the Chevette, keeping the hatchback just within sight, counting on Elizabeth Palmer not to check her rearview mirror too closely. He knew she wouldn't. She was on the hunt, or so she thought. Her attention would be fixed on what lay ahead.

She led him to the seedy strip of trailer parks, cheap motels, and bars called, inevitably, Miracle Mile. The district was crowded even at this late hour. Young men in ponytails and buzz cuts stood in angry clusters under the streetlights. Tattooed and miniskirted women walked past, eliciting the usual simian responses.

The area was a center of prostitution and drug use. Many of the motels were rented by the hour. An adult bookstore competed for business with a gospel mission. There was a great deal of neon everywhere, and there was darkness in the places where the bright lights didn't reach.

It had been two weeks since Cray's last visit to Miracle Mile. Had Elizabeth Palmer been tailing him even then? Had she shadowed him for that many nights before he became aware of her?

The establishment he'd patronized was a topless

bar, not his usual sort of place, but he'd been in a restless mood, the first phase of his killing cycle.

He watched as the Chevette pulled behind the building and made a quick circuit of the parking lot. The persistent Miss Palmer was looking for his Lexus.

Failing to find it, she continued down the street. Cray cruised well behind her, past a department store that had shut its doors and was now a garish mausoleum of dead hopes, spray-painted with taggers' signs, the parking lot a wasteland of asphalt inside a sagging security fence.

At a bowling alley the Chevette again performed a quick search of the perimeter. Cray, parked at a curb a block away, tried to fathom why she would look there. He was no bowler, for God's sake. The activity was far too déclassé for his tastes.

And yet . . .

He *had* gone there, hadn't he?

Cruising the strip, he'd seen a woman enter the bowling alley on a Friday night. She had a golden fall of hair, and a wide, laughing mouth that intrigued him. He'd parked and sought her out inside. But predictably she had proven to be of no interest whatsoever, merely a glorified barfly, chortling raucously at the coarse jokes of her companions, using foul language, embarrassing herself. After eavesdropping on her conversation long enough to determine her true character, Cray had left.

Yes. He'd done that. But not very recently. Perhaps as long as a month ago.

Elizabeth Palmer could not have tailed him for a month. She wasn't good enough, slick enough. He would have spotted her long before tonight.

Or would he?

Making eye contact with her at the street fair had been pure accident. If it hadn't been for that split second of awareness, the instant when he saw her and sensed she was watching him, would he even have noticed her in the resort bar?

She could have been after him for thirty days, thirty nights. Staking out his home, then following him whenever he left in the evening. Following remorselessly, tirelessly, night after night. Following and watching.

For a month. A month . . .

It had been only a little more than a month ago that Sharon Andrews' body had been found.

The discovery had been Cray's fault. For the first time in twelve years, he'd gotten careless.

Ordinarily he was meticulous in the disposal of his victim's remains. But Sharon Andrews had led him on a long chase, and by the time he ran her down, night was ebbing. He had used a collapsible shovel to dig a shallow grave near the stream bank. Sealed inside an extra-large, heavy-duty trash bag to discourage scavengers, she was laid in the hole and covered over.

That should have been the last anyone saw of her, but Cray hadn't counted on the summer flash flood season. In late August, torrential rains had fallen in the White Mountains. The stream had overflowed, the rush of water widening the banks, and Sharon Andrews had been dislodged from her grave and swept downriver.

He had buried her too close to the stream. A stupid error. Had he been less tired and more clearheaded, he would have moved her higher up the hillside. Or perhaps he should have simply left her in the open for the scavengers to find.

The trash bag, knotted shut, had kept her body dry. Without moisture, bacteria could not thrive. Some mummification had taken place, but little decay. And because the body was well preserved, no one could miss the obvious mutilation.

WOMAN'S FACELESS CORPSE FOUND IN WHITE MOUNTAINS.

That had been the headline in the Tucson *Citizen* on the day after the storm, when, at a campground three miles from the site of the kill, Sharon Andrews was found entangled in a floating deadfall, bobbing amid ribbons of shredded plastic. A pair of forest rangers fished her from the water.

Nothing about the corpse or the plastic bag could lead investigators to a suspect. The bag was a common type, available anywhere. The two bullets imbedded in Sharon Andrews' leg and hip were 9mm semi-jacketed hollow points, untraceable.

No real harm had been done. Even so, Cray hated having his work uncovered. He endured two weeks of media speculation on the twisted psychology of the killer.

The coverage enraged him. He felt violated.

Oddly, every expert assumed that the mutilation was postmortem. No one seemed able to conceive of the truth—that Sharon Andrews had been alive to witness her own final unmasking.

Pain had killed her almost at once, but not before Cray had shown her the trophy he'd taken. She had stared at her own face in his gloved hands, and it had stared back in eyeless mockery, the last thing she would ever see.

That was the whole point, and it was so very obvious, yet not one of them could see it. Not one.

Cray shook free of those thoughts and focused on recalling the exact date of the body's discovery.

August 17. Five weeks ago.

Elizabeth Palmer had begun following him just afterward. Or so it would appear.

He pondered this sequence of events as he chased the little hatchback into South Tucson, a blighted barrio landscape of rusty lowriders and security-barred windows and brick walls tattooed by gang graffiti.

Brave Elizabeth risked a look into a bikers' bar and then a noisy pool hall.

Cray had been to both places within the past month. He could not recall exactly when.

She couldn't have followed him inside on every occasion. She would have attracted notice in the rougher places—the notice of the other patrons, certainly, if not of Cray himself. Perhaps she had sat outside, watching from her car as Cray entered and left.

If so, the tableau was reversed now. It was Cray who sat and watched, sunk deep in the Lexus' leather seat.

She did not give up until Cray's dashboard clock read 2 A.M. The bars were closing. There was nowhere left to look.

Now she could only go home. She must be worn out, poor thing.

The Chevette headed north on Park Avenue, then west on Silverlake Road, toward the interstate. Cray, staying far behind, watched the red rectangles of her taillights.

Elizabeth drove steadily, never exceeding the speed limit. At every stop sign and red light she came to a full stop. She never ran the yellows. She used her turn signal even when no other vehicle was near.

Such caution seemed out of character for a huntress sniffing John Cray's spoor.

Then abruptly she turned down a side street, the move so quick it had to be unpremeditated. Cray worried that she'd seen him behind her and was trying to shake him off.

No. There was a simpler explanation.

A few blocks ahead, the light bar of a Tucson PD patrol unit shimmered at the curb. A police car was making a traffic stop.

Cray did not take the side street. He continued past the police car and the motorcyclist who'd been pulled over, then waited at an intersection until he saw the Chevette reappear a quarter mile ahead.

Elizabeth Palmer had gone out of her way to avoid passing a police car.

And now Cray knew why she drove so timidly.

She was afraid of being stopped. Afraid of the police.

Now why would that be, Elizabeth? he wondered. What would a nice girl like you have to fear from an officer of the law?

He couldn't guess, but he began to understand why she would follow him on her own. If the police were off limits for some reason, then she would have no choice but to handle things herself.

It seemed a heavy burden for such frail shoulders.

He would be glad to lift it from her, to give her peace.

He expected her to get on Interstate 10, but instead she passed beneath it, then pulled into a motel on the frontage road.

She was not even a local resident. And the motel, a ramshackle one-story building amid miles of desolation, looked as seedy as the car she drove. Whoever she was, she had no money.

She was nobody. Nobody at all. A stranger from out of town, alone, engaged in a secret quest. Who would miss her when she disappeared?

Cray parked on the frontage road, then retracted his side window and stared at the motel parking lot across a waste of weeds and flat, parched land. Trucks howled past on I-10, shaking the world.

He watched as Elizabeth Palmer got out of the car and headed toward the motel. Halfway there, she stopped, lifting her head to look around sharply.

"Do you know I'm here, Elizabeth?" Cray asked in a whisper. "Do you feel my gaze?"

With a dismissive shake of her head, she resumed walking. At the side of the building she fumbled in her purse for her keys, then unlocked the door of her room.

The door shut behind her, and a light came on behind closed drapes. There was a pause, and suddenly her shadow passed over the drapes, sweeping like a pendulum. Again. Again.

She was pacing. Upset.

"You're tired, child," Cray said. "You need your rest."

She would fall asleep eventually. Cray could wait.

Another bevy of trucks roared past, and then in a stretch of sudden stillness, Cray heard the distant wail of a coyote somewhere on the flats, another predator like himself.

7

The room was quiet, at least. Elizabeth was grateful for that. She had spent much of the afternoon trying to block out the pornographic sounds from the adjacent units.

The motel, if she could judge by the scarcity of cars in the parking lot, was largely empty now. Apparently it did most of its business during the day.

Many times in the past twelve years she had been holed up in a place like this. Sometimes it was a motel just off the interstate, and sometimes an apartment house that rented single rooms by the week, with a common bathroom down the hall.

There had been a nice cottage in Santa Fe, which she'd rented for nearly a year while doing clerical work at an accounting firm. Trellises of climbing roses had garlanded the patio; she would sit outside in the soft springtime air.

That had been one of the good times. Colorado Springs had been good also. She'd spent six months there, in a two-bedroom apartment with modern appliances and quiet, respectable neighbors. She had been tempted to buy a cat and settle in, but then things had gone wrong and she'd had to clear out fast, loading up her Chevette in the night.

So much running, twelve years of it, crossing state lines, moving from the desert to the mountains, from cities to small towns.

A month ago—had it been only a month?—she'd been living at the edge of a Navajo reservation in the Four Corners area, where the sculpted buttes took great jagged bites out of the turquoise sky. She had been a waitress in a truck-stop diner, a job that always seemed strangely glamorous in the movies. Her feet were sore every night, and in her sleep she would dream of balancing stacks of dishes.

She'd run and run, and now here she was in southern Arizona, not fifty miles from where her zigzag trek had started.

Elizabeth kicked off her shoes, tossed her jacket on the armchair by the standing lamp. It was a nylon jacket, red with silver and white trim, bearing the insignia of the University of New Mexico Lobos. She'd bought it in Albuquerque, on an excursion from Santa Fe—just one of many things she'd picked up in her wanderings.

Barefoot, she paced the floor. A window air conditioner rattled and hummed, stirring a lukewarm breeze. The spotty beige drapes shivered in the current of air.

She ought to sleep, but worry had her in its clutch and wouldn't let go.

Worry . . . and guilt.

"Shouldn't feel guilty," she murmured. "Not your fault."

She'd done her best. She had methodically revisited every one of Cray's hangouts from his previous outings. A wasted effort, and an exhausting one, but at least she had tried.

Still, trying wasn't good enough when a woman might be in danger, somewhere in this city or its outskirts.

"Well, maybe he won't do it tonight. Maybe he went straight home."

She hoped this was true. But if it wasn't—if Cray was a killer and tonight was his night to strike—then she wouldn't be there to stop him when it mattered.

She wondered how many he had killed. She knew of only two. One case was recent, and the other was from many years ago. But there had to be more.

The recent case was the murder of Sharon Andrews. The corpse swept downriver in a flash flood. A corpse without a face.

The story of the body's discovery, sufficiently gruesome to make the news wires, had appeared in the August 18 edition of *The Dallas Morning News*.

On the nineteenth of August a trucker left the paper at the diner where Elizabeth worked. She kept it. Dallas might be a place to go, when she had to run again. She wanted to check the classified ads, get a feel for the job situation.

She didn't get around to looking at the paper until the evening of August twenty-first. As she flipped through the coffee-stained pages, an AP story datelined Apache County, Arizona, caught her eye.

She read it.

And she knew.

That night she left for Tucson. She drove south on two state highways, then on Interstate 17, stopping only once, at 7 A.M., to call the diner and quit her job.

It was best to leave no loose ends. She didn't want her boss to file a missing-persons report.

When she arrived in town, taking a furnished apartment on the south side, Tucson's morning and afternoon papers ran daily stories on the Sharon Andrews case, and the TV news led with the story for a week. But no progress was made, and the fear and excitement subsided. Tucson was not quite a metropolis, but it had grown a lot since 1987, when she had last seen it. The metro area population—city and suburbs and unincorporated county land—was pushing one million.

People were busy. Life went on.

Except, of course, for seven-year-old Todd Andrews, and Sharon's parents and friends, and the police detectives and sheriffs' deputies working the case in two counties, and Elizabeth Palmer herself.

Elizabeth's life had not gone on. It had been stalled and frozen in a compulsive routine.

Every day she watched Cray's residence. She followed him in the evenings. He had gone out a dozen times, with increasing frequency throughout the month.

She watched. She waited. She took no job, earned no money.

As her savings dwindled, she found it hard to make the weekly rent even on her barrio apartment. Last week she'd switched to a one-star motel on Miracle Mile. She'd stayed until even twenty-five dollars a night seemed a little steep.

Two days ago she had found this place by the interstate. Nineteen dollars a night. She could afford to stay here another three days. Then she would be sleeping in her car.

And if Cray was not, in fact, the man who'd murdered Sharon Andrews . . .

Then all the expense and risk she had assumed by returning to Tucson would have been wasted. She would be broke and homeless and jobless, with nothing to show for it but a paranoid delusion.

Well, if so, she would go about rebuilding her life, that's all. She had done it before.

And though she was tired now, she knew exhaustion would not last. There was something in her that pushed her forward even when the massed resistance of the world seemed to be driving her back. In her worst moments, in flophouses and alleyways, when all hope should have been gone, she'd felt it—some living power, an energy that seemed to renew itself even when she fought against it, preferring despair.

She would survive. But some other woman might not.

The thought made her weary, or more precisely, made her suddenly aware of how weary she already was.

She stretched out on the soiled bedspread and shut her eyes, but sleep would not come.

She knew what she needed. And though it was past two-thirty in the morning, she didn't hesitate as she reached for the bedside phone and called her father-in-law.

She made it a collect call, charging it to his account, because her money was running low. He wouldn't mind.

He answered on the second ring. The phone must have awakened him, but she heard no grogginess in his deep, slow voice.

"Anson McMillan."

"It's me," she said.

"Figured as much."

"I'm sorry to call so late."

"Don't bother yourself about that. How are you, darling?"

"Going along."

"Any trouble?"

She wanted to say yes, all kinds of trouble. She wanted to tell him everything, but she couldn't. The truth would be too hard for him. He was a strong man, but everyone's strength had its limits.

"No," she said lightly. "I was just feeling restless, that's all."

"Got a job?"

"Sure." Another lie.

"Enough money? There are ways for me to get you money, you know."

"I'm fine, Anson."

"I'll bet you don't get enough to eat. You always were all skin and bones."

"I've put on a few pounds."

"I doubt that. Where are you now?"

She smiled at the clumsy way he tried to sneak that question in. "You know I won't say. And you don't want to be told."

"I guess I don't. Best not to know. You could come by sometime. For a visit."

"I can't chance it."

"They're not looking anymore. It's been too long."

"They'll always be looking. And people know me there. It's too dangerous."

"All right, that's so, but there are other places you could go and settle down. You don't need to stay on the move, not forever. You can't live that way."

"I've done okay so far."

"If you call it doing okay, living from day to day."

Don't we all live that way? she wondered, but she didn't ask this question.

Instead she made him tell her what he'd been up to, and he obliged, knowing why she wanted to hear it.

She curled up against the pillows and listened to him speak of the rusty porch door he'd replaced, and the new gun he'd added to his collection, and the food he put out for the rabbits every morning. She heard him light a cigarette as he went on talking.

"Went to the cemetery the other day," he said. "Placed a new wreath on Regina's grave. Nice day, warm and clear. No rain yet, and it's still too early for snow, even in the high peaks of the range."

He spoke more about the weather. Elizabeth noticed that he had said nothing of visiting Justin's grave. She wondered if he'd laid a wreath there also. She doubted it.

After a long time she said, "I'd better let you get back to sleep."

"You don't have to. You know me. I can talk all night."

"It's okay, Anson. I just wanted to hear your voice."

"Always a pleasure hearing yours. I wish . . ."

He didn't finish. She knew everything he meant to say but couldn't.

"So do I," she whispered. "But we play the hand we're dealt. Isn't that what you used to say?"

"I said it. Don't know that it means much."

"It does to me."

They said their good-byes. She held the receiver to her ear long enough to hear him click off, and the sad silence after.

She cradled the phone, feeling calm again. Things were bad, but she would go on. If she had to sleep in her damn car, she would. She'd faced worse problems and endured.

And as for Cray . . .

Tomorrow she would watch Cray again. Tonight there was nothing she could do.

At this very moment he might be lurking outside his next victim's window, preparing an abduction and another kill.

If so, she couldn't stop him.

She stretched out on the bed, hearing the creak of old mattress springs, and turned off the bedside lamp. The sudden darkness was heavy and hot, and she let herself fall into it, as into a deep hole. When she reached the bottom of the hole, she was asleep.

Her last half-waking thought was of Sharon Andrews.

Who's next? a voice asked, a voice that might have been Elizabeth's own.

But she heard no answer.

8

Cray waited an additional half hour after the motel room's window went dark, giving Elizabeth Palmer sufficient time to fall asleep.

Then he pulled on black leather gloves and removed his Glock 9mm from the rear storage compartment of the Lexus.

Cray never handled the Glock bare-handed. There were no prints on the gun or on any of the seventeen rounds loaded in the magazine. The gun itself was unregistered and untraceable. It could never be linked to him.

Also in the storage compartment was a canvas satchel—black, of course—with a drawstring clasp. His little black bag. Cray smiled.

Time to make a house call.

Slowly he drove into the motel parking lot and found a vacant space near Elizabeth Palmer's room. He switched off his lights and engine, then sat for another long moment, allowing his eyes to readjust to the dark.

He had excellent night vision. Though the moon had long since set, he could see every detail around him. He could even read the unilluminated dial of his watch without strain.

The time was 3:30 when Cray got out of the Lexus.

He stood with his satchel in hand, breathing the warm, dusty air. The parking lot was a flat stretch of asphalt amid a flat stretch of desert under a huge sky dizzy with wheeling stars. Cray felt the immensity of the world and his smallness in it. He felt lonely and almost afraid.

It was always this way for him, at these moments. At heart a human being was only a small, scared animal in the night. When death was a safe abstraction, this fundamental dread could be evaded.

There was no evasion now.

Elizabeth was in an unfamiliar apartment, a place she'd never been before. Yet strangely she felt certain it was her place; she lived here, and parts of it were known to her.

The tiny efficiency kitchen with the compact fridge under the stove—it was like the kitchen of her studio apartment in Taos.

The living room opened onto a patio very similar to the one she'd loved in Santa Fe.

The bathroom with the dripping faucet was straight out of Salt Lake City, where she'd spent three cold months.

I guess this is all the places I've lived, Elizabeth thought. A composite of my life.

She wandered from room to room, the view through the windows constantly changing, then found an open door that led to a one-car garage, the type that came attached to a modest house.

The garage was part of her life too, but she couldn't recall quite how. There was no car parked in it, and she explained this to herself by saying aloud, "He's out."

But she didn't know who *he* was.

Didn't know—yet part of her did, or almost did, and suddenly she was sure she didn't want to be in the garage.

And she wasn't. She was in a park, someplace green and hot, under a tree, just sitting, and this was much better, except there were ants, so many of them, a flood tide of crawling red.

She jumped up and brushed them off her bare legs, and her hands came away red and sticky, glazed with some viscid awfulness that smelled like copper pennies.

She turned away and smelled the ocean breeze as she walked along the seashore, her hands clean again, cool water lapping her bare feet. The sea surged, pulling in sheets of seaweed.

One green clump, bobbing in the foam, caught her attention. She bent to retrieve it, lifting it in both hands, a flat, limp oval. As she raised it to the sun, she saw that it wasn't seaweed at all.

It was a woman's face.

Cray approached the door of Elizabeth Palmer's room and studied the lock. As he had expected, it was a dead bolt, key-operated. He knew the type. The bolt had a one-inch throw and no beveled edge, and it was not spring-loaded. Even with one of his locksmith tools, he would find the lock almost impossible to pick.

He could break a window or force the lock, but either way he would make noise, perhaps enough noise to be audible above the rattle and hum of the air conditioner.

There might be a better approach.

At the rear of the building, near a stairwell where a soda machine cast its lurid glow on an intaglio of obscene graffiti, Cray found a door to what was evidently the custodial storeroom, secured with a Yale padlock.

He opened the satchel and took out a stainless steel canister, the approximate size and shape of a thermos but with a spray nozzle and trigger. He had purchased it from a chemical company specializing in hospital supplies. The canister held two liters of liquid nitrogen pressurized at 135 p.s.i., with a temperature of minus 320 degrees.

Cray positioned the nozzle against the padlock and released a jet of mist. The air crystallized in a cloud of fairy-dust sparkles, and through his gloves he felt a stab of sheer cold, arctic and unreal, in his fingers and wrists.

When he withdrew the canister, the padlock was shiny with ice.

There was a hammer in the satchel. Cray tapped the padlock once. Chilled and brittle, it shattered magically. The pavement at his feet glistened with a shower of bright metal shards.

Inside the storeroom, amid mops and slop buckets and other filth, he found a set of master keys.

Every room in the motel was now open to him. But he had an interest in only one.

A woman's face.

Elizabeth saw it, and the shock was fresh and vivid, and for a moment she was startled half-awake. Dimly she knew she was in bed somewhere, a room, one of the countless way stations she had visited.

The ocean was gone, and the foam, the seaweed, the mask that had drooped in her hands.

But she saw that mask still. She had seen it for years, in dreams and in memories.

It was the face of a woman she had never known, a woman whose name was a mystery. A young woman, probably, and pretty, or so it seemed.

She might have had a lover, a family, sad moods, secret fears. But all Elizabeth knew of her was the wrinkled remnant she had held so briefly under the flicker of a sixty-watt bulb.

The woman, whoever she was, had meant nothing to Elizabeth, and yet, in a different way, she had meant everything. She had changed Elizabeth's life, made her an outcast, taught her fear. She was the reason for all the peril and suffering of the last twelve years. Elizabeth ought to hate her for that, and for the nightmares she brought.

But it was wrong to hate her, of course. She was only another victim.

The first victim. Far from the last.

The dream receded, and Elizabeth yielded to a new and better sleep, a sleep without nightmares.

9

Cray tested three keys on the chain before finding the one that opened the motel room's door. He eased the door an inch ajar before a security chain stopped him.

Such chains were useless. Any hard impact—a shove or a kick—could snap the chain at its weakest link or pull the anchor bolts out of the door frame. But the noise might wake the woman inside.

Eager to proceed, he was almost willing to take this risk, and then the air conditioner clicked off.

Silence.

He couldn't break the chain now. She was sure to hear it.

Well, there was another option.

Rummaging in his satchel, Cray produced a bent wire hook. Carefully he inserted the hook in the opening, then snagged the chain and lifted it free of its frame.

No more obstacles.

In his pocket he kept a vial of chloroform, purchased from the same medical-supply house that had sold him the liquid nitrogen. He unscrewed the lid and moistened a washcloth.

With the cloth wadded in one fist, Cray pushed gently on the door and slipped inside. He stood for a moment just inside the doorway, a shadow amid shadows, scanning the layout of the room.

A suitcase rested on a folding stand. A television set, glass panel gleaming in the faint ambient glow, was bolted to a counter. Some sort of cheap artwork hung slightly askew on one wall.

All of this was on his left. To his right was the bed, flanked by nightstands with matching lamps, their conical shades dark. Elizabeth Palmer had not bothered to unmake the bed, even to turn down the rumpled spread. She lay across it, supine, her head on a pillow.

Fast asleep. Cray heard her breathing, the sound low and regular.

She did not snore. That was good. He disliked women who snored.

The air conditioner switched on again, the thermostat registering the warmer air flowing in through the open door.

Elizabeth stirred, half-awakened by the machine's rattle and roar, then settled into sleep again. He heard her low groan, and he knew she was dreaming, and that the dream was unpleasant.

A dream of him, perhaps.

Gently, Cray shut the door.

Like a lover he approached her. He thought of myths. Of Cupid coupling with Psyche in the dark. Of the incubus that hovered wraithlike over its beloved to take her while she slept.

At her bedside he stopped. He stood looking down at her.

She intrigued him. She was a mystery.

He studied her face. Her blonde hair, formerly tied in a ponytail, was loose now, fanning over the pillow. She had a high forehead and soft, gently rounded features. Her mouth was small, the lips pursed in sleep. He saw her eyelids twitch and knew she was dreaming. Of what? he wondered.

Her skin was pale. He saw freckles. A dusting of them on her nose and cheeks and forehead.

And then he knew.

She had changed her hair. It used to be red, worn in a pageboy cut.

And she had grown up, of course. Twelve years was a long time. She had been a teenager then. Must be thirty now. No, thirty-one.

She was slimmer than she'd been—the baby fat was gone—and in its place he saw lean muscles in her arms and in the curve of her neck.

From a girl, she'd become a woman. Nearly everything about her had been altered, but she still had her freckles, and they gave her away.

Cray released a shudder of breath. He was shaking.

He had been calm until this moment. He had been focused. But abruptly there was something tearing at him, some blind confusion, a howling turmoil, and he needed a moment to understand that it was rage.

He thrust his arm down, clapping the wet cloth on her face, pressing it to her nose and mouth, and her eyes flashed open.

In the dark he couldn't see their color, but he knew they were blue.

From her throat, a strangled noise of panic, good to hear.

Her arms thrashed. He held her down, not even

straining. He was far stronger than she was. She had never been any match for him. It had been sheer suicide for her to go up against him on her own.

With a shiver of surrender, she went limp.

Her eyes closed slowly. Cray held the cloth in place until he was certain she was unconscious.

"I have you, Kaylie," he whispered. "After all these years, I have you at last."

10

Whiteout.

The world was erased behind a brilliant screen of pure white, no depth or texture anywhere, only the perfect whiteness of snow on snow.

Elizabeth struggled to understand it, and then she knew it was a dust storm, like the one that had caught her by surprise on Interstate 10 on her way from Las Cruces to Lordsburg five years ago.

She'd been driving the rattletrap Dodge she owned back then, a car that had never been very reliable, when without warning the highway had disappeared in a sheet of windblown sand, even the hood of her car wiped from sight, and for a few terrifying seconds she had coasted at sixty miles an hour, seeing no road and no traffic, praying she would not be part of a chain collision that would leave her mangled in the wreckage.

Then the dust storm blew past her, and she was in a motel room in Tucson, slumped in an armchair.

And Cray was there.

"Hello, Kaylie," he said.

She blinked, focusing on the tall man in black, his gloved hands, the shiny pistol aimed at her. The room was very bright. He'd turned on every lamp.

"Your first instinct will be to fight or flee." Cray's voice was low, nearly inaudible over the buzzing drone of the air conditioner. "Resist the impulse to do either. I don't want to shoot you here, but I will, if you make it necessary."

She shifted in the armchair and heard the creak of old wood. Her bare toes curled into the carpet's short nap.

Cray hadn't tied her to the chair, but he had dressed her in her red Lobos jacket, zipping up the front, knotting the long nylon sleeves to trap her hands across her midsection.

Like a straitjacket. Yes. He would have been amused by that.

"Do you intend to be sensible?" Cray pressed, impatience seeping through his cool smile. "Well, do you?"

Slowly she nodded. It was the only way for her to answer. Her mouth was gagged with what felt like a washcloth, tied in place at the back of her head.

"Good. Then just sit tight. We'll be leaving soon."

He wedged the gun in the beltless waistband of his slacks, then turned away. She saw that her suitcase lay open on the folding stand where she'd left it.

He was rummaging through her things.

She became aware of the need to breathe. But she couldn't breathe with the towel clogging her mouth. For an awful moment she was sure she would suffocate or choke to death.

No, wrong, she could breathe, and to prove it she inhaled slowly through her nostrils, feeding her lungs.

When she was calm again, or almost calm, as calm as she could be under the circumstances, facing death at the hands of the man who was her worst enemy—

when she was able to think, she tried to reconstruct what had happened.

She'd talked to Anson, then gone to sleep. Bad dreams . . .

Then Cray must have broken in, sedated her somehow.

She remembered an instant of alertness, of disorienting terror, and after that, a long stomach-wrenching fall.

And now . . .

She was his prisoner.

Again.

In the suitcase Cray found the clipping from the Dallas newspaper. She saw him study it in the lamplight. His lips formed a circle. "So." The clipping, neatly folded, went into his pants pocket. He resumed searching.

Her gaze traveled around the room and settled on the bed. The bedspread was a rumpled mess, the pillows strewn. Amid the disorder she saw a canvas satchel, something of his, which he'd tossed there.

Just behind it, on the nightstand where she'd left it, lay her purse.

In one lunge she could reach the purse, grab the gun inside. But first she had to free her hands. She tugged at the knotted sleeves. Cray had tied them tight.

She couldn't break free, and so the gun would do her no good, and she had no hope and no chance at all.

"I intend to dispose of your luggage, of course." Cray said it casually, merely for the sake of conversation. "I'll put your suitcases in your car and drive into a bad neighborhood, then leave the doors unlocked and the key in the ignition. The car and its contents will disappear quickly enough."

He was foraging in the bottom of the suitcase. She watched his hands, gloved in black, slip like twin snakes among her undergarments and toiletries.

"But just in case your personal effects are somehow recovered by the police, I need to ascertain that they include nothing that links you to me."

Finished with the first suitcase, he closed the canvas lid, then walked to the closet and removed the second one.

"You know the sort of item I mean. A diary or journal, a torn-out page of a phone book with my name circled. Perhaps I'm being paranoid. But even paranoids have enemies. Isn't that right, Kaylie?"

The second suitcase was large and heavy—she'd never unpacked—but with one arm Cray hefted it easily onto the counter. His strength dismayed her. She had forgotten how powerful he was.

Still, she saw a weakness. Cray looked very much like a man in cool control, but it was an act. His hands were not as steady as they should have been, and there was a twitch at the corner of his mouth.

He was fighting for composure. Fighting against an emotion so strong it threatened to overmaster him.

Hatred. Hatred of her.

She'd hurt him deeply, and now it was his turn to inflict pain.

Cray unzipped the suitcase and rummaged in it. At the bottom he found a thick manila envelope.

"Well, well. What have we here?"

My life, she wanted to say. *That's what you have.*

He opened the envelope and tamped a clutter of papers and laminated cards onto the countertop.

"Let's see. A New Mexico driver's license issued to

one Ellen Pendleton. Miss Pendleton looks rather like you, Kaylie, except for the brown hair and the rather mousy librarian's glasses." He flipped the card aside. "An obvious fake. I hope you didn't pay too much for it."

She hadn't. It was the first false I.D. she'd obtained after going on the run. A man with a camera had stood her up against a life-size posterboard display of a driver's license form, the details filled out by hand in large block letters that looked almost like type. He'd taken her picture, then simply laminated the photo.

The results had been terrible, but for fifty dollars she couldn't complain. Later she'd done better.

"Here we go," Cray said. "This looks more professional. You were Paula Neilson for a while." He studied the Colorado driver's license, the Social Security card, the birth certificate, credit cards, even a voter-registration card, all in Paula Neilson's name. "These documents are genuine. You got her name from a death roll, didn't you?"

She nodded.

Knowing that the Ellen Pendleton I.D. would never hold up to scrutiny, she had stopped at a cemetery outside Colorado Springs and found a young woman's grave. It had been easy to obtain the deceased's birth certificate from the local department of records; she'd handled the transaction by mail.

With the birth certificate in hand, she had applied for a driver's license, then obtained a Social Security card and the other items. As Cray had said, all the documents were authentic. For six years she had been Paula Neilson.

"And one more document. Elizabeth Palmer's birth certificate. Another return from the dead?"

He didn't want an answer. If he had, and if she could have spoken, she would have told him that Elizabeth Palmer was a name she had made up, and the documents establishing her reality had been created with the aid of a desktop computer, a scanner, and a color printer.

She had done the job herself, during the period in Santa Fe when she did clerical work and had access to the proper equipment. She'd been wary of retaining any one identity for too long.

Later, upon returning to Arizona, she had exchanged her fake New Mexico driver's license for a genuine one, issued by the Motor Vehicles Division. From that moment forward, she had been Elizabeth Palmer. It was who she was now. It was her real identity, as far as she was concerned.

She had created Elizabeth, and she had become Elizabeth, and she never—never—had been anything else.

Cray would not see it that way, of course. He knew her only from her former life.

He was studying the birth certificate, generated with a desktop publishing program. "Elizabeth was born on October third, 1967. Her birthday is coming up. She'll be thirty-two. I'll have to remember to send a gift. The other items under Miss Palmer's name are in your wallet, I suppose."

She stiffened. She didn't want him to look in her purse.

He didn't. He merely shrugged. "Well, you've been a busy girl, I'll give you that."

Cray dumped the assorted cards and papers back into the envelope, then put the envelope in his satchel.

"I'll take these with me. Nobody will find them. They would raise too many questions. I don't intend to have people looking into your disappearance very closely, if at all."

Rapidly he worked his way toward the bottom of the suitcase, speaking in a low, informal tone.

"I've already replaced the set of master keys I stole from the storage closet. The damage to the closet's lock will be attributed to vandalism. Since nothing was taken, probably the management won't even bother to file a report."

He found a favorite book of hers, *Watership Down*, the one about the rabbits, which she'd bought at a junk sale in Las Cruces and carried with her ever since. Indifferently he riffled the pages, looking for marginal notes or hidden messages. There were none.

"As for your disappearance, I doubt any questions will be raised. In an establishment of this kind, the guests must frequently check out at odd hours. I'll leave the door unlocked, the room key on the counter with a two-dollar tip. They'll think you left in a hurry. And they'll forget you immediately."

He reached the bottom of the suitcase and took out her photo album. It was a slim spiral-bound volume, only half-filled.

She disliked having her picture taken, for obvious reasons, but at a few parties and picnics over the years she'd been caught on film.

Cray flipped through the sheets of photos, his face unchanging. She wondered what the pictures looked like to him—the silly poses struck by her friends, the sliced watermelon and paper airplanes and big, goofy smiles.

"As long as your car isn't found in one piece," he

was saying, "no one will have any reason to look for you at all. You'll have vanished, and no one will even know it."

The photo album went into his satchel also. He shut the second suitcase. He was done.

"It's what you've wanted, Kaylie. Isn't it? To disappear completely? Never to be sought, and never found? Why, it's a dream come true."

The smile he showed her was so bright with malice, she actually shrank back into the chair.

"Now," he went on casually, "we'd better be going. I'll return later for your car and luggage. There's no hurry about that. Right now I want to get you out the door and on your merry way. But first . . ."

From his pocket he withdrew a long strip of black fabric.

A blindfold.

"First I need to be sure you won't run. I've been awaiting our reunion for a long time, Kaylie. I would hate to see it cut short."

He took a step forward, and she knew this was her last chance. Once her eyes were covered, she would be helpless, and Cray could do anything. Anything.

In that moment she remembered how much she hated this man, hated him more than he could possibly hate her, and a flash of raw fury jolted her out of the chair and straight at him with no thought, no plan of action, only the senseless need to attack.

Lightly, with one hand, he shoved her backward. She fell across the bed, and before she could lash out with a kick, he was on top of her, smiling, God damn him.

"There's that fight-or-flight instinct I warned you of," Cray said.

Her hands thrashed inside the jacket's nylon sleeves, and behind the gag she was screaming, but the screams were only stifled sounds that nobody would hear.

The blindfold came down, her sight blotted out in a fall of darkness, and Cray slapped her, the leather glove stinging her cheek.

"No more of your nonsense now," he said sternly. "If you struggle, if you give me any trouble at all, I'll hurt you. You'll win yourself nothing but pain."

He pulled her off the bed. The darkness tilted around her. She swayed, her knees liquefying, and then Cray's arm was supporting her, and he was hustling her across the room.

He paused once, apparently to collect something. She heard a rustle of fabric.

The door opened. She felt the balmy night on her face.

As Cray escorted her outside, the sudden sense of air and space was shocking, disorienting. She imagined herself a space traveler ejected from the safety of the capsule into the terrifying emptiness beyond.

The walkway felt cool and smooth against the soles of her bare feet. She tried to count her steps, though she didn't know why. It was something people did in the movies. They remembered every detail of their kidnapping, and later they could lead the police to the place where they'd been taken.

Jingle of metal, a soft click, the sound of an automobile's door swinging wide. Cray had brought her to his SUV.

"In you go," he said.

She prayed someone was watching from one of the motel windows, some insomniac who would see a gagged, blindfolded woman being pushed into a Lexus sport-utility and would call 911.

Cray lifted her in both hands, shoved her roughly into a passenger seat. The front seat, she was fairly sure. He pulled a lap belt tight across her waist, and she heard the snick of the buckle.

Behind the gag, she made a very small sound, something like a moan.

"No need to be scared yet," Cray said, his voice close to her ear. "We've got a good half-hour ride ahead of us before things get interesting."

Half an hour was not nearly enough time to reach the White Mountains, where Sharon Andrews had been killed. Cray must be taking her someplace nearer to town.

The desert, she guessed. The empty vastness, where he could do whatever he liked, and no one would see or hear.

Something thumped on the floor of the passenger compartment. A second item, less heavy, followed it.

Then the door banged shut, and for a moment she was alone in the Lexus while Cray circled around to the driver's side.

Her toes probed the floor and felt rumpled canvas. The satchel.

And the other item?

She felt worn fabric and a tangled strap. Her purse.

No doubt he'd brought it for the same reason he'd wanted the envelope with her birth certificates and Social Security cards. The purse contained her identification, which he intended to destroy.

It contained a gun also. A gun now less than three feet from her grasp, if she could only reach it.

Savagely she pulled at the jacket's knotted sleeves, fighting to rip the nylon and liberate her hands.

No use.

The driver's door opened, and the Lexus shifted on its springs as Cray slid in beside her. "All ready for our little outing?" he asked cheerfully.

He shut his door. The engine started, its hum low and ominous.

"I know I am," he added. "I've been ready for years."

There was motion, the Lexus reversing, and Elizabeth felt her last hope sliding inexorably away.

11

Cray was ten miles west of the motel, driving down a two-lane strip of blacktop through the flat, unforgiving desert, when he decided it was time for a real conversation.

He reached over to the woman in the passenger seat who called herself Elizabeth Palmer, and loosened the washcloth that had stoppered her mouth.

"Penny for your thoughts," he said.

She coughed weakly and repeatedly, a typical reaction to the strain of being gagged. He waited for her to recover her composure, feeling no impatience.

His rage had cooled. He had no reason to be angry now. She was going to die, and first she would know terror and then pain.

It was all he could have asked for, all he had wanted throughout the past twelve years.

When her spate of coughing was finished, she raised her head, turning her blindfolded face toward him, as if she could see through the opaque fabric.

He thought she might start screaming, or plead for mercy, or thrash in her seat the way some of them did. But to her credit she seemed almost calm. He kept thinking of her as the teenager she had been, but she was older now, and the years had made her stronger.

A long moment passed, filled with the hum of the engine and the beat of the tires on the rutted road.

"Where are we going?" she asked finally.

He was disappointed. The question was too obvious.

"Is that the first thing you say to me," he chided softly, "after all these years?"

"What should I say?"

"How much you've missed me. I've missed you. I'm so very glad to see you again. Really. You do believe that, don't you?"

"Yes. I do."

Her voice was as he remembered it. A soft, girlish voice, strikingly innocent. He had spent many hours in conversation with her, in the days when they had been bound together so intimately, and he had always been intrigued by the childlike quality she projected. He hadn't expected it to last.

"Little Kaylie," he breathed, "back from the dead. At least, I thought you might be dead. So much time had passed, and you had disappeared so utterly. As if you had vanished into some Bermuda Triangle, leaving no trace."

She made a ragged throat-clearing noise. "You thought I'd been killed?"

"To be honest, I wondered if you'd killed yourself. You have definite suicidal tendencies."

"No, I don't."

"Then why have you been following me?"

She said nothing.

Another desolate mile sped by. The dashboard's glow lit his gloved hands on the wheel, her face in profile. The car's interior was a bubble of light, and around it in all directions lay a great and brooding darkness.

He wondered if Elizabeth Palmer, whose name when he had known her had been quite different, was thinking of that darkness and of the destiny that would soon make her part of it forever.

"You didn't answer me," she said. "Where are we going?"

"Not much farther."

"Where?"

"There's a dirt road a few miles ahead. It dead-ends in the desert. Must have served a ranch once, or perhaps a ranch was planned for that site but never built. In any case, nothing's there now. We'll have privacy, you and I."

"Why not the White Mountains?"

"I'd prefer to take you there, I really would. There, or to some destination even more remote. Sadly, the hour is late. Daybreak's coming. We don't have as much time as I'd like."

"Time for what?"

"Aren't you the inquisitive one. Brimful of questions. You know what they say about curiosity and the cat."

"Time for what?" she repeated, her voice low and toneless.

"You'll see. It's a kind of game I play. But much more than a game."

"What game?"

"Patience."

He was proud of her. She had not done the usual stupid things. She hadn't tried kicking at him, or twisting wildly in her seat to grope for the door handle in a hopeless attempt to throw herself from the car. She hadn't cried, not even silently.

Best of all, she hadn't retreated into a comatose state and left him with a mere simulacrum of a woman.

He hated it when they did that. He wanted alertness, vitality, the animal instincts healthy and strong. He wanted a taut and quivering hare to chase.

This one would do nicely. He should have expected no less.

"Exactly how long have you been after me?" he asked her.

"Twenty-seven days."

"Watching me, waiting for me to make a careless error?"

"Yes."

"To catch me in the act."

"Yes."

"Bold of you. But I suppose, given the dictates of your conscience, you felt you had no choice. You couldn't go to the police."

"No. I couldn't."

"You might have phoned in an anonymous tip, of course. But on a case this highly publicized, the authorities must get hundreds of crank calls. And there are so many people who might carry a grudge against a man in my position. Disturbed people angling for revenge. . . ."

"I know."

"They wouldn't have believed you."

"Of course not."

"So you had to do it all yourself, with no help from anyone."

"I'm used to it."

"Poor Kaylie. Poor dear child."

She didn't answer.

He saw that she was gathering herself, her head lowered, lips pursed. That was good. She didn't yet know what sport he planned for her, but she knew that all her resources would be required, and she was marshaling them for this last, doomed effort. He respected her for it.

A saguaro cactus rose on the roadside, then fell back in a long, slow windshield-wiper motion. The cactus was a tall one. It might be a hundred years old. Cray wondered how many small, meaningless deaths it had witnessed in the nightly dance of predator and prey.

He looked again at his passenger, saw the ripple of her throat as she swallowed the taste of fear. The freckles on her cheeks stood out against the paleness of her skin.

She was pretty. Oddly, he had never noticed it before, not when he'd known her, not when he'd looked at her photograph and wondered if she was still alive and if he would ever have revenge.

He found it strange to think of men kissing her mouth, whispering endearments, bringing pleasure to her. There was one man he knew of, but had there been many others?

Well, there would be no more.

"I like your hair," Cray said. "You're much better as a blonde. You weren't the redhead type. You lacked the requisite personality."

"How can you say that," she whispered, "when you never knew me?"

"But I did know you. I knew you intimately. I knew your secrets. I knew your mind. I still do."

"I wasn't myself then. You didn't know *me*."

Cray considered his response as he slowed the Lexus, turning the wheel. A dirt road swung into the windshield.

"Perhaps you're right," he allowed at last. "But I'll get to know you tonight, won't I?"

The road was a narrow, rutted track bordered by swarms of prickly pear and jumping cholla. Cray's high beams played over floury swirls of dust as the Lexus rolled forward.

"Oh, yes, Kaylie," he said. "You'll be surprised how well I'll know you before we're done."

12

Elizabeth thought she was holding up pretty well so far. Her mind, her body, the whole of her being had been focused on the single task of staying alert and in control.

She had felt the Lexus turn onto another road, a dirt road that punished the suspension.

At the end of this road, her death was waiting.

Fear rose in her, a fierce wave of fear almost overpowering her will, but with a shudder of effort she forced it down. To panic would be fatal. Some of the others must have panicked. She would not.

"Why am I blindfolded?" she asked, holding her voice steady.

"It minimizes your mobility."

"I'm not very mobile anyway, right now."

"There's nothing much to see. Cactus of all kinds. The moon has set. It's very dark."

"Darker for me," she said.

Cray made a soft sound like a chuckle. "In every sense."

Her hands shifted inside the nylon sleeves. It was so much like wearing a straitjacket. She had worn one for three days not long after her arrest. The attendants had refused to remove it even when she used the toilet. They had wiped her off when she was done. She remembered the latex gloves, the cold touch.

"I strip away the mask," Cray said.

The words came from nowhere, startling, baffling. She turned her head in the direction of his voice. "What?"

"You asked what I do. The nature of the game. It's just that simple. I strip away the mask."

She flashed on an obscure image, seaweed in the tide that became a woman's face. "I know about . . . that part of it."

"No, that's not what I mean. What I do at the end is merely symbolic, a kind of private ritual. Primitives take scalps or heads. But what they're after is the soul. So am I."

It was hard to think of something to say. "I never thought of you as religious," she ventured.

"Oh, I'm not. Not in the least. There is no ghost in the machine. We're chemicals, nothing more. Mere vectors for our genetic endowments. The whole glorious human animal is only a Rube Goldberg contraption, jury-rigged by natural selection to dump our complement of DNA into the gene pool. We exist to fuck and die."

"Then I'm not sure where the soul comes in."

"Soul—well, perhaps it's a misleading term. Think of it this way, Kaylie. A human being is an onion, layer upon layer. Social norms and religious archetypes, shame and guilt, repression and evasion, personae we adopt and discard as mood or moment dictates. Peel the onion, strip off the mask, and what's left is the naked essence. What's left is what is real."

Anger stirred in her, pushing back fear. "You keep calling me Kaylie. It's not my name. Not anymore."

"Isn't it?" Somehow, though she couldn't see him, she could feel his slow, cool smile. "Well, that's one more layer of illusion I intend to peel away."

The Lexus slowed. Stopped. The engine clicked off.

"We've arrived," Cray said. "Now the real fun begins."

Unexpectedly she felt him lean close to her, and her vision returned as the blindfold was pulled away.

She blinked at the surprise of light and color. Cray had left the key in the ignition, the high beams on. Long rays of halogen light fanned across an oval of dirt, the cul-de-sac at the end of the road.

There was nothing beyond it but the land's flatness and spiny humps of cacti and, here and there, tall saguaros like scarecrows in a field.

"Take a good look," Cray whispered. "It's your final resting place. The end of all your journeying, at last." He smiled. "What are you thinking? Perhaps that you stayed hidden for twelve years, and you could have gone on hiding?"

"Something like that."

"And now you're going to die. But perhaps not."

She was sure he wanted to see an uplift of hope in her face. She wouldn't give it to him. She merely narrowed her gaze and waited.

"I'm giving you a chance. The same chance I gave the others."

"It didn't do them any good."

"Maybe you'll be lucky. You're due for some luck in your life, aren't you?"

"Overdue," she said, her voice low.

"All right, then. You have miles of open space. No houses or roads nearby. A wilderness, and do you know how many small animals are being hunted in this wilderness tonight? You'll be one of them. You're prey. And you know what I am."

She looked around her, taking in the emptiness of a place without lights or people or doors to lock and hide behind.

"You'll have a fifteen-minute head start. I promise not to watch you when you go. I'll pick up your trail, and hunt you down, if I can. I use no special technology, only a pistol, and it's not even equipped with a night-vision scope. And you should know that I will shoot to wound, not kill. The killing is done with a knife. The last thing I'll do is take your face. I get to keep that, as my trophy. And, by the way, I carry smelling salts, which sometimes prove necessary. You'll be alive and conscious right to the end. That's the game I play. The game I've played for more than twelve years."

She registered the words. She knew all of it was true, and it would really happen to her. She would be hunted like an animal, and she would die in pain, and there was no hope for her.

"Why?" she asked.

On his face she saw a flicker of surprise, and she knew that none of the others had thought of asking that particular question.

He was silent for a moment. Perhaps he would not answer. Then she realized that he was gathering his thoughts, like a conscientious teacher composing the clearest possible reply.

"Because this is life," he said simply. "Kill or be killed. Eat or be eaten. All our most powerful emotions are reducible to the instinctive responses of animals in the fight for life. Anger pumps us up for battle. Fear sharpens our reflexes and perceptions. Have you noticed how preternaturally alert you are right now? And love, the poets' favorite, is only an expression of the need to find safety in communal ties. Burrowing animals—that's all most of us are. And then there are a few who do not choose to burrow and hide. It's one or the other, predator or prey."

"There's more to life than that."

"Really? Has there been more to your life for these past twelve years? Haven't you been running, hiding? Doesn't your heart beat faster when a siren goes off or there's a knock at your door? No wonder you like that silly book, *Watership Down*. What are you, if not a timid rabbit in her hutch?"

"Do you talk to all of them like this?"

"No. Never. You're the first. I thought you might understand."

"You were wrong."

"Evidently." Cray frowned, and though it was crazy, for a moment Elizabeth felt certain she had disappointed him somehow. "Well, let's get started."

He unlocked her door with the power button on his console, then left the car and walked around to the passenger side. She watched as he passed through the high beams, every detail of his features and form jumping into sudden clarity, then melting into a blur of shadow once more. He was careful to avert his face from the light, and she knew why, of course.

He was protecting his night vision. He would need it for the hunt.

She looked down at her purse, tantalizingly near. The clasp was still secure. Cray must not have looked inside.

He wouldn't know about the gun. The gun that was so close. . . .

Again she tugged at the sleeves, but her efforts only pulled the knot tighter.

Then her door swung open, and Cray leaned in, his face inches from her own.

Reflexively she drew back. She could see flecks of amber in his gray-green eyes, his nostrils flaring with an intake of breath. He was clean-shaven, but a ghost of beard stubble was materializing on his lean cheeks and narrow, angular chin.

The gun was in his hand again. She studied it—a large, black, dangerous thing, unpredictable as a snake. The gun he would hunt her with.

Shoot to wound, he had said, not kill.

She had never been wounded by a bullet. Distantly she wondered how it would feel.

"It's a nine-millimeter Glock," Cray said, "if that means anything to you."

"Not a lot."

"I'm going to hold this gun to your head, Elizabeth, or Kaylie, or whoever you think you are."

The muzzle touched her forehead. She had expected it to be cold, but Cray must have worn it close to his body, and his own heat had warmed it.

"My finger is on the trigger. All I need to do is squeeze."

She drew a tight breath. "So do it, then."

"Oh, no. That's not the game I play. I simply want you to understand that you have no options here. No freedom of choice. Not that you ever did. Free will is only another illusion."

She wanted no more philosophy from him. She waited.

"In a moment I'll release your hands. Then you'll climb out."

"All right."

"Any deviation from my instructions, and—bang—you're dead."

"You'll kill me anyway. This would be faster."

"Indeed it would. Quick and perhaps painless. But you don't want me to shoot you, and do you know why? Because while you live, you have a chance. A slender chance, a chance hardly worth considering, it's true—but a chance. You might outrun me, evade me, survive this night. You won't give that up. Will you?"

"No."

"I thought not. You see? I *do* know you."

With his left hand Cray reached for her sleeves. The knot he'd tied was clever, expertly made. With one pull it came apart, and she was free.

"Now get out," Cray said.

This was the critical moment, her last opportunity. Once she left the vehicle, the purse would be beyond her reach forever.

Cray was leaning back, his big black gun floating a few inches from her face.

She unbuckled her lap belt. Cray had pulled it to its full extension before securing it. The retractable portion was a three-foot strap, the buckle's steel prong lolling at one end.

As a weapon, it wasn't much.

But it was all she had.

With a jerk of her arm she flung the strap at Cray, whipping the steel prong at his gun hand, then dived to the floor and seized the purse, popping it open—

And Cray laughed.

"It's not there, bitch."

He was right.

The Colt was gone.

She looked up at Cray and saw his bland, cool smile.

"Your purse was the first thing I looked at," he said. "I found your stupid little toy. I took it with me when I returned the master keys to the storage room. On my way there, I tossed the gun into the desert brush, where no one is likely to find it for months or years. What did you think I was doing while you were out cold?"

She dropped the purse. There was a kind of numbness in her, an absence of any sensation.

"Now," he added, his smile unchanged, "exit the goddamned vehicle, you little piece of shit."

The black gun, the Glock or Grock or whatever it was called, drifted down to fix her in its sights.

"Okay," Elizabeth whispered. "You win."

She started to rise, and without conscious intention she slipped her hand into the satchel beside the purse, closing her fingers over the first item she touched, a steel canister with a spray nozzle.

There was a trigger, and she found it as she sprang at Cray.

From the nozzle—a jet of hissing gas.

She had time to think the canister was useless, only a can of compressed air for fixing flat tires, and then she felt the atmosphere around her turn suddenly cold with a mist of ice crystals, and Cray screamed.

He spun out of the doorway, and she pumped the trigger again.

His left arm came up to protect his face. Frost glittered on his sleeve.

Whatever was in the canister, it was cold, as cold as dry ice, and she could hurt him with it, and she wanted to.

She held down the nozzle, spraying him with arctic cold, and his knees gave out, dropping him to the dirt.

For a moment she knew a wild sense of power, of victory, and then his pistol swung at her.

He had a clear shot, and there was nowhere for her to hide.

But he didn't fire.

It seemed as if his hand wouldn't work, or maybe it was the gun itself that had jammed or locked or—

Frozen.

She could see the glaze of ice on the black barrel.

The gun had been disabled, and Cray was defenseless.

She could punish him.

Kill him.

"Son of a bitch!" she shrieked. *"You son of a bitch!"*

She depressed the trigger, aiming for his face, his eyes.

But this time there was only a feeble hiss, then silence.

The canister was empty.

Cray knew it. Already he was already struggling to rise.

She threw the canister at him. Missed.

There might be other weapons in the satchel, but she had no time to look.

Into the driver's seat. Crank of the ignition key. The motor bursting to life as the high beams momentarily dimmed.

Cray lurched upright, his face wild, and grabbed for the open door.

She saw his gloved hands seize the door frame, and

then the Lexus surged forward as she wrenched the gear selector into drive and stomped the gas pedal.

Cray's gloves, shiny with ice, slipped free of the door, and he fell again in the dirt.

Elizabeth watched him fall, then looked ahead, and there was a low wall of cactus rushing at the Lexus, no way to dodge it or even slow down, and she screamed as the chassis bucked with impact, the foliage sliding under the wheels, dirt rising everywhere in thick spiraling drifts.

Then she was in a clear patch, steering between obstacles, and behind her Cray dwindled in the rearview mirror, a dusty, staggering figure, all in black, so small now, smaller than she could have imagined, and finally gone in the night.

She kept driving, the accelerator on the floor, the big Lexus careening like a carnival ride.

There was a dirt road somewhere and a paved road beyond it, but she knew she couldn't find either of them, not now.

She raced through the trackless desert, plowing up clumps of prickly pear, skirting the big saguaros, barely able to see, because her control had shattered at last, and she was crying.

13

Cray walked for two hours through the desert, following the Lexus' tire tracks. His hands still ached with cold from the liquid nitrogen spray, and he found it difficult to flex his fingers.

Only the black leather gloves had saved him from serious injury. The gloves—and his reflexes. Had he been less quick to react, she would have sprayed him in the face, and he would have been permanently blinded.

As it was, he had shielded his eyes, and the gloves and his long shirtsleeves had absorbed the worst of the spray. The gun, too, of course. The Glock remained frozen, its trigger immovable, the slide locked.

Tonight's misadventure was his first defeat. In years of deadly sport he had never lost to an adversary, had never known the embarrassment of failure.

Still, he would overcome this setback. He would find a way to win. He would bring Kaylie down.

The task posed challenges, to be sure, but he had faced and surmounted many challenges already. A lifetime of challenges.

What he was now, he had made of himself by a concerted and persistent exertion of will. He was not a born predator—at least no more than any man.

At the beginning, he had been only a precocious little boy, a boy kept soft and sheltered, doted on by his mother and grandmother, his sole caretakers in a household barren of a father.

Johnnie Cray had been told that his daddy was a policeman killed on duty, a story that sustained him in his earliest years, until he learned that it was a well-intentioned lie, and that his father was, in fact, a television repairman who had run off with his mother's best friend when Johnnie was six months old. He left a note explaining that childbearing had made Johnnie's mother fat.

As a small boy, Johnnie knew nothing of such unpleasantness. He knew nothing of ugliness or pain. His mommy and grandma did their best to protect him from life's stronger jolts. They kept him apart from other children, fed him sweets, ruffled his hair, and praised his blossoming intelligence.

You're special, Johnnie, his mother would tell him. *You're so smart. You'll do great things with that mind of yours.*

And Cray, so small, had puffed with pride at the words and the future that was their promise.

Then, at the age of seven, he started school. And things changed.

School was a different world, a universe of coarse humor and petty tests of manhood for which he was utterly unprepared. He became the goat, the class joke, the universal victim. The pack smelled his weakness. They pounced.

His nemesis was Billy Curtis. Billy hounded him. And Billy was everything Cray had been protected from, everything despicable in human nature. He was unintelligent and crude. He spit food. He made farting sounds. He kicked people. He notched stick-figure graffiti into the bathroom wall.

And he hated Johnnie Cray. *Johnnie Cry-baby,* he called him. *Johnnie, who wears diapers. Johnnie, who's such a good little girl.*

Cray was nine years old, a third grader, having endured two years of this torment, when one day at recess Billy Curtis tackled him for no evident reason and threw him helplessly to the ground. It had rained that morning, and the pavement was wet and muddy. Cray fell in the slop and lay there, gasping, as all the other boys and even a few unkind girls gathered in a circle to laugh.

Billy Curtis, performing for his audience, capered in triumph and yodeled a singsong doggerel: *Johnnie, Johnnie, better call your mommy!*

And Cray, on his knees, stared up at Billy, chanting and cavorting, swinging his loose arms, an ape in triumph, and he knew suddenly that Billy Curtis was quite literally an ape—an animal, mindless and savage.

Hating Billy, Cray conceived his revenge.

The next evening he climbed the fence to the Curtises' backyard, where he stole Billy's dog, a half-blind, arthritic schnauzer named Shoe. Cray took the dog into the woods, carrying it bundled in his arms. He would always remember the dog shivering in confusion and fear, yet staying quiet—too old, it seemed, to present any resistance.

In the woods he tied a leash around Shoe's neck, and then with cold intent he pulled the leash tight and slowly, very slowly, he strangled the dog to death.

Shoe took a long time to die, wheezing and pawing at the damp, clotted earth. Finally a shudder of surrender hurried through the small body, and the schnauzer was dead.

In that moment Johnnie Cray's anger left him, and he was just a little boy, poking at the dog, both fascinated and horrified by the simple phenomenon of its lifelessness.

He had meant to throw the dead dog over the fence into Billy's backyard, but he found he couldn't do it. Abruptly he was stunned by his own savagery, ashamed, unwilling to advertise the act. Instead he dug a shallow grave near an oak tree and buried Shoe in secret, crying as he filled in the hole.

He did not sleep that night. He lay awake in the great darkness which seemed so unnaturally still, and he thought about the thing he had done and the reasons for it.

Billy Curtis was an animal, yes. But Johnnie Cray was no better, was he? He too was nothing but an ape, driven by anger to an act of violence he could not justify.

Strangely, this thought, when it finally formed itself in words, eased his distress. If he was only an animal, then he couldn't be blamed for what he'd done. He might be no better than Billy Curtis, but at least he was no worse. No worse than anyone, because they were all like that, everybody on earth. All of them were animals, even the grownups in their business suits and cars and offices. All of them, at heart, were no different from Johnnie Cray.

He was not an outcast, then . . . or if he was, it was only because he saw a truth that others didn't. Saw it and acted on it.

All this he had understood at the age of nine. In the

thirty-seven years since, he had not wavered in his fundamental faith.

By degrees, year after year, Cray had pursued a higher understanding of this truth, peeling away humanity's pretensions to greatness, sloughing off any notion of human dignity as a mere antique curiosity. He had explored the deepest dimensions of his bestial inheritance, confronting it even though it scared him, even though at times he felt he couldn't bear the truth he faced—until finally he had broken through to a new, exhilarated self-acceptance, the end of denial, full and grateful surrender to the predator within, a surrender so complete that in its throes he would crane his neck and bay at the moon like a mad animal.

Few had traveled so far. Few had stared into the depths of the well of darkness, the abyss as Nietzsche called it, and had stayed true to what they'd seen.

He was a pioneer—yet not the only one. Today there were others exploring territories close to the land he had mapped. There were geneticists who ascribed all human action to an instinct of reproduction mysteriously encoded in DNA. There were anthropologists who sought the origins of morality in the social instincts of lower primates. There were psychologists who dispensed with both the conscious mind and the subconscious, focusing instead on reflexes trained through operant conditioning.

Different paths, but they led in the same direction. They led to the new millennium just dawning in all its bright but alien promise.

Cray saw the future sometimes. It would be a world stripped of illusions, a world where no outdated ethical precepts would hold sway, where no one would judge or be judged, ever.

There could be no such thing as conscience in the world he saw, and therefore no guilt, no shame. And no hours lying lonely in the dark.

That world was very real to Cray. He was committed to it, utterly.

He had to be.

At dawn he found the Lexus, abandoned in the desert.

He approached it slowly, aware that there was no need for haste. His quarry must be long gone by now. Long gone, and laughing at him.

Inside his gloves, his hands curled into fists, and because he performed the action without strain, he knew that the last effects of the cryogenic gas had worn off.

The front end of the Lexus was canted at an absurd angle. The left front tire was flat. More than flat. It was shredded. Cactus needles had punctured it—he could see a clump of prickly pear clinging to the ribbons of rubber—and the bitch had gone on driving until the tire had disintegrated and she was riding on the wheel rim.

The doors were unlocked. There was no key in the ignition. She'd taken it, no doubt hoping to leave him at least temporarily stranded, unable to start the engine. If so, she'd miscalculated. As long as the vehicle was still drivable, he could get it moving.

He walked around the Lexus, surveying the damage to the exterior. Scratches were grooved into the side panels, where the mesquite brush had stripped away the finish. A few cactus spines were stuck like porcupine quills in the other tires, but none had penetrated deeply enough to cause another flat.

All right, then. He would change the tire, and then he would drive away.

Drive where? Home, he supposed. There was no place else to go. He surely wouldn't find her at the motel again.

Cray looked around him. The Tucson Mountains lay to the south; somewhere west was the Tohono O'Odam reservation. East, there was a road. He saw a sparkle of traffic.

Sandario Road, probably. A two-lane strip of blacktop running north-south. Not a major artery, but crowded enough in the first phase of the morning rush.

She would have walked there. The distance couldn't be much more than a mile. And at the roadside she would have stuck out her thumb and waited.

She might be waiting still. Might be, but he knew she wasn't. Not too many cars would pass before someone stopped to pick up a pretty blonde woman in distress.

Afterward, what would she do? Call the police, identify him as Sharon Andrews' killer? Possibly.

But the authorities were unlikely to believe her. They might carry out a perfunctory investigation. He could handle it.

Cray nodded, his lips pursed tight. Yes. He could handle anything Kaylie McMillan could do to him.

In his wallet he carried a duplicate key to the Lexus. He used it to open the rear compartment, where he kept a full-size spare tire and a jack.

Kneeling in the dust, he changed the tire. The wheel itself was slightly bent, but he could drive on it.

He replaced the jack and shut the trunk, and then very calmly he jacked back the slide on the Glock, taking aim at a tall saguaro.

But it was not a saguaro.

It was Kaylie.

"Die," Cray said.

He snapped the trigger once, and a bullet pockmarked the saguaro's trunk, scaring a cactus wren from its burrow.

"Die."

A second shot nicked one of the long, drooping arms.

"Die, you little whore. Die as you should have died, twelve years ago. Die and die and die and die. . . ."

He went on firing until the gun was empty and the saguaro was a punch card of drilled holes.

It, at least, would die.

Something had to.

Cray got into the Lexus and turned on the engine, then began the long drive home.

14

"Bad night?"

Elizabeth took a moment to register the question.

She knew the driver was looking obliquely at her, sizing up this strange, scared, barefoot woman who had appeared on the shoulder of Sandario Road in the predawn darkness, carrying a purse and a canvas satchel and hoping for a ride.

"You could say that," she answered finally.

Something more was obviously required, some narrative to satisfy the man's curiosity. She could claim she'd had a fight with her boyfriend and run from his parked car. Or that her own car had broken down on a back road.

There were many things to say, but she had no strength for any of them. She remained silent.

Daybreak bloomed over the mountains. A glaze of pink light spread across the pale, tired land.

"So where am I taking you?" the driver asked.

She looked at him. He was an Indian, perhaps sixty. Age had filled out his face and grayed his ponytail. His hands on the steering wheel of the old Dodge Rambler were thick and meaty and lightly liver-spotted.

He reminded her of Anson, her father-in-law. There was no physical resemblance, only a similarity of character. Both of them were men well worn by the years, men whose squinting eyes had seen too much darkness ever to fully trust the light.

"I'm staying at a motel." She couldn't remember the name. "It's off Interstate Ten, near Silverlake Road. But if it's out of your way—"

"Not really."

"I appreciate this."

"Don't worry about it. What's your name?"

"Paula Neilson," she said, using one of her old identities. Lying about such things had become habitual with her.

"Wallace Zepeda. What brings you to Tucson, Paula?"

"Just . . . personal business."

"Personal business. Well, that's clear enough. Me, I'm in the security field."

She flashed on the fear that he might be a cop, a detective or an undercover officer or something.

"Airport security," he added, and she saw a smile crease his cheek. "You wouldn't get past my checkpoint."

"Wouldn't I?"

"Not when the mere mention of the word *security* turns you as pale as . . . well, as a paleface, pardon the expression. You on the run from the law, maybe?"

"Of course not."

"Good. I'd hate to be aiding and abetting. Mind if I turn on the music?"

"Music would be fine."

"Better than talking, huh?"

That smile again.

She didn't answer.

There was an audiocassette half-inserted in the Rambler's tape deck. Zepeda pushed it in and thumbed the on-off knob, and Creedence Clearwater Revival pumped through the cheap speakers at moderate volume.

The song was "Who'll Stop the Rain."

Elizabeth thought it was a good question.

She looked at the desert. Cray was out there. Cray, who hunted women in the wilderness the way other men hunted mule deer and javelinas. Cray, with his erudite, impeccably pedigreed opinions on the nature of the human mind.

No ghost in the machine, he had said. No spirit, no soul, only chemicals.

And if that was so, then what was murder except a rearrangement of those chemicals into a new form? And where was the crime in that? There was no right or wrong, no good, no evil. There was only better living through chemistry. There was death as sport.

Blood sport. She tried to imagine what it would have been like. Cray had said he would give her a head start. She would have fled through the alkali flats, cutting her legs on cactus needles, stumbling, falling, rising. She would have fought against panic, but in the end panic would have overtaken her, and then she would have made some thoughtless mistake, and a bullet would have brought her down.

How long, from start to finish? An hour, maybe. Or less time even than that.

Elizabeth felt a shudder pass through her as it became real to her—the fate she would have suffered, and how narrow had been her escape.

And Cray would not give up. She was sure of that. He must have followed her. Perhaps he had reached the Lexus by now.

She had taken the ignition key, but he probably carried a spare. Even if he didn't, he was smart enough to hotwire the vehicle.

If she had been thinking more clearly, she would have let the air out of the other tires or stolen the distributor cap to disable the vehicle. As it was, he could change the tire and get away.

And then what? Would he prowl the city night after night in search of her car?

She knew he would.

Well, she could leave town, of course. Head to Texas, possibly. A new name, new life. She'd been Elizabeth Palmer for too long anyway. It was smart to change I.D.'s at least once every few years.

But Cray would go on killing. He might never be caught.

Call the police, then. Tip them off.

She doubted they would believe her. Sure, she could tell them what had happened, but it would be the claim of an anonymous caller. The damage to Cray's Lexus might help substantiate her story, but she was fairly certain Cray would come up with an explanation.

She had his ignition key. She could mail it to the police. But what would it prove, except that she had stolen the key somehow?

In her mind she heard Cray smoothly answering every question. *Why, yes, Officers, as a matter of fact, my sport-utility was stolen the other night. Someone must have found the spare key I keep in a magnetic case under the chassis. . . .*

I know, I know, it's the first place a thief will look. I suppose I just never thought it would happen to me. In any event, the vehicle was taken for a short joyride. I was lucky enough to find it a mile from here, on a dirt road. One of the tires had gone flat. . . .

A report? There seemed to be no point in filing a report. My insurance deductible is quite high, so I'm paying out of pocket for the new tire and some other repairs. . . .

He could persuade them. Unless . . .

She remembered the satchel in her lap.

Carefully she opened the satchel and took out her photo album and the manila envelope containing her I.D. documents. Then she probed deeper inside, using the flat of her hand to rummage through the items, touching nothing with her fingertips for fear of leaving prints.

It felt good to look. Cray had violated her privacy by examining her luggage. Now she would return the favor.

She saw a small pocket flashlight with a red filter. A jewel box with a transparent plastic lid, holding what looked like locksmith tools. An unlabeled vial of clear liquid, probably chloroform. A package of what must be smelling salts. Duct tape. A suction cup. A glass cutter.

The satchel was Cray's tool kit.

And it would incriminate him.

Burglar's tools for breaking and entering. Chloroform for carrying out a silent abduction. Duct tape to bind the victim.

She dug deeper and found a spare clip for that pistol of his, the Gock, Grock, whatever it was called.

Had he shot Sharon Andrews with the pistol? If so,

the cartridges in this clip were probably of the same caliber and design as the two slugs found in her body.

There was one more item, at the very bottom of the sack. A leather sheath. And in it, a knife.

She cupped the sheath in the palm of her hand and lifted it. Spots of discoloration freckled the careworn leather, spots that were brown and black and rust-colored. Some were dirt, and some were blood.

Sharon Andrews' blood? Almost surely.

Cray had used this knife to—well, she knew what he'd used it for.

Seaweed in the tide. Green and limp.

A woman's face.

She almost dropped the knife in a spasm of repugnance.

"You okay?" Wallace Zepeda asked over the music.

"Fine. I'm fine."

She was. Really.

Because she had Cray now. She had him.

All she needed to do was get the whole package to the police—Cray's tools and, with them, his damn car key. The key would link the satchel to him almost as effectively as a fingerprint.

The cops must receive dozen of anonymous tips, but this was one tip they couldn't ignore.

And let Cray tell any smooth lie he liked. It wouldn't matter. He was finished, the murdering bastard.

Her hands were shaking as she knotted the satchel's drawstring clasp.

When she looked up, she was surprised to see that the Rambler was heading west on Silverlake Road, and her motel was dead ahead.

"It's there," she said, pointing.

Zepeda pulled into the parking lot and turned off the cassette. He cast a sour gaze on the ramshackle building and the nearby freeway.

"Great place. You find out about it in the Triple-A guide?"

Elizabeth smiled. "Not exactly. Look, I really want to thank you—"

"Forget it. I don't want your gratitude. I just want your attention for a moment."

"I'm kind of in a hurry."

"You've got time for some old Indian wisdom, don't you?"

"Sure. I'm sorry. Of course I do."

"Then here goes. You're in some deep shit, lady. You can't handle it alone. You need to get some help, or the next person who finds you in the desert will be looking at a corpse."

She was shocked for a moment, and then she had to smile. "That's old Indian wisdom?"

"It's wise enough. And I am one old fucking Indian."

"I'm going to get help, Mr. Zepeda."

"You wouldn't be selling me a string of beads, would you, Paula?"

"I wouldn't dare."

"Okay, then. Get some rest. And find yourself some damn shoes."

He let her out and watched her as she hurried to her room and went quickly inside. He noticed that she hadn't needed a key; the door had been left unlocked.

Unlocked—in this neighborhood.

It was just another thing Wallace Zepeda didn't want to think about as he drove away, Creedence loud over the speakers, the sun a haze of glare in the red east.

15

Cray was heading south on Interstate 10, two miles past downtown Tucson, when his glance strayed to the floor of the passenger seat and he realized that it was empty.

Kaylie's purse had been there. She had taken it, of course. That didn't matter.

But the satchel did.

He had forgotten it entirely. Exhaustion and anger had fogged his mind.

She had carried off his little black bag, perhaps without even knowing what it was. But she would know before long. She would look inside, paw through the satchel's contents. She would find the knife.

Cray had cleaned the knife after each kill, but he knew that microscopic traces of blood could still be found on it, perhaps in the narrow crevice where the blade met the hilt.

Sharon Andrews' blood. And the blood of others.

The knife posed the worst threat to him, but the other items were incriminating as well. Once in the possession of the police, the bag's contents would fairly scream his guilt.

"God damn her," he said with sudden violence. "God damn that meddlesome girl to hell."

He took the next exit and doubled back toward town, driving fast. There might not be much time.

Elizabeth spent less than two minutes in the motel room, long enough to put on her shoes and collect her two suitcases.

Before leaving, she entered the bathroom, switching on the vanity lights over the counter. The sink was old and yellowed with deposits of chemical residue, and there was hair, not her own, in the drain.

She cupped her hands under the lukewarm stream from the tap and splashed her face, wanting to feel clean.

When she looked at herself in the mirror, she saw sky-blue eyes and a pale, freckled complexion. She found the strength for a smile. "Still here," she said aloud.

Cray had wanted to wipe her out. He had failed. Now he would pay the price.

She loaded her luggage into the Chevette, then remembered her gun. Cray had said he pitched it into the brush outside the motel.

She spent a few minutes combing the weeds before conceding that the gun was lost. It could be anywhere within the dense foliage. She would need hours to perform a thorough search, and even then, finding the gun would be largely a matter of luck.

Well, maybe she wouldn't need it. Maybe her role in all this was almost done.

The hope buoyed her as she hurried to the front office, fishing the room key from her purse.

The clerk was watching an adult video on a portable TV with a built-in VCR. He glanced at her and asked perfunctorily, "Room okay?"

"Fantastic."

He heard sarcasm and shrugged. "For nineteen a night, whatchoo expect? The Ritz friggin' Carlton?"

On the TV, a nude woman with breasts like water balloons was urgently requesting, *"More."*

Elizabeth was at the door when the clerk said, "Hey, wait a sec. You see anybody funny hanging 'round here last night?"

"Funny?" There was nothing funny about John Cray. "No."

"Kids, maybe? Troublemakers?"

"I didn't. Why?"

"Some shithead busted inna our storage closet, is why. Didn't take nothing, but they fucked up a goddamn expensive padlock. Broke it all in pieces."

"Broke it?"

"Like it was glass. I don't know how the hell they pulled that off."

She thought of the cold stream hissing from the canister's nozzle. Cold enough to freeze a padlock solid and render it vulnerable to a shattering blow.

"Me neither," she said. "You call the police?"

"Cops?" The clerk pantomimed spitting. "All them assholes do is hassle me. You know?"

"I know. Well, good luck."

She was glad the crime would go unreported. She didn't want the police somehow connecting the break-in with Cray, then tying him to her.

The police. She really was going to contact them. The thought seemed strange, unreal, after so many years of evading every patrol car, every blue uniform.

Although it was only a few minutes past seven o'clock, already the morning was warm. The Chevette, unprotected from the sun, baked her as she cranked the engine. The car was equipped with air-conditioning, but that particular feature had never worked. She rolled down the window and tried to breathe.

Pulling out of the lot, she anxiously checked the frontage road, looking for a black Lexus. It was doubtful Cray could get here this fast, but she wasn't taking anything for granted.

The road was clear. She took the 22nd Street on-ramp to Interstate 10 and let it carry her north.

Cray rolled into the motel parking lot at 7:10. The Chevette was gone. Kaylie had left.

He had expected as much. Driving here, he had pieced together her most plausible plan of action.

She would call the police. It was her best move, the one he would have made had their positions been reversed. She would call from a pay phone and identify him as the killer, offering the satchel as proof of his guilt.

Or she might simply leave the satchel outside a police substation with an unsigned note. But he didn't think so. He expected her to call, because only by talking to another person could she be certain her message had gotten through. And, high on the adrenaline rush of survival, she would do it as soon as possible.

From a public phone. She wouldn't call from the motel. She still didn't want to be identified, didn't want to get directly involved.

Having made the call, she would need to make a quick getaway before the police responded. The fastest escape route was the interstate. Cray was betting she would stay close to I-10, either a few miles north or south of the motel.

Which direction?

South, the city turned mean. Barrio streets, crime, danger. More police cars cruising. More cops on the beat.

She wanted to be in a less populous, less heavily patrolled area.

North, then. She would go north. Past downtown Tucson, into the near suburbs.

Of course, she might have made the call already. By now it might be too late.

Perhaps he ought to run. Race for the border. He knew enough Spanish to get by. He could live in the mountains if he had to, at least for a month or two, until the urgency of the search abated.

No.

He would not permit himself to lose. It was bad enough that he had let her get away. To allow her this ultimate victory was unthinkable.

Cray found I-10's entrance ramp and sped into the northbound lanes. The time was 7:15.

16

Elizabeth drove three miles on the freeway, until the crowded part of town was behind her. She considered taking the Speedway Boulevard exit, but decided to go a little farther.

At Grant Road, a mile north of Speedway, she exited, heading east. Within two blocks she found a Circle K convenience store. Two phone kiosks were stationed at the side of the building, away from the main entrance.

Perfect.

She wondered if she was reckless to try this. It would be safer to simply mail the satchel to the police.

But mailing it would take more time. She was determined to have Cray arrested as soon as possible. Today, even.

He was a monster, and she wanted him caged.

She parked a block away from the convenience mart—close enough so she could run to her car after making the call, but not so close that somebody loitering near the phones might happen to see the Chevette and link it to her.

Her luggage was in the hatchback compartment.

She opened the larger suitcase and found her winter gloves, pulling them on.

No fingerprints on the phone handset.

She was thinking of everything. This would be an error-free performance. It had to be.

She shouldered her purse and picked up the satchel. Her heart was drumming fast, and the air seemed very hot, but she was all right. She was going to do this and do it perfectly, no mistakes.

Halfway to the phone she stopped with a sudden thought. Slowly she opened the satchel, and inside she found her photo album, twenty-eight pictures of herself in various guises throughout the years, and alongside it, the manila envelope containing the false documentation she had purchased or created.

She'd nearly forgotten about those items. Nearly left the satchel for the police with her photos and her phony birth certificates inside.

"Oh, Christ, Elizabeth," she whispered, feeling something worse than fear—a kind of disorienting embarrassment, a sense of humiliation so deep it was almost physical pain.

She hurried back to the car. In the driver's seat she fumbled open the satchel and took out the damn photo album and the damn envelope, and then she searched it thoroughly with her gloved hands, checking to be sure nothing else of hers was in there.

When she was done, she checked again. She no longer trusted herself.

Wallace Zepeda had been right. This was too much, this burden she carried. It was making her—

—*crazy*—

—a nervous wreck, and she couldn't bear up under it much longer.

Cray passed the exit for downtown without slowing. Kaylie wouldn't go into the heart of the city. Too much traffic. Too great a risk of encountering a delay after she had made her call.

The next major street was Speedway. He got off there, heading west for six blocks, looking for the Chevette.

Nothing.

This was hopeless. He would never find her. She would call, and even though the police would surely be skeptical, a squad car would be dispatched to pick up the package she had left.

Squad car.

Of course.

Cray pulled onto the roadside and opened his glove compartment, hoping fervently that Kaylie McMillan, clever as she was, had not thought to look inside and clean out its contents.

She hadn't. The police-band transceiver was still there.

Six of the channels were preset to Tucson PD frequencies. He activated the scan mode, dialing the volume high. Coded cross talk chattered over the speaker. If the patrol unit had not yet been dispatched, he might hear the call go out.

The scanner, roaming among the various frequencies, buzzed and chirruped with ten-codes and half-intelligible inquiries and responses. He listened for the particular assignment he was waiting for.

Obviously there was a chance Kaylie had gone outside city limits, in which case the call would be handled by a sheriff's department cruiser. Cray wasn't monitoring those bands; he couldn't listen to a dozen channels at once.

Or, if she had called already, he might have missed the dispatcher's signal. Or the assignment could have been conveyed electronically via the mobile computers installed in TPD cars. Perhaps even now the police had the satchel in their hands, and an evidence technician was examining each separate, incriminating item.

He pulled back into traffic and made a U-turn, then headed east on Speedway. He would travel it for a mile or two beyond the freeway. If he still hadn't found her car, he would continue north.

Grant Road was the next exit. Maybe he would find her there.

Elizabeth almost got out of the car again, and then in an excess of self-doubt she opened the satchel and checked its contents one last time.

She was sure there was something she'd forgotten. But no, it was all here.

Chloroform. Duct tape. Smelling salts. Pocket flashlight. Locksmith tools. Glass cutter. Suction cup. Spare clip for the gun. And the knife in its sheath.

Okay. She was set. She was ready to go.

No, she wasn't.

Cray's ignition key. That was the item she'd overlooked.

The key to the Lexus was the one item that could be definitively connected to Cray. And it was still in the pocket of her blouse.

"You're cracking up," she told herself, and she wasn't sure if it was a joke or not.

If she could overlook so many obvious details, what else was she failing to see? Maybe she ought to wait, have some breakfast. She hadn't eaten since—when? —since yesterday afternoon, actually. She could find a coffee shop, have some eggs, some coffee. Clear her head.

That was the smart thing to do, but she knew it wasn't a real option. She had to get this over with. Her fear would only get worse the longer she delayed.

She found the key in her pocket and placed it in the satchel, then carefully knotted the drawstring.

This time she was ready.

She looked at herself in the rearview mirror. Her pale, freckled, frightened face.

"Ready," she said, confirming the fact, just in case there was any doubt.

Out of the car again. She approached the convenience store. The two phones at the side of the building were both unused at the moment. Good.

She checked out the street. No patrol cars. She looked through the glass wall of the store. No cops inside. Not even a security guard, from what she could tell.

Better and better.

She placed the satchel on the ground below the kiosk, pushing it against the brick wall of the building to hide it from a casual observer. Then she lifted the telephone handset in her gloved hand.

Calling the police. She was really doing it, really calling the police.

She took a breath, fighting for composure, and then with a trembling finger she stabbed three digits.

A long ring. Another.

She was shaking so hard she could barely breathe.

A third ring, cut off early as a businesslike male voice came on the line.

"Nine-one-one. What is your emergency?"

The bitch wasn't on Speedway.

Cray had covered the wide, well-traveled boulevard in two directions. Twice he'd seen a red hatchback that might have been the Chevette, but both times the sighting had been a false alarm.

At the corner of Grant and Campbell he hooked north. Returning to I-10 would take too long. He would take Campbell to Grant Road and head west.

On the passenger seat, the transceiver stuttered and crackled, his lifeline to the police—and just possibly his last hope.

17

"I'm calling with information," Elizabeth said, her mouth pressed close to the handset, "about Sharon Andrews, the woman who was killed in the White Mountains. I know who did it."

"All right," the man on the other end said in a low, neutral tone.

She'd heard that tone before, though she wasn't quite sure where.

"His name is John Cray." She spelled it. "He lives in Safford. Just outside Safford, I mean. Lives there and works there."

The words had come out in curiously disjointed blocks of speech. She had rehearsed this conversation many times, but now she couldn't remember a single thing she'd meant to say.

"Go on," the man said.

If he was impatient or skeptical, he hid it well. He sounded interested, open to whatever she might say. A calm, reassuring, practiced voice, a doctor's voice. . . .

Then she remembered where she'd encountered that tone before. It was the quiet, unstressed monotone a psychiatrist used when humoring a difficult patient.

For a moment she froze up, old memories blasting her like a cold wind, and she couldn't say anything.

"Ma'am?" the 911 operator prompted.

"John Cray," she said again, just to kick her mind into gear. "He killed Sharon Andrews."

"And how do you know that?"

"Because he tried to kill me, too."

No, God, that had come out wrong. It sounded paranoid, delusional.

"Tried to kill you?" the man asked with the faintest lilt of skepticism.

"I've been watching him, following him." Still all wrong. She could hear the desperate craziness in her words. "No, look, forget about that. It doesn't matter how I know. All right? It doesn't matter. . . ."

She was screwing up, blowing it. If she got this wrong, she might never have another chance. Cray would go on killing, and she couldn't stop him, couldn't do anything.

There was too much at stake, and she was too scared. After what she'd been through last night, she wouldn't have thought she could ever be scared again, but here she was, in a state of stupid panic over a phone call.

Eyes shut, she fought for calm.

"I'm sorry to sound so flustered," she said softly. "This is hard for me."

"Of course it is."

There it was again, that psychiatrist's voice of his. She hated that voice. It mocked her, and without thinking she snapped, "Damn it, I'm not crazy."

Shit.

That was exactly the sort of thing a crazy person would say.

She was messing up so badly. She'd had no idea she could be such a fool.

"No one's suggesting—" the man began, but she cut him off.

"Cray drives a black Lexus sport-utility vehicle. If you look at it, you'll see it's pretty banged up. I drove it through the desert to escape from him."

"You were in the desert?"

"Yes, he took me there. He always takes his victims into the wilderness. Mountains, desert—he *hunts* them. It's a sport for him. He lets them go, and he tracks them, hunts them down like animals. It's what he was going to do to me, but . . . but I got away."

This sounded rather unlikely even to her.

"I have proof," she added.

"What sort of proof?" The voice sounded almost bored now.

Had he already dismissed her as a nut? Maybe she shouldn't have called 911. Maybe it would have been smarter to try talking to one of the detectives. Or a desk officer. Maybe . . .

"A bag," she said. "A satchel. Cray's satchel—I took it from him. It's got all his stuff, the stuff he uses to break into places and kidnap women. There's some ammunition in it, and a knife. The knife he used on Sharon Andrews and the others. And the ignition key to the Lexus. It's all in here, the proof you need, and all you have to do is come and get it."

"Perhaps you could bring it in."

"I'm leaving it for you. Here, at this phone. You already know where I'm calling from. You do an instant trace on nine-one-one calls."

"Actually, our trace equipment is malfunctioning at the moment. If you could tell me your location . . ."

This had to be a lie, and why would he lie to her, if not to buy time?

The squad car had already been dispatched. It was coming.

Coming right now.

"Ma'am?"

Elizabeth slammed down the handset, and then she was running to her car.

Cray was cruising west on Grant Road in heavy traffic, scanning the roadside for a parked Chevette, when the call came over the transceiver.

"Mary Twelve"—the dispatcher was calling for a patrol unit—"requesting a ten-twenty."

"Uh, we're at Oracle and Prince," the unit answered.

"Okay, we need you to make contact with a female RP at a pay phone, Circle K store, Grant and Fifteenth Avenue. This is a code two incident, code two."

"Ten-four."

An RP was a reporting person.

It was Kaylie. Had to be.

Cray locked in that channel on the radio, then accelerated, weaving between two cars into a clear stretch of road.

Fifteenth Avenue was twenty blocks away. Near the interstate.

She was calling from a phone at a convenience store, and she meant to make a quick escape and leave the satchel for the cops to find.

The plan might work. He wasn't sure he could beat the squad car to the scene.

"Mary Twelve, we got some additional information

on that RP. She's not expecting to be contacted. Nine-one's holding her on the line. It's a—sounds like it could be a disturbed individual."

"Ten-four."

Disturbed individual. Cray smiled at that diagnosis as he maneuvered from lane to lane, blowing past slower traffic.

Ahead, the stoplight at First Avenue cycled to red, stopping a logjam of cars. He couldn't afford to be stuck at the light. With a spin of the wheel, he whipped into the right lane and cut north on First, then veered west on the first side street.

He sped through a residential neighborhood, past rows of one-story homes with dirt yards and RVs in the driveways.

"ETA, Mary Twelve?" the dispatcher asked.

"ETA in two minutes."

Two minutes.

It would be close.

The next major street was Stone Avenue. Traffic was running north and south, but he skidded into a gap, southbound, and immediately hooked onto Grant again, racing west.

"Mary Twelve, we got a nine-one hang-up on that RP."

She'd fled.

"ETA one minute," the patrol unit responded.

They were still hoping to catch her.

Probably they wouldn't succeed, but they would find the package she had left for them—unless Cray found it first.

He looked ahead. Coming up was Oracle Road, the six-lane highway he'd taken last night when he followed the Chevette south from the foothills.

A red light at that intersection would last a good two minutes, and he would have no chance.

The light was green as he approached, but the DON'T WALK sign was solid red, and he knew a change was coming.

Yellow.

He floored the gas, and his tachometer buzzed into the danger zone.

The car in front of him was stopping, damn it, and the lane to his left was jammed.

On the shoulder, then.

He swung the wheel, and the Lexus bounded around the slowing traffic and streaked through the intersection under a red light. Somewhere a horn blared.

Close now. Fifteenth Avenue was within sight.

The Circle K appeared in waves of shimmering heat, a mirage of hope.

Patrol car? He didn't see one. Not yet.

Then he saw a flash of red shoot away from the curb a block past the Circle K, and he knew it was the hatchback with Kaylie McMillan at the wheel.

For an insane moment all he wanted to do was follow the little car, yes, follow it at a distance, unseen, follow until Kaylie thought she was safe, and when she pulled over—

Grab her. Take her away. Kill her slowly. And at the climax, lift her face from her skull, a freckled mask, his greatest prize.

But he couldn't do that.

The satchel was what mattered.

She must have left it by the phone.

The Chevette disappeared down the road, streaking toward the freeway, and Cray let it go.

Cutting speed, he hauled the Lexus into the Circle K's parking lot and killed the engine.

Then he was out and looking around desperately for a pay phone. None was in sight. But there had to be one here. At the side of the building, perhaps. He checked one side—nothing. Ran to the other.

Two phone kiosks, neither in use.

The satchel, where was the satchel?

There. On the ground beneath the nearer phone.

He seized it, then looked outside and saw a Tucson PD Crown Victoria roll into the lot.

They were here.

And he was trapped at the side of the building with the evidence in his hands.

The store's brick wall loomed on his left. A hurricane fence, too high to climb, faced him to his right.

Directly ahead of him, the two cops were getting out of the car.

He could ambush them, kill them both.

Except he couldn't. He'd left his Glock in the Lexus.

Anyway, the bitch would have mentioned his name over the phone. Killing these two errand boys would serve no purpose except to confirm her story.

Run, then.

He turned and sprinted toward the rear of the store, the satchel thudding against his hip. Between the back wall and the fence protecting the adjacent vacant lot, there was a narrow gap, barely wide enough to squeeze through.

Cray eased into the gap and came up against a clutter of planks and cinder blocks, the remnants of some minor construction job, thrown back here and forgotten. The mess was high enough to block his path. He couldn't advance.

Breathing hard, he hugged the wall and listened as the cops came around to the phones.

"—said there was some kind of bag she left," one of them was saying.

"What are we, UPS, picking up parcels?"

"I'm just telling you what it said on the MDT."

Mobile Data Terminal. The squad car's computer. A fuller explanation must have been transmitted electronically, and the cop riding shotgun had read it while his partner drove.

"Well," the driver said, "I don't see any damn bag."

"She was probably a mental case anyway."

"Did they say what kind of bag?"

"Nah."

"Like a shopping bag? Or a suitcase?"

"They just said bag. What difference does it make? Nothing's here."

There was a pause, long enough to let Cray think they had gone away, and then the driver said, "Think she could've taken off around back?"

"We can check it out."

Cray stiffened.

They would come back here and find him boxed in by a wall and a fence and a mound of discarded refuse.

He untied the satchel's drawstring. Reaching in, he touched the leather sheath of his knife. He could kill one of them, at least, before the other opened fire.

It was better to go out that way than to be carted off to prison, a freak and a laughingstock.

"Ah, fuck it." That was the driver. "I'm getting too old for this shit. Let's get out of here."

"We can ask in the store if they saw anything."

"Let's just go," the driver said, then added in his radio voice, "Mary Twelve."

He was on his portable, calling in. Cray heard a soft sizzle of static, then the driver again, his words fainter as the two cops walked away.

"The RP is GOA." Gone on arrival. "Negative on the ten-thirty-one. . . . Yeah, she didn't leave anything behind. . . . We're code four here."

Cray did not move until he heard the double slam of the squad car's doors. Then he stepped out from behind the wall. Hidden in shadow at the rear of the alley, he watched the car pull out of the parking lot into the traffic stream on Grant Road. Finally he exhaled a slow breath and lowered his head.

He saw the knife in his hand. It was unsheathed, and his fingers were curled tightly over the handle, holding the weapon poised for a lethal thrust.

He hadn't even known he'd removed the sheath. The act had been carried out unconsciously, by instinct.

Well, he of all people could hardly be surprised by the limitations of the conscious mind.

Cray sheathed the knife and replaced it in the satchel, then left the alley. Before driving off, he bought a thermos of coffee at the Circle K.

It had been a long night, and if Kaylie had indeed given his name to the 911 operator, then he could expect an equally long day.

18

"I steal their faces."

"You already told us that. But you haven't said why. Hey, Mitch? Mitchell? You hear me? Tell us why."

The raggedy man named Mitch didn't answer. He had zoned out again, his drawn face going blank, his pale, rheumy eyes losing focus. He stared out the window of the moving car at a blur of strip malls and burrito stands, a trickle of saliva on his chin.

Roy Shepherd sighed. This wasn't the guy. He was sure of it.

Almost sure.

He didn't put a great deal of faith in psychological profiles. They were mostly guesswork, and often not very good guesswork at that. He'd worked the streets long enough, first as a patrol cop and now as a plainclothes detective, to know that human nature was too complicated, too multifaceted, to be reduced to a series of simple formulas.

Still, the profiles were reliable in some respects. If the killer was careful and methodical, leaving few clues or none at all, covering his tracks, defying capture, then he almost certainly was not schizophrenic.

The schizos could be violent—oh, yes, Shepherd

knew about that—but their violence was apt to be spontaneous, frenzied, splashy. They weren't organized in their thinking. They were inept at concealment.

Whoever had killed Sharon Andrews in the White Mountains five months ago—killed her and cut off her face and taken it as a grisly souvenir—was surely crazy, a psycho, but not a schizophrenic like glassy-eyed Mitch.

Mitch might have killed somebody, though. He seemed to think he had.

Shepherd settled back in the rear seat of the unmarked car. Two other detectives, Janice Hirst and Hector Alvarez, sat up front. Hirst was driving. Alvarez was rather noisily chewing gum. He always had a stick of Juicy Fruit in his mouth. Shepherd had never seen the man actually eat anything.

He glanced out the window. After fifteen years in Tucson, his whole professional life, he knew the town better than most cabbies. He didn't even need to check the street signs to know that the unmarked car was crossing the intersection of 22nd Street and Park Avenue.

The warehouse was two blocks away. If there were faces or any other body parts in Mitch's possession, Shepherd and his colleagues would know soon enough.

"I steal their faces," Mitch mumbled in a sleepwalker's voice, and a smile briefly animated his expression.

He'd said the same thing to the patrol cops who arrested him for creating a public disturbance at 6:30 this morning, after Mitch was found directing traffic on Wilmot Road.

I steal their faces.

It had gotten the cops' attention, at any rate.

Shepherd had taken their report at 7:15. Possible confession in the White Mountains case. Street person saying he took people's faces.

He hadn't believed it, and his skepticism had only deepened after a thirty-minute interrogation of the suspect. Mitch was indigent. He lived off handouts and soup-kitchen charity. He slept at shelters and in alleys. He had no driver's license and no means of transportation.

How was he supposed to have abducted Sharon Andrews and taken her to the White Mountains, roughly a hundred miles northeast of Tucson?

Mitch hadn't answered that question or very many other questions. He had merely reiterated his mantra with tiresome regularity while his expression varied between epileptic twitches and utter blankness.

The one bit of solid information Shepherd had coaxed from the man was the place where the faces could be found.

CDS, Mitch had said.

When pressed, he carefully repeated the acronym, enunciating each letter with exaggerated precision.

CDS stood for Central District Supply. The company, now defunct, had operated a warehouse near South Tucson. The three letters, painted ten feet high, still adorned the side of the abandoned building.

Looking ahead, Shepherd saw those letters now rising over the roof of a lower building at the end of a dead-end street south of 22nd. "That the place?" he asked Mitch.

Mitch nodded. "CDS."

"The faces are in there?"

Another nod. "I steal their faces."

Shepherd looked away. "We'll see."

Hirst parked in a vacant lot alongside the looming bulk of the warehouse. She and Alvarez climbed out of the unmarked Crown Victoria, then helped Mitch to exit.

He stood vacantly, swaying and humming, his wrists handcuffed behind him. Shepherd had insisted on the handcuffs. He knew you couldn't take any chances with these people.

Shepherd himself got out last, unfolding himself from the close confines of the sedan's rear compartment. He was tall and slim, and at thirty-eight he kept himself in shape by rising at 5:30 every day to play vigorous handball at Fort Lowell Park. This morning, after his game, he had driven directly to Tucson police headquarters and showered there. Somehow he had misplaced his comb, and he'd had to smooth and part his close-cropped brown hair with his fingers, a procedure that had left him slightly unkempt.

As he stood by the car, a dusty breeze kicked up and made mischief with his hair, and he knew that if Ginnie were here, he would catch gentle hell from her for the state of his appearance. Ginnie had been the one who'd always straightened his tie, exclaimed over loose threads in his slacks, and made tut-tutting noises when he came down to breakfast in a week-old, unwashed sweatshirt and Jockey briefs.

He smiled, thinking of his wife, but the smile turned to sadness as the wind blew harder. He had not been able to think of Ginnie without sorrow for a long time now. There was a hurt in him, deep and raw, and even an hour of pounding the handball until his palms were numb could not assuage it.

"Show us how to get in," he told Mitch, hoping the man was sufficiently lucid to comprehend the order.

He was, for with a nod, Mitch led the three cops through knee-high weeds and swirls of windblown dust toward the tall chicken-wire fence surrounding the warehouse. He took long, stiff, clumsy strides. He hummed louder.

At the rear there was a gap in the fence, professionally cut. Mitch hadn't done that. The work was too clean, too competent.

The four of them slipped through the gap and came to the back of the building, where Mitch pointed at a door that had been chained shut.

The chain links had been severed—again, a neat, professional job.

"Somebody busted in here," Hector Alvarez said, "probably hoping there was still some merchandise inside."

Janice Hirst studied the broken chain. "Long time ago. See? The links are rusty even where they were cut through."

Mitch just stood, waiting.

"So they're inside?" Shepherd asked him. "The faces?"

Nod.

"Anybody else in there? Friends of yours?"

Head shake.

It was probably true. But Shepherd unholstered his Beretta anyway.

"Janice, stand post out here with our friend Mitch. Hector, give me some cover."

Alvarez snapped his Juicy Fruit. "Right."

Shepherd tested the doorknob. It turned freely. He eased the door an inch ajar, then took out his flashlight.

Flash in one hand, gun in the other, he pushed the door wide and sidestepped in, not lingering in the doorway where he was silhouetted against the glare. Then he turned on the flashlight, holding it away from his body, and panned the beam over the windowless, cavernous room.

He saw them.

Faces.

They leaped out of the shadows, face after face, tacked to walls and support columns, faces young and old, in many hues, all staring eyelessly.

Mitch had cut out the eyes. Perhaps his trophies' lifeless gazes had disturbed him.

"Jesus," Alvarez muttered.

Outside, Mitch released a giggle. "Told you," he said. "I steal their faces. I steal their faces."

Shepherd nodded. "You sure do." To Alvarez he added, "Hang back for a minute. I want to check it out."

His flashlight leading him, Shepherd advanced into the gloom.

The ceiling was high, the walls far away, his every step on the concrete floor echoing from distant corners. Clusters of trash were piled here and there like atolls in a sea of dust. Magazines, mostly. Mitch must have scavenged them from Dumpsters. He—

There was movement to Shepherd's left, and he swung the flash at it, glimpsing a pink tail and a scurrying blur.

Nice place, he thought grimly.

When he was satisfied that the warehouse was

empty except for the rats and the faces, he approached the nearest pylon. It was steel, reinforced with concrete, and Mitch's artistry had made it a totem pole of faces.

Most were women, but there were a few men. Shepherd recognized some of them. Fashion models, actresses, other celebrities.

Nearly all the photos were in color, glossy, and large enough to be almost life-size.

Mitch had cut them out very neatly, omitting the eyes, and with thumbtacks or finishing nails he had mounted the photos around the warehouse, scores of them, hundreds of them, the work of a lifetime.

"This is quite impressive, Mitch," Shepherd said. "You're an artist."

"I steal their faces," Mitch informed him from the doorway.

"It's good you told us. Work like this deserves an audience."

"I steal their faces."

"Yes. We got that."

Shepherd loitered in the warehouse for a minute or two. He truly was impressed with the man's achievement. Mitch was like those people who build monuments out of junk or amass the world's largest ball of string. He was crazy, to be sure, and compulsive or obsessive or whatever the term was, but he had demonstrated a degree of diligence and sheer persistence that few sane people could equal. The warehouse was a kind of art gallery, and stamped on it was Mitch's personality, fascinating and unique.

"You could charge admission," he told Mitch as he rejoined the others in the sunlight.

Mitch only blinked, but Shepherd thought he detected a hint of shy gratitude in the man's twitchy smile.

They returned to the car, easing their prisoner into the backseat. Janice Hirst looked sad.

"It's almost a shame," she said.

Shepherd asked what she meant.

She lowered her voice. "Well, they'll put him away, at least for a while. It's too bad. He's harmless, don't you think?"

Hirst was a transfer from the sheriff's department in Pinal County, and there were a lot of things she didn't know. Alvarez, though, had been with Tucson PD nearly as long as Shepherd himself, and he turned away, uncomfortable.

Shepherd ought to have let it go, but he couldn't. "When they're this far gone, they're not harmless."

"But you said he ought to charge admission."

"What he's done here is harmless. Interesting, even. But who knows what he might do next?"

"You mean violence?" Hirst frowned. "That's rare among schizophrenics."

"So I've been told. You handle a lot of street people in Pinal?"

"Not really. Rural area, you know. Illegals camping out in the woods. . . ."

"Mental patients? Deinstitutionalized? Mainstreamed?"

"Hardly ever." She lifted her chin. "But I've read up on it. I know—"

"You don't know a fucking thing," Shepherd said without emphasis. "Now let's get out of here."

There was silence on the drive back, except for Mitch, who hummed an unmelodic tune and stared at distant visions only he could see.

19

Elizabeth had eaten nothing in twenty hours. Her last meal had been a couple of granola bars consumed while she staked out Cray's residence late on Monday afternoon.

She had not realized how utterly famished she was until she opened the menu at the coffee shop and read the list of selections. She wanted one of everything. She wanted breakfast, lunch, and dinner all at once.

The bored waitress drifted back to Elizabeth's corner table after serving a tray of steaming dishes to a boisterous group of utility workers across the room. "Decided yet?" she said without interest.

Elizabeth, who had waited tables in a coffee shop not very different from this one, appraised the woman's technique as poor. You got better tips with a cheery welcome and a smile.

She ordered two eggs, scrambled, with hash browns and sausage links and toast with jam and a large orange juice and coffee with cream and sugar and a cinnamon roll on the side.

"Did I remember to say hash browns?" she asked.

The waitress jotted down a few scribbles. "Sweetie,

you remembered to say every darn thing on the menu. How do you keep your figure?"

"I run marathons."

It was true, in a sense. She'd been running for twelve years, and that had to be some kind of record.

She shifted anxiously in the leatherette bench seat, awaiting the food's arrival. Her hunger, now that she had permitted herself to notice it, was like a living thing inside her, a restless animal clawing and twisting in her belly. She felt weak and faint.

But it didn't matter. The discomfort was only physical, and it couldn't compete with the sheer elation lifting her like a concentrated adrenaline rush.

She'd done it.

Called the police.

Left the satchel.

The 911 operator hadn't believed her, but so what? The package would prove her story.

She just hoped the patrol cops didn't paw through the contents and smear any fingerprints Cray might have left.

Even now the satchel would be on the desk of some homicide detective at Tucson PD's downtown headquarters. Or maybe it was in the criminalistics lab, its contents being photographed and measured by careful people with gloved hands. How long would it take before they realized this was the real thing? The knife would surely confirm it. Probably they could match the blade to nicks on Sharon Andrews' skull.

Even if they weren't absolutely convinced, they would have to delve deeper. Their next step would be to talk with Cray.

There were two possibilities. Either he had already

fled, hoping to lose himself across the border or in another state, or he was waiting for them, intending to brazen out their interrogation.

If he'd fled, his guilt would be established by that fact alone. If he tried to match wits with the investigators, he would be hard-pressed to explain the key to his Lexus in the satchel, or the damage to the vehicle itself.

He was finished, either way. The turnaround was so complete, so perfect, as to leave her almost disoriented. She felt as if she had been spun in circles.

By all rights she should have been Cray's victim. She should be dead now, a body in the desert, perhaps buried, perhaps merely kicked into the mesquite brush, a meal for scavengers that would come in the night to tease apart her bones.

And her face . . .

Reflexively she touched the skin of her cheek, her forehead. She knew what Cray would have done with her face.

Instead, she'd beaten him. She'd put him on the defensive, boxed him in, and he would never escape.

The waitress returned with a high hill of food. "Dig in," she said grumpily.

Eggs had never tasted so fine. Elizabeth ate them all in a sustained ravenous burst, then turned her attention to the side dishes and beverages.

She was halfway through the meal when chairs scraped the floor at the table next to her. Glancing up, she saw two men in blue uniforms seating themselves. Cops.

Fear froze her. For a moment she lost the ability to breathe. All she could think of was that they had seen her leave the pay phone, they had followed her, they had tracked her to the coffee shop, and now they were playing a game with her, a sadistic game.

No, that wasn't what had happened, of course not.

They were just two patrol cops on a break. The coffee shop, not far from downtown, seemed to cater to city employees. The utility workers across the room, for instance.

The waitress said hello to the cops, her attitude improving noticeably around them. These guys were regulars. They called her by her first name, Lois. They made jokes about the menu.

So everything was okay, and Elizabeth could stop shaking.

Except she couldn't.

Fear of cops was not a rational thing with her anymore. It was a habit of mind, a way of being. She had spent too many years avoiding blue uniforms and two-tone sedans with light bars. Even a businessman in a blue suit could spook her, or a car with a ski rack that looked, in silhouette, like a patrol unit's dome light.

The cops were wearing their portable radios, the volume dialed low. She heard the soft crackle of police codes. She hated that sound. She would rather hear the whine of a dentist's drill, the yowl of an alley cat, anything but the cross talk of prowl cars on the hunt.

Stop this.

She had lost her appetite. Half her meal remained before her, uneaten. She had to finish it. To leave now, so soon after the police had appeared, would look suspicious.

She drank her orange juice. The pulp felt slimy in her mouth, and when she swallowed, she experienced a momentary thrust of nausea.

The room was hot. She had trouble holding her silverware. The problem was the damn Formica tabletop; it was too shiny; it reflected the glow of the overhead fluorescents.

And there were ceiling fans, the blades lazily rotating; they flickered.

It was the flicker and shine that were getting to her, and the noise—a cascade of laughter from the utility workers, a clatter of cutlery somewhere from the rear of the coffee shop—noise and brightness and the sultry heat, the bubbling indigestion in her gut, all of it.

The cops were talking about last night's football game, Panthers and Saints: "What the hell were they thinking of when they went for it on fourth down . . . shit, I woulda kicked it away, pinned 'em deep . . ."

Come on, Elizabeth. They aren't paying any attention to you. Just ignore them. They're no threat. You're okay.

She wasn't sure who was saying these reassuring words. The voice was familiar, a deep, slow, male voice. Anson's voice? Could be.

But Anson just didn't know. He didn't understand how it was to be a hunted rabbit every day and every night for twelve years, hiding behind false names and false documents, waiting for the fatal slip or the trick of fate that would leave you helpless before the hounds.

They were six feet from her. Closer, maybe.

She reached for the coffee, wanting something hot in her belly, and her trembling hand knocked over the ceramic cup.

The cup didn't break, but it rang like a bell as it struck the tabletop, spewing a flood of coffee over the Formica.

And people were looking.

Everyone was looking.

The two cops—looking.

One of them turning in his chair, offering a paper napkin, saying something, his face polite, nice smile, kind eyes, but still he was the enemy and he was *seeing* her.

"That's okay," she managed, using her own napkin to swab up the mess. "I've got it. Thanks."

Then the waitress was there with a sponge, and the rest of the spill disappeared under the quick circling motion of her hand.

"Want a refill on that?" the waitress, Lois, asked.

"No, just . . . just the check, please."

God, listen to her, she sounded so damn scared.

She risked a glance at the cops again. One of them, the one who'd volunteered his napkin, was still watching her. "Happens all the time," he said kindly. "Don't fret about it."

She had to say something, anything. "I'm just clumsy today," she tried.

"No big deal," the other cop said. "Clumsiness is only a misdemeanor in this town."

It was a joke, and she laughed, but even the word *misdemeanor*, with its connotations of arrest and punishment, prodded her into a new spasm of panic.

The waitress came back with the bill, and Elizabeth paid in cash, overpaying somewhat, not caring.

"Keep the change. I'm sorry about the—you know."

"Not a problem. Don't you want that cinnamon roll?"

"Guess my eyes were bigger than my stomach." The cliché came from nowhere, rescuing her from a self-conscious silence. She got up, grabbing her purse, trying not to look at the cops, feeling like such a fool.

After twelve years she was still this afraid. After last night. After the phone call an hour ago. After all she had done, all she'd been through—still the fear was with her, clinging like a shadow.

She left the coffee shop. Outside, she glanced through the window, and for a moment she was sure she saw one of the cops, the one who'd made the misdemeanor joke, watching her.

But maybe not.

It could have been her imagination.

She hated this life. Running, hiding. Hated it, and she was tired of it, too, just tired, worn out.

Her Chevette was parked on a side street, away from the main thoroughfare. She slipped behind the wheel and sat for a long moment, breathing harshly through her mouth, letting the fear subside.

After a while she slotted the key into the ignition cylinder and ran the battery, then turned on the radio. She dialed through the AM bands, wanting to hear a soothing voice, something to distract her. She found a news update. The time was exactly nine o'clock, and the ABC announcer was talking about a battle in Congress over Medicaid funding.

This was good. This was a safe topic, far removed from her life and her concerns. She listened, grateful for the illusion of escape.

There were more news headlines, then a spate of ads, then the stock market numbers at this hour, and after the ABC sign-off, the local news came on.

"The top local story, a possible break in the White Mountains Killer case . . ."

Elizabeth sat upright, her fear forgotten.

This soon? Word had gotten out already?

It seemed impossible, too much even to hope for.

But . . .

"Police sources say they may have apprehended the man who killed single mom Sharon Andrews in the White Mountains wilderness last April. There is, as yet, no official word . . ."

They had him.

Somehow, only an hour after she'd left the satchel, *they had arrested Cray.*

". . . a man believed to be in custody and linked to the crime that shocked southern Arizona. Reports are still sketchy, but it appears that a telephone tip to nine-one-one earlier this morning may have been instrumental in identifying the suspect . . ."

Her call.

There was no doubt, then.

It was incredible that they had moved so fast, but somehow they had.

The report ended with a request to stay tuned for further details as they developed, and then a political talk show came on, and Elizabeth switched off the radio.

She felt immensely better. She felt fine. She wished she could march right back into the coffee shop and finish that cinnamon roll she'd left uneaten.

Cray was in custody.

In custody.

Words that had haunted her, frightened her, for the past twelve years—but not this time.

"I won," she told John Bainbridge Cray, who hovered before her in her mind. "I beat you, you evil son of a bitch. *I beat you.*"

20

At 9:30 A.M., a meeting of the White Mountains Killer task force convened in an interrogation room at Tucson PD's downtown headquarters. Captain Paul Brookings, commander of the Homicide Division, presided. He looked unhappy, but he always did.

"Got a shit storm coming," he said by way of opening the conclave.

His gaze panned over the seven men seated around the long mahogany table and lounging on the metal bench against one wall. The bench was fitted with steel rings, suitable for securing handcuffed prisoners when the room was used for its primary purpose.

"So what else is new?" a detective named Rivera sighed.

Marty Kroft tossed a Styrofoam coffee cup at a wastebasket and missed.

The task force was decidedly informal in both its organization and its membership. A core group of four homicide detectives had stayed with the case since the discovery of Sharon Andrews' remains last August, but other investigators drifted in and out of the task force as their caseloads dictated.

Roy Shepherd had been there from the start. He had

investigated Sharon's disappearance even before she turned up dead. He'd met her boy, Todd, the seven-year-old now being raised by his maternal grandparents in Sierra Vista. He'd gone to Apache County to share notes with the sheriff's department there and to see the creek where the body had been found.

The killing belonged to him, really, not to Brookings, not to anyone else. Other cops had worked it to varying degrees, but he had lived it. And he wanted the case cleared. More than anything in his sixteen-year career in law enforcement, he wanted to find the man who had peeled off that woman's face and taken it with him as a souvenir.

"Don't hold back, Captain," he said from the far end of the table. "Share the bad news."

Brookings found a smile at the corners of his mouth. "You telling me you don't already know? Shep, I'm surprised at you."

Shepherd permitted few people to call him Shep, a nickname he detested, but Paul Brookings could get away with it.

"I admit it's a lapse in my customary omniscience," he answered mildly. "But Hector and Janice and I were all tied up with that freak who said he stole people's faces."

Janice Hirst wasn't part of the task force, but Hector Alvarez had been on the case almost as long as Shepherd. Alvarez nodded. "We thought we had something, maybe."

Marty Kroft looked puzzled. "Guess I'm not so, uh, omniscious either. What's this all about?"

"False alarm." Shepherd explained about the magazine photos, the warehouse that had become a gallery.

Steve Call snorted. "Sounds like a man who could use some serious downtime."

"He's on vacation in the psych ward now," Alvarez said.

"These street people," Don Rivera muttered, "man, they just get weirder. . . ."

Then he fell silent, and for a moment so did everyone else, because they had remembered that Shepherd was in the room.

Brookings was first to speak. "Anyway, that's the shit storm I referred to. Some idiot leaked the story. Major break in the White Mountains case, blah blah blah. Local radio picked it up and ran with it. Story will be in the *Citizen* too, unless we squelch it fast."

The Tucson *Citizen*, the city's afternoon paper, was just now going to press.

"They give any details?" Yanni Stern asked. Stern worked vice. He'd been drafted by the task force to find out about any local perverts who had a yen for snuff films or an interest in mutilation beyond the body-piercing variety.

Brookings filled out the story. "You can see what happened here. Some jackass blabbed about crazy Mitch's arrest."

"Radio said it was a nine-one tip-off," Rivera said. "What's that all about?"

"Something different entirely. We'll get to that part of it in a few minutes." Brookings sighed. "Bottom line, it's a royal mess. Graves has been on the phone ever since the story broke." Graves was the sergeant who handled public relations. He knew every local reporter. "We'll get a retraction, but hell, it still looks bad. People get all worked up, and then when they're disappointed, look who takes the blame."

Shepherd was bored. He tuned out Brookings and listened to the sounds of the station house. Phones rang in a shrill cacophony. Somewhere a woman was talking loudly in Spanish, her voice rising operatically. He made out enough words to know she was not making threats, just venting. She was upset. Most of the civilians who paid a visit to police headquarters were upset.

Brookings and the others were still hashing out the media strategy. Shepherd had never felt any interest in the media. To his way of thinking, reporters always got everything wrong, and anybody who listened to them was a fool.

His wife had found his attitude harsh. He smiled a little, thinking of Ginnie. She had believed in people. She had thought most folks, even reporters, tried honestly to do their best and deserved encouragement for it. There had been nothing cynical in her, nothing sour.

Maybe if she had been less trusting, less sure of the fundamental goodness in people, she would still be alive.

Brookings moved to the second item on the agenda, the latest in a series of jurisdictional squabbles between the Apache County Sheriff's Department and TPD. The dual investigations were not always impeccably coordinated.

Another waste of time. Shepherd shifted in his chair, the metal legs scraping on bare tiles. The room had been carpeted once, but too many agitated prisoners had puked or peed on the floor. It was the innocent ones who got the most nervous. The guilty took arrest in stride.

The discussion was winding down when a community service officer, one of the civilian volunteers who relieved the department's manpower shortage by doing clerical tasks, wheeled in a reel-to-reel tape player on a cart.

Brookings set the player on the table. "This brings us to that nine-one call our friends in the news media got so excited about." He glanced at the service officer, an affable septuagenarian named Rudy. "All cued up?"

Shepherd knew Rudy. A week after his retirement from the insurance business, the man had simply shown up for TPD's civilian training classes, explaining that seven days of inactivity had nearly brought on premature senility, and he could stand no more.

"Yes, sir, Captain." Rudy nodded. "I matched it to the entry in the nine-one-one log." All 911 calls were recorded, and the time of each call was marked by the operator in a duty log.

When Rudy was gone, Brookings explained what they were about to hear. "We got an anonymous tip this morning. RP was a woman. She gave us a name. Of course, this had nothing whatsoever to do with crazy—what's his name?"

"Mitch," Shepherd said.

"Right. Crazy Mitch. But the call and the arrest happened pretty much at the same time, and you know how things get put together even when they have no connection. Tip-off in the case, and then an arrest of a guy who says he steals faces—bingo, the killer's in custody."

Alvarez snapped his gum.

"Now we all get to hear what our anonymous source had to say." Brookings smiled. "Pretty exciting, huh, Shep?"

"I'm thrilled," Shepherd intoned with the required ironic frown as he pushed back his chair.

The truth was, he did feel a mild rush of adrenaline. So far the various tips that had come in by phone and mail had proven worthless, but somebody out there might know the killer's identity.

Maybe this woman was the one.

Brookings played the tape. Shepherd listened, jotting notes on his memo pad, as the voices of the 911 operator and the nameless female caller trembled through the tape deck's tinny speaker. He liked the woman's voice. It was soft and breathless, suggestive of vulnerability. He wanted to believe her. But belief got harder as the tape played on.

"I'm not crazy," she blurted out at one point.

Shepherd wrote down the words. The crazy ones were always quickest to assert their sanity. A normal person never imagined that anyone would doubt his basic rationality, but a person with a history of mental problems, a person accustomed to being prodded and poked by psychologists, learned to be defensive on that subject.

The call lasted less than three minutes. It ended with a click, and the 911 operator saying, "Ma'am? You there? Hell."

Brookings shut off the machine. "So what do we think?" he inquired of the room.

Rivera looked bored. "Probably a squirrel."

"That's what the nine-one operator thought. It's why he wanted her picked up, and Bentley concurred." Bentley was the watch commander on the morning shift. "But she was GOA when the beat car got there."

"And the satchel?" Call asked.

"*Nada*. She didn't leave anything at the scene."

Rivera grunted. "Squirrel," he said again.

"I'm not so sure."

Shepherd hadn't known he was going to speak until the words were out of his mouth. Everyone looked at him.

"Maybe she did have the evidence," he went on slowly, "but she got scared off before she could leave it for us."

Brookings frowned. "Other than pure wishful thinking, is there any basis for that supposition?"

There must be, but Shepherd hadn't worked it all out yet. He knew that he wanted the tip to pan out. He wanted proof that somebody named John Cray, who lived and worked near Safford, had sliced off Sharon Andrews' face and taken it home with him. He wanted this case cleared, justice done. He wanted closure for Sharon's young son and her grieving parents.

But none of this was a reason or an argument or a logical basis for anything at all.

To organize his thoughts, he glanced at the notes he'd scribbled in his pad. "She said this man Cray lives near Safford," he began. "Safford is roughly halfway between Tucson and the White Mountains. It makes sense."

"There are lots of places between Tucson and the White Mountains," Stern said.

"And Safford is one of them. It doesn't prove anything. It's just interesting—potentially interesting, at least. Then there's this bit about hunting. You know how scratched up the Andrews woman was. Like she'd been on the run through the brush."

Brookings shrugged. "She got away from the guy, and he went after her."

"Or maybe he let her go and then followed. Made a game out of it."

"Pretty far-fetched."

Shepherd was undeterred. "She said Cray drives a Lexus SUV. That's a pretty good all-terrain vehicle, and we've always known our guy has four-wheel drive. He didn't kill Mrs. Andrews anywhere near a paved road."

"Car's all banged up, she claimed," Alvarez added. "It's something we can check out easy enough."

Rivera, holding to his squirrel theory, grunted with heavy irony. "Yeah, she banged it up when she escaped from him in the desert. After he tried to hunt her, I guess. She's a regular Indiana Jones, isn't she?"

"People get away from bad guys sometimes," Brookings said, though he seemed dubious.

"Sure." Rivera shrugged. "And crazy people make up stories about bad guys. The bogeyman's always after them, and they're always just barely getting away."

Stern nodded. "He's right. This gal's got nutcase written all over her. She says she's been following Cray. Why? If she suspects him, why doesn't she go to the cops right off?"

"She's afraid of cops," Call said. "Come on, Yanni, we see it all the time."

Stern held his ground. "Not in cases like this. She's delusional. Paranoid."

Shepherd could see that Rivera and Stern had won over most of the group. But he was still unconvinced. He tried another tack.

"How about the rest of what she said?" In his memo

pad he had jotted down *break-in*, *kidnap*, and *others*. "She claimed there were tools in this satchel for breaking and entering. But in the White Mountains case there was no break-in. Mrs. Andrews was snatched right outside the auto dealership, probably forced into the killer's car."

Mercado shrugged. "Doesn't that undercut the credibility of the call even further?"

"Not necessarily. Not if there were break-ins in other cases."

Marty Kroft looked at the ceiling. "We're back to this again."

"She said there were others," Shepherd went on implacably. "Others Cray had killed."

"Oh, Christ," Rivera said, "she's your frigging soul mate. No wonder you believe her."

Shepherd clamped down on a spasm of anger. "I'm just saying her version of things might turn out to be pretty close to the truth."

"Close to your idea of the truth," Stern said. "Your theory." He put a dismissive emphasis on the word.

"Yeah, my theory. Let's just say I'm right about my theory. Let's say Sharon Andrews was not an isolated incident. Let's say this psycho has been in the game for a while, and we never knew about it because none of the earlier victims turned up anywhere. There are plenty of unsolved missing-persons cases—"

"You can't go pinning every unsolved juvenile runaway on the White Mountains freak," Kroft said.

"I'm not talking just runaways. I'm talking kidnappings too. Break-ins, and the woman of the house gone, never found again. There have been six I've turned up so far—"

"All in different localities," Rivera interrupted. "Not just different neighborhoods, I mean different counties."

"The man travels. Most serial killers do."

"Never the same MO. Method of entry, time of day, choice of victim—no similarities."

"He varies his methods. He's smart. He doesn't leave an obvious trail."

"Time span of roughly a decade, as I recall. That's a lot of dead girls, man."

"He's not constantly active. The urges follow a cycle. You know about that."

A serial killer—if this was indeed what Shepherd was dealing with—tended to operate in a long, rhythmic pattern. The killing phase was followed by a period of dormancy. Then the urges would resume, and the killer would begin fantasizing, then stalking, and finally he would kill.

The length of the cycle's inactive phase varied significantly. Often the killings became more frequent as the urges intensified or earlier caution was abandoned.

It had been five months since Sharon Andrews' disappearance. She had been murdered within hours of her disappearance; that day's lunch was found in her stomach at the autopsy.

Five months—and now the female caller claimed the killer was ready to strike again. The time fit Shepherd's profile.

Actually, *profile* was too technical a term. He wasn't a psychologist, and he had no training in behavioral science. But he'd been a cop for a long time. He had an intuitive sense of the man he was looking for.

That man would be sadistic, obsessive, capable of

animalistic violence—yet self-controlled, careful, intelligent. He would know the danger in striking too often or too recklessly. He would moderate his urges, suppress or divert them for as long as possible, draw out the period of dormancy until he could restrain himself no longer.

A month was too little time; a year—probably too long.

"One kill about every six months is what I'm guessing," Shepherd said. "If so, the body count wouldn't be unrealistically high, not for a guy like this. He could go on doing it for ten years or even longer, assuming he's good enough."

Rivera brushed this aside. "No one's that good."

"It's been known to happen."

"In the movies. Look, Roy. You're dealing with a bunch of completely unrelated cases with absolutely nothing to link them to the White Mountains thing or to one another. There's no pattern, except the one you want to see."

Shepherd considered a counterargument. He knew several he could use. But the effort would be wasted. Kroft, Rivera, and Stern were hostile to the very idea of connecting the Sharon Andrews case to any earlier crime. The others in the room had no opinion. And Brookings would sway with any majority, never holding firm.

"You may be right," Shepherd said, spreading his hands. "On the other hand, this man Cray just might be the son of a bitch we're looking for. We'll have to check it out, that's all."

Brookings speared him with his gaze. "*You'll* have to. Thanks for volunteering."

"Wouldn't have it any other way."

"Of course," Alvarez ventured, "it might help to find out if there really is anybody named John Cray in the Safford area."

The captain nodded. "Might save Shep a long drive. Hey, Kroft—don't you know a guy over at Graham County Sheriff's?"

Kroft shrugged. "Chuck Wheelihan, yeah. Met him a couple years ago when I was working vice. There was a meth crew operating out of Safford, hauling the shit into Tucson to sell on the street."

"Why don't you give him a call, see if he can find out anything about this Cray."

"What the hell. My caseload's empty. I got nothing but time to waste."

He left the room, and the meeting proceeded to the issue of Baxter Payton, a salesman at the auto dealership who, according to several employees, had aggressively pursued Sharon Andrews, only to be repeatedly rebuffed. Brookings felt Payton was a strong candidate for the role of suspect.

It's an O.J. thing, he had argued to Shepherd in the earliest stages of the case. *This Payton guy, he was obsessed with her, and if he couldn't have her, no one could.*

Shepherd had interviewed Payton and come away with the impression that the man was a loser, obnoxious and insecure and intensely dislikable, but no murderer. Still, after the body turned up, Brookings had pushed hard for a second look. Shepherd had foisted the job on Lou Mercado and Steve Call, two younger detectives who had just made rank.

Now they had the unpleasant duty of informing their captain that there was no way, positively no way, that this creep Payton had done Sharon. They alternated in their presentation, Call leaning forward to tick off points on his blunt, meaty fingers, Mercado sitting ramrod-straight in a dignified courtroom pose.

"We checked out every angle," Call began. "Day of her disappearance, Payton worked late, writing up a sale. We found the buyer, and he confirmed it. So Payton's alibied. But we say, okay, even so, maybe he could get away for a minute, snatch her, stash her in his car."

Mercado took over. "We asked him about it. He let us do a search. Forensics vacuumed his vehicle—trunk, backseat, everything. They turned up nothing they can tie to Sharon, no fibers from her clothes or her carpet at home, no blood, no hair. She wasn't in there."

" 'Course," Call said, anticipating an objection, "Payton had access to every vehicle on the lot. It's a used-car shop, you know. Salesmen take cars home with them sometimes. But they keep a log of cars signed out, and he didn't sign out anything that week."

"So he's alibied," Mercado concluded, "and there's no physical evidence, and he didn't do it."

Call wanted the last word. "Plus, the guy is a little weasel who wouldn't have the balls to snuff a housefly."

Brookings processed this information, then shrugged. "Yeah, I never figured it was him. Too obvious."

Shepherd smothered a grin. That was just like Brookings. The captain was a certified specialist in covering his ass. He knew how to deflect blame and absorb credit, how to alienate nobody and be everyone's best friend. Shepherd ought to hate him for it.

But hell, CYA was an art every cop had to learn—a survival skill, no less than proficiency with firearms. Cops were civil servants, and civil servants who flouted the rules and dissed their superiors were just begging for a dead-end career.

Anyway, he couldn't dislike Paul Brookings, and not just because they'd gone fishing together more often than the other men in the squad needed to know.

Shepherd owed Brookings. He wasn't sure he could have endured the past two years without the captain's calm, steady support.

Kroft returned, a peculiar look on his face. "Talked to Wheelihan. Hell, you know he's made undersheriff now? When's my promotion coming up, Captain?"

"When you tell me what the hell your pal said to you."

"Well, there's a John Cray in the Safford area, all right. Chuck didn't even have to look it up. He knows the guy. Whole department knows him. Fact is, he's sort of famous, at least locally."

"Famous how?"

"Mainly 'cause he wrote a book that sold pretty well. *The Mask of Self*—that's the title."

Shepherd had never heard of it, but the word *mask* pricked his interest. He thought of Sharon Andrews' faceless corpse.

"Some kind of mystery novel?" he asked, his tone even.

"Nonfiction." Kroft looked at him, and Shepherd tried to read his expression but failed. "About how who we think we are is only an illusion. 'Least, that's how Chuck described it."

"So he's an author," Brookings said, perturbed. "What does that tell us?"

Kroft shrugged. "Nothing, I guess. That's not how the local cops know him, anyway. They knew him a long time before he ever got into print. They work with him."

Shepherd felt his optimism slipping away. "Do they?"

"Yeah."

Then Kroft's face reshaped itself in a huge, unfriendly smile, and Shepherd realized why his expression had been so oddly strained. He'd been holding back that smile, fighting it like a man warding off a sneeze.

"Dr. John Cray," Kroft said, "is the director of the Hawk Ridge Institute for Psychiatric Care."

Kroft let a moment pass while this information registered.

"He runs a goddamned mental hospital," Kroft finished, not trusting subtlety where this point was concerned. "He takes in all the loons who've gotta be held for observation. And, Shep—he's made a lot of enemies, Chuck says."

Enemies. Yes.

Every psychiatrist made enemies, and a man like Cray, a man who supervised a mental institution harboring scores of patients, would make more enemies than most.

Rivera laughed. "Man, I told you she's a squirrel."

Stern, at least, was polite enough not to say a word.

"Sounds like you were right," Shepherd said without rancor. "On the other hand, just because he's a shrink doesn't mean he's not a killer."

This was, in part, bravado. But he couldn't shake free of that word *mask*. It fit the case too well.

"You happen to ask if Cray drives a Lexus?" he added.

Kroft's smile slipped a little. "Yeah, I asked. He's got one—an SUV, like the woman said. But any of his patients could know that. It doesn't prove anything."

"No," Shepherd said. "It doesn't." He scraped back his chair and got up. "Better get moving. It's still early. I might be able to catch him before he goes to lunch."

Kroft looked baffled. "You figure it's even necessary to do a meet-and-greet? I mean, you could phone the guy, or I could have Wheelihan send some deputies to chat him up."

"I can't tell much from a phone call. And it sounds like the local deputies are a little too friendly with this guy."

Stern spoke. "You don't still think there's anything to this?"

"I'll know soon enough when I talk to Cray. And when I take a look at that Lexus of his."

Brookings looked unhappy. "I'm betting it hasn't got a scratch. Face it, Shep. The lady's a head case."

"My second one today. Looks like I hit the jackpot. Lucky me."

He meant it as a joke, but it hit too close to home, and nobody was laughing as Roy Shepherd walked out the door.

21

The Hawk Ridge Institute for Psychiatric Care was a large, rambling complex of brick buildings, none higher than two stories, set amid rolling greenery in the foothills of the Pinaleno Mountains. Route 366 was nearby, feeding traffic into Safford, but the institute lay on a desolate back road, and its neighbors were farms and ranches and, a few miles distant, a federal prison camp.

From the road, the institute looked something like a prison itself, with its high iron fence and the guardhouse at the gate. But once inside the grounds, visitors were surprised to see flower beds, neatly tended, and sparkling fountains and birdbaths and colonnades of eucalyptus trees. The less severely afflicted patients were free to roam the property, and they could be seen here and there, some clustered in companionable groups, others solitary.

The administration building and one ward of the institute had been built in 1942. By the mid-1960s two more wards had been added, both of them L-shaped one-story structures well removed from the heart of the complex.

Then the trend of deinstitutionalizing mental patients

had begun, and over the next thirty years Hawk Ridge's population dropped by more than half. Today the institute housed one hundred and thirty-three patients, most of them considered chronic and untreatable—the hard cases who did not respond to medication. Only two of the three wards were in use; the third, Ward C, had been shut down as an economy measure. It stood in decrepit isolation, a windowless shell, one of its doors padlocked, the other bolted shut. Occasionally a staff member with a passkey slipped inside to smoke a joint or indulge some other secret vice.

Hawk Ridge was a peaceful place, and remarkably picturesque. The staid facade of the administrative center was softened by closely trimmed fir trees. Behind and above the building were the tall mountains, brownish at the lower elevations, rising to green, the details of even the highest ridgeline visible in the pellucid air.

Sometimes a hawk or, more seldom, a turkey vulture could be seen riding the high thermals, circling above a hidden gorge, and at night the cries of coyotes were heard, shrill and ghostly and unmelodic, though all too often they were drowned out by the screams.

There were screams, of course. In Ward B, known as the violent ward, where the hardest of the hard cases were kept, the screams seemed never to end. There were patients who could be prevented from screaming only by the massive application of tranquilizing drugs, and even then they would eventually learn to tolerate the medication, which would lose its effect.

Some patients would scream all the time if there were no sedatives to quiet them. Others, who cycled through stages of illness, had their lucid periods, when they could be transferred to Ward A, the admitting ward. Here they were installed as temporary guests, until their precarious mental balance was upset, and they had to be drugged and restrained in a private cell.

So nearly always there was somebody screaming, but the staff—three psychiatrists, seven supervising nurses, two dozen therapy aides, eight security officers, three cooks, and assorted groundskeepers and maintenance personnel—had learned to pay no attention to the noise.

Only the hospital director, John Bainbridge Cray, M.D., did not ignore the screams.

He rather liked them.

This had been a hectic morning for Cray. He had arrived at his home on the hospital grounds at 8:45, exhausted after his long night and only moderately revived by the coffee he'd consumed during the drive from Tucson.

Quickly he showered and changed, then spent some time in his garage, taking care of a few unpleasant but necessary details.

By 9:20 he was in his office. To his secretary, Margaret, he excused his tardiness by saying he'd forgotten to set his alarm clock.

His first order of business was a conference call involving an allegation of misconduct by a therapy aide, David Wilson. Wilson was accused of having beaten an unruly patient, Jocelyn Beatty, who had checked into the hospital voluntarily after experiencing symptoms of manic-depressive illness.

He spent half an hour on the phone with the patient's mother, the attorney she had retained to represent her daughter, and a case officer employed by the

Arizona Health Services Department. Cray informed them that David Wilson already had been placed on paid leave pending the outcome of an internal investigation. He offered to turn over Wilson's duty logs to the attorney. He promised his full cooperation. And he meant it.

Cray took any allegation of misconduct with the utmost seriousness. The patients in his care were never to be mistreated. In the performance of his duties, he adhered to the most conscientious standards of professionalism. It was a point of pride with him.

Was this an inconsistency in a man of his predilections? He supposed so. But in truth he did feel something special for his patients. The women he had killed—they were nothing, merely lab rats, experimental animals set loose to run a deadly maze. The patients at the hospital, on the other hand, were his charges, almost his children, and he would not let them be hurt.

Well, there had been one exception. One patient he had meant to harm. But he'd never had the chance.

At least, not yet.

When the phone call was done, he hosted a meeting in his office. A patient, Dennis Callaghan, was set to be discharged. Cray served coffee and pastries to Dennis and his grateful parents. The atmosphere was cheery, and the strong morning sun poured through the spotless windows like a benediction.

"We just don't know how to thank you, Doctor," Mrs. Callaghan said, holding tight to her son's hand. "Dennis has been in and out of places like this for . . . well, all his life. You've managed some sort of miracle cure."

Her husband said the same, and Dennis mumbled an echo.

Cray accepted the compliments graciously. To be honest, he did not think that either he or his staff had contributed greatly to Dennis Callaghan's recovery. The treatment prescribed for him had been entirely routine, not much different from the strategies employed by other hospitals throughout the patient's history. A loading dose of Haldol—ninety milligrams—had been administered, then tapered to fifty milligrams, at which point Dennis' condition had stabilized.

Why had the pharmaceuticals worked here and now, but not before? There was no reason. More precisely, the reason was unknown, owing to the mysterious complexity of the human organism. A certain chemical would work in one instance, have no results in another, produce crippling side effects in the third, and there was no logic to it, no pattern, only the randomness of accident.

Dennis Callaghan had been cured—at least for the moment. This was enough for his parents and for Dennis himself, and it was enough for Cray. He had learned humility in this field. He had learned not to expect to understand too much.

Once the Callaghans were gone, Cray asked Margaret to send for Walter Luntz. "There's an errand I need him to run," he added quite unnecessarily.

Walter Luntz resided in a guest room adjacent to the kitchen area, quarters intended originally for a live-in cook. But Walter was not a cook. He was a permanent resident of the Hawk Ridge Institute, a man of forty-nine who had spent the last twenty-five years of his life under psychiatric care.

His was an unusual case. He had responded quite well to pharmacological treatment in certain respects. His thought processes were fairly lucid, and he suffered from no evident delusions. Within the structured environment of the hospital, or outside it for brief forays into the larger world, he was fine.

But send him to a halfway house or ask him to fend for himself in a rented apartment—two strategies that had been tried in the early years—and he quickly decompensated, reverting to an acute psychotic state.

Cray was just as glad that Walter could not leave the institute. The man was useful here. He did clerical chores, even ran errands, driving a used Toyota Tercel that Cray had paid for out of hospital funds. His driving was quite good, and his license had never been revoked throughout all his years of hospitalization.

The institute was understaffed, and Cray could use all the help possible.

Today Walter would perform his greatest service.

Cray heard him coming—fast, clumsy steps—and then Walter Luntz appeared in the office doorway, a tall, stoop-shouldered wreck of a man, with long, ropy, simian arms and a potbelly and a conical, hairless head.

Unlike the other patients, Walter was permitted to wear street clothes. His taste in fashion was idiosyncratic at best. Today he wore khaki trousers, a turquoise-encrusted belt, and a lime-green open-collar shirt.

"Dr. Cray?" he asked hesitantly, afraid to cross the threshold without permission.

His voice was reedy and weak, a wind instrument breathlessly played.

"Yes, Walter. Come in."

Cray shut the door after him, then ushered Walter to the couch. The door was oak, solid-core, and it ensured privacy.

Then he explained to Walter what he wanted. He explained more than once, keeping his words simple. Walter was not unintelligent, but he was naive and prone to childish misunderstandings.

The assignment Cray offered was a challenge, perhaps too great a challenge for a man whose tasks rarely required driving more than a few miles into nearby Safford for some office supplies. But curiously Cray felt sure Walter was up to it, so long as he had clear instructions and a couple of visual aids.

One of these was a photo Cray had downloaded from the Internet during a brief on-line session this morning, and the other was a slip of paper filled out with a few letters and numbers in a large, careful hand.

"Do you understand?" he asked the man who sat with him on the sofa.

Walter nodded. His head gleamed in the sun. "I can do it, Dr. Cray."

Even so, Cray reviewed the matter one last time before sending Walter Luntz on his way.

At 10:30 he toured the facility, opening a succession of locked doors with his passkey, checking in with the psychiatrists and supervising nurses on duty in the two active wards. He had heard of hospital directors who stayed in their offices all day, inaccessible and aloof. This was not Cray's approach.

Anyway, he needed to keep moving. There was a restlessness in him today, a droning background hum of frustration, of fury.

He had come so close with Kaylie. Had his reflexes

been a few degrees sharper, or had he simply put the canister of liquid nitrogen in the backseat, safely out of her reach . . .

A hundred times he had replayed the scenario in the desert, always with himself as the victor.

God damn that woman. Still alive.

But perhaps not for long.

In Ward A, Nurse Killian reported a problem with a recently admitted patient who was not responding to a rather high dosage of Haldol.

"Let me talk to him," Cray said. "What's his name?"

"Roger."

"Bring him out."

Cray met Roger at the nurses' station. The man was young and tall, and he had the moist, limpid eyes of a suffering artist.

"Have you been hospitalized before, Roger?" Cray asked kindly.

"Yes, sir."

"And they gave you pills?"

"Yes."

"Which ones?" Cray swept his hand over the metal tabletop, where he had laid out a variety of standard neuroleptics. "The red? The yellow? The green?"

"All of them."

"Which ones worked?"

A ghostly smile lit up Roger's pale face. "The red ones were pretty good. I got better on the red."

"Then that's what you need. Thank you, Roger."

When the man was gone, Nurse Killian objected to the procedure. A patient could not be allowed to prescribe his own medication.

Dorothy Killian was a good RN, and Cray was lucky

to have her, but she was new at Hawk Ridge, and she didn't know how he did things.

"It's been my observation," Cray said, "that the patient, especially an experienced patient like Roger, often knows which pharmaceuticals have been most beneficial to him. Let's take him at his word."

He prescribed ninety milligrams of risperidone—the red pills—and left Nurse Killian shaking her head.

Next he visited the day hall, where those patients who were not confined to their rooms congregated throughout the morning and afternoon. The room was large and airy, although the high, arched windows were unfortunately crosshatched with iron bars. Open doors led to a veranda, which had been screened in for security reasons.

Cray was quite serious about security. In the fourteen years of his directorship, there had been just three significant escape attempts, only one of which had been successful.

Cray pursed his lips. Yes, only one.

He surveyed the day hall. Ceiling fans turned languidly overhead, and sunlight gleamed on the tile floor. The room would have been exotic and beautiful, if not for the TV set babbling behind a clear plastic shield, and the patients lolling on cheap lounge chairs and badly worn couches, and the ubiquitous smell of Lysol.

A therapy aide informed Cray that a patient named Lawton, known for disruptive behavior, was demanding a Bible. This was a common request at Hawk Ridge. An obsession with religion characterized more than half the patients at any given time.

It was Cray's hypothesis that religious impulses

originated not in the cerebral cortex, the seat of thought, but rather in the more primitive limbic system, where primal emotion held sway. The limbic brain—specifically the septal region—was known to be dysfunctional in most schizophrenics.

He had expounded on this idea in *The Mask of Self*. If humanity's deepest and most reverent feelings were the product of a chemical imbalance or a neurological malfunction, then was any aspect of human life truly sacred? How about life itself? And if not, then was there any reason—any logical reason—not to kill one's fellow human beings, if one could get away with it?

Of course he had not made these last points in his book. Tactfully he had left his readers to draw their own conclusions.

"Give Lawton a Bible," he told the attendant indifferently, "if he wants one. But make him understand that he can't annoy or harass the others."

"Dr. Gonzalez was afraid having the Bible might get him more agitated."

Cray ordinarily did not overrule the psychiatrists working under him, but he saw no merit in Gonzalez's concern. "If he gets agitated, tell him the meek will inherit the earth. That one has done the trick for centuries." He started to move away, then added, "If he still won't calm down, sedate him."

A great many of Hawk Ridge's patients were sedated throughout their stay. Some had been heavily tranquilized for years. The other psychiatrists, Cray's subordinates, had been critical of this approach, believing that it impeded the patients' recovery.

This might be true. But Cray would not have a lot of

lunatics raising hell in the public parts of the hospital. They could scream all they liked while in seclusion, but the common areas must be kept safe and civilized.

He wandered among the patients in the day hall. They were men and women, young and old, all different, yet all curiously alike in their white sneakers and white socks and light blue, two-piece cotton garments, which looked very much like pajamas. At some institutions the patients were permitted to wear their street clothes, but Cray sniffed the dangerous scent of anarchy in this policy.

He ran a tight operation. His hospital was clean. The food in the commissary was nutritious and filling and sometimes even tasty. Discipline was enforced on both the patients and the staff. He made few mistakes.

But Kaylie—innocent little Kaylie with her freckled schoolgirl face and shy, hushed voice . . .

He'd made a mistake with her. And he was paying for it even now. He had paid for twelve years.

At 11:15 his pager buzzed, displaying his secretary's number. He called her from a phone in Dr. Bernstein's office.

"One of the groundskeepers was working near your house," Margaret said, worry in her voice. "He found your garage window broken. He says it looks like someone tried to get in."

Cray did his best to sound concerned. "I'll be right over to take a look."

The morning had been routine so far, but all of that was about to change.

22

"Cornflakes."

Shepherd stopped at the front steps of the Hawk Ridge Institute, facing a pair of gray-haired patients in matching cotton outfits.

"Excuse me?" he asked the one who had spoken, a chinless man with a face made of wrinkles and liver spots.

"Cornflakes," the man repeated. "Cornflakes with milk."

He smiled. His two front teeth were missing. He looked like a mischievous child.

The man's companion, a woman with glazed eyes, asked Shepherd if he had ever been to Venice.

"No," Shepherd said. "Never."

The woman nodded, satisfied. She and her friend returned their attention to an empty ambulance slant-parked in a loading zone. They stood staring at it raptly, and Shepherd headed up the steps.

The front doors opened on a small lobby, musty and inadequately lit. Another patient was inside, this one a middle-aged woman who sat curled on a wooden bench and studying her sneakers as she hummed to herself.

She had a proud, photogenic face, and Shepherd felt a touch of sadness when he thought of the person she might have been, if illness hadn't stolen her mind.

At the front desk sat a receptionist, paying no attention to the patient. Her concentration was fixed on the flickering amber monitor of an antique computer terminal. For a moment she reminded him of Ginnie. There was no physical resemblance, only the pose she had struck, the air of intent concentration as her careful hands worked the keyboard.

Somewhere deep inside him there was a revival of the old pain. He felt it, hated it, and at the same time, oddly, he was almost bored with it, because the pain had been with him for so long now, and had gotten tiresome.

Maybe this was what people meant when they spoke of healing. He hoped so.

"May I help you?" the receptionist asked without looking up.

"I'd like to see Dr. Cray."

"Do you have an appointment?"

"I'm afraid not."

She frowned. The garish amber light glinted on her granny glasses. "Which patient is this regarding?"

"None." He showed his badge. "I need to talk to Dr. Cray about a police matter."

The woman barely glanced at the badge. She seemed unimpressed. It occurred to Shepherd that the institute's staff must be accustomed to police inquiries. Kroft had said the hospital had regular dealings with the local sheriff's department. Certain obviously unstable suspects—transients, arsonists—were held here for psychiatric evaluation.

"You'll have to sign in, please."

Shepherd filled out the sign-in sheet fastened to a clipboard. The receptionist put it away without looking at it.

"Dr. Cray's in his office. Second floor, Room Twenty-two. Elevator works only if you've got a key, and anyway, it's busted. Take the stairs."

She jerked her head at a door with a steel handle and a posted sign that read STAFF ONLY.

Shepherd thanked her, but she was already bent over her keyboard again.

The stairwell smelled of disinfectant. Shepherd disliked that smell. It reminded him of hospitals—well, of course, this was a hospital, wasn't it?—but he was thinking of the other kind of hospital, the normal kind, like the University Medical Center in Tucson, where, two years ago, he had spent a long series of days and nights, praying, eating too little, crying when he was alone and no one could see.

God, he wanted to be out of this place. He would talk to Cray, size him up, and go.

The door at the top of the stairs opened on a hallway. Shepherd had thought that mental hospitals were always decorated in light green or blue tones to soothe the patients, but the walls here were white, and so were the doors—everything, white.

Some of the doors were open. Walking past, he glimpsed staff members on the phone or typing at actual typewriters, IBM Selectrics or some similar equipment. He hadn't thought anybody used typewriters anymore. He wondered if Hawk Ridge's employees used carbon paper too, and mimeograph machines.

In one room, marked ADMISSIONS, the two paramedics who had arrived in the ambulance stood flanking a disheveled teenager in an overcoat. A woman who must be a doctor was interviewing the kid, jotting down notes on a clipboard.

"And what did you do after you got home?" she asked.

"I watched TV, and the guy in the car commercial told me I needed to start a fire in the toolshed. He told me I had to burn the fucker down. I didn't *want* to. I'm scared of fire. But the guy was on TV, you know? When they're on TV, you gotta do what they say. . . ."

Room 22 was at the end of the hall. This door was also open. Shepherd entered an anteroom furnished with a desk, a few file cabinets, and a couch. A plaque on the desk read MARGARET. Cray's secretary, or assistant, or whatever she should be called.

Her swivel chair was empty. The clock on the wall pointed to 12:15. She must have left for lunch.

But Cray was here. Shepherd saw him through the doorway of his office, seated at his desk, a telephone in one hand and a file folder in the other.

"The chart's in front of me now," he was saying. "Moban, two hundred milligrams. Maintain him on that dosage for two weeks, and then, if necessary, we'll take another look."

He hung up, raised his head, and noticed Shepherd in the anteroom. "Yes?" he snapped.

Every cop was good at assessing people. Shepherd processed what he could see of Dr. John Cray—sharp eyes, high forehead, small mouth, hollow cheeks—and decided the man was intelligent, arrogant, controlling, and very tired.

"Dr. Cray." Shepherd stepped through the doorway into Cray's office. "I'm Detective Roy Shepherd, Tucson PD."

He watched Cray's face for a reaction. Cray merely frowned.

"Tucson? I was expecting someone from the sheriff's department."

This response baffled Shepherd. He let a moment pass as he approached the desk. Automatically he noted Cray's age, approximately mid-forties, and a few other details.

He wore no wedding band. His complexion was sallow; he did not get out in the sun very much. He wore a brown suit of good quality, in need of being pressed. His shirt collar was unbuttoned, revealing a taut, muscular neck.

"I'm not sure I follow you," Shepherd said finally.

Cray looked impatient. "This is about the vandalism, isn't it?"

"Vandalism?"

A sigh leaked out of Cray, the sigh of a man who was smarter and better organized than everyone around him, and weary of this burden. Shepherd decided he disliked John Cray.

But the truth was, he disliked all psychiatrists, disliked the profession of psychiatry as such. He had his reasons.

"Apparently," Cray said, "we've got our wires crossed. You see, my sport-utility vehicle was vandalized last night. I called the sheriff's department about it just half an hour ago. They said they'd send someone to take a report. But of course that's not at all why you're here."

"No."

"Still, I have a feeling your visit could be related to my little problem." Cray leaned back in his chair, studying Shepherd over the neat stacks of paper on the desk. "It's about *her*, isn't it?"

"Her?"

"Kaylie McMillan. Isn't she why you've come to see me?"

"I guess I'm a little slow today, Doctor. Who exactly is Kaylie McMillan?"

"The person who trashed my Lexus—or so I believe." Cray smiled, a surprisingly warm smile that illumined his face and made him look younger. "I'd better start at the beginning, hadn't I?"

"That might be good."

"Please have a seat. Care for some coffee? It's quite good. One-hundred-percent fresh-ground Kona. There's a coffee house in Tucson that sells it."

So he went into Tucson now and then. Hardly a startling admission, but Shepherd took note of it as he pulled a metal chair close to the desk and sat. "No, thanks. I'm fine."

"Then perhaps, before I tell you about Kaylie, you might enlighten me as to why you're here. Since, quite obviously, my guesswork on the subject was all wrong."

Shepherd kept his answer vague. "Someone's made some rather serious allegations, Doctor. Allegations concerning yourself. Now, I'm just looking into this on a purely preliminary basis—"

"Kaylie," Cray said.

He was nodding, his expression curiously content, like a man who'd found the answer to a riddle and was pleased with his own cleverness.

Shepherd shrugged. "Excuse me?"

"These allegations were made anonymously, isn't that so?"

"Well, yes."

"Kaylie did it. What precisely did she accuse me of? Kidnapping parochial-school girls and selling them into slavery? Using my basement as a torture chamber? A series of ax murders, perhaps?"

"You're taking this kind of lightly."

"I'm not taking it lightly at all. She vandalized my Lexus. She's evidently spreading false accusations of a nature sufficiently serious to require your presence in my office. And she's stalking me."

"Stalking you?"

"Yes. What did she accuse me of?"

Shepherd hadn't wanted to reveal the charge too soon, but he saw no way around it. "She said . . . Well, she said you were the White Mountains Killer. You know the case—"

"Yes, of course. Her claim is original, at least. But hardly unexpected. That crime has received a good deal of publicity, and psychotics are highly suggestible."

"Kaylie's a psychotic?"

"Oh, yes. She was a patient here, you see. One of the more difficult ones."

The woman's voice on the 911 tape spoke in Shepherd's memory: *I'm not crazy.*

"When was this?" he asked.

"Twelve years ago, when she was nineteen. The sheriff's department placed her in our care after her arrest."

"On what charge?"

"Homicide." Cray took another sip of his Kona coffee. "She and her husband, Justin, had been married less than three months when dear, sweet Kaylie shot him in the heart."

23

Murders were rare in Graham County. A year could pass, even two or three, without a single homicide. For that reason Shepherd was sure Cray would remember the details of the case.

"Tell me how it happened," he said.

Cray swiveled in his chair, sunlight catching the flecks of amber in his grayish eyes. "All that's known with certainty," he answered, "is that Kaylie killed Justin with his own revolver, then panicked and fled in their car. A deputy found the vehicle on a back road the next day. She'd lost control and driven into a ravine. Search patrols were organized. A helicopter spotted her two miles from the crash site, wandering in the brush. When the police reached her, she was on her knees, sobbing."

Slowly Shepherd nodded. Twelve years ago he had been a patrol officer riding shotgun with Gary Brannigan. He and Gary'd had their hands full with drug shootings and gang fights, and neither of them had paid much attention to crimes outside Tucson city limits. But dimly Shepherd recalled the case of a teenage wife in Graham County who'd murdered her husband and had been found in the desolate foothills, soiled and dehydrated and distraught.

"They never found out why she did it," he said, more to himself than to Cray.

"Unfortunately, no. When the sobbing subsided, Kaylie entered a catatonic state. Essentially, she had suffered what the layman calls a nervous breakdown. So the deputies brought her to us. She was admitted to our forensic ward—Ward C, which is no longer in use. She was kept in seclusion, and was utterly uncommunicative."

"Catatonic?"

Cray shook his head. "Initially she exhibited unpredictable outbursts of violence. She had to be kept under restraint, for both her own safety and the safety of the other patients."

"Under restraint? You mean, in a straitjacket?"

"Only at the beginning. The first few days."

"How long was she here?"

"Four months."

"Who treated her?"

"I did. They delegate the more challenging ones to me." Shepherd caught the lift of pride in the statement. "After a few weeks she recovered the ability to communicate. We had many long talks, Kaylie and I."

"Do you remember anything distinctive about her voice?"

Cray hesitated, seemingly bewildered by the question. "Her voice?" Then his eyes narrowed. "Oh, I see. It was a telephone call, wasn't it? That's how she contacted you. Well, her voice is rather girlish, actually. She sounds like a sweet little thing. Shy and sensitive and vulnerable. Her true personality profile, however, is rather more complicated than that."

The description matched the voice Shepherd had

heard on the 911 tape. "Okay. Sorry for interrupting. You were talking about the progress Kaylie made in your therapy sessions."

"She seemed to be getting better. But she professed complete amnesia when it came to the killing of her husband."

"Professed? You think she was lying?"

"She's certainly capable of carrying off an elaborate deception. As subsequent events were to prove."

"What events?"

Before answering, Cray paused for another long swallow of coffee. Shepherd waited, casting his gaze around the office.

Papers and folders were everywhere, all stacked tidily, with no impression of disorder. There were a couple of framed paintings on the walls, but otherwise the office was bare of decoration—no knickknacks or mementos, no family photos on the desk.

Did Cray have friends, a lover? Shepherd doubted it. The man seemed too distant to inspire affection.

He could inspire hatred, though. Especially in a patient consigned to his care, wrapped in a straitjacket, imprisoned in a cell. . . .

"The events," Cray said at last, "of the night of June twenty-third, 1987. The night when Kaylie escaped."

Old bitterness laced the words. Shepherd heard it in Cray's tone, saw it in the angry twist of his mouth.

"If she'd been watched more closely, she never would have gotten away. But she'd fooled us into dropping our guard. We had no idea that she spent every night loosening the bolts on the grille over the air duct in her room."

The air duct. Yes, Shepherd remembered that detail.

It had stuck in his memory because it was so much like something in a movie. He had rarely heard of anyone actually escaping that way.

"She took off the grille," Cray said, "and crawled into the duct. Kaylie is a small woman, and there was room for her, though it must have been a tight fit. She belly-crawled to the midpoint of the building, a distance of eighty feet, and ascended a short vertical shaft to a rooftop vent. She kicked out the wire-mesh panel at that end of the duct system, then emerged onto the roof. She was able to climb down and run to the perimeter fence, which she scaled easily. Later we found her footprints in the dirt."

"And then," Shepherd said, more facts of the case returning to him from some long-forgotten mental file, "she proceeded on foot to a farm or a ranch, something like that—and stole a car."

"A pickup truck."

"Hot-wired it."

"Yes. I have no idea where she learned that particular skill. But you see, that's the thing you need to understand about Kaylie McMillan. Despite her illness, she's smart and determined and . . . unexpectedly resourceful."

Shepherd noted the hesitation. Cray, it seemed, was still upset about having been bested by one of his own patients, even after twelve years.

The man liked to be in control. He would not forgive anyone who challenged him successfully.

"She drove to the house where she'd lived with Justin," Cray said. "It had been four months since the killing, but the place was still unoccupied and largely undisturbed. She changed out of her hospital-issue garments into her regular clothes, packed a couple of suitcases, and left. By the time we discovered she was missing from her room, she must have been miles out of town. The pickup was found on the following evening at a rest stop along Interstate Eight. Where she went from there is anyone's guess."

"Without money she would run out of options pretty fast."

"She must have had money. I can't imagine how she got it. Possibly there was some cash hidden at the house. Or perhaps she stole money, or got it from a friend who's remained silent. I can't say. But she vanished. She's been missing for all this time. I thought she might have died. The suicide rate among unmedicated schizophrenics is quite high. But I was wrong. She's very much alive. And apparently, at long last, she's decided to lash out, hurt me in any way she can."

"You seem pretty sure she's the one who's harassing you."

"Quite sure."

"How can you know?"

"Because I saw her."

The phone rang. Cray let his message machine answer. He listened to the faint, tinny voice over the speaker for a moment, then shrugged.

"Nothing urgent. Where was I?"

"You saw Kaylie."

"Yes. Just last night, at a resort hotel in the Tucson foothills."

"Which resort?"

He named the place. Shepherd knew it well. One of the city's best.

"Why were you there?" Shepherd asked.

"I was in the mood for their chicken quesadilla. It's a favorite dish of mine. They serve it at the bar and grill."

"You went alone?"

Cray met Shepherd's gaze. "I'm not the most sociable of men, Detective. When I was younger, it was different. But I've spent two decades at Hawk Ridge. I've been director of this facility for the past fourteen years. As director, I live here, on the grounds. I spend every day, nearly every waking hour, hemmed in by doctors, nurses, orderlies, guards, patients, visitors, all making demands on my time. . . ."

The phone rang again, as if to punctuate the point. Cray ignored it.

"To cut to the chase, I've learned to rather relish the opportunity to get away by myself. Do you think that's so eccentric?"

Shepherd didn't, and he said so.

"Well, then." Cray resumed his story. "I went there for dinner. But before I could order, I became aware of being watched. A woman across the room was looking at me. She was alone, as I was. I might have taken it as an invitation to approach her, but something about the woman was . . . unsettling."

"You didn't recognize her?"

"Not at the time. She's changed. As a teenager, she was red-haired; now she's a blonde. And she's older, of course, and slimmer, I'd say. And I saw her only from a distance. Still, I knew the woman was familiar, and some sixth sense warned me of a threat. I left the bar. She followed me. Finally I worked up the nerve to confront her—but when I tried, she melted away into the dark and was gone."

He drained his coffee cup. Shepherd noted the deep

crescents underscoring Cray's eyes. The man was weary. No wonder he needed caffeine.

As if anticipating this thought, Cray nodded. "I didn't sleep well last night. Couldn't get that woman out of my mind. I knew I'd seen her before, but where? Then, early this morning it came to me. Kaylie. Of course it was Kaylie. You know, I really should have expected that she would come after me someday."

"Should you?"

"Certainly. She hated her confinement here. Though we tried to help her, she must have felt humiliated and abused. She would never forget . . . or forgive."

"So you think she's still crazy?"

Cray smiled indulgently. "*Crazy* is not a term of art in my profession, Detective. What we're dealing with in Kaylie McMillan is chronic, unmedicated psychosis that can escalate unpredictably into an acute, florid episode. She has demonstrated a capacity for lethal violence. She displays cunning and foresight and monomania. She is a danger to herself and others. And now"—the smile was long gone—"she appears to have targeted me."

Shepherd wasn't sure what to say. But a response seemed unnecessary. Cray was already rising.

"Words can't tell the whole story," he said. "Let me show you what she did to my Lexus."

He led Shepherd into the anteroom, where the secretary was just returning from lunch.

"I'll be gone a few minutes, Margaret." Cray shrugged. "Police business."

Margaret was no more impressed than the receptionist downstairs had been. She glanced at Shepherd only long enough to ascertain that she didn't know him.

"Walter back yet?" she inquired of Cray.

"No. He may be gone awhile."

He and Shepherd left together. In the hall Shepherd asked, "Who's Walter?"

"A patient. One of our long-termers. He's functional up to a point, but he can never be deinstitutionalized. He's been here too long."

The thought of a lifetime spent inside these drab walls was insufferably depressing to Shepherd. "Where is he now?" he asked.

"Running an errand for me."

"You use your patients to run errands?"

"Only this one patient. Walter is special. You'd be surprised how adept he is at certain rather simple tasks." Cray reached the stairwell door and paused with his hand on the knob, a long-fingered, elegant hand with perfectly manicured nails. "Schizophrenia can be something of an asset, you know."

Shepherd thought this was a joke, but he saw no humor in Cray's face.

"It's quite true," Cray said. "Every adaptation of the human organism must have some survival value, or it would have been bred out of the gene pool."

"What survival value?"

"Well, take Walter, for instance. Like many schizophrenics, his sensitivity to visual stimuli is acute. He's tireless, resistant to fatigue. And single-minded. Give him an assignment, and he won't stop until he gets it done. In many ways he's far superior to us normals."

"I'm not sure I'd buy that."

"But think about it, Detective." There was Cray's smile again, cool and bland and somehow secretive. "This is a man who misses nothing around him, who never loses his focus . . . and who never, ever quits."

24

"Find the red car. Find the red car. Find the red car. Find the red car."

Walter Luntz repeated the words in a steady monotone as he drove the Toyota Tercel down Tucson's streets.

He loved the Tercel, which Dr. Cray had bought for him—think of it, just for *him,* a gift from the great Dr. Cray. It was the car he used for running errands, a wonderful car, though too small for Walter, who stood six foot three and had to stoop in doorways.

Hunched in the driver's seat, his callused hands wrapped around the steering wheel, his bald head bent low under the roof, he devoted his full concentration to the job he'd been given.

"Find the red car. Find the red car."

He was unaware that he was speaking. He heard the instructions in his mind, spoken not by his own voice but by Dr. Cray's.

"Find the red car."

It was the last thing Dr. Cray had told him before sending him forth on his mission. It was the only thing that mattered, and Dr. Cray had stressed the importance of the red car, of *finding* the red car, over and over again. He had even shown Walter a picture of a very similar car, which he had found in a place called the Internet.

The car in the picture was not red, but Dr. Cray had told Walter to imagine it as red, and with effort, Walter had been able to do so.

Find this car, Dr. Cray had said as they sat together in his office with the door closed. *It could be anywhere in Tucson, but most likely you'll find it at a motel, in the parking lot. Do you know how to recognize a motel?*

Walter knew. He had even stayed in a motel once, years ago, when he was a young man. He remembered that there had been a slot by the bed that you put quarters into, and the bed would quiver. Fun.

There are many cars like this in Tucson, Dr. Cray had told him. *You can't check every one, so just check the ones in the motel parking lots. The special car, the one I need you to find, has a license plate with this number on it.*

Dr. Cray had handed him a slip of paper with a string of letters and numerals written carefully by hand. Walter had studied the paper for a long time before nodding.

Can you do it? Dr. Cray asked, his voice more gentle than Walter had ever heard it.

Sure I can, Walter had said, feeling a lift of pride at the statement.

He could, too. It was rare for him to drive as far as Tucson, much less to explore the city one street at a time, and the excursion would tax his capabilities—but he could do it.

For Dr. Cray, he could do anything.

Because Dr. Cray was the greatest man in the world. Dr. Cray might even be God.

Sometimes, especially at night when Walter lay alone in bed in the small guest room that was his home, he thought that Dr. Cray had come down from heaven to help all the sad, ill people like himself, and when they were cured, every one of them normal again, then Dr. Cray would ascend to the clouds in a burst of glorious light.

Walter had not shared these thoughts with Dr. Cray. He was shy.

The car belongs to a woman, Dr. Cray had said, keeping his voice low and conspiratorial. *She's a very dangerous woman, Walter. If you find her car, you must not let her see you. Do you understand?*

Sure, he'd said, though in truth he had some trouble following this.

Just call me. Use the phone I gave you. Dr. Cray had kindly supplied Walter with a fine telephone that he took with him whenever he ran an errand. Walter had used the phone only once, when he became confused by a proliferation of street signs and had to pull over in a panic. *Call me, and tell me where the car is, and I'll take care of it from there.*

But she's dangerous, Walter had protested. *You said so.*

I can handle her.

You'll get hurt.

No, Walter, I'll be fine, just fine.

Walter, who did not like the thought of anything bad happening to Dr. Cray, the great Dr. Cray, Dr. Cray who was his hero and savior and maybe God, had made a soft mewling noise.

Are you okay, Walter? Walter? Are you okay?

I'm okay, Walter had said.

Dr. Cray seemed to think for a moment. Then he said very softly, *Listen, Walter. I think I'd better tell you who this woman is. You know her. Or at least, you knew her once. She was a patient here.*

There have been lots of patients, Walter said. It made him dizzy to think of how many there had been, coming and going, getting well sometimes, or other times dying. The dead ones were buried in the graveyard, and there was nothing left of them but bronze plaques and flowers.

Yes. Dr. Cray's face was calm and expressionless. *Many patients, but you may remember this one. Her name was Kaylie. Kaylie McMillan. She was just a girl when she came here, and you were thirty-seven.*

Kaylie, Walter said, and he nodded.

Do you remember?

I remember. The girl's face came to him, sharp and vivid. He had a photographic memory. He might have been looking right at her. *She was pretty.*

Very pretty, Dr. Cray agreed. *I was trying to help her, but before I could, she ran away. Do you recall that night, Walter? She ran away, and there was trouble.*

Walter stiffened. He remembered the trouble. There had been police and other people, people with cameras and microphones, and later it had been on TV, and they made it look like it was Dr. Cray's fault. They said bad things about Dr. Cray and the hospital, and they kept using the same strange words, *breach of security.*

It had been bad. And Kaylie had caused it. She had run off, abandoning Dr. Cray, who only wanted to make her better. She had run, and Dr. Cray had been blamed.

She's a bad person, Walter said.

Dr. Cray nodded gravely. *Yes. She is.*

I hate her.

You don't need to hate her. You only need to be careful that she doesn't see you. She looks a little different now, but not too much. Her hair is blonde, not red as it used to be. Do you think you would know her if you saw her again, Walter?

I'll know her.

Good. If you find the car, don't let her see you. Because she may remember you too. Do you understand?

Walter had been silent, thinking hard, a fierce frown stamped on his face.

Do you understand, Walter? Dr. Cray asked again.

Walter had responded that time. *I understand.*

But Dr. Cray had not seemed sure, and so he had repeated the instructions, then repeated them again.

The last thing he said before opening the office door was the most important thing of all: *Find the red car.*

"Find the red car," Walter said to himself as he cruised along 22nd Street in the slow lane. "Find the red car. Find the red car."

He had seen many red cars in the parking lots of many motels during his search, but none of the cars had been right. Some had been the wrong shape, not at all like the picture from the Internet, and some had been the wrong kind of car—a Toyota, like the car he drove, or a Hyundai or a Honda. Funny names.

Repeatedly he'd actually stopped to check the license plate of a Chevrolet Chevette, comparing it with the number Dr. Cray had written down. Every time his heart had been beating fast and hard with excitement, because he was so very eager to complete his mission and please Dr. Cray, but every time he had been disappointed. The license plates had been wrong.

The last time it happened, in sheer frustration he had banged his fist on the side panel of the Chevette, and a man coming out of the motel had stopped to look at him.

That was bad. He was not supposed to attract attention. Dr. Cray had been very clear on that point.

"Find the red car. Find the red car." For variety he altered his emphasis on the words. "Find the *red* car. *Find* the red car. Find the red *car*."

He would find it. He knew he would. There were countless things he was no good at. He couldn't write more than a few words without losing track of what he wanted to say, and he couldn't get the jokes on TV comedy shows, even when they were explained to him, and he couldn't do laundry or have long conversations or eat soup without getting it all over himself.

But this job he could do.

He would find the red car.

But he would not use the telephone to call Dr. Cray.

He would take care of Kaylie McMillan all by himself.

She had hurt Dr. Cray once before, simply by running off. How much worse could she hurt him if she really tried?

Walter didn't intend to find out. After all, the great Dr. Cray might be God, but he was a human person too, and Walter didn't want anything bad to happen to him. He didn't want Dr. Cray to . . . die. He wouldn't be able to stand it if Dr. Cray died.

Kaylie McMillan, on the other hand . . .

She could die, and no one would care.

Killing her would be easy. She wasn't big, and he was. He would ambush her, leap up and take her by surprise, clap his hands to her head, and with one twist of his wide shoulders he would snap her neck.

Then she would never hurt anyone ever again, and everything would be fine, just fine.

"Find the red car," Walter Luntz said, nodding in obedience to the command. "Find the red car. Find the red car. Find the red car."

25

Cray lived in a house at the rear of the hospital property, screened by hedges and served by a private drive. The director's mansion, it was called, although it was actually no more than a modest two-story home in the Southwestern style.

Shepherd followed Cray down a winding path to the house, past a small well-tended cemetery where two dozen patients—"the unclaimed ones," Cray explained offhandedly—were interred. The air was warm and still, and there was birdsong in the high branches of the trees.

At the side of the house was a two-car garage with a single window at shoulder height. The pane had been smashed.

"One of our groundskeepers reported this to me about two hours ago. The break-in must have occurred last night."

"When you were home?"

"Yes. But my bedroom is upstairs, on the other side of the house. I never heard the sound of breaking glass. Or any other sound." Cray shrugged. "Perhaps that's just as well. It wouldn't have been advisable to directly confront Kaylie—not in her present condition."

He unlocked the side door and flipped a light switch. Two bare bulbs in the ceiling of the garage snapped on, casting a pale yellow glow over Cray's Lexus.

Shepherd circled the vehicle. It had been savagely abused. Someone had slashed all four tires and grooved deep scratches in the black finish. The front window on the driver's side had been shattered; Shepherd saw a large, jagged rock on the bucket seat. The seat cushions were sliced in tatters, and the lid of the glove compartment hung open, the contents strewn. Shepherd saw a scatter of CD cases on the floor. Symphonies, operas. Every disk had been defaced.

"Did she make any attempt to enter the house itself?" he asked.

"No. But of course all the doors were locked, even the door from the garage."

"Is there a burglar alarm?"

"I've never thought it necessary to install one. Not in a gated compound patrolled by armed guards."

"How about the Lexus? Doesn't it have a security system?"

"An antitheft system is standard. But I'm afraid I had it disabled soon after I bought the vehicle."

"Why?"

"Too many false alarms. The system was overly sensitive to vibrations or casual contact. The horn was constantly blaring. I just got tired of it."

"But Kaylie wouldn't have known the system was turned off."

"I doubt she would have thought about it at all. In the throes of her obsession, she would not be functioning rationally." Cray waved a hand at the vehicle. "As you can see."

"Did she take anything from the car or the garage?"

"Yes. A spare medical kit I kept in the vehicle."

"A kit?" Shepherd remembered the 911 tape. "Like a satchel?"

"I suppose one could describe it that way. I think of it as my black bag. Occasionally I'm called out to see a released patient on an emergency basis. Why do you ask?"

"The caller said she had a satchel of yours, which contained your . . . instruments of murder."

"A delusion. What else did she say?"

Shepherd saw no reason to hold anything back at this point. "She claimed that you kidnap women and hunt them. Like animals."

Cray shrugged. "Unsurprising, really. Most paranoids develop elaborate fantasies that have some basis in their personal experience. Kaylie associates me with the authorities—the police, I mean—who have indeed been hunting her for the past twelve years. You see how her mind might expand the truth of her situation into an imaginative metaphorical construct?"

"She also said we'd find your Lexus in bad shape, because she had to drive it through the desert to escape from you."

Cray chuckled. The sound echoed off the corners of the garage. "No doubt she believes as much. Of course, if she had taken my vehicle, it would hardly be here in my garage."

"She expected you to have it, though. She told us to check it out."

"The inconsistency would never occur to her. You have to understand a person like Kaylie, Detective Shepherd. She's fundamentally out of contact with reality. She can break in here, vandalize my property, and an hour later she'll be fully convinced that I'm the villain. She rewrites history from moment to moment."

"Yet she's evaded the law for more than a decade."

"I'm not claiming she's been this severely irrational throughout that entire time period. She must experience intervals of near-lucidity. Perhaps such intervals persist for months, even years. But always there will be a relapse. Stress or a hormonal change or some neurotic obsession will trigger a crisis, and she'll regress to acute psychosis. She will decompensate, as we doctors like to say."

Shepherd surveyed the ruined Lexus. "Looks like she's decompensated now."

"I'd have to concur in your diagnosis."

Cray locked up the garage and walked with Shepherd to the parking lot. Strange laughter rained down from a second-floor window in the administration building. Shepherd wondered if it was the young man who'd set fire to a toolshed because the TV had told him to, or if it was somebody else.

At his car, he stopped, facing Cray in the bright daylight.

"All right, Doctor. It seems clear that this woman is harassing you, and that she made a false report. The case, though, belongs primarily to the jurisdiction of the local sheriff. Breaking and entering, vandalizing your vehicle, theft of your medical bag—all those crimes were committed here in Graham County, not in Tucson. The only aspect of the case that's properly within my purview is the phone call to the nine-one-one line. And we get lots of phony tips. We could never prosecute them all."

"I understand. As I said, I called the sheriff's office. I'm sure a deputy will be along shortly to take my statement."

"Relay any information that might be helpful. Pay particular attention to the changes in Kaylie's appearance. You said she's blonde now, and more slender. Any other details you can remember will be helpful."

"I'll try. But I got only a glimpse."

"Do your best. And please, could you have the deputies fax the report to me at Tucson PD?"

"I thought it wasn't your case."

"I'd like to stay up to speed anyway." Shepherd handed Cray a card. "Here's the fax number where they can reach me. Ask them to dig up the file on Kaylie McMillan and fax that too. Okay? Now, there's one other thing."

"My safety," Cray said.

"It could be an issue."

"In my line of work, Detective, it always is." Cray smiled. "I suppose we both know something about that."

"Even so, you need to take precautions."

"I intend to be vigilant, believe me."

"Do you have any experience with firearms?"

"None, and I don't plan to acquire any. Guns scare me."

"All the more reason to carry one. If she shows up armed, you need to be able to defend yourself. There are classes in firearms safety—"

"Out of the question. I won't become a lone gunman, toting a six-gun like some character out of the Wild West. Besides, I could never harm Kaylie. She was my patient, you see. She was entrusted to my care."

Shepherd gave up. There was nothing he could say to that.

"As you wish, Doctor." He shook Cray's hand. "Thanks for your time."

Cray was walking away when Shepherd remembered one more question to ask.

"That book you wrote—*The Mask of Self*. What was it about?"

Cray turned back, then thought for a moment. "Icebergs," he said.

"Come again?"

"Have you seen an illustration of an iceberg, Detective? The tip is just one-tenth of the whole, yet it's all we see above the surface. I think that what we call the personality, the ego, the self, is the iceberg's tip. The remaining nine-tenths of human nature, the enormous submerged mass, is our great store of inherited drives and instinctual, automatized responses. It is these which really move us. We are animals at heart. The self is mere window dressing. A mask, a false front. We hear about 'mind over matter.' It would be more true to say the mind doesn't matter."

"Kind of an unusual position for a psychiatrist to take."

"Not really. It's my job to delve beneath appearances. To ignore the surface and dive deep."

"How did the book sell?"

"It's in its fourth printing."

"Congratulations. Do you think Kaylie's read it?"

Cray's face darkened, and Shepherd knew this was one question the man had not thought to ask himself.

"I can't say," Cray answered slowly. "I doubt she would. Is it important?"

"Something set her off. Maybe she took offense. Maybe she didn't like her own doctor saying that his patients are animals at heart."

"I wasn't referring to her, specifically."

"But you do think of her that way?"

"I think of us all in that way, Detective. You and me and any poor bastard screaming in his isolation cell. Saints and sinners, heroes and knaves—we are, all of us, actors in our own dream, playing roles our minds script for us, while our bodies go their own way, following their innate will."

"Sounds like a quotation."

"*The Mask of Self*, Chapter Three, page thirty-nine." Cray at least had the grace to smile.

"So long, Doctor. And take care."

Shepherd got in his car and drove away, watching Dr. John Bainbridge Cray in the rearview mirror, a tall, neat man in a brown suit, lord of this small, sad fiefdom.

A lonely man. Proud. Not easy to like.

But a killer?

No.

It was Kaylie McMillan who was the killer, and she was on the loose, and violent, and perhaps capable of killing again.

26

Elizabeth woke in a strange room, a room that was hot and musty and limned in a strange half-light that fell through windows veiled in translucent drapes.

It took her a moment to understand that she was in a motel, yes, another motel in Tucson, her third in the past ten days. She had left the first motel because it was too expensive, and she had left the second because of Cray.

The memory surprised her into full alertness. She sat up too quickly, then spent a moment recovering from a tug of dizziness.

She remembered everything now. She'd had breakfast at a coffee shop, where some cops had frightened her, and then she'd heard the news—the wonderful, impossibly good news about Cray.

He was in custody. They had him. They must have picked him up immediately after examining the contents of the satchel. The damaged Lexus had confirmed her story.

Blinded by relief and joy, she had driven to the first motel she could find, a two-story structure a half mile from the coffee shop, with a red VACANCY sign and a nightly rate of thirty-seven dollars.

The place was an unmistakable improvement over her usual accommodations—a swimming pool, cable TV, definite luxuries—and the price was a bit steep for her diminishing reserve of cash, but she had been both too tired and too happy to argue.

Checking in so early, she'd had to wait for the maid to finish making up the room. For a few minutes she had stood in a corner, watching the young woman vacuum the carpet and replace the towels, thinking vaguely that there was something familiar about her —the dark complexion and round, serious face—her face . . .

And suddenly she had realized that the maid reminded her of that other woman whose name she didn't know, the woman whose disembodied face haunted her dreams.

But there would be no more dreams. She was sure of it. Cray had been vanquished, and the last residue of his evil had been swept away.

Finally the maid left with a smiling good-bye, and Elizabeth was alone.

Sleep had taken her almost instantly. She closed the drapes, lay on the bed, and dropped away into the dark.

The dreamless dark. No nightmares. Never again.

That had been at ten in the morning. Now the plastic clock on the nightstand read 2:49. She had slept for nearly five hours, cocooned in the cool hum of the air-conditioning and the smoothness of freshly laundered sheets.

Her first priority at this moment was a shower. Not having bothered to undress, she still wore the clothes she'd put on last night, wrinkled and sticky with a paste of sweat. Her hair felt dirty, matted, lumpy. She needed to be clean.

She undressed, then stood under a cone of spray in the tiled stall, inhaling steam.

Remarkably, shampoo was provided free of charge, an amenity she had not enjoyed in her previous lodgings. She squirted a dollop into her hand and worked the creamy foam into a lather, rubbing the suds deep into her hair, massaging her scalp until her exhaustion was gone.

It felt wonderful.

At 3:10, when she was clean and dry and dressed in fresh clothes, she turned on the radio and traveled around the dial in search of a news station.

She wanted to hear Cray's name. Her final doubt would be dispelled when the announcer said that it was John Bainbridge Cray, noted psychiatrist and author, who was under arrest.

That was how they would put it too. Noted psychiatrist and author.

She knew about Cray's psychiatric methods. His talents as an author were more difficult for her to judge. Although she had seen magazine write-ups on his book, she had been unable to bring herself to actually read the damn thing.

It was hard enough just knowing that he was famous—well, moderately famous anyway—and successful.

She didn't like to believe there was no justice in the universe. She had seen what such a belief did to people, the bitterness it bred, the cynicism and ugly despondency.

But when she thought of Cray writing about the human psyche and finding an audience for his views, she almost couldn't stand it. There was a limit to the unfairness a person ought to be asked to accept.

She was unable to find a news station, only a lot of

pop music and a couple of talk shows dealing with national affairs.

There would be local news updates at four o'clock, she supposed—nearly an hour from now.

Too long to wait. How about the TV? She turned it on and used the remote control to search through more than twenty channels. She found news, but again nothing local.

"Damn," she muttered.

She switched off the TV and felt herself trembling with impatience and frustration and the desperate need to know.

She told herself to relax. It was over now. That was the thing to remember.

Cray had not won in the end. All his triumphs had been temporary. She had outsmarted him, and now he was in custody, in custody, in custody, where he belonged.

But she had to be sure.

Well, there might be a way.

Tucson had two newspapers, and one of them, the *Citizen,* came out in the afternoon. It was just barely possible that the details of Cray's arrest had been reported in time to make today's edition.

She grabbed her purse and the room key, then left in a hurry.

The day was warm and bright. Blinking at the glare, she fished sunglasses from her purse, then headed east on Speedway Boulevard in search of a newspaper.

Traffic rushed past in an impatient stream. The street was wide, six lanes with a landscaped median, and lined on both sides with strip malls and family restaurants. Not a ritzy neighborhood, to be sure, but in comparison with the grime of Miracle Mile and the blighted desolation of the frontage road along the interstate, it seemed like Rodeo Drive.

She felt herself smiling. Things had worked out. Last night had been a close call, very close, but she had survived, and she had won.

Then she passed an auto dealership, and abruptly she remembered that Sharon Andrews had worked at a car lot somewhere on Speedway Boulevard.

This car lot? Elizabeth didn't know, couldn't recall.

But if not this one, then another just like it.

Sharon had left at the end of her workday and had simply disappeared, and no one had known what became of her. Even after her body was found, nobody could say precisely how she had died. Even Elizabeth hadn't been sure.

But now she knew. Cray had told her.

He had driven Sharon Andrews high into the White Mountains and set her loose on a desperate run, and in the starlight he had tracked her, remorseless as any predator on the hunt, and he'd shot her, and as she lay wounded, he had used his knife—the knife from his satchel, the knife in the leather sheath—to strip her face away.

Elizabeth wasn't smiling anymore. It felt wrong to be happy. Disloyal, somehow.

Disloyal to Sharon and to the other women, however many there might be—all of Cray's victims, down through the years.

At the corner of Speedway and Wilmot, in a small shopping center, she found a row of newspaper vending machines.

The Tucson *Citizen* was displayed in the nearest one. She bent for a closer look, her heart pounding hard and fast in her ears.

Through the Plexiglas panel she read the headlines.

A road project was over budget and behind schedule. A senator was under investigation for campaign irregularities. A local software firm was hiring two hundred new employees.

Nothing else.

Maybe the news had come in too late to allow the front page to be redesigned. There still might be a story inside.

She found coins in her purse and fed them to the machine, then pulled open the bin. The paper in the display window was the last copy left. She slid it out of its bracket and tried to flip through the pages, but the wind kept crumpling the newsprint and she couldn't see anything.

Calm down, Elizabeth. Take it easy.

The soothing words came to her in a calm male baritone. It took her a moment to realize that it was Anson's voice she had heard.

His advice was sound, as usual. She drew a deep, slow breath, then another.

When she was back in control, she found a bus-stop bench shaded by a kiosk and sat down with the paper. The kiosk sheltered her from the wind, and she was able to flip through the pages methodically, hunting for any reference to the Sharon Andrews case.

On the second page of the *Tucson & Arizona* section, she found it.

POLICE DENY BREAK IN WHITE MOUNTAINS CASE.

Deny.

She had to read the words three times before they made any sense.

A shudder rippled through her, and she felt a bulge of nausea at the base of her throat.

There had to be some mistake. But of course there wasn't. Her hope had been only an illusion.

With effort she refocused her eyes on the trembling newsprint in her hands and read the article itself.

A Tucson Police Department spokesman was quick to dismiss reports of a major break in the ongoing White Mountains Killer investigation.

Earlier today, three Tucson-area radio stations reported that a suspect had been arrested and charged with the slaying of Tucson resident Sharon Andrews, whose mutilated remains were found by campers in the White Mountains last August.

The department's official spokesman, Sgt. Benjamin Graves, called the reports inaccurate. Graves speculated that the misunderstanding may have arisen after the arrest of a homeless man on unrelated charges.

A homeless man.

It was never Cray.

The story never had anything to do with Cray at all.

She almost stopped reading, too tired to continue.

But on the radio, they'd said it was a 911 call. *Her* call—it must have been.

Scanning the article, she saw *911* embedded in the text two paragraphs down.

The story may have been blown further out of proportion by a separate incident involving a 911 call. Graves confirmed that the department received a call early this morning from an anonymous tipster claiming to know the identity of the White Mountains Killer.

"Somebody's wires got crossed," Graves said. "It looks like the arrest and the phone call were both reported at around the

same time, and the impression was left that there was some connection between the two. It's an unfortunate example of the confusion that sometimes occurs in a high-profile case."

Graves said that the 911 tip was unlikely to represent a legitimate break in the investigation. "Without going into detail, all indications are that the call was one of many false leads we've received in connection with this matter. There is no evidence, absolutely none, that would give any credibility to this particular call."

Graves stressed that members of the public are encouraged to phone the department with any information that may be of value . . .

Elizabeth lowered her head.

For just one moment she wanted to toss aside the newspaper and walk away, leave town, hear nothing more about the White Mountains case, and never, ever know if the man who had killed Sharon Andrews had been brought to justice.

One of many false leads, the cop had said. *No evidence. Absolutely none.*

But she had given them all the evidence they could possibly need.

All they had to do, the damn fools, was look at the satchel, just *look* at it, for God's sake—was that too much to ask? Was it unreasonable? Was she wrong to expect any help at all, from anyone, ever?

Maybe she was wrong. Maybe she had to do everything herself.

Catch Cray. Kill him. Deliver his body to the front steps of the police station, with the faces of his victims pinned to his hide as incontrovertible proof of his guilt.

The faces of his victims. . . .

She blinked, then slowly lifted her head with a thought.

A crazy thought. Yes, crazy. Of course it was.

But for once that word didn't scare her. Because she wasn't crazy. She knew that now.

It was the world that was insane.

27

Shepherd was cruising the interstate, three miles from Tucson city limits, when his cell phone chirped. He fumbled it out of the side pocket of his jacket. "Shepherd."

"Roy, it's Hector. Something's come up. Something sort of interesting."

Alvarez was the phlegmatic type, slow to show excitement, but Shepherd heard a rare intensity in his voice now.

"Don't keep me in suspense," he said mildly.

"Well, the fax came in from Graham County." The sheriff's file on Kaylie McMillan. After leaving the hospital, Shepherd had called Alvarez and summarized Cray's story. He'd told Alvarez to watch for the fax. "I took a look at it."

"And?"

"Decided to post a copy of the lady's arrest photo on the bulletin board. What the hell. She's a fugitive, after all. Well, guess what."

"I'm a real bad guesser, Hector."

"Couple of patrol guys saw the pic and made her. I mean, they eyeballed her just this morning in a greasy spoon over on Speedway."

Shepherd's heart froze for an instant, then kicked into high gear. "They're sure?"

"Real sure. They said she started acting nervous when they sat down at the next table. Even spilled a cup of coffee all over the table, made a real mess—then left in a hurry. They didn't think too much of it at the time, but when they saw the photo, it was like, bam, that's her."

"What time this morning?"

"About nine."

"What's the name of the place?"

"Hold on." Alvarez shouted the question, got an indistinct answer, and said, "Rancheros Cafe."

Shepherd knew it. "Cross street is Woodland."

"Yeah."

"Okay, I'm about five minutes east of town right now. I'm going to detour over to the coffee shop and see if I can talk to anybody who remembers her."

"You want company?"

"It's not necessary. She must be long gone. But maybe I can take a statement from someone who works there. Who are the patrol cops, by the way?"

"Leo Galston—he's a T.O.—and Kurt Bane."

"I know Leo. I want a statement from him and his partner."

"They're already writing it up."

Shepherd took the Kolb Road exit and shot north to Speedway.

He remembered telling Cray that this wasn't his case. The Graham County sheriff had primary jurisdiction. There was no urgent reason for him to get involved.

But he hadn't told Cray the whole truth, had he?

Shepherd's mouth pinched. No. He'd said nothing about Ginnie.

His wife. His late wife.

Roy and Virginia Shepherd had lived on a cul-de-sac off Fort Lowell Road, in a modest brick house, ranch style, with pebbles and cacti in the front yard and a small, thirsty, carefully tended garden in the rear. The neighborhood was typical of Tucson—middle-class, quiet except for one neighbor's dog that never quit barking, bare of shade on hot summer days, untouched by any crime more serious than graffiti.

Shepherd and his wife had been happy there, or happy enough. The marriage hadn't been ideal. Sometimes Roy had gotten angry with Ginnie for the amount of time she spent in the den, hunched over her computer keyboard, working on her project.

The project was a Web site she had created, a clearinghouse of information submitted by dozens of local agencies and organizations, public and private, all committed to aiding the poor and homeless. Ginnie's goal was to coordinate the efforts of municipal and county relief agencies with the activities of private charities and churches.

Restaurants could check the inventories of local food banks and allocate surplus cuisine more intelligently. Schedules of AA meetings throughout Pima County were posted daily; printouts were posted in shelters. People needing assistance in a variety of foreign languages could be matched to appropriate relief workers who might be working across town or outside city limits.

A worthwhile endeavor, but endlessly time-consuming. Every evening, after a day's work, Ginnie had downloaded her e-mail from all these scattered sources, then had spent hours updating the site before uploading the new pages to the host server.

Shepherd had worried about her. She wasn't getting any sleep. And she had no time for him—or for anyone.

It was ironic, in a way. Ordinarily a cop's wife would complain that he was never home, but Shepherd had always made time for his personal life, and he wanted his wife to share it with him.

After some weeks of argument, an agreement had been reached. Ginnie would give up her job downtown and take on the Web site as a full-time occupation. She would earn no money for the work, but money had never been the point. Anyway, she was paid little more than minimum wage at the health clinic where she worked from eight to five every weekday.

Shepherd thought of the Tuesday night when she told him she'd given notice. *They just need me to stay on till they find a replacement,* she said. *Another week or so.* And, smiling, she'd added, *You can live with that, can't you?*

As it turned out, Ginnie was the one who couldn't live with it.

They celebrated her decision with wine and take-out meals from the best Italian restaurant in the world, just down the street. Drunk and laughing, they made love in the living room, progressing in giddy stages from the couch to the rug to the bare hardwood floor in the foyer.

And the next day Timothy Fries had visited the clinic.

Fries was a street person who had spent most of his life shuttling from one psychiatric ward to another.

Doctors had variously diagnosed him as acutely psychotic, manic-depressive, paranoid, and schizophrenic. Every pharmaceutical treatment had been tried; none had achieved more than transitory success. He had periods of lucidity, then relapsed into craziness. His family had given up on him. He had no friends, no home, no job, no life.

When his path had crossed Virginia Shepherd's, Fries had been thirty-two years old, penniless, ragged, and constantly afraid.

Ginnie did clerical work at the clinic, freeing up the staff nurses for more important duties. Part of her job was to interview incoming patients to elicit their medical histories.

On that Wednesday morning two years ago, Fries had entered, complaining of a headache. He had visited the place twice before, but always on weekends, when Ginnie wasn't around.

Had she been familiar with his case, she would have known that his headaches were psychosomatic, a product of his belief that larval worms had crawled into his skull via his ear canal and were presently feeding on his brain.

As it was, she knew only that the man in the anteroom was emaciated and scared and in pain. She asked him the standard questions, marked down his more intelligible replies.

He was mentally ill—this much was evident from his scattershot thought processes and muted affect—but she didn't judge him to be either paranoid or dangerous.

And so she made an error, a small error, hardly important.

She turned away from him to put her clipboard in the out basket. That was all.

In that moment Timothy Fries lunged at her, and she felt something sharp and hot burst through the bunched muscles at the base of her spine, and there was a rush of numbness in her legs, a dizzy collapse, an impression of chaos as nurses and doctors filled the anteroom and dragged the shrieking man away.

He had found a knife, a rusty treasure scavenged from the trash, and had concealed it under his coat when he entered the clinic. Apparently he'd become convinced that the clinic itself was responsible for the worms in his brain, and he had determined to take revenge.

Anyone who worked there could have been his target. Ginnie just happened to be convenient.

The blade had severed her spinal cord but hadn't killed her. She lingered in the hospital for two weeks.

During that time Shepherd left her room only once a day, for an hour, to go home, shower, shave, and change his clothes.

The doctors did what they could. They injected Ginnie with massive doses of methylprednisolone to minimize the swelling that could choke the blood vessels near her spine. They gave her morphine when her legs spasmed. They ordered soft-tissue massages to prevent the loss of muscle tone in her legs, and antibiotics to ward off infection.

Even so, after ten days they knew enough to tell Roy Shepherd that his wife was unlikely ever to walk again. Having suffered a complete transection of her spinal cord, she had neither feeling nor voluntary movement below the waist.

Shepherd remembered the blank stretch of time that followed his conversation with the doctors. Numb, disoriented, he walked blindly out of the hospital and stood on a walkway near a stand of palo verde trees. He blinked at the sun. He tried to think.

Then he saw a hummingbird alight briefly on a green branch before launching itself in hectic motion.

It flew so fast, with such ease, darting from bush to bush in search of nectar, wings strobing in the sun.

Ginnie had been like that once. Always moving, a blur of energy and purpose. Shepherd had loved that quality in her. He recalled walking with her in Reid Park when she abruptly challenged him to a race and started running, her legs swallowing distance in long strides, and her dark hair billowing behind her.

Shepherd had caught up with her and won, but what he recalled more vividly than the race itself was the electric charge that shivered through him when he saw her spring into action, this lithe creature who was all speed and air and laughter.

He thought of this, watching the hummingbird until it had darted away into a blue haze of distance and he was alone.

Then he went back inside the hospital to tell Ginnie the news. He said it gently, of course, but the truth was sharp-edged, and it could not be softened. When he was done speaking, he held his wife's hand. Ginnie was silent for a moment, and then she said she wasn't really surprised.

It looks like I'll be spending more time in front of that computer than I'd counted on, she added, and incredibly she managed a brief, wan smile.

The smile told Shepherd that things would be all

right. His wife's spirit was intact, even if her body was not. She would recover.

That night, at Ginnie's urging, he went home to sleep in his own bed. He was exhausted. He'd had perhaps twenty hours' rest in ten days.

Yet he woke in the middle of the night, his heart racing, a headache inflaming his skull.

And he knew.

Something was wrong.

He threw on his clothes and drove to the hospital. When he got there at 4 A.M., he found a team of doctors and nurses engaged in a frantic rescue operation in Virginia Shepherd's room.

Later he learned that she had suffered a condition called autonomic dysreflexia, common in cases of spinal cord injury. Despite the antibiotics, her urinary tract had become infected; because she had no sensation in the lower portion of her body, there had been no burning discomfort to serve as a warning of the problem.

Thirty minutes before Shepherd's arrival, at perhaps the exact moment when he had awakened with a premonition and a pounding migraine, Ginnie's blood pressure had spiked, stopping her heart, and her cardiac monitor had triggered an alarm at the nurses' station.

Epinephrine and defibrillators were used to restart her heart, but her blood pressure continued to climb, and again she went into cardiac arrest.

The second time she could not be revived.

At 4:45, Shepherd was informed that his wife had died.

He stood in the hallway, trying to take in this news

that was at once so simple and so impossibly complicated.

Did she feel anything? he asked the doctor finally. *I mean . . . any pain?*

The doctor said a sudden, severe headache was normally the only symptom the patient reported.

Shepherd nodded. His own headache, which had blinded him with pain for more than an hour, had gone away at 4:33 precisely.

It was the exact moment when Ginnie had gone away too.

He lived alone now, in the modest brick house in the cul-de-sac off Fort Lowell Road. His friends advised him to sell the place, put the memories behind him, but he wanted those memories, painful though they were.

He had changed nothing in the den where she worked. The computer was still there, untouched in two years. Sometimes he stood in the doorway of the small, untidy room stacked with books and paperwork, and he imagined that he saw her sitting at the keyboard, perhaps in a wheelchair, perhaps not.

The wheelchair didn't matter one way or the other. Only she mattered, and she was lost to him.

And Timothy Fries?

He was back in an institution, no threat to anyone—at least until some new doctor recommended his release.

Someone would. Because there were too many people with soft hearts. People who didn't know how to hate.

Shepherd wasn't one of them, not anymore. He had learned hatred. There might be virtue in forgiveness, but there was no vigilance in it. Those who were quick to forgive, who prided themselves on their tolerance, were the ones who had dropped their guard and let the mad dog Fries out of his pen.

Now there was another Tim Fries on the loose. Not a man of thirty-two this time, but a woman of thirty-one.

She had shot her husband, escaped from an asylum, and she was obsessed with the doctor who had treated her, just as Fries had been obsessed with the clinic where Ginnie worked.

It was not Shepherd's case, at least not primarily. But hell, he was handling it anyway.

He would get Kaylie McMillan off the street and see that she was locked up, in a jail cell or a mental ward, for the rest of her life.

28

He had found the red car.

Walter knew it. From the moment he saw the car in the motel parking lot—the red car, it was a red car, just like the picture from the Internet—yes, from that very moment he'd had a feeling that it was the one.

And he never, ever had feelings. He had heard people speak of such things—intuition, hunches—but he'd never had the least idea of what they were talking about.

Yet this time he himself, Walter Luntz, had experienced a genuine premonition, and he had even said aloud in the cramped confines of his Toyota Tercel, "This is it. This is the right red car."

Wary of calling attention to himself, he parked on a side street, not in the parking lot, then doubled back on foot. Although he had been driving for what must have been a long time, he was not tired in the least. He could have driven for hours, for days.

In truth, Walter had little concept of time at all. Time was something he measured mainly by the meals he was served in the hospital commissary. There was breakfast time and lunchtime and, his favorite, dinnertime.

But today he'd had only breakfast, no lunch, no dinner, and so time, for him, had simply stopped, and there was only the task of driving and searching and now, finally, the delicious reward.

He crossed the parking lot to the red car and stood behind it, staring at the license plate until he remembered the slip of paper Dr. Cray had given him.

Carefully he unfolded it and compared the license number with the string of letters and numerals on the plate.

The same.

He checked again. He checked a third time. Then, because he was a conscientious person and he did not want to fail in his important mission, he checked once more.

It was her car. Kaylie McMillan's car.

His big hands flexed. He thought of last Christmas, when he and some of the other patients had been treated to a turkey dinner, and he'd gotten to play with the wishbone. It had snapped so easily in his fingers, just the way Kaylie McMillan's neck would snap when he wrenched her head sideways on her shoulders.

He was not prone to violence. He'd never killed anybody, never even hurt an animal. Still, he didn't imagine it would be too hard.

He just had to find her. She could be behind any of the motel room doors. He supposed the easiest way was to just knock on every door until eventually she answered. Then he would break her neck and walk away.

The nearest door had the number 27 on it in big letters. "Twenty-seven," Walter said, for no particular reason. He often announced the names of things.

He knocked, but there was no answer. Nobody home.

"Twenty-eight," he said at his next stop.

This time a person did answer, but it wasn't Kaylie. It was some guy in a bathrobe, who said, "Yeah?" in a belligerent way.

"Is Kaylie in there?"

"I don't know no fucking Kaylie. You got the wrong fucking room, asshole."

The door slammed.

Walter nodded. The man had been helpful. He had made it very plain that Walter had the wrong room. If everyone in the motel was equally cooperative, he would find Kaylie in no time.

His knocking drew no response at Rooms 29, 30, and 31.

The door to Room 32 was already open. A maid was at work changing the sheets. "Is Kaylie in here?" Walter asked.

The maid was a young woman with dark hair and a round, dark face. She did not speak English. Walter was temporarily flummoxed. Then he thought of a way to get his point across.

He took a pad of motel stationery from a bureau and in a few deft strokes he sketched Kaylie's face, as he remembered it.

Drawing was one of his few talents. He had heard Dr. Cray remark several times that his skill in this area was *really exceptional*, which Walter took to mean *good*. Some of the other patients couldn't draw at all, couldn't draw even a stick figure or a cartoon face, and some of them couldn't recognize a human portrait when they saw one.

Walter might have his problems, but this was not

one of them. The drawing he produced was a perfect likeness of Kaylie McMillan at age nineteen, an image culled from a library of faces in his photographic memory and put on paper without a single smudge or wasted line.

He showed it to the maid, and her face brightened.

"Ah, the *señora,*" she said. "I make up room for her. Very pretty, very nice."

Walter nodded. He thought Kaylie was pretty too. He thought he might even kiss her once, smack on the lips, after she was dead.

"Where is she?" Walter asked. "I'm looking for her." He rarely lied, but the importance of this moment inspired him to a brilliant prevarication. "I'm her brother, and I'm here to pick her up."

This sounded convincing, though he wasn't sure the maid quite understood.

Whether she did or not, she seemed happy to help. "She is in Room, uh . . . how you say *nombre?* Three and seven."

Three and seven? Room 10? No, that couldn't be right.

Then Walter understood.

Room 37. Just a few doors down.

"Thank you," Walter said. He took the drawing with him when he left.

Well, that had been easy. Now he would kill Kaylie and go home. His stomach was getting a little restless, and he suspected that lunchtime had passed. He hoped he would not miss dinner.

"Thirty-seven," he said, and rapped on the door.

No answer.

He knocked again. "Kaylie," he called. "Are you there? Come out, Kaylie."

Nothing.

He was rather disappointed. It appeared she was out.

The idea that she might not open the door never occurred to him. At the hospital, the only world he knew well, people always responded when he knocked on their doors or called out to them or pressed a buzzer for help.

If Kaylie was not responding, then she wasn't home. But she would be back. He could wait.

Waiting was another thing he was good at. He could sit in the same position for hours without moving.

Next to Room 37 there was a stairwell. A good place to hide.

Walter retreated into the far corner of the stairwell and leaned back against the wall, his arms at his sides, his gaze focused straight ahead on nothing, no thoughts in his mind, no distractions, and he waited for Kaylie to return.

29

"Ma'am? You okay?"

Elizabeth heard the words and looked up.

Two small boys, no older than ten, stood watching her with wary concern. One had a book bag slung over his shoulder, and the other wore a Diamondbacks baseball cap cocked on his head.

"Ma'am?" the boy with the book bag said again, his face scrunching up in a puzzled frown.

"I'm fine," she answered automatically, wondering why he and his friend had stopped to ask.

Then she realized that unconsciously, while sitting on the bus-stop bench, she had begun to shred the newspaper in her hands. Long curling strips lay everywhere on the bench and sidewalk, a scatter of confetti.

"You're not s'posed to litter," the boy in the baseball cap said sternly. "It's against the law."

He seemed less helpful than the other boy, and more afraid.

Elizabeth found a smile for him. "I'm sorry. You're right." Her gaze widened to include them both. "I won't do it again."

The second boy did not return the smile. He just stood silently appraising her, worried by what he saw.

His companion, more trusting, said, "That's okay. You didn't mean to. What's your name?"

Before Elizabeth could answer, the other boy cut in. "I don't think we should be talking to her, Tommy."

Tommy ignored this. "You waiting for the bus?"

"No. Just sitting down. I wanted to get out of the wind for a while." She got up, taking care not to scatter the loose strips of newsprint in her grasp. "Guess I'd better get going."

"We go to Sewell Elementary," Tommy said.

"Come on." The other boy tugged at Tommy's arm. He seemed even more concerned now that Elizabeth was on her feet. "Let's go."

Tommy reluctantly yielded to the pressure. "Okay, well . . . we'll see you."

He produced a slightly goofy, lopsided smile, and Elizabeth realized that he was enamored of her, in his boyish way. That was why he'd stopped to talk.

She was charmed, yet at the same time oddly saddened. It took her a moment to realize that she was wondering how much time had passed since anybody had smiled at her like that.

She hadn't dared intimacy in years. A serious relationship posed the risk of exposing her safeguarded secrets, or of drawing another person into the dangerous mess of her life.

"Bye, Tommy," she said, with a smile of her own.

She glimpsed a red tinge inflaming his cheeks as he turned quickly away.

The two boys walked off, and she heard the one in the baseball cap saying, "What's the matter with you, man? You nuts or something?"

She watched them go. They were heading west on

their way home from school; her motel lay in the same direction. She didn't want them to think she was following them. She had a feeling Tommy's companion wouldn't care for that development.

When they were well down the street, she wedged the newspaper under her arm and started walking. She knew what she had to do, and she had better get moving if she intended to do it tonight.

The risk was high, but she'd tried everything else.

She could run, of course, just run away and let Cray kill again and again, never to be stopped.

But then she would dream every night of the ride into the desert in the black Lexus, knowing that other women were taking that journey, women she might have saved. And one of those women might have a boy like Tommy, a boy who would grow up without his mother. Sharon Andrews, the last victim, had left a son behind.

"So do it, then," she whispered to herself. "Do it, and get it over with."

She thought of Tommy's serious friend, who'd scolded her for littering. What would he say if he knew her plans for the evening?

In her mind she heard him saying sternly, *It's against the law.* But littering was only a misdemeanor. Tonight she would commit a felony.

Well, so what? The law had never helped her. The law had been her enemy for twelve years. The law was obtuse and stubborn and blind, and to hell with it.

The two boys had cut down a side street now. Walking past, Elizabeth saw Tommy's friend run up the driveway of a small house nestled in tall evergreens.

She envied him. He had a home and friends, and he ran only for the joy of it, not for survival.

The boy waved to Tommy, who yelled something indistinct and continued down the street. His house must be somewhere in the neighborhood.

She thought she saw him turn back once, perhaps looking for her, but probably it was only her imagination.

A boy of ten. If she and Justin had been married for the past twelve years, they might have a child of that age. A child who ran home from school with a book bag on his shoulder.

But Justin was dead, of course.

And she had killed him.

She had shot him in the chest and left him to bleed to death in the garage.

She still remembered—she would always remember—the stunned look on his face when he sank to his knees, the empty disappointment in his eyes, and the awful trembling of his lips as he tried to form words and failed.

The memory moved through her like a shudder, and briefly she was dizzy.

Too much sun. She needed to sit down. Well, her motel was close now. She could read the sign, outlined against the bright sky. The Desert Dream Inn.

It seemed appropriate. A desert dream was a mirage, wasn't it? An illusion. A false hope.

She had been fooling herself to expect the police to believe her. She had been the victim of an illusion.

But not anymore.

30

Lois Belham had been on her feet from seven in the morning until three in the afternoon, and now, at 3:15, after shedding her waitress uniform and counting her tip money, all she wanted to do was go home and soak in a tub.

But first she had to talk to the cop.

He was a plainclothes guy, and he'd introduced himself as Detective Shepherd. She was grateful to him for suggesting that they sit in a corner booth. At least she could get off her feet.

"I remember her," Lois said when Shepherd mentioned the incident of the spilled coffee. "Cute little thing, but all fluttery, like a bird."

"You hadn't seen her before?"

"No, never. Guess Leo and Kurt told you about her, huh?"

"That's right."

Leo Galston and Kurt Bane were the two patrol guys who came into the coffee shop now and then. Lois knew them pretty well. Nice guys, good tippers, and that Leo had a linebacker's shoulders. Lois was big on shoulders. Her ex-husband Oswald had been built that way, and it might've been the reason she married him.

"Can you describe her?" Shepherd asked.

"She's a blonde. Fair skin, freckles—like a schoolgirl."

"Color of her eyes?"

"Didn't notice. Might've been blue. Blue would work well for her, with the blonde hair and all, but I can't really say."

"Anything else?"

"Let me see. Her hair was fairly mussed, I remember. There was some dirt on her clothes, too. Not that she was, you know, slovenly." She was proud to use this word, which she'd learned doing her crosswords for relaxation in the evenings when her feet were sore. "She needed to wash up, is all. She looked like she'd spent some time outdoors."

Shepherd jotted this in a memo pad, appearing unsurprised. "What was she wearing?"

"She had on a jacket, one of those vinyl ones with a zipper. It was dark in color, as I recall." Cops on TV were always saying things like that—*dark in color*, not just *dark*. Sounded more official, somehow. "And a skirt, a white skirt. I remember because I thought it looked nice, and I was going to ask her where she got it."

"Did you?"

"Never got a chance. After the wet cleanup, she was so upset, she just paid her tab and scrammed."

"How old was she, would you say?"

"Lord, I'm not a good judge of age. Middle twenties, maybe." She almost added something, but reconsidered.

Shepherd seemed to sense her hesitation. "And?"

"It's just—well, I'd bet she didn't go far."

He looked at her. "Why do you say that?"

"Because she was tired. She looked like she'd been up all night and had just wore herself out. I know how that feels." She surely did. She was bone-tired right now. "You just want to crawl into a bath or a bed and shut your eyes. This lady you're after had that same look about her."

"So you think she's close by?"

"Right in the neighborhood. That's what I think."

In the neighborhood.

Shepherd emerged from the coffee shop, blinking at the glare, and scanned the rows of strip malls lining Speedway Boulevard. He knew of two motels on Speedway within a half-mile radius of the Rancheros Cafe. If the McMillan woman had indeed been ready to crash in a nice, warm bed, she might have checked into one of those motels after leaving the coffee shop.

It was a long shot, but any shot at all was better than none.

Which motel? One lay to the east, the other to the west.

West seemed right. Going west, she wouldn't have had to make a difficult left turn onto Speedway. She would have simply eased into the traffic flow and let the current carry her to the first available lodgings.

Worth a try.

He got in his sedan and pulled out of the parking lot, driving fast out of habit.

Of course, it was possible that she had checked into a motel days ago, in an entirely different part of town. But he didn't think so. If she'd had a place to stay, she would have gone there directly after making her 911 call in order to wash up and change. Women hated dirt.

He smiled, imagining what Ginnie would have said if she'd heard such an obvious example of stereotypical thinking.

The motel appeared on his right, two blocks ahead. Drawing near, he could read the sign out front, advertising CABLE TV and AIR CONDITIONING, as if both features were exotic luxuries.

In larger letters the motel's name was spelled out: THE DESERT DREAM INN.

31

Near the motel office, in an alcove, there was a soda machine. Elizabeth knew she shouldn't waste any money, even sixty cents, but after her walk in the sun, she was hot and fatigued.

She fished a few coins from her purse, then fed them into the slot and pressed the Coke button. A frosty can rolled down the chute with a thud. She popped the tab and took a long swallow, leaning against the wall.

There were plans to be made. She would have to stop for dinner somewhere; she needed to be well fed and alert. And maybe she ought to pick up another flashlight. Her little pocket flash was probably inadequate for the job she had in mind. Also, she'd better remember to take her gloves and the vinyl jacket.

It was too bad she'd lost her gun. She would have liked the protection it provided. But the gun was gone, and she had no money for a replacement. She would just have to hope she didn't need it.

Still organizing her thoughts, she stepped out of the alcove, just in time to see a dark sedan pull into the parking lot.

And she knew.

Cop car.

There was no doubt. She knew it with her nerve endings and reflexes, before her mind even had time to process the reasons.

Cops always drove either a Ford Crown Victoria or a Chevy Caprice, and the sedan was a Ford straight out of the police motor pool, complete with a stubby, telltale antenna jutting out of its rear.

Instantly she ducked back inside the alcove, her heart booming, the can shaking in her hand.

Had they seen her? She wasn't sure.

She had emerged from the alcove only momentarily, and the overhang above the doorway had kept her in shadow.

They might not have noticed her. She prayed they hadn't.

If they had, she was finished. There was nowhere to run. The alcove had no exit except the one that led to the parking lot.

She hugged the wall and listened.

The sedan rumbled to a stop not far away. The motor died. She heard a car door open and shut.

One door.

One cop, then. Alone.

Had to be a detective. It was the detectives who drove the unmarked cars.

He was here, looking for her. He must be.

She had been stupid, so stupid, to check into this motel. She should have known that the cops at the coffee shop would remember her. Should have left this neighborhood, gone outside city limits entirely. But she'd been exhausted, distracted by the news on the radio, not thinking clearly—not thinking at all.

Twelve years of caution, and now it all might have

ended for her because of one mistake, one moment's inexcusable carelessness.

Footsteps on asphalt. The man . . . approaching.

He was coming for the alcove, straight for the alcove, and coming fast.

God, this was it.

Arrest.

The word she hated most in the world.

Would they put her in another mental institution, or would it be jail this time? She might almost prefer jail. Either way, she would be trapped, caged, and they would never let her go.

He was close now. A few yards away.

Wildly she thought of making a break for it, sprinting across the parking lot, perhaps losing him in a back alley.

Ridiculous. She could never outrun him.

He stepped onto the walkway outside the alcove.

Then a door opened—the door to the motel office—and she heard a male voice say, "Excuse me. I'm Detective Shepherd, Tucson PD."

The door swung shut.

He was in the office. He'd had no interest in the alcove. He hadn't seen her, after all.

Relief weakened her. She dropped the soda can, and its contents painted an ink-stain splash on the cement floor.

Moving fast, she left the alcove and doubled around to the rear of the motel, praying she had time to salvage her belongings and flee.

The manager was in her office, smoking a cigarette and arguing with somebody on the phone. She hung up quickly when Shepherd entered. He'd heard enough of the conversation through the door to know she'd been in a dispute with her bookie, but he didn't give a damn about that.

He introduced himself, showed his badge. She was no more interested in it than the receptionist at Hawk Ridge had been.

"How can I help you?" she asked indifferently. She had narrow, suspicious eyes and three chins.

"I'm looking for a woman, a fugitive, and it's possible she's staying here."

"What woman?"

"She's blonde, looks to be between twenty-five and thirty, and if she checked in, it probably would have been this morning, before ten."

"We don't get many check-ins at that hour. . . ."

"It could have been later. She was wearing—"

"Whoa. Hold on. What I was gonna say is, we don't get many check-ins at that hour, which is why I remember the lady in question."

She was here.

32

Elizabeth came around the back of the motel at a run and nearly collided with a maid's cart outside Room 29.

"Señora," the maid called from just inside the doorway.

A note of urgency in her voice made Elizabeth stop. "Yes?"

The maid came forward, struggling to find words in English. Elizabeth remembered her from this morning, when she changed the room after the early check-in.

"There is a man who looks for you," the maid said finally. "A tall man."

A man? Detective Shepherd? Had he been here earlier, snooping around? Or was it some other cop?

Elizabeth didn't know, had no time to think about it.

"It's okay, thanks," she said meaninglessly, and again she was running for her room.

She reached it and found her key and flung open the door. Crossing the threshold, she realized distantly that the shredded newspaper was still in her hand. She dropped it on the floor and found this morning's outfit scattered on two armchairs and a table—skirt, blouse, jacket.

Quickly she scooped up all three items and ran to the big suitcase on the folding stand. She thrust the clothes inside.

Maybe it was stupid to take the time to salvage her things. Maybe she would be better off just running now, leaving everything behind.

But she had almost no money left. How could she replace her wardrobe? She didn't have much as it was. She had to save what she could. She—

A presence.

Behind her.

She sensed it, felt it.

Detective Shepherd—he was here, he was in the room with her, and she'd lost her last chance, she was finished, she could never get away.

Slowly Elizabeth turned, dread numbing her, and she saw the man in the doorway, limned in the afternoon glare.

Not a detective.

Detectives wore suits and were neatly groomed and said things like *Don't move, you're under arrest.*

This man was clad in khaki trousers and a lime-green shirt, and there were deep sweat stains under his armpits, and he wasn't saying anything at all.

A tall man, as the maid had said. A man who, like Shepherd, had come looking for her.

Elizabeth stood frozen, staring at him, uncertain what to think or what to do.

"Kaylie," the man whispered.

The bottom dropped out of her stomach, and she knew him suddenly. She remembered.

He was one of Cray's patients—yes—the one who was a permanent fixture at the hospital. He'd entered her room—her cell—several times to change the bedding, while she huddled in a corner, watching, hoping he wouldn't notice the marks of tampering on the grille of the air duct.

Walter. That was his name. She used it now, in the feeble hope of establishing a connection with him.

"Walter," she said. "Hello."

He took a step forward.

Somewhere an impatient voice was screaming at her that she had no time for this, because the policeman would be coming, might be on his way already.

She ignored it.

The policeman was not her biggest problem at the moment.

Walter was.

Walter, who held her pinned in his unblinking stare. Walter, who was so tall, so powerfully built, whose large hands hung at his sides, the fingers slowly curling and uncurling.

"Kill her," Walter said, his tone quite normal, the words stated casually and calmly. "Break her neck."

Then with astonishing speed he closed the gap between them, his big hands rising, and she ducked and pivoted away from him, grasping the first object within reach, the large suitcase, and swung it at him, the lid still open, clothes and toiletries spilling everywhere as the heavy canvas case struck him solidly in the gut.

He grunted, grasped the suitcase in both hands, yanked it away, tossed it on the bed.

"Kill her," he said again. "Break her neck."

He lunged. She stumbled backward. The bathroom door was behind her, and she pushed it open and darted inside, then shut the door and fumbled for the lock, but there was no lock, damn it, the door didn't have a lock and now Walter was pressing hard against the other side, his weight and his strength overpowering her, forcing her back, the door easing open and nowhere to run, the room so small and no window and no exit.

"Kill her. Break her neck."

Stop saying that! she wanted to shout. *Just shut up and stop saying it and go away!*

He was in the bathroom with her, no expression on his face, no light in his eyes, a huge man who was an automaton in the grip of a trance, and he swiped at her, clutching at her hair, loose strands whisking through his fingers as she spun away from him, trying to maneuver in the tight confines of the room.

Flash of action, his left arm streaking toward her face. She whipped sideways, the blow connecting only with the mirror above the sink, silvered glass fracturing, and she had time to think *I'm okay* before pain walloped her hard on the back of her head—his right hand, delivering a palm heel strike—and in a plunge of dizziness she staggered through the doorway and collapsed on the floor between the bed and the TV stand.

She was aware of numbness alternating with jolts of pain, and of the feeble clawing movements of her hands on the short-nap carpet, and of bubbles of nausea popping in her throat and leaving a sour taste.

Aware of all this, but not really, because there was no person to register these separate facts. There was no Elizabeth or Kaylie or whoever she thought she was. There was only pain and desperation and then, strangely, one lucid thought.

This is what Cray does to them.

To his victims. That was what she meant.

He'd told her how he liked to strip them to their essence. She hadn't understood. She did now.

Then the pain was gone, replaced by a cold anger that cleared her mind.

She wouldn't let him win. Had to get up, run, run now.

But her body wouldn't obey. Her arms and legs trembled with weakness. She could not find the strength to stand.

Blinking, she turned her head. Walter was still in the bathroom, wrapping his left arm in a small hand towel. He'd cut himself on the mirror's shards.

He tied the towel in place, then looked benignly at her. He seemed to be in no particular hurry, and of course he wasn't, because he was a schizophrenic and time did not exist for him.

"Kill her," he said, as if reminding himself. "Break her neck."

She was getting tired of hearing that.

"You remember her?" Shepherd said, keeping his voice calm.

The manager shrugged. "Sure do. Maybe nine-thirty, she comes sashaying in here, asking for a room. So I think she's a hooker, right? And I don't want hookers. My husband and me, we run this place, and it's not the Hilton, I grant you, but it's respectable."

"Did you give her a room or not?"

"Room Thirty-seven. Left side of the building, first floor. Sort of close by, so I could walk past now and again and check on it. Any noise, any funny business, and she'd be out of here. But it's been quiet all day. What'd she do?"

"Never mind that. I need a spare key."

"You bust up the place, you pay for it."

"I'm not going to bust up anything." Shepherd took his cell phone from his pocket and used the speed dialer to call Alvarez at his desk. As the phone rang at the other end of the line, Shepherd asked, "What name did she register under?"

"No name. No registration. She paid cash up front. That's another reason I pegged her for a whore. Now, seeing how you're after her, I'm guessing maybe she's something a whole lot worse."

Shepherd heard a click as the phone was picked up, then a snap of chewing gum and a laconic voice saying, "Alvarez."

"I found her."

"What took you so long?"

"That's funny. I need you and a patrol unit right away."

"I'll bring Galston and Bane, the ones who I.D.'d her. They're still here filling out the report. It'll be a nice little reunion for Miss McMillan, don't you think?"

Shepherd nodded. "She'll be thrilled."

33

Walter came out of the bathroom.

Elizabeth twisted onto her side, making one last effort to stand, knowing it was hopeless.

"Kill her," Walter said.

Where was Detective Shepherd anyway? For the first time in twelve years, arrest was not her greatest fear.

Walter bent over her. His hands, so huge, loomed like figments of a nightmare.

"Break her neck."

She drew up both legs and delivered a double kick to his midsection, aiming for his groin.

He only blinked, perfunctorily acknowledging the blow.

She scooted back, banging her head on the base of the TV table—another shimmer of pain—but fleeting, insignificant, as Walter stooped lower, closing for the kill.

Nowhere to retreat. Behind her, only the table and the wall and a tangle of insulated wires—the power cord and cable connection for the color TV.

She grabbed the wires with her right hand, not knowing why. They couldn't help her, not when Walter was reaching out, his eyes level with hers, his bald head gleaming like a bullet.

Her grip on the wires tightened, and she pulled, straining, the muscles of her arm and shoulder bursting with sudden, desperate exertion.

The wires were screwed into the back of the TV, and the TV was bolted to the tabletop, and the table was tall and narrow and just a bit unsteady, and she felt it move.

Hands on her throat.

Walter on top of her, foul breath in her face, pressure shutting off her windpipe.

"Kill her. Break her—"

The table rocked, tilting back, banging the wall.

Walter glanced up.

The table swayed forward, top-heavy with the weight of the TV, and Elizabeth tore free of the hands that held her and gave the taut cords a final, violent yank.

She heard Walter make a small noise, something midway between a grunt and a groan—a scared, childish noise that made her feel almost sorry for him.

Then the table pitched forward, the TV cracking free of its bolts, and the picture tube exploded around Walter's head in a brief, sizzling fury of sparks and smoke.

He slumped, maybe unconscious, maybe dead.

Elizabeth was pinned beneath him. She thrashed and flailed, fighting to wriggle free. The man was two hundred pounds of dead weight, with the table and the ruined TV fixing him in place.

He stirred.

Alive.

Regaining consciousness.

And she was still stuck beneath him, his heavy midsection and legs draping hers.

She had to liberate herself, and do it now.

Gasping, she twisted onto her side and dug her fingers into the short carpet fibers and clawed until she had a secure handhold, then dragged herself forward an inch at a time.

Walter murmured, his face showing a flicker of animation before going slack again.

She got one leg free, then planted her shoe against his shoulder and used the leverage to pry loose her other foot.

Now get out. Get out now.

She tried to stand, but at first the effort overwhelmed her, and she fell on one knee.

Walter moaned.

On her second try she stood without falling. Some blind reflex guided her to her purse, which she had dropped on the counter when she was packing her suitcase in a rush.

There was no time to salvage her belongings now. Half of them lay scattered across the bed and the floor. The purse was all she could take with her, all she had left.

She sprinted for the door, then heard a clatter of wood and glass behind her, and turned instinctively to look back.

Walter was on his feet. He'd come fully alert, swept clear of the table and the smashed television set, lurched upright. And he had done all this in less time than she had taken to cross ten feet of carpet.

Run.

Outside, into the glare and heat, fishing her car keys from her purse and stumbling, gasping, her shoes pounding asphalt, heart vibrating like a plucked wire, currents of dizziness all around her.

Then she was at her car, thrusting the key at the keyhole of the door on the driver's side, and Walter was loping toward her in a coltish, loose-limbed gait, covering ground with deceptive speed.

The key turned, the door unlocked, and she was behind the wheel, trying to find the ignition slot, missing it, missing again.

Her hand was shaking wildly, and strands of hair had fallen in hectic disarray across her face.

Finally she got the damn key in the slot, and she cranked the ignition and heard the motor rev and fail.

It wouldn't start, the damn car *wouldn't start*.

This had happened before. The Chevette was old. It had been used hard for many years. Sometimes she had to nurse the engine to get it to turn over.

Walter was ten feet away.

"Come on, Kaylie," she whispered, "do this right."

Distantly she realized that she had just called herself by her true name for the first time in a dozen years.

She took a long, slow breath and forced herself to turn the key slowly while gently, gently depressing the gas pedal.

A feeble growl, the motor coming alive, then a cough and a rattle and silence.

Slap of a hand on the windshield, Walter's left hand, leaking blood from the cuts on his arm, leaving long pink smears on the glass.

Elizabeth pumped the accelerator slowly, slowly.

The door shook. Walter had grabbed the handle, but miraculously she had locked it after entering, though she had no recollection of doing so.

She pumped again, in a careful rhythm, the way she had taught herself. No panic. Panic would kill her.

Walter snarled.

His face had been empty of expression before, but there was rage stamped on it now, a crazed fury born of years of frustration, of being unable to follow directions or answer simple questions or understand what other people were talking about, and now even in the simple task he had set for himself—*kill her, break her neck*—he had failed, he had once again been humbled by the world, and he hated her for it.

Elizabeth keyed the ignition. The motor struggled. Wavered.

Walter smacked the driver's-side window with his fist, and a loose mosaic of hairline cracks shivered through the safety glass.

Another blow would open the window, and his hands would plunge inside and tear her apart.

The motor caught.

She slammed the gear selector into reverse, and the Chevette squealed backward, her foot flooring the gas.

Through a fog of tears Walter watched the red car drive away.

He tasted defeat, a familiar flavor. He had been defeated at nearly everything, and now this too. But this time the sting of defeat was worse. On past occasions when he had disappointed himself, he had known only shame. This time there was fear also.

He had ventured well beyond the narrow boundaries Dr. Cray had circumscribed. He had taken a risk and had lost.

Dr. Cray would be angry.

The thought started Walter running in a clumsy, loose-limbed trot. He had no particular destination in mind. He merely had need of speed and exertion, so he ran across the parking lot, finally reaching the curb, where he found himself at the side street where he had parked.

His car, the car Dr. Cray in his kindness had purchased for him, waited a few yards away.

Walter hoped Dr. Cray would not take back the car. He hoped Dr. Cray would not be too terribly upset.

Most of all, he hoped Dr. Cray would not take matters into his own hands, would not attempt to track down the dangerous Kaylie McMillan all by himself.

"She's vicious," Walter said, finding the exotic word somewhere in the lower reaches of his memory. "She's a vicious, vicious person. She could *hurt* Dr. Cray."

Maybe she was on her way to Dr. Cray's office right this very moment. Maybe she meant to kill him.

With that thought, all concern for himself vanished from Walter's mind, and he hurried to his car, eager to return to Hawk Ridge and protect Dr. Cray, protect him from Kaylie McMillan, protect him at any cost.

34

"We're on our way," Alvarez said. "ETA in fifteen."

Shepherd ended the call and pocketed the phone. The manager handed him a passkey.

"Like I said, Room Thirty-seven."

"Left side of the building?"

"Yeah. You're not going in alone, are you?"

"I'm not that much of a hero. Think I'll just walk past her room, see if I hear any activity inside."

"She's been quiet all day. You plan on telling me what she's wanted for?"

Shepherd remembered the phone conversation he'd interrupted. "Illegal gambling," he said, keeping the smile off his face. "Placing bets with a bookie. We're really cracking down on that."

The manager frowned, unsure whether to believe him. Shepherd left her to think about it.

Outside, he took a moment to readjust to the glare and open space. Then casually he started walking toward Room 37, where a woman who'd been a fugitive for twelve years was about to end her run.

Room numbers glided past on his left. 42 . . . 41 . . .

He turned a corner.

40.

Her room was three doors down.

39.

He could see her door now.

38.

Her open door.

"Shit," Shepherd breathed, and he knew right then that he'd lost her.

He turned, his gaze sweeping the parking lot for any sign of a blonde woman. There was no one.

Slowly he approached the open door. His gun was in his hand, its weight reassuring. He had slipped it free of his armpit holster without conscious intention.

At the door he called loudly, "*Police.*"

No answer.

She could be inside, could be hiding, could even be lying in ambush. The prudent thing was to wait for Alvarez and the two street cops.

Hell. He knew she was gone. Call it intuition.

He entered the room, the pistol high and leading him, and saw an overturned table, a smashed television set, a suitcase flung open on the bed, clothes and sundries strewn over the floor.

Distantly he recalled the manager telling him not to bust up the place. He hadn't planned to, but Kaylie seemed to have had other ideas.

Shepherd searched the room with swift efficiency and determined that Kaylie was not hiding anywhere. He noted the broken mirror in the bathroom, the rust-colored dabs of blood on the carpet.

"She had a party, all right," he murmured grimly. He thought of the Lexus vandalized in Cray's garage. The pattern here was similar.

Touching nothing, he cast his gaze over the scattered items on the floor, focusing on two objects of interest: a spiral-bound book that looked like a photo album, and a manila envelope stuffed with paper.

In his pocket he carried a pair of latex gloves. He put them on, then flipped through the photo album. Snapshots of parties and picnics riffled past. Most of the faces were different, but in nearly every photo there was a woman—sometimes blonde, sometimes dark-haired—but always the same.

Hello, Kaylie, he thought with a tight, fierce smile.

He could see why the waitress at the coffee shop had described her customer as looking young. Kaylie had a slightly round, almost childlike face that had not aged much in the past twelve years.

And freckles, as the waitress had remembered.

An innocent face. Pretty, in fact.

Shepherd thought of her voice on tape, the hushed urgency, the shyness. He had liked her voice. He had wanted to believe her.

Studying the photos, he wished . . . he almost wished that he . . .

The thought felt dangerous. He blinked it away.

To feel anything for this woman was just stupid. Worse than stupid—disloyal. A betrayal of his wife, or of her memory. Kaylie McMillan was just another Timothy Fries, a psychopath, violent and unstable and obsessive, and sympathy for her was an affront to Ginnie.

Shepherd tossed the photo album on the bed. His hand was shaking just a little.

He picked up the manila envelope. Inside it was a sheaf of documentation establishing a series of false

I.D.'s. Different names, birth dates, backgrounds, but all of them were Kaylie McMillan.

She had been busy, these past twelve years.

"Roy, what in Christ is going on?" That was Alvarez, at the door, Galston and Bane behind him.

Shepherd looked up from the documents in his gloved hands, surveyed the wreckage in the room, and said simply, "She flew."

35

A mile from the motel, Elizabeth pulled onto a side street and parked at the curb, then sat for a long moment, shaking all over as fear and relief and anger throbbed through her in a sequence of vivid aftershocks.

Too much had happened in the past twenty-four hours. She couldn't absorb it all, couldn't make it real.

Obstacles and threats everywhere. Danger, pursuit, the walls of her life closing in.

If Cray or his henchmen didn't get her, the police would. The police, who were there to protect and serve. Who were they protecting now? Cray? Who was served by that?

She raised a trembling hand to her throat and felt the memory of Walter's fingers tightening like a vise.

Close call. Really close.

She'd faced death twice since yesterday evening. She'd risked arrest when she made her 911 call, and again this afternoon.

So far her luck had held, but she knew she could press it no further. Anyway, she couldn't stay in Tucson. Everybody here was after her. She had to leave town. Leave Arizona entirely.

It was time to go to Texas, as she'd thought of doing before all this bad business began. Dallas had been her original destination, but the city seemed too big, too complicated. She could try San Antonio, maybe. It was supposed to be nice there. They had a riverwalk. She would like to see that.

In San Antonio she could obtain or forge a new I.D. Elizabeth Palmer would have to go. That was all right. Names didn't matter. She'd had many names.

As soon as possible, she would ditch the Chevette, obtain another car. She had no idea how she would manage this, with no money and no credit history and no collateral, but she would find a way.

She had to. Because the police would search her things. They would find the documents that established her various false identities. They would run a motor-vehicles check on Elizabeth Palmer. The make and model and license plate number of her car would be known to them immediately. The information would go on a hot sheet, or whatever they called it, and she would be at perpetual risk of being spotted and pulled over.

In the short term, she might be able to steal somebody's license plate, put it on the Chevette, buy some time.

All right. Get to Texas. Tonight.

In the glove compartment she kept a map of the western U.S. She unfolded it and checked the route she'd have to take. Interstate 10 would get her all the way there. A fifteen-hour drive, no problem.

She checked her purse, counting bills. Fifty-four dollars.

Most of that would be spent on food and fuel. And she had no luggage, no change of clothes, not even a toothbrush. Nothing to fall back on, nothing to pawn or barter.

In San Antonio she would need a job immediately. Well, she had waitressing experience, clerical skills. She could find something.

This was bad, so bad. She'd been down-and-out at other times during her twelve years on the run, but never had she felt so completely beaten, so lost.

Could be worse, though.

She could be in handcuffs.

She could be dead.

The thought lifted her, just a little. She would get through this. And after all, she was not entirely alone. There was Anson. She could reach him, calling collect, at any hour and hear his grave, slow voice. And though she hated asking him for money, she had done it before, and he'd wired it to her without hesitation.

Strange behavior for the father of the man she'd shot in the heart and left to die, but Anson had his reasons.

She checked the map again, steadying herself in the study of its clean, logical lines. Everything made sense in maps, it was all laid out for you, and you always knew just where you were going.

Driving the interstates was like that, too. A straight road, no surprises, the destination dead ahead.

"Okay," she said aloud, "so get going."

And forget about Cray.

It was her only option at this point. The police had boxed her in. She couldn't pursue her quarry any further.

Anyway, damn it, she'd done all she could. She'd done everything that could have been asked of her.

San Antonio.

A fresh start.

"Oh, hell," Elizabeth said, and she crumpled the map and tossed it on the floor.

She wasn't going to Texas. She knew that.

Whatever the risk, whatever the consequences, she had started this game of cat-and-mouse with Cray, and she would see it through.

She put the Chevette into gear and pulled away from the curb, heading east to Safford and the Hawk Ridge Institute, where she would make her stand.

36

Alvarez and the two beat cops entered the room slowly, taking in the damage.

"Looks like a goddamn tornado hit the place," Leo Galston said.

"More like a hurricane." Shepherd shrugged. "Hurricane Kaylie."

"You think she's cleared out for good?" Alvarez asked.

"Yeah."

"But she left her stuff."

"She was in a hurry. She must've sprinted out of here. Left the door wide open."

"Why would she trash the place and run?"

"Way I see it, she realized she'd made a lot of noise, and somebody might call the manager about it. She didn't want a confrontation, so she panicked and fled."

Alvarez frowned. "That doesn't explain why she made all this mess in the first place."

Shepherd didn't answer. He was staring at an item he'd overlooked earlier, a crumpled newspaper on the floor near the bed.

Carefully he picked it up in a gloved hand. It was today's edition of the Tucson *Citizen*, open to the *Tucson & Arizona* section.

The page had been partially shredded. It appeared Kaylie had made a furious effort to obliterate an offending article. But the headline, at least, was still intact.

"Here's your answer," he told Alvarez. "About why she trashed the room. She's still upset about the White Mountains case. She went nuts—more nuts than usual—when she read this story."

Galston asked, "What story?"

"It's got to be the retraction of the false lead that went out over the radio. She must have heard there was a breakthrough as a result of a nine-one tip. She got all excited. She thought we'd bought her story, arrested Cray. That's what she wants. She hates him. Then she reads this, finds out it was all a mistake, Cray's not under arrest, there are no breaks, no suspects, nothing—and she loses it."

"And *we* lose *her*," Galston said grimly.

"Looks that way."

"How about her car?" Alvarez asked. "Did the manager see it?"

"Not that I know, but we can run it down easily enough. It's registered to Elizabeth Palmer." He found the birth certificate in the sheaf of papers. "That's one of her three fake I.D.'s—the current one, I think."

Bane, the rookie, asked how Shepherd knew it was current.

"Because the documentation she kept on the other two includes her driver's license and Social Security card. Those items are missing for the Elizabeth Palmer alias." Bane still looked puzzled, so Shepherd spelled it out. "She's carrying them in her purse."

"If we know what I.D. she's using, and we know

what she's driving," Alvarez said, "then she won't get far."

Shepherd sighed. "Sure she will, Hector. It's a big country. Plenty of places to hide. And she's been on the run for years. She's damn good at it. She can run and hide . . . if she wants to."

"But you don't think she does."

"No."

"What else would she do?"

"I don't know. But she's gone over the edge, that's for sure. Cray said psychotics go through cycles, phases. He said Kaylie was in the acute phase now. Maybe it's been building for the last twelve years. Like a volcano—more and more pressure—then *bang*. Eruption."

"You sound worried," Alvarez said.

"I am."

Galston tried to shrug it off. "She was just a little bit of a thing. She didn't look so dangerous."

"Tim Fries didn't look so dangerous, either," Shepherd snapped, not quite realizing the words were spoken aloud until he heard their echo in the room.

Bane asked who Tim Fries was. Alvarez and Galston both knew, and they both shushed him, Galston with a clamp on his arm, Alvarez with a look.

Then there was silence. Shepherd was thinking.

"She'll go after Cray," he said.

Alvarez said she already had. But that wasn't what Shepherd meant.

"I'm not saying she'll stalk him or wreck his car. She'll go after him personally."

"Try to take him out, you think?"

Shepherd's shoulders lifted. "She shot her husband.

Why not Cray? She seems to think he's a serial killer. In her mind, she'll be performing a public service."

"Graham County Sheriff's will have to handle it," Alvarez said. "Patrol the area near the hospital. Get Cray to lie low for a few days. Maybe he'll even leave town."

"I doubt it. He's stubborn."

"Well, it's their problem, not ours."

Shepherd didn't respond directly. He scanned the mess in the room—the scatter of clothes, the broken TV, the shards of glass in the bathroom, the blood spots on the floor. He thought of the frantic voice on the 911 tape, accusing Cray of murder, saying he entrapped his victims and hunted them like animals in the moonlit wilderness.

He couldn't walk away from this. Ginnie's ghost would never forgive him.

"So," Alvarez said, "you're gonna call Graham County. Right?"

Slowly Shepherd nodded. "I'll call that guy Kroft knows—Chuck Wheelihan—the one who was promoted to undersheriff."

"I don't think you need to talk to the undersheriff."

"Oh, yeah." Shepherd smiled, a secret smile that puzzled the two patrol cops and worried Alvarez. "Yeah, I think I do. But first I need to get in touch with somebody else."

"Who?"

"Cray."

The phone in the room might have Kaylie's prints on it, so Shepherd used his cell phone instead. He stood outside for a clearer transmission and found the number he needed in his memo pad.

There were four rings at the other end of the line, and then a receptionist—no doubt the woman in the lobby who'd been bent over her computer keyboard, the woman who'd reminded him briefly of Ginnie at her desk—answered. "Hawk Ridge Institute."

He identified himself. His call was transferred to Cray's secretary, then to Cray himself.

"Yes, Detective?" The man sounded harried and tired. "How may I help you?"

"We just had a close encounter with your former patient."

"With Kaylie?" Instantly the weariness was gone from Cray's voice. "Is she under arrest?"

"I'm afraid not. She eluded us, but just barely. Before she left, she did a lot of damage to her motel room."

"Damage?"

Cray seemed surprised by the news. Distantly Shepherd found this odd. The man knew what Kaylie had done to his Lexus, after all.

"She messed up the place pretty badly," he said. "Apparently she's still in a violent frame of mind."

"I see." Peculiar hesitation there. "Well, I suppose you intend to warn me again that I need to watch out for her. I do appreciate your concern—"

"Actually, I'm calling for a slightly different reason." It was Shepherd's turn to hesitate. "I want to ask you for help."

"Help?"

"In apprehending this woman. Tonight."

"You want my assistance . . . in catching her. I see."

There was something new in Cray's tone, something Shepherd could not quite define. Under other circumstances, he might have thought it was a note of sly amusement. But the cell phone's reception was muddy, and he was sure he'd misinterpreted what he heard.

"It may entail some risk," Shepherd said, choosing his words with care. "And I haven't contacted the sheriff's department to work things out with them. But if I can get their cooperation, can I count on yours, as well?"

He waited. On the other end of the line, Cray exhaled a long, slow breath.

"Detective," Cray said, "when it comes to putting Kaylie safely in custody where she belongs, I assure you I'll do everything I can."

37

Chuck Wheelihan, undersheriff of Graham County, stood by the side of his Chevy Caprice cruiser in the desert night.

Three deputies loitered nearby. They wore tan short-sleeve shirts, open at the collar, and brown trousers encircled by gun belts, and they had yellow-bordered patches on their shoulders and silver badges on their chests. They were young. Damnably young, Wheelihan thought.

One was smoking a cigarette, another had just returned from taking a whiz in a creosote patch, and the third was drumming his fingers restlessly on the hood of Wheelihan's car.

"So, Chuck," the drummer said, "what do you think the odds are of this working?"

Wheelihan took a moment to think it over. The great quiet of the desert loomed around him, and above the high peaks of the Pinaleno range the stars dazzled.

"One in three," he answered at length.

"That guy from Tucson seems to think our chances are a good deal better'n that."

"That's because he thinks the girl is watching Cray's house."

"And you don't?"

"Way I see it, she ran to the border or to another state. Or she's layin' low."

"If she's sensible, sure. But she's crazy, they say."

There was eagerness in the young man's voice. He wanted to go up against somebody crazy, somebody dangerous, even if it was only a woman.

Not much action here in Graham County. The militia types stirred up a fuss from time to time, setting off explosives in the desert or scaring folks with their silly war games, and there was that local man who'd taken a tire iron to his girlfriend's skull one drunken night, but that was about it, as far as excitement went.

So Chuck couldn't blame the boy for straining at his harness. Still, he preferred to keep things low-key, which was why he took his time in making his reply.

"Sure she's crazy. I know that. I'm one of the ones that nabbed her, way back when. I was part of the search-and-rescue team. We came across the gal, out in the desert about twenty miles from here, and you should've seen her, all dirty and crying, and she wouldn't say nothing. She was just kneeling there, kneeling like she was at her prayers. Her eyes were empty. Nobody home. You know what I mean?"

The boy didn't. "I guess."

"She's a psycho, all right, like all the other nutcases they got there in the loony bin. But she's not stupid, see? She escaped from the nuthouse, didn't she? She's stayed on the lam for twelve years. Am I right?"

"You're right, Chuck."

"She's not so dumb. Some of these fruitcake types, they can be pretty damned shrewd. So I'm saying, she's nowhere near this spot, is my guess. She's off in

Sonora, maybe, or cruising up to Salt Lake. Or she's gone to ground like the scared bunny rabbit she is. Whatever. Point is, she's not gonna risk coming anywhere near Dr. John Cray."

The smoker, who'd been listening to this, tossed his cigarette away with an impatient flick of his wrist. "So why're we here, earning overtime," he asked, "when some of us would rather be at home getting a hot meal?"

Wheelihan shrugged. "Because I could be wrong, Mel. I have been before. And I know the sheriff would dearly like to close the book on the McMillan case. He comes up for reelection next year, you know."

"Sheriff don't have to explain to my wife why he missed her pot roast," the smoker groused.

"Pot roast makes good leftovers," commented the man who'd relieved himself, contributing this thought for no particular reason.

"Just get comfortable, boys." Wheelihan smiled at the high canopy of the sky. "It's a nice night, and we're getting paid to do this, and who knows? We just might get lucky. Like I said, it's one in three. She might be on the run. She might be hunkered down. But if she's here—if she's staking out the place like this man Shepherd thinks—then we'll get her."

He surveyed the gravel road visible through the scrim of mesquite trees that concealed the three department vehicles, the road that John Cray soon would travel in his Lexus sport-utility, the road Kaylie McMillan would have to take if she meant to follow Cray from his house. He nodded.

"Heck, yeah," Chuck Wheelihan said. "We'll get the crazy little bitch."

38

On her belly, hidden on a ridge of the Pinaleno foothills, Elizabeth watched Cray's house.

The evening was balmy, with a light breeze. The dry air had a velvet texture, soothing on her skin. There were no clouds anywhere, and the stars were sharp and brilliant, and in the far distance a coyote sang its lonely refrain, to be answered by echoes from deep canyons.

Strangely, she liked this spot, her special hiding place. She knew it well. It was home to her, really—more like home than any motel room she could remember. She'd spent a great deal of time here on this ridge, under the open sky.

On every evening of the past twenty-seven days, she'd come here, steering her Chevette partway up a twisting fire road, then leaving the car to traverse a trail on foot. By five o'clock she was always settled near the rim, lying on a blanket she carried in her car, waiting to see what Cray would do.

Sometimes he would go out, and she would follow in her Chevette. On other occasions he would stay home, but even then she would keep her vigil until after midnight, returning to her motel only when she was certain Cray would not prowl the streets.

His house lay at the rear of the hospital compound, served by a private, gated driveway. The foothills, all scrub and stunted trees and windblown confusions of cactus, rose up instantly beyond the road.

Elizabeth's perch on the slanted ridge placed her at eye level with the upper story of Cray's home, about two hundred feet away.

The curtains of his bedroom windows were rarely closed. With the aid of binoculars—one of the few possessions she had left, and only because she had forgotten to remove them from the Chevette's glove compartment—Elizabeth could see him clearly whenever he entered the room.

He was there right now.

She watched him in the wobbly oval of the binoculars' field of view. He was removing his suit jacket, his shoes.

Normally he arrived home earlier than this. Tonight some business at the hospital must have delayed him. She hadn't seen any lights in the windows of the house until twilight was settling over the mountains.

Although he was late, he appeared to be following his usual routine in other respects. Invariably he changed out of his business attire after a day's work.

If he meant to stay in, he would don a charcoal dressing gown and slippers, then pass the night reading or perhaps jotting notes in a pad while music, faintly audible even at this distance, would spill from the window of his downstairs study.

But if he meant to go out . . .

Then it was always the same outfit, the black pants and shirt, nighttime camouflage for a creature of the shadows, a creature on the hunt.

She waited, holding Cray fixed in the twin lenses of the binoculars.

He was naked now. She had seen him this way many times. It scared her, repulsed her, to be voyeuristically acquainted with his body.

He stretched, and she saw the play of his muscles, the rippling strength in his long, corded arms and crosshatched abdomen. Like a yawning tiger he seemed to luxuriate in his own boundless vitality.

She thought of Sharon Andrews, numb and dead, and she hated him so much.

Abruptly Cray turned away from the window, disappearing into another part of the bedroom. From prior observations, she knew he had gone to his closet to select his outfit for the evening.

She waited.

When she saw him again, he was all dressed in black, sleek as a panther.

Going out.

She wasn't really surprised. After all, she was still on the loose, and she doubted he could rest until he found her. He had sent poor Walter to hunt her down, but Walter hadn't finished the job, and now Cray meant to do it himself.

How he expected to find her, she couldn't imagine. Perhaps he would search aimlessly. Perhaps he had some better plan.

Or perhaps he wouldn't look for her at all. He might go in quest of some new victim, fresh prey. Another Sharon Andrews to abduct at random and chase in the cold moonlight.

She gritted her teeth against a new wave of anger. Trembling, she stood.

He would leave shortly. She knew what she had to do.

Moving fast, Elizabeth scrambled off the ridge and headed down the trail toward the fire road, where her Chevette was parked.

39

Cray knew she was watching him.

Naked in his bedroom window, he had sensed the pressure of her gaze. It had required all his willpower not to turn and stare into the night, seeking some sign of her.

She must have watched him on many previous evenings, but he had not been attuned to her presence. Now he was, and her proximity to him was as real and immediate as an electric shock.

Kaylie had come. Brave girl.

He'd never needed to send Walter after her. He could have waited, secure in his home, until she arrived, drawn to him like a mouse to a baited trap.

Smiling, Cray picked up his medical bag and looked inside to ascertain that its contents included two vials of sedative and several syringes. He might need the sedative to restrain Kaylie, if she became hysterical—or if she threatened to say too much.

His equipment in order, he descended the stairs to his living room, then paused before a mirror for a final check of his appearance.

He was again a man in black, just as she would expect him to be.

Throughout the day he had been fatigued. Coffee

and a handful of amphetamines pilfered from the hospital supply room had kept him alert enough, but an undertow of exhaustion had threatened continually to drag him away.

Now his lethargy was gone. He was exhilarated.

The snare had been laid, the quarry was in sight, and the best part of it all was that the plan was not even his. He had Detective Shepherd to thank for it.

Shepherd—perfect name, a palatable irony. He was a poor shepherd indeed, to lead the choicest member of his flock straight into the wolf's ravenous embrace.

Cray had met with Shepherd this evening, at the hospital. The conference had lasted thirty minutes. Shepherd had told Cray what was expected of him, the performance he was to deliver. What was particularly important, Shepherd had said, was that Cray must not leave the house until after dark.

It was dark now. Night, Cray's friend, had visited him again.

He found it amusing that both he and the police needed the darkness. And poor Kaylie—she needed it as well, didn't she? She needed the shadows, the concealment of the night.

Nocturnal animals, all of them. By day they hid in their burrows—Kaylie in her cheap motel, Cray in his office, the police in squad rooms and courthouses. They did safe, meaningless things. But at night they came alive.

At night the heart quickened. Danger, a night-blooming flower, opened its petals and released its subtle, enticing perfume. Risks were taken. Hunters stalked.

" 'Come, seeling night,' " Cray quoted in a whisper, " 'scarf up the tender eye of pitiful day. . . .' "

Macbeth. A reference, as Cray recalled, to the Elizabethan sport of falconry; the bird's eyelids were sewn shut—scarfed up—while it was in training. By metaphorical extension, day was the time for seeing and being seen, and night, blinding night, was when the unseen ruled.

Shakespeare must have loved the night. All poets did, and all killers too.

At the end of their meeting, Shepherd had given Cray a portable radio preset to a frequency used by the Graham County Sheriff's Department. The radio was now clipped to Cray's slacks, its dark shape nearly invisible against his clothes.

He glanced at it. The power LED was lit, but the radio was silent.

He hoped it would not be silent for long.

With his medical bag in hand, he crossed the kitchen swiftly, his black shoes clacking on Saltillo tile, and reached the door to the garage. Before opening it, he tossed a curt glance out a side window, into the small arbor that bordered his property.

What he saw pleased him, but he deferred a smile.

His Lexus waited for him in the garage. What he'd done to the vehicle had been painful—grooving deep scratches into the finish, slashing the upholstery and tires. Still, the task had been necessary, and most of the damage was superficial.

He surveyed the car in the light of the bare ceiling bulb. It was still a mess, of course, but at least it was drivable once again. After Shepherd's phone call, Cray had sent for a mechanic, who had replaced all four tires, hammered out some minor damage to one of the wheel rims, and checked under the chassis and the hood.

The front seats remained a travesty, the leather hacked and torn, and the front window on the driver's side was gone, leaving the vehicle's interior open to the elements, but Cray didn't mind.

Comfort was not a prime consideration. Tonight's drive would be short. He expected to travel no farther than a mile or two.

Even so, he took a moment to find a relatively unscratched CD in the pile of discs on the floor of the passenger compartment. Puccini's *Gianni Schicchi*. It would do.

He started the engine, then slid the disc into the player and let the rich strains of the opera's overture fill up his world.

With the remote control, he opened the garage door. As it rose, he settled back in the tattered seat and prepared himself.

There was risk, naturally. Kaylie might be sufficiently frustrated—maddened, even—to try something desperate.

In their meeting Shepherd had raised this possibility. Of course, Shepherd believed Kaylie McMillan to be psychotic. He thought she had wrecked her motel room in a fit of rage, while Cray had already learned the truth of the matter from Walter Luntz, who had recounted the narrative in a low, shamed voice upon his return.

You weren't supposed to attack her, Cray had said, holding his anger in check. *I told you to find the car, that's all.*

Find the red car, Walter said glumly.

I thought you were more reliable, Cray chided softly.

Walter hung his head. *I'm sorry, Dr. Cray.*

We'll speak of this later. In the meantime, you are to tell no one what happened today. Do you understand me, Walter? No one at all.

Walter had said he understood, and Cray had let him leave, his shoulders hunched, head down, a large man diminished by disgrace.

So Kaylie, of course, had not trashed her room, any more than she had vandalized the Lexus. Still, she might well have been driven to the point of blind rage, even derangement, by all that had transpired in the past twenty-four hours.

She was unstable, after all. Cray had never doubted it. Psychotic? No. But hardly well adjusted, either.

If she was armed—if she had recovered her gun from the weeds where he'd thrown it, or had obtained a substitute firearm—then she might attempt an ambush. Might take a shot at him from outside the fence, or from the roadside.

Unlikely. Not impossible. A gamble. One he was willing to take.

The garage door had risen. Cocooned in Puccini, Cray backed slowly into the driveway, where Kaylie McMillan just might be waiting with a gun.

Wheelihan got the message on his handheld radio and signaled to the deputies.

"He's leaving. Get ready."

The three men climbed into their patrol cars and started the engines, then waited, headlights off.

At the roadside Wheelihan knelt in the mesquite brush and tipped a night-vision scope to his eyes. He peered at the long strip of gravel.

Cray would be coming this way. Cray—and maybe someone in slow pursuit.

"Come on, Kaylie," Wheelihan whispered, a cold crawl of sweat glazing his neck. "Don't disappoint us now."

The gate at the end of Cray's driveway swung open in the red glow of his taillights. He eased the Lexus onto the road.

His heart rate was steady at sixty-eight beats per minute. His respiration was slow and deep. Puccini wavered over the speakers.

The road was empty in both directions.

Cray headed west, toward Highway 191.

A bullet might snap out of the darkness at any moment, but he felt no fear. He fiddled with the controls on the CD player, skipping a few damaged tracks before settling on the opera's best aria, one of the peaks of Puccini's art.

Then he settled back, listening as the soprano's first notes trembled from the audio console in luxuriant stereo.

"O mio babbino caro . . ."

Cray let the rich waves of sound wash over him, a tidal flow of high emotion, of love and longing, passionate yet civilized.

There was dignity in this music, and sadness also. Puccini had composed *Gianni Schicchi* at the end of World War I, when the naive optimism of the Romantic era was fading to ashes. The world never again would cherish the illusion of an immortal soul, a ghost in the machine. And things would change.

At rare times, upon waking in the dawn twilight, Cray would wish he'd been born earlier in history, when no one knew that a human being was only a basket of chemical compounds, a glorified ape disguising its basic animality behind layers of personae that could be all too easily stripped away.

He might have fit into that earlier era, had he been given the chance. He might have proved himself elegant and mannered and even dashing, like the gentlemen of that vanished world.

And not knowing any better, he might even have found a way to believe in something great, something higher than reflex and instinct, hormones and encoded instructions in the genes.

The mood always passed. Heartsickness was not for him. He was a realist. He took life as it was.

At his hip, the handheld radio squawked.

Cray grabbed it. "Yes?"

The rough masculine voice sizzling on the radio belonged to Undersheriff Wheelihan. "I've spotted her. She's a quarter mile behind you."

Cray glanced at the rearview mirror. "I don't see anything."

"She's got her headlights off. I'm using a night-vision scope. Maintain your speed till you're past the checkpoint. We'll take it from there."

"I understand," Cray said.

He set down the radio on the passenger seat next to his medical kit, feeling vaguely disappointed. It hardly seemed sporting of the law enforcement authorities to hunt poor Kaylie with a night-vision scope. Cray himself had never used such equipment when he chased down his prey.

He drove on. The aria reached its climax. *"Mi struggo e mi tormento,"* the soprano sang. Her suffering, her torment.

Kaylie had struggled so hard to evade capture, all these long years.

Soon her torment would be over.

But in another sense, it had only just begun.

40

Wheelihan watched the Lexus cruise past. He waited another twenty seconds, watching the car with no headlights as it approached in the green fog of the night scope.

A small car, subcompact, not new, in poor condition.

Lone occupant, hunched over the wheel, a smeared glow of green.

Close now.

Almost here. . . .

Wheelihan lifted his rover radio and scrambled his troops with a one-word command: *"Go."*

Three pairs of high beams instantly snapped on, bright fans of light crisscrossing the desert brush, and a moment later the dome lights burst into whirls of furious color.

The trio of patrol cars skidded around clumps of mesquite and careened onto the gravel road, then halted, forming a disorderly row that blocked both lanes. They waited there, garish in the pulsing varicolored light, but silent; Wheelihan had told his men to keep their sirens off.

The little car was still coming, confronted now by a barricade of steel.

For a tense moment Wheelihan wondered if Kaylie

would stop and surrender peacefully, or panic and try to ram through the roadblock.

His men were ready for that eventuality. If Kaylie offered resistance, they were under orders to shoot.

Shoot to kill.

He didn't want it to end that way, and so he was relieved when the subcompact slowed, brakes squealing, and finally stuttered to a stop a few yards from the blockade.

His men stayed in their vehicles, as they'd been told. Every one of them had his weapon sighted on the suspect huddled behind the wheel. From the ground by his feet, Wheelihan picked up an electronic bullhorn, a toy he'd rarely had the opportunity to use.

"Turn off your engine," he said, speaking normally. It was a mistake to shout into one of these things.

There was a moment's hesitation, and the little car shuddered as the motor died.

Good. Very good.

"Now raise your hands. Raise them where we can see them."

Another pause. Then slowly two pale, trembling hands were lifted out of the shadows.

"Keep them raised. Do not move. You will not be harmed."

His men were emerging from their vehicles now, first using the open doors for cover, then approaching fast and low, their guns leading them.

When the subcompact was surrounded, Wheelihan allowed himself to breathe.

"Got her," he whispered.

He was still congratulating himself on a smooth operation, damn smooth, when Mel Baylor, who had missed his wife's pot roast this evening, called out, "Chuck, we got a problem here."

Problem?

Wheelihan set down his bullhorn and hurried to the car, a battered and dented Toyota Tercel. As he drew near, he saw what the problem was. Yes, indeed.

Hunched in the front seat was the driver, who was not Kaylie McMillan, but instead a very large, very bald man blubbering like a child.

Cray reached the scene at a run, his medical bag swinging at his side, and found Walter standing in tears by the side of his car. He kept repeating two words, "Dr. Cray," with imbecilic insistence.

"This guy seems to know you, Doc," Undersheriff Wheelihan said, disgust souring his voice.

Cray hated being called Doc. He pushed his irritation away.

"He's a patient," he said, trying to be calm, but afraid suddenly—terribly afraid of what Walter might say. "He lives at the institute. But he's not confined there. He has a car, this car, and he runs errands."

"Runs 'em at night? With his lights off?"

"That isn't standard procedure, obviously. Let me speak with him."

"He's all yours."

Cray hoped the undersheriff and his deputies would move away, afford him some privacy with Walter, but none of them moved.

Gingerly he touched the big man's arm. "Walter," he began in his best professional tone, "why don't you tell me what's happened here."

"Got arrested," Walter said, his eyes hollow with fear.

"No, you're not under arrest. There's been a misunderstanding. A mistake. Now, why were you out driving around after dark?"

A pendulous thread of mucus dangled from Walter's left nostril. With an equine snort, he sniffed it back.

"Following you," he whispered.

"I see. That's why you had your headlights off. So I wouldn't see you?"

"That's right, Dr. Cray."

"Now, why was it so important to follow me?"

"Because of Kaylie. I thought you'd go looking for her, like I—"

"Yes, I understand now." It was imperative to cut off this dangerous line of discussion. "You asked me earlier today why the police had come by, and I told you about Kaylie. You were worried that I'd try to find her somehow. You were hoping to protect me."

"Protect you." Walter seized on these words, as Cray had hoped he would. "Yes, protect you, it's all I wanted to do, just protect you, Dr. Cray."

"That's fine, Walter."

"Because I know how dangerous she is."

"Yes, fine."

"She could hurt you. She tried to hurt—"

"That's enough, Walter. We all understand you. You're not in any trouble. You haven't broken any laws."

Wheelihan coughed. "Well, Doc, he was driving without his headlights."

Doc again. Cray was growing tired of this man. "Write up a ticket," he snapped. "I'll pay it for him."

Walter's lip trembled in the prelude to another sob.

The undersheriff looked at the big man, then at Cray, then shrugged. "Aw, to hell with it. I'm just pissed off, is all. I thought we had her. As it turns out, probably she was never even here."

"She was here. I—" *I felt her,* Cray almost said. *I sensed her presence with the tips of my nerve endings.* But he couldn't say that. "I know her well enough to anticipate her behavior patterns. She came here tonight."

Wheelihan looked dubious. "Well, if so, she's gone by now. All this commotion would've scared her off for sure."

"Unless she wasn't on this road, because she never meant to follow me in the first place."

"The house, you mean?"

Cray nodded. Of course. It would be the house. Now that he thought about it, the house was the only thing that really made sense.

She hadn't come here to kill him. She wasn't a killer, not really, though neither Shepherd nor Wheelihan knew it. She had come for evidence—hard evidence, conclusive, impossible for the police to ignore.

His trophies.

That was what she was after, crafty Kaylie. The faces of his victims, the totems he had collected during twelve years of nocturnal sport, which she hoped to find in his residence while he was away.

"Yes . . ." he murmured, and then remembering he was surrounded by people, he added more loudly, "yes, she'll try to break into my house."

41

Security at the Hawk Ridge Institute was tight. The hospital compound was entirely fenced in, patrolled by a small but vigilant guard detail. The front gate was monitored by a guard in a gatehouse.

But the gate across Cray's private driveway was not monitored by anyone.

Elizabeth had thought about that gate many times on the long nights when she watched Cray's house. She thought of it again now as she left her perch on the ridge and descended the foot trail to the fire road.

Her car was parked on the road, but she wouldn't need it. She paused only long enough to stow her binoculars inside. Then she jogged down the winding road toward flatter ground. Had to hurry. She needed to be in position near the gate by the time Cray left for the evening.

When he departed, the gate would briefly swing wide, and for a few seconds the sealed perimeter of the institute would open just a bit.

She reached the main road, a strip of washboard gravel with no streetlights, illuminated only by the stars and the faint glow of the hospital complex.

At the roadside she paused. The director's residence

was directly across the way. She saw movement in a first-floor window. Cray, slipping past. Heading for the garage, it appeared. On his way out.

She crossed the road at a run, then hunkered down in the bushes at the edge of the driveway, ten feet from the spear-pointed gate with its elaborate torsade of wrought-iron curlicues.

There was nothing to do now but wait for Cray's Lexus to emerge from the garage.

The night was still, the air velvety and fine. She wished she could be somewhere else, in the arms of a lover, perhaps, or swinging on a hammock on a veranda, a cool drink in her hand.

Instead she was crouching in the weeds like an animal, hunting the faces Cray collected like totems, like scalps.

The idea had come to her as she sat on the bus-stop bench with the crumpled newspaper in her hands.

The police had not believed her. Either the satchel had not persuaded them, or they had never received it. But suppose she found evidence they could not ignore. Evidence so compelling it could not be open to any possible doubt.

The faces.

She was sure Cray kept them. She could even guess how they would be preserved.

She could guess—because she had seen one, many years ago.

That one must be in Cray's possession now, along with the others he had collected since.

How many victims? She couldn't guess. Six or ten or more. . . .

A bevy of faces, skinned from their victims' skulls,

preserved like parchment, perhaps pressed like leaves between the pages of a book—or hanging from a wall, pasted under glass—or pinned on mounting boards, like prize butterflies.

He had them.

In his house, almost certainly. Where else would he keep his treasures?

They would be hidden away, safe from accidental discovery by a housekeeper or a dinner guest. She would need time to find them. From experience she knew that Cray, when on the prowl, would be gone for hours.

When he got back, his beauties would be gone.

And then? The next step?

She didn't like to think about it. But there was only one thing she could do.

No phone call this time. No frantic pleading with an anonymous officer on the 911 line, who would dismiss her as a crank.

She would take her evidence directly to the police, take it in person. She would give herself up—Kaylie McMillan, wanted fugitive, desperado—surrender to the authorities, with the trophies as proof that she was not crazy and not a criminal.

And she simply would have to trust in the representatives of law and order to hear her out, to believe her at last.

Trust. A difficult idea to embrace, but she had no choice. She had gone nearly as far as she could on her own. She was tired. She was worn out. She needed to set down her burden, and she would.

After tonight.

At the far end of the driveway, the garage door rumbled open. Cray was leaving.

Elizabeth peered through a veil of foliage and saw red taillights throwing dim cones of light through a haze of dust.

The Lexus backed out. She crouched lower.

Faint music reached her. An opera. Pretty.

Then the gracious notes were erased behind the low squeal of the gate, swinging wide in response to an electric eye within the grounds.

The gate was hinged on one side only, the side farthest from her. It opened with ponderous majesty, the iron spikes catching the taillights' glow, dripping blood.

Still she didn't move. She couldn't risk Cray seeing her.

She squeezed herself compactly against the shrubbery, trying to blend in, wishing she hadn't lost her luggage, because she would have liked to change into darker clothes that melded with the night.

The gate was wide open now, the Lexus easing through.

She saw Cray at the wheel, his face in profile, the glow of the dashboard filling in the hollows of his cheeks.

Was he thinking of her at this moment? Was he asking himself where she was hiding, where he might find her?

The Lexus emerged fully onto the road, its headlights bright, their spill creeping close to her hiding place.

If she was speared in the glare, would he see her? She thought he might. She bent lower, compressing herself into a tight, shivering huddle of fear.

Then the headlights swung away as the Lexus pivoted toward the open road.

She was safe.

But the gate was closing.

She uncoiled from her crouch and hurried forward, hugging the fence, staying low, still afraid Cray would glance back toward the driveway and glimpse a pale, moving shadow amid the bushes.

The Lexus started forward, down the road. A wisp of an aria reached her through the open window on the driver's side, then trailed off into silence as the big black vehicle receded.

She was near the gate now, less than two yards away, but it was swinging shut too fast, and she didn't think she could slip through in time.

Only a narrow gap was left between the leading edge of the gate and the masonry gate post, a post also topped with spikes to discourage intruders.

In a moment the gate would slip into place against the post, the latch fastening automatically, and she would be locked out.

She dived headlong for the opening, aware that if she misjudged her jump she would be caught between metal and stone, with a crushed leg or snapped ribs as her reward—immobilized, stuck here to wait for Cray's return.

The ground came up fast and shocked her with its impact, and she heard iron squealing on its hinges on one side, felt cold stone on the other, and with a gasping effort she scrambled through, pulling both feet clear just before the gate clanged shut.

Made it.

She lay on the lawn near a flower bed, gulping air, wishing she were on the road to San Antonio right now. Then she raised herself to a half-crouch and carefully made her way down the driveway to the front of the house.

She had no idea how to break in. The last time she'd trespassed on somebody's property, she had been on the run after escaping from this hospital. She'd found a truck in a farmer's barn and hot-wired it, a skill she'd learned from Justin, of course—Justin, who knew so many things he shouldn't have known.

Justin could have told her how to break into Cray's house, if he were here, if he were alive, if she hadn't shot him in the heart.

But of course, had she not shot him, she wouldn't be on the trail of John Cray's secrets. Had she not shot him, she would still be Kaylie McMillan and not Elizabeth Palmer or Paula Neilson or whoever she was now.

Anyway, there had to be some way in.

She tested the front door, hoping absurdly that it was unlocked. No luck, naturally. The front windows, too, were locked. Cray was careful.

Through the windows she could see his living room, part of the house that had not been visible from her vantage point on the ridge. She noted a fireplace, bookshelves, an overstuffed sofa and armchair, plush carpet, soft lighting, all the graces and amenities she had been denied in her long flight from what the world called justice.

But somewhere in this house there was the evidence that would take Cray's comforts away from him, put him in a cell with a steel toilet and bunk beds.

The thought—the hope—buoyed her as she crept around the side of the residence, to the garage.

Somewhere close, a mockingbird announced its presence, running through a litany of bird calls. A breeze stirred the leafy branches of an arbor looming on her right. She smelled fresh-cut grass, a rarity in the desert.

Birds and trees and green lawns—she'd never imagined any of these things when she was imprisoned in this hospital, confined to a windowless isolation room in Ward C, the oldest ward, now abandoned to the deer mice and scorpions.

For her, there had been only concrete and steel, loneliness and terror, and the gibbering complaints of other patients down the hall.

The bird stopped singing. She heard a rustle of wings, and it was gone. Something had scared it off. A predator perhaps. The night was crowded with them.

There was a side door to the garage. She tested it. Like the front door and front windows, it was locked. But nearby, almost at eye level, was a window.

A broken window.

Elizabeth stared at it, baffled. It was like an invitation to enter.

And suddenly she knew something was wrong.

She didn't know what, precisely. She knew only that the window, open and welcoming, was a stroke of fortune too good to be believed.

She had learned suspicion over the past twelve years. She had learned to trust the tingle at the back of her neck, warning her of danger.

She felt that tingle now.

Get away, she told herself. Get away now, run, hide—

She turned from the window, and the lights came on.

Two lights from the arbor where the mockingbird had sung, the mockingbird that had not been scared off by any predator, except the human kind, the kind that hunted her.

Flashlights.

A pair of them, beams wavering through a scrim of leaves, and from the shadows—a voice.

"Don't move, Kaylie. Just stay where you are."

42

Past shock, past panic, she knew she'd heard that voice before, and she remembered where: at the motel this afternoon, while she hid in an alcove and a man entered the manager's office, announcing himself as Detective Shepherd.

He was here, and this was some kind of trap, and Cray—

Cray was part of it, was in on it, was helping the police to catch . . .

"No," she whispered, and she waved her arms at the lights in a frantic effort to make them disappear, make this stop happening. "No, you can't, *you can't!*"

"Don't move!"

The flashlights swam toward her, two dark figures limned in their backsplash—Shepherd in his dark suit, and another man, a deputy, tan shirt and brown pants and a gun belt.

Closing in.

She had to run, her every instinct insisted that she run, but there was nowhere to go. She was cornered, her back against the garage wall and the two men drawing near, pinning her in the wavering circles of light.

"No, please," she said, speaking not to them but to whatever justice there might be in the universe. "Please, this isn't right."

"Calm down, Kaylie."

That was Shepherd, Shepherd who was showing her a smooth, false smile, the smile she had seen on doctors' faces, on Cray's face, and why not? Cray and Shepherd—they were in league together, allies united against her, smiling killers working hand in hand.

She felt the pressure of a scream welling in her throat.

"Kaylie . . ." Shepherd said again in his deceitful, soothing voice.

"Not my name," she whispered, and then the scream broke out of her in a rush of furious words: *"That's not my name, I'm not Kaylie, stop calling me that, stop calling me—"*

Abruptly they were all over her, their hands, their hot breath—too strong for her—the deputy and Shepherd overpowering her frenzied resistance, twisting her around, then grabbing her arms, wrenching them behind her back, pain in her shoulders, metal on her wrists, handcuffs, they were cuffing her, and she was struggling, thrashing, refusing to surrender even as they pressed her face to the wall and wood splinters pricked her cheek.

"Christ, she's a fighter," the deputy said.

Shepherd answered, "Just hold her down."

She whipsawed wildly under their restraining hands, but she couldn't break free, and what she had to do was talk to them, talk quietly, try to persuade them, maybe they would believe her, or at least pretend to believe. . . .

"Search his house," she gasped. "Search his house."

"Cray's house?" Shepherd was leaning close, his voice loud in her ear. "Why?"

"You'll find . . . you'll find their faces. The women. . . . He kills them and . . . Like Sharon Andrews."

"You need help, Kaylie." He sounded so kind, but they always did.

"Just search. He keeps them there. I know he does."

"Kaylie . . ."

"For God's sake, wasn't it enough—what I gave you? The satchel? The knife? How much more do you need?"

Gently: "There wasn't any satchel, Kaylie."

The words reverberated in some hollow part of her, nonsensical words.

"I left it for you," she said blankly. "At the phone."

"There wasn't anything there."

This was impossible. "They didn't look hard enough. Or they went to the wrong phone or . . . or Cray . . . he got there first and took it. . . ."

"How could he do that?"

"I don't know. It doesn't make sense. But he's the one you want. He's the one who killed Sharon Andrews. He tried to kill me. I know it sounds crazy. I know you think I'm insane."

"We just want to help."

She was crying. "Well, don't. Don't help me. Just let me go. You're no good at helping, any of you. You just make things worse. You never believe me and you never do anything, and now you're working with him, with . . ."

Cray.

Approaching out of the dark at a fast stride. Behind him, other deputies.

She heard herself moan.

"It'll be all right," Shepherd told her, and God, she hated him for uttering those words—such a stupid, meaningless thing to say.

Then she saw something in Cray's hand. A black kit of some kind. The satchel?

It had to be the satchel, he was carrying it in plain view of everybody, and in a spasm of excitement she nearly opened her mouth to alert Shepherd and the others—but no.

No, it was a different sort of bag, not the one he'd carried into her motel room last night. A doctor's bag, that's all, and if she started yelling about it, she would only look that much more foolish and desperate and crazy.

Cray strode into the outer ring of the two flashlights' glow, his face lit from below, his eyes in deep wells of shadow. "Congratulations, Detective," he said crisply. "Your plan appears to have proven an unqualified success."

Shepherd shrugged. "Not much of a plan. Just common sense. Either she would follow you—or she would stay behind and try to get inside the house. And she broke in through the garage window once before."

But I didn't, Elizabeth almost said, but she knew her protest would be wasted. The broken window was part of Cray's scheme, in some way she couldn't quite understand. He had laid a trap for her, he and the police together.

She said nothing, merely stood trembling, her wrists cuffed behind her, the garage wall hard against her shoulders, and Shepherd holding on to her left arm with a steady hand.

"Well," Cray said, inspecting her from a cautious distance, his gaze cold and sly, "she had to slip up eventually. In the acute phase of her illness, she's not capable of thinking clearly."

This broke her silence. "You piece of shit," she breathed.

Cray ignored her. "She'll do better once she's on a program of medication and intensive therapy. She'll get the best care here."

Here.

She stiffened. They couldn't leave her here . . . with Cray.

She opened her mouth to say so, but remarkably Shepherd said it first.

"I'm not sure that's such a good idea," he said quietly.

"Oh, but it's the only way, Detective. She needs psychiatric help. Surely you can see that."

"But under the circumstances, don't you think some other doctor at a different institution—"

One of the sheriff's men, who seemed to outrank the others, cut Shepherd off. "Afraid there isn't another institution in this county, Roy. Oh, I guess the county medical center handles a few psychiatric cases, but the ones that can't be treated on an outpatient basis are always transferred here to Hawk Ridge."

Cray smiled, charming as a snake. "Undersheriff Wheelihan is entirely correct. We're the only show in town."

Shepherd wouldn't give in. "She could be remanded to a Pima County facility."

Elizabeth listened, aware that her fate would be decided by this conversation, this casual exchange among men free to go home to their beds and their wives tonight.

The one identified as Wheelihan shook his head. "I doubt a judge would go for that idea, Roy. Not unless Dr. Cray were to testify it's necessary."

"And I won't," Cray said. "Institutionalization at Hawk Ridge is the best thing for her. She needs to confront her fear, deal with it. Only by seeing that I pose no threat will she begin to recover from this paranoid delusion."

"Don't listen to him," Elizabeth whispered in a voice so low that only Shepherd could hear.

"Really, Detective," Cray said, "there's no other option."

"Don't listen . . ." Elizabeth's voice dropped to a hiss of breath, inaudible even to her.

There was a pause, a stillness, everything suspended, and then very softly, Detective Shepherd said, "I suppose you're right."

She'd lost.

Cray had her.

She was his patient again, his prisoner.

No escape this time.

His prisoner forever.

A wave of fear broke over her, and she was screaming.

Shepherd grabbed her, said something, more words that didn't matter, more protestations of helpfulness and compassion, but she wasn't listening anymore, couldn't hear him or hear anything except the ululant glissando of her own voice as she screamed and screamed and screamed, Shepherd and the deputy holding her fast, and Cray rummaging in his bag and now coming toward her, and in his hand, in his hand . . .

A syringe.

Gleaming.

She saw his lips move, his thin bloodless lips.

This will calm her, he was saying. *This will make her sleep.*

She didn't want to sleep. Sleep meant darkness, and she was afraid of the dark.

Her screams became speech, a last plea thrown at the uncaring men around her and the vast night beyond.

"Don't let him do this, please don't let him, he'll kill me, he'll kill me—"

Cray reaching for her, the needle rising, huge and shiny and as terrifying as the gun he'd trained on her in the Lexus last night.

"He'll kill me!"

Flash of pain in her neck, the needle biting deep, and at once all strength left her, and where there had been screams, there was silence.

Silence and the onrushing dark.

Silence and falling, a steep plunge, nothing at the bottom.

"She'll be fine now." Cray's voice, so far away, a voice from the shadows that swam around her and inside her, everywhere. "We'll look after her, I assure you. We'll give poor Kaylie the very finest care."

Kaylie.

Not my name, she wanted to say.

But of course it was. It had always been her name, and though she had imagined she could run from it, in the end it had caught up with her, as it must.

Elizabeth Palmer was dead. Paula Neilson, Ellen Pendleton—the other people she'd been—they were all dead.

Only Kaylie was left.

It's who I am, she thought as shadows folded over her. *Can't fight it. Not anymore.*

I'm Kaylie . . . again.

PART TWO

GOOD THINGS OF DAY

43

On Tuesday afternoon, one week after the arrest of Kaylie McMillan, a burial service was held on the grounds of the Hawk Ridge Institute.

John Cray stood in a gathering of mourners at the small cemetery near his house. Ordinarily such a ceremony would attract only a handful of staff members, but today's occasion had brought out nearly everyone who worked at the institute, whether on duty or not.

Even the press had come. A reporter from the local newspaper stood at the back of the crowd, jotting notes in a steno pad. Before the ceremony he had asked Cray for his thoughts.

"It's always difficult to lose a patient," Cray had said, his tone cool and steady, "but in this instance it's especially hard."

He thought the words would look good in print. He hoped the reporter remembered to identify him as the author of *The Mask of Self*, and not merely as the institute's director.

At the head of the grave, the minister of a local church stood with a leather-bound Bible open in his hands, reading from Paul's letter to the Romans. "None of us lives to himself," he said in his calm, clear voice, "and none of us dies to himself. If we live, we live to the Lord, and if we die, we die to the Lord. . . ."

The day was cloudless and bright, but for the first time there was a taste of autumn in the air. Cray wore a greatcoat over a somber suit. He kept his face expressionless, careful to betray nothing.

Everything had gone so well up to this point. It would be a shame to spoil it all by laughing aloud.

His greatest worry had been the autopsy. The county coroner routinely investigated any death at an institution that received state funding. A cursory examination posed no dangers, but there had been the possibility of toxicology tests.

Luckily no tests had been done. Death by natural causes had been the ruling.

And now all evidence to the contrary had been sealed in a mahogany casket, hanging in a sling over a newly dug grave.

" 'Whether we live or whether we die, we are the Lord's. For to this end Christ died and lived again, that he might be Lord of both the dead and of the living.' "

The Bible clapped shut, and a portable winch operated by one of the groundskeepers hummed into action.

Cray and the others watched as the sling was lowered, the casket committed to the earth.

There was a soft thump as the casket touched bottom. The minister poured sand from a bottle into his open palm, then ritually spilled it into the grave.

" 'Earth to earth, ashes to ashes, dust to dust.' "

Cray hadn't cared much for St. Paul's effusiveness, but he liked this older sentiment. It was the hard, honest dogma of a desert people. What was a person, after all, except earth and dust? What was a life, in the end, except ashes scattered in the uncaring wind? No romanticism here. No illusions. Man was clay.

When the ceremony was over, Cray lingered awhile, watching the groundskeepers remove the sling and fill in the hole with shoveled dirt. One of the men misinterpreted his continued presence as a sign of grief.

"Don't feel too bad, Dr. Cray," the man said kindly. "It's just one of those things, you know?"

There was wisdom in this, too—the unstudied fatalism that got most human beings through the pointless maze of their lives.

"I know, Jake." Cray smiled. "Still, I wish I could have done more."

"Nothing you could do. Just happened, is all."

"I feel it's my fault, in a way. If I hadn't agreed to cooperate with the police—"

"You can't think of it like that. You did what was right. Anyway, you couldn't have her running around loose."

"No. No, that wouldn't have been good . . . for anyone."

"The McMillan girl's better off now," the man said.

"I suppose she is."

"And as for Walter . . ." The groundskeeper cast a glance at the grave half-filled with dark, damp soil. "Well, maybe he's better off, too."

This was the fellow's first concession to sentiment, and it disappointed Cray. "Maybe so," he said curtly, and then he left the two men to their work.

Walter was not better off. Walter was dead, and Cray saw no honor in death, no cheer to be found there.

Certainly Walter had not wanted to die. He would

have pleaded for his life, if he'd had the wits to do so, on the night Cray killed him.

Cray had waited three days to carry out this necessary task. If Walter had expired immediately after Kaylie's arrest, questions might have been raised. By Friday, Cray had felt safe enough to act.

He'd made his preparations in the evening. Come midnight, he had visited Walter in his room. At that hour the administration building had been largely empty, and no one had seen him enter.

Even so, he had carefully shut the door behind him, and had kept his voice low. . . .

"Hello, Walter," Cray said.

Walter, still awake with a single lamp lit, was sulking on the edge of his fold-out sofa. He looked up with a guilty start when Cray entered.

"Hi, Dr. Cray," he answered softly, a fearful flutter in his voice.

"You didn't come to work today, or for the past two days. You hardly even leave this room anymore."

Walter was silent.

"I hear you've been skipping meals at the commissary."

"Not hungry."

"Is that it? Or is it that you've been afraid to come out and face me?"

No answer.

"You did cause an awful lot of trouble Tuesday night."

"I know it, Dr. Cray," Walter agreed morosely. Then, as a plaintive afterthought: "I was just trying to help."

"Of course you were. But don't you see, Walter, that

you can't help anybody by thinking for yourself? Your brain is all muddled. What comes out of it is so much goop, of no value to anyone."

"Kaylie's dangerous," Walter muttered. "She could hurt you. I didn't want you getting hurt."

"Yes, well, you needn't worry about Kaylie anymore."

Walter lifted his head in surprise, showing his first, faintly hopeful smile. "Is she . . . dead?"

"Why, no. She's our guest. Hadn't you heard?"

"I haven't been talking to anybody."

"I see." Cray had suspected as much, but he was pleased to obtain confirmation of this fact. "Well, Kaylie is staying with us now, locked up tight."

"So you're helping her get better?"

"Oh, I'm helping her, all right. But we're not through talking about you, Walter."

"I won't do it again, Dr. Cray."

"Won't do what again? Try to kill Kaylie? Follow me when I go out for a drive? Say too much to the wrong people, as you almost did on Tuesday night?"

Walter was confused by the fusillade of questions. "I—I won't do any of it anymore."

"But you will. Oh, not right away. You're too badly cowed at the moment, too humiliated even to emerge from your room for more than one meal a day. But eventually your shame will ebb. You'll be back to your old self again, won't you? But not quite your old self. You'll be different. You'll have changed."

"I . . . I haven't . . . I didn't . . ."

"Oh, yes. You've changed, whether you know it or not. You've acquired a taste of independence. You know how it feels to act on your own initiative. After all these years of doing what you're told, running errands on command, eating at assigned times—after all that, you've finally discovered your glorious ego."

"I have?"

"It's remarkable, really. On your own, you've retraced the course of human evolution over the past several thousand years. Have you read the *Iliad*, Walter? Oh, of course you haven't. It hasn't got Curious George in it, so how could you? But if you had read it, you'd know that the Greeks of that period possessed no concept of an integrated person. Limbs and breath and blood, yes—but not a person, a totality, moved by a single will. The arm tensed, or the breath came fast and shallow, or the blood pulsed quicker in the veins, but where was the unique, conscious personality, the mind and self that were the unifying principle of it all? There was no person, not in the modern sense. Imagine living with no notion of a self. But you don't have to imagine it, do you?"

Walter blinked, plain bewilderment showing on his face.

"Then later," Cray went on as if he'd heard an answer, "came the more sophisticated Greeks—Sappho the poetess, Archilochus the warrior. They discerned a will in themselves, a will to love or fight. What a find this was! They glorified their newfound will, and subsequent Greeks built avidly on this discovery, until you hear of an inscription on the Delphic oracle's temple that read simply, *Know thyself*. A platitude now, but originally a new and dizzying insight. Ever since that day, poor humanity has been striving to know itself, to analyze and organize and prioritize its endlessly fascinating inner life. Today we have built a great, towering edifice of self, a skyscraper of Babel, and we worship at its cornerstones, while neglecting and forgetting and denying what animals we really are. Denying the primal truth for the sake of an ever more elaborate illusion, a game of words, abstractions, superficialities. We've cut ourselves off from our true nature, from the instincts that really move us. We deny the earth that made us, while striving after a divinity that doesn't exist."

Cray allowed himself a smile, a kindly smile directed at the man who had been, in some way, his friend.

"Now you've become one of us, Walter. You've become a person with a will and a mind and all the tormented conflict and narrow self-absorption attendant on such things. You've arrived, Walter. You're a man of the modern world at last. Congratulations."

Walter, dazed under this onslaught, comprehending none of it, merely nodded in stupid gratitude. "Thank you, Dr. Cray."

Cray laughed. Poor Walter.

"The point is," Cray said softly, "you're not what you once were. You've become unreliable, a random variable, capable of disrupting all the careful equations of my life."

"I didn't mean to," Walter said with the perfect genuineness of a child.

Cray sat on the couch, comfortingly close to the huge, stoop-shouldered man. "Will you take your medicine?"

Walter blinked. "I always do."

"No, this is new medicine. It's used only in very special cases, like yours."

"I'll take it, Dr. Cray."

"You haven't even asked me what it is."

"I trust you."

"Yes, of course you do."

"I trust you," Walter said again, more softly. "I think . . . I think you're the greatest man in the world. I think you're like . . ." He turned away, bashful in this moment of absolute sincerity. When he finished his thought, he was blushing. "I think you're like God."

Cray uncapped a vial and spilled a few small dark pills into his hand.

"I always wanted to tell you," Walter went on, his voice hushed with embarrassed reverence. "But I was afraid you'd say I was crazy. I mean . . . more crazy than usual."

"We're all crazy, Walter," Cray said without emotion. "The mind itself is our disease. We seek a cure. Now take your medicine."

Humbly: "Yes, Dr. Cray."

With the practiced skill of a lifelong patient, Walter dry-swallowed the pills.

"You'll be feeling tired soon," Cray said. "I'll let you rest."

"Don't go, Dr. Cray."

"No? Well, I suppose I can stay a little while."

As things turned out, Cray lingered in the room for hours, while Walter first blinked at his blurring vision, then clutched his belly in a spasm of pain. Finally Walter closed his eyes and slept.

Even then Cray maintained his vigil. He monitored his patient's pulse, observing the onset of bradycardia, the most common symptom of a digitalis overdose.

Walter's heart rate dropped below sixty beats per minute, then below forty, then became irregular.

At dawn his heart stopped. Supine on the sofa, his mouth open, head lolling, the big man shivered all over like a wet dog and lay still.

Watching him, Cray reflected that he was indeed like God, in at least one way.

He could take a life.

He remembered that stray thought now, as he crossed the grounds of the institute under the clean blue sky and the crisp peaks of the Pinaleno range.

He felt whole. He felt strong. He felt—

"Dr. Cray!"

Cray stopped.

He knew that voice.

Damn.

He looked down the long driveway toward the front gate, where a guard had detained a burly, bearded man of seventy.

"Dr. Cray, I *demand* to speak with you!"

The man's voice carried easily. Several patients were staring in his direction. An orderly pushing a woman in a wheelchair had stopped on the greensward, his gaze swinging between the unwelcome visitor and Cray himself.

"I know you can hear me!"

"Oh, hell," Cray muttered.

He would have to acknowledge this man, much as he hated to. Straightening his shoulders, he marched along the driveway toward the gate, where Anson McMillan, Kaylie's father-in-law, waited by his pickup truck, glaring at Cray through the wrought-iron bars.

McMillan had gray hair and a gray beard. He was all squares and rectangles—hard, blocky face, squat frame, wide shoulders. In his denim shirt and corduroy pants he looked like an aging cowhand, lacking only a lasso and a wide-brimmed hat.

Cray had expected him to return eventually, but not so soon. McMillan had visited the hospital only last week, immediately after Kaylie's arrest.

"Dr. Cray," McMillan said again, with dangerous courtesy, as Cray drew close.

"Good afternoon, Mr. McMillan." Cray kept his voice even. "What seems to be the problem?"

"The problem is that this glorified night watchman"—McMillan threw a contemptuous glance at the guard, who stiffened under the insult—"won't let me pass."

"Don't denigrate my employees, please," Cray said, reaching the gate at last and coming face to face with McMillan across the iron barricade. "Officer Jansen here is doing his job."

"His job is to keep me out?"

"I'm afraid so."

"Why?" McMillan barked the word, baring his teeth in a threat display. Cray thought he looked like an ape in a cage.

"Surely, Mr. McMillan, you don't need it explained to you. It's my policy to deny access to any visitor who might be reasonably expected to disrupt this hospital."

"I'm not here to disrupt anything."

"Your behavior last time suggested otherwise. Perhaps it's slipped your mind that you had to be escorted off the premises by several members of the institute's security detail."

"Slipped my mind—hell." McMillan chewed the

words and spat them out. "Don't talk to me like I'm a senile old fool."

Cray kept his expression blankly formal. "I'm merely explaining why Officer Jansen is under orders not to allow you readmittance to this facility."

"Damn it, I wouldn't have raised a ruckus if you'd acted sensible about things."

"Mr. McMillan, I know what's best for the patients treated here—"

"And visitors aren't what's best? Family?"

"You're not a blood relation." Cray spread his hands. "Frankly, given the circumstances, I'm surprised you care to see her at all."

"Well, I do." McMillan hesitated, then added in a gentler voice, "She needs to talk to someone."

"She talks to me every day. I see her for therapy. And there are nurses and orderlies to chat with, if she lacks company."

"That's not what I mean. She needs somebody who'll listen to her. Who . . . who believes in her."

"No, Mr. McMillan. That's precisely what she does not need. A sympathetic listener would only encourage the persistence of her delusions. What's necessary for her right now is a structured, supervised, carefully controlled environment." Cray found a smile, cool and calm, and unsheathed it like a blade. "I only want what's best for her, you know."

McMillan was not charmed. He took a step closer to the gate, and Cray could see his eyes, coal black, strikingly intense.

"What's best for her," McMillan whispered, "is a shoulder to lean on. That's what she's always used me for. We're close, her and me. She's like a . . . like my daughter."

"A daughter? She murdered your son."

McMillan was unfazed. "There were reasons."

"An odd thing for a bereaved father to say. What would possibly induce you to forgive Kaylie for what she did?"

McMillan brushed this question aside. "I didn't come here to be psychoanalyzed. I came to talk with her. You're going to let me."

"No." Cray shrugged. "I'm not."

McMillan's hands were large and callused, and when they squeezed into fists, they became blunt instruments packed with force, meaty hammers that could have opened Cray's skull in a cascade of blows, if not for the dual barriers of the iron gate and McMillan's precarious self-restraint.

A moment passed, and then the hands relaxed, weapons no more, and McMillan asked softly, "How long do you intend to keep me away from her?"

"Until she's ready to face her past."

"How long?"

"It could take weeks. Months. An indefinite period of time. There's no way to predict the length or efficacy of a course of treatment."

McMillan absorbed this, then rejected it with a shake of his shaggy head. "No, sir. Not weeks, months. I'll see her sooner than that. She's my daughter-in-law. She's family. I have an interest. I can force the issue."

"It would not be advisable—"

McMillan cut him off. "Screw what's advisable. I've been talking to a lawyer. He's the one who told me to come on over here and give you a second chance to be reasonable. Seeing as how you won't cooperate, we'll just have to go over your head."

"I run this institute," Cray said sharply.

"But you don't *own* it. One of these big health-services companies in Phoenix has got title. You're their hired hand, is all. And they don't like bad publicity, do they? I've been reading up on this place. Patient got beaten here last month, state government's investigating. Another patient, Walter somebody, died just three days ago."

Cray said nothing.

"That's not the kind of track record your bosses probably want to see. And now here I come—me and my lawyer—demanding action. You think they'll side with you? If they do, I'll go to the papers. I'll get a court order. I'll make a stink."

"I'm sure you will."

"No, I'm sure I *won't*—because it'll never get that far. They'll overrule you and let me in, pronto, just you wait and see."

"You're a determined fellow, Mr. McMillan."

"Damn straight I am, where Kaylie's concerned. Now one more time I'm asking: do I get in to see her?"

"I think not," Cray answered mildly.

"Then we'll do it the hard way. I'll be back."

"No doubt."

"Soon. Maybe tomorrow, if my lawyer can open the door to the corporate boardroom quick enough, and I'm betting he can. Good day, Doctor."

Cray watched Anson McMillan walk to his truck and swing open the door on the driver's side.

"Why are you doing this?" Cray asked suddenly, the question coming as a surprise even to him.

McMillan paused, half-inside the truck, looking at

Cray over the door frame. "Because she's not crazy," McMillan said. "She never was."

Cray was silent. He stood motionless as McMillan slammed the door and started the engine. Even when the pickup reversed out of the entryway and vanished down the road, he did not move.

"Some kind of nut, huh?" Officer Jansen said finally, for no reason other than to break the long silence.

Cray nodded. "Yes."

"Think he was serious about all that lawyer business?"

"Yes."

"So . . . what are we gonna do?"

"We'll handle it." Cray took a step back from the gate and repeated the words. "We'll handle it."

He turned and headed back toward the administration building. His mind processed the dilemma, evaluating options, ordering priorities, weighing risks.

McMillan could not be allowed any contact with Kaylie. She knew too much. She would tell him everything. And given what McMillan must know or guess about his son Justin's past, he might very well put the whole story together, then persuade the sheriff to take a fresh look at the case.

"Dangerous," Cray murmured, mounting the staircase of the administration building.

Yes. Much too dangerous.

Cray had not avoided arrest this long by taking chances. His survival instinct was finely honed. To save himself, he would do whatever was necessary.

There was only one way to defuse this latest threat. It was a course of action he disliked, one that carried risks and smelled of desperation.

He would dare it, though. He had to. And quickly, before McMillan returned.

Pausing at the front door, he nodded slowly, in silent endorsement of his decision.

Kaylie must die.

Tonight.

A shame, really. He enjoyed having her as his prisoner. He looked forward to their daily sessions, the intricate mind games he played with her. And he would have relished the opportunity to watch her for just a few weeks longer.

To watch her—as she finished going insane.

44

Kaylie, alone.

That was who she was. She was Kaylie now. She had always been Kaylie, and the rest of it was all lies.

Her head was buzzing again. Wasps in there. A hive between her ears.

Craziness.

She shuddered, hating the disorder of her thoughts. Was insanity a germ? Could you inhale it, like the flu bug, from an infected atmosphere?

She had not been crazy on the night of her arrest. She was sure of that.

But now . . .

No longer could she seem to keep her thinking straight. She had periods of sharp clarity, when she knew what day it was and how she'd gotten here, but there were other times—more and more frequently—when she was adrift on a raft of strangeness, in a calm yet angry sea.

Losing her mind.

Like last time.

Fear rose in her, a peculiar disembodied fear that clutched at her sense of self and made her small and helpless and not a person, somehow.

The fear was what she hated most of all.

The fear . . . and Cray.

Cray, yes. Hold on to that. Cling to the certainty of evil. Evil was something hard and real, and she could not lose herself wholly as long as there was one real thing in her world.

She blinked the fear away, and looked around her at the room where she had spent her incarceration. An isolation cell, they called it. Nicer, newer, than the one she'd had last time.

Back then, twelve years ago, they'd kept her in the oldest wing of the hospital, Ward C, and the rooms were poorly heated at night and the cement walls sweated during the day, and there were bugs, brown and shiny like scurrying pennies.

This room was better. It was clean. It had no bad smells. Its furnishings, though meager, were not the stuff of dungeons.

An improvement, yes.

But a cell nonetheless.

The room was small. She had paced it today—or last night? She didn't know. Time had blurred, melted. Hours were minutes were days.

But the room . . . Stay focused. Look at the room.

Small. Three paces by four.

A bed—just a cot with rubber sheets—rubber so that if she should wet herself, the sheets could be hosed clean.

Steel toilet in a corner, not hidden, no privacy, and any nurse or orderly who wished to look through the plate-glass window in the door might catch her squatting there. Cray himself might see her.

A shiver hurried through her body like a fever chill.

She hugged herself, rocking on her haunches as she crouched on the linoleum floor.

The round hole in the door was the room's only window. She had no view of the outside world. She never saw daylight. There was no clock, and they had taken her wristwatch. Morning was when the attendant came with a breakfast tray, noon was the lunch tray, evening the dinner tray.

A single chair rested in a corner. It was plastic, with wobbly legs and no armrests and no seat cushion. Cray used the chair when he came for their therapy sessions once a day.

And that was it. That was all there was for her—the bed and the commode and the chair where Cray sat, and the tile floor that was cold against her bare feet.

She had kicked off her slippers, but she still wore the blue cotton outfit they'd dressed her in, the uniform of the condemned.

For the first day—Wednesday, it must have been, the day after her arrest—she had been strapped face-down to the bed, and when the sedative wore off and she started screaming, they had wedged a rubber throttle in her mouth.

Then there had been nothing she could do except lie motionless on the waterproof sheets, hearing the howls from down the hall, waiting for the nurse to enter with the syringe.

Injections every day. Always in her left arm, now purple with bruises. Medicine, they told her. She wondered.

Cray had visited her on that first day also, Cray who had shown such solicitous concern while the nurse was present, but when the nurse was gone and he was alone with Kaylie . . .

Then it had been like last time, no difference at all, and she had known for sure that she was Kaylie again, Kaylie the scared teenager, Kaylie in pain.

Later, she had been set free.

A nurse and some orderlies had unstrapped her from the bed, leaving her at liberty within the room's close confines.

She believed it was three or four days ago that this modest emancipation had occurred. She wasn't certain, though. It might have been yesterday—or tomorrow. It might have been next month or a million years in the future.

You're in sad shape, girl, a voice said.

Anson's voice.

She'd been hearing him a lot lately. At first she had welcomed him. But now an unmistakable hostility had seeped into his speech, and he frightened her.

Everything frightened her.

The small room and the rubber bedding and the nurses with their needles and the screams from the far end of the ward and Cray, of course, always Cray, never forget Cray.

You won't be wriggling out of this, Anson said. *You're a wily one, sure, kept the bloodhounds at bay for twelve years, but you're done for now.*

"Done for," Kaylie murmured.

Got what you deserved, you vicious little bitch. Serves you right for killing my boy.

"Don't say that. . . ."

You killed my boy, and now you expect comfort from me? Rot in hell, whore. Better yet—rot just where you are.

Eyes shut, she drew her knees up against her chin and huddled in the tight knot of her pain.

If even Anson had turned against her, then there was no hope left.

45

Shepherd was at his desk, eating a chicken taco with too much sour cream, when his phone rang.

"Homicide," he said through a mouthful of shredded lettuce and cheese.

"Roy?"

He recognized Undersheriff Wheelihan's voice and took a swig of Diet Coke to clear his throat. "Chuck, what's up?"

"Just wanted to tie a few loose ends into Boy Scout knots. We found Kaylie's car, day before yesterday. It was parked on a fire road in the foothills near the hospital. Looks like she hiked to a ridge from there and scoped out Cray's house. We found her shoe prints in the dirt, and a pair of cheap binoculars in the car."

"What kind of car?" Shepherd asked, for no reason except curiosity.

"Chevy Chevette, real piece of crap, easily a couple hundred thousand miles on it. According to the registration, she bought it in Flagstaff two years ago. We would've found it sooner, but we thought she must have parked somewhere right off the road, so we had our guys going through the arroyos. Finally we had a chopper do a flyby, and the pilot spotted the car in the hills."

"Anything in the car?"

"One thing that was interesting. Notebook in the glove compartment. She was following Cray for about a month, and she kept a record of all the places he went." A chuckle came over the line like a dry cough. "Our man Cray gets around, it appears."

"Does he? Where?"

"Well, if Kaylie's notes can be believed, he visited a strip club on Miracle Mile. Maybe you know the place—strictly in your professional capacity, of course."

There was only one club of that kind in that district. Shepherd nodded. "I know it. Where else?"

"Bikers' bar in South Tucson, for one. I happen to have spent an evening there once, some years ago, definitely *not* in a professional capacity, and please don't ask me for any details. Fairly rough clientele, as I recall. I was glad to get out of there with my privates intact."

Shepherd's lunch lay cooling on his desk, long forgotten. "Doesn't sound like a place where a man like Cray would want to hang out."

"You never can tell about people, though."

"I guess not."

"I mean, hell, look at Kaylie's father-in-law."

Shepherd frowned. "What about him?"

"Didn't I tell you? He's dropped by our office three times since we informed him of Kaylie's arrest. You'd think he'd be happy she's finally back under wraps, where she belongs."

"But he isn't?"

"Far from it. He seems mightily pissed off, don't ask

me why. First time he comes in, he asks how they can hold her in the institute without an arraignment. So I explain to him that she's still under the original indictment, and she's being kept for observation to determine her competency to stand trial. He goes away, but a couple days later he's back."

"Why?"

"Seems he went over to Hawk Ridge, tried to get in to see her. They wouldn't let him. I think Cray personally nixed the idea. Said she was in no condition to receive visitors, and seeing Justin's father would only upset her."

"Makes sense," Shepherd said.

"I thought so too. But not him. He's red in the face, he's so ticked off. Keeps saying they're keeping Kaylie from him, and it's not right. Weird, huh? So I ask him, why would you want to talk to that little bitch anyhow, after what she did to your boy?"

"And?"

"He doesn't answer. He just asks me if I know any good lawyers. Which, as a matter of fact, I do. I told him about this attorney from Scottsdale who keeps a vacation home in Kimball, northwest of here."

"You said there were three visits."

"Yeah, he put on a repeat performance just this morning. Dropped by to thank me for recommending that attorney. Looks like he's hired the guy to help him force his way into the institute. He's obsessed with seeing Kaylie. Won't let it go. But that wasn't the weirdest thing."

"Then what was?"

"How he looked. He had Justin late in life, and he's maybe seventy now, but until this morning he could've passed for twenty years younger. Now it's like—like he was up all night crying."

"Crying?"

"Well, his eyes were red as hell. He said it was allergies. I don't know. He said to me, Kaylie's all alone in the world. She's got no folks—they died when she was growing up. No relatives by blood. There's only him." Wheelihan exhaled a deep, thoughtful sigh. "I just hated seeing him that way. Anson's always been a rock. Even when his kid died, he took it like a man. So why's he all teary-eyed now?"

Anson, Shepherd thought, noting the name. Anson McMillan.

"Well," he answered, "you said it yourself. You just never know about people."

"Isn't that the damn truth. Hey, I'd better let you get back to your lunch. I could hear I interrupted you."

The taco was cold by now. Shepherd figured he'd throw it out. "Okay, Chuck," he said. "Thanks for the update."

"Hey, thank *you*. After all the local coverage this case has gotten, the sheriff thinks he's a shoo-in for reelection. And since you're not around, he's showering his gratitude on me." Wheelihan laughed. "Sometimes it's better to be lucky than good."

Shepherd cradled the phone, then stared at the cold taco in its nest of wax paper, not quite seeing it, not seeing anything around him.

Cray had gone to a strip club, a barrio bar. No crime in that, but it seemed out of character, or perhaps Shepherd simply didn't know Cray's true character.

And there was Anson McMillan, showing a solicitous concern for the woman who'd shot his son in the heart.

Unusual name. There couldn't be more than one Anson McMillan in Graham County. Easy to find him. Easy, maybe, to get him to talk. . . .

"It's not your case, Roy."

The voice belonged to Hector Alvarez, who'd appeared at the desk without so much as an audible footstep or a snap of chewing gum to warn of his approach.

Shepherd blinked, wondering if Alvarez was psychic. "What?"

"Kaylie McMillan." Alvarez grinned. "I overheard you say good-bye to Wheelihan. And now I see the expression on your face."

"What expression?"

"That lost-in-thought, grim-determination, unfinished-business look. Last time I saw it, you were getting ready to run the sting that nabbed Kaylie. If you recall, I said to you at the time . . ."

"It's not my case."

"Right."

"Sound advice."

"But you didn't take it."

"Well, I'm stubborn that way." Shepherd rose and picked up the half-eaten taco. "You ought to know that by now, Hector."

"Roy." The smile was gone from Alvarez's face. "Just let it go, huh? The girl's guilty. She's a nut. She's in the crazy house, where she belongs. God's in his heaven, all's right with the world. And you got a full caseload."

Shepherd almost argued, but hell, Alvarez had a point. Didn't he?

"You hear me, Roy?"

"I hear you." Shepherd wadded up the wax paper and pitched his lunch into the trash. "And you're right. Really."

He meant it, too.

At least he was almost sure he did.

46

Ward B of the Hawk Ridge Institute for Psychiatric Care—the back ward, as it was called—was reserved for the chronically ill, the violent, and those patients known as forensic cases.

The latter cohort consisted of patients held for observation in advance of a criminal proceeding. Wally Cortland had been sequestered here in 1996 after he slit his mother's throat with a letter opener and blamed it on the Devil. In 1992, shortly after the old forensic ward—Ward C—had been permanently closed, Sylvia Farentino had made an appearance, on charges of poisoning her boyfriend with a cup of lye in the pancake batter.

There had been others, generally less colorful. Drifters arrested for vagrancy, whose thought processes were too disorganized to be called normal. Drug addicts whose brains had been perhaps permanently scrambled by PCP or crack. Petty criminals with IQs so low that it was impossible to determine if they were competent to assist in their own defense.

And now there was Kaylie McMillan. Murderess, fugitive, and the only patient ever to escape from Hawk Ridge.

She'd been away for quite some time. Now she was

back. But this time her visit would be briefer than before, and she would leave in a zippered bag.

Cray smiled at the thought as he used his passkey to open Ward B's exterior door. The door was steel, and like all ward doors it was key-operated on both sides. A turn of the passkey was required both to enter and to exit. This precaution ensured that no patient could slip past an inattentive nurse or orderly and simply walk away.

It meant also that any staff member who mislaid the passkey would be imprisoned in the ward until help arrived. Cray had no problem with this. A certain measure of fear kept the staff alert. And he was pleased to note that in the past ten years not a single key had been lost by any institute employee.

Antiseptic smells, common throughout the hospital, greeted him as he let the door swing shut. The floor and walls of each ward were scrubbed daily. Antibacterial sprays were applied to desktops and door handles. Every metal and tile surface gleamed.

He moved forward, past the alcove that led to the O.R., where nonpharmaceutical methods were occasionally employed on especially recalcitrant patients. Beyond the alcove was the nurses' station—a desk and a couple of folding chairs, a few file cabinets, and a closed-circuit television monitor that switched between two grainy black-and-white images of the ward's two intersecting halls.

The nurse on duty was Dana Cunningham, just beginning her three-to-eleven shift. A tall, large-boned woman, she was capable of wrestling a two-hundred-pound patient to the floor. Cray had always thought she bore a certain resemblance to Walter, though he was tactful enough to avoid making the observation.

He waved at her, passing the desk, and she stopped him by rising from her chair. "Doctor? May I speak with you a moment?"

"Of course, Dana. What is it?"

"It's about Kaylie McMillan."

"I'm on my way to see her right now. Her daily therapy, you know."

"Usually you're earlier."

"Well, there was Walter's funeral. And an unwanted visitor who required my attention."

"I see. It's just that I don't often have the chance to consult with you about her. I'm getting concerned."

"In what way?'

"The dosage she's on—it's really very high."

"Not extraordinarily so, for a loading dose."

"I'm seeing side effects. Tremors, agitation, restlessness. . . ."

Cray waved off this objection with a flutter of his elegant hand. "If we lowered the loading dose for every patient who exhibited those symptoms, we'd have a hospital full of unmedicated florid schizophrenics."

"But we may be *over*medicating in this case. And the treatment program doesn't seem to be having the desired effect. If anything, she's become more agitated over the past week. I'm told she refused her breakfast this morning, and at lunchtime she threw the tray at the tech who brought it in. She hasn't eaten anything all day. She's clearly decompensating."

"Well, then the dose should be increased, not reduced."

"We're already maxing her out. Doctor, what I

was thinking was, maybe we should cut back to eight hundred milligrams of chlorpromazine and forty milligrams of trifluoperazine. That still ought to be high enough for a loading dose. If her condition continues to deteriorate, we could try a different strategy. . . ."

Cray was growing bored. "I'll tell you what," he said smoothly. "Why don't we continue with the current dosage schedule today, and tomorrow we'll look at a reduction?"

Cunningham didn't like it, but she had sufficient sense not to argue. "Okay, Doctor."

Cray smiled. He had no concern about Kaylie's treatment tomorrow. For her, there would be no tomorrow. He would see to that.

"Fine, then," he said, and headed briskly down the hall, glad to escape a discussion that was, after all, not only irrelevant but premised on an entirely faulty supposition. Kaylie McMillan was indeed becoming more agitated and disturbed, but not as a consequence of any antipsychotic drugs.

She was not, in fact, receiving any antipsychotic drugs.

The vials used by the nurses for Kaylie McMillan's three daily intramuscular injections—vials Cray himself had mixed—contained no chlorpromazine, no trifluoperazine. They contained only methylamphetamine, the most potent amphetamine available, in an extraordinarily concentrated dose.

Speed, in street parlance. That was the medication dear Kaylie was on.

She had been taking the drug for the past week, receiving more than three hundred milligrams of meth each time she was injected by the unwitting nurses. Three injections daily. Nearly one thousand milligrams in total, day after day after day.

Methylamphetamine's psychotropic effects were gradual and cumulative. During the first two days Kaylie had been lucid. For that reason, Cray had kept her strapped down, with a bite block in her mouth. He didn't want her saying too much, raising doubts among the staff.

On the third day the drug had begun to take hold. By now it had taken nearly full control of her.

The symptoms of amphetamine psychosis were almost identical to those of acute schizophrenia. Kaylie was hearing voices, harsh and accusatory. The close weave of her thought processes had unraveled. She was scared, scared all the time.

Even the most experienced nurses and ward attendants would not be able to distinguish her behavior from that of a genuine psychopath. No one could doubt that she belonged here, in the ranks of the insane.

Cray reached the end of the hall and turned down the intersecting corridor. Rows of numbered doors passed him on both sides. Not every door was locked, even in Ward B, and not every room was occupied. Many of the patients, including a few who had displayed violent tendencies, were allowed to mingle with the others in the day hall, and to return in the evening, just before the lights-out bell.

The policy was humane and modern. Contemporary medical standards discouraged the practice of shutting a patient away in an isolation room. Cray accepted these standards. Hawk Ridge was not a prison, after all.

Except in Kaylie's case.

The institute would be her prison for the rest of her life.

Still, as matters had developed, she would not be a prisoner for long.

47

Kaylie heard him coming—the rapid clack of his hard-soled shoes on the corridor's tile floor.

A moan escaped her. She knelt on the bed, hugging her knees, waiting.

There was a soft thunk as a pneumatic bolt released, and then the steel door opened, and Cray was there.

"Hello, Kaylie."

That smile. How she hated that smile.

"It's so good to see you again," he went on, stepping inside, carefully leaving the door ajar. "I really do look forward to our daily talks." He came closer, studying her, then put on a sympathetic face. "I'm quite concerned about you."

This was too much to bear.

"Just shut up," she snapped, despising the childish petulance in her voice.

Cray made a tsk-tsk noise. "That isn't very nice."

Grinning, he sat in the chair, a yard away from her. She drew back slightly on the bed, wanting more distance between them.

"I hear you're not eating," Cray said. "You should. No matter what our emotional travails, we should always maintain our bodies at optimal efficiency. Our bodies are the only part of us that matters, in the end. Mind, ego, personality, all these pretty layers of decorative embroidery that we knit around the primal essence of our being—all of it is an illusion, nothing more. A kind of mask."

"The mask of self," Kaylie murmured, watching him with narrowed eyes.

Cray registered surprise with a subtle lift of one eyebrow. "You've read my book? How delightful."

"Didn't read it. I wouldn't—I would never . . ."

She had to take a breath. It was hard to speak in complete sentences. Her thinking was all cloudy. Her head ached.

"I'm disappointed to hear it. I'd hoped to include you among my readers." Cray leaned back in the plastic chair, and his smile widened. "Now, of course, there'll be no chance of that. No chance and no hope, Kaylie—no hope for you at all."

Such familiar words, an echo of her memories from twelve years ago.

Back then he had been a younger man than the John Cray who sat in the room with her now, a John Cray with a goatee and bright mischievous eyes. He had come in for therapy three times a week, and in each session he had told her there was no cure for her illness, no hope of improvement, and no chance that he would ever let her go.

And though she had been shell-shocked by trauma, though she had been numb inside and confused—even so, she had sensed the undistilled evil in him, and the hatred, raw and pungent. Only later had she thought to ask herself why he hated her, and why he was so desperate to keep her at Hawk Ridge, away from the outside world.

"You've been our guest for one week," Cray was saying quietly, hands folded in his lap. "Doesn't it feel longer? How desperately you must yearn for your freedom. For escape, Kaylie. Escape—a sweet dream, isn't it? Or perhaps not a dream after all."

This surprised her. It was not what she'd expected him to say.

"Why not?" she whispered. "Why not . . . a dream?"

"Because there may be a way out."

She tried to draw a breath, but her throat was tight, and she managed only a cough.

Cray rose abruptly from the chair. Smiling, he approached her. He reached out with one hand, and though she tried to retreat, he was too fast for her. With his long fingers he cupped her chin and tilted her head to face him.

"That's what you want, I'm sure. A way out. To flee all this, to be liberated. What's the alternative? Only to linger in this sunless, airless room for months and years and decades. And you know what will happen in that case, don't you?"

He bent lower, his eyes locked on hers.

"You'll go insane."

A shudder ran through her, a spasm of the fear that seemed to come out of nowhere at times and harass her. Involuntarily she shook her head.

Cray smiled. "No? You don't think so? But it's true, Kaylie. It will happen. It's happening already. Isn't it?"

He released her chin and stepped back, but even now she could not look away from him, because he had named it just then—named her real terror.

Not death. Death was nothing.

Insanity.

"You know I'm right," Cray said. "You've been hearing voices, haven't you? Perhaps seeing things that can't be real? You try to think, but your thoughts are all tangled. After so many years of telling yourself you're not crazy, it turns out that you are."

I'm not! she wanted to scream, but she heard Anson's low growl: *Who are you kidding, girl?*

Anson, who'd deserted her. Anson, who was in her head, calling her names like *bitch* and *whore*.

"You're losing your mind," Cray said, and Anson echoed him: *Losing your mind, that's for sure.*

"Not true," she muttered, and finally she found the strength to break eye contact with Cray. "Not, not, not."

Cray paced before the bed, remorseless as a shark. "Of course it's true. You're sliding into the precipice, and who'll save you?"

She squirmed farther back on the bed, until she was pinned against the wall, Cray before her, roving, roving.

"Will I?" Cray asked. "Will anyone? No one can save you, Kaylie."

At the foot of the bed, he stopped abruptly, his voice dropping to a hush.

"Unless you save yourself."

She listened, rapt.

It was so tempting to think that somehow she could save herself . . . that she was not powerless . . . that there was something, anything, she could do.

Cray folded his arms. "You're interested, I see. Good. Then let's talk about your escape."

She won't escape, Anson said cruelly. *She's right where she belongs.*

A new voice seconded the thought. *That's for damn sure.*

Justin's voice.

Oh, God, was he here too? Was he inside her?

He couldn't be. He was dead. She'd killed him. She'd shot him, watched him die. . . .

"You're a clever girl, Kaylie. You're good at getting out of a jam."

Which one was that? Anson? Justin?

No, it was Cray. Live and in three dimensions, not a disembodied voice. She focused on him, because he was real.

"Now you're in the worst jam of your life," he said, "and you'll need all your cleverness to see your way clear. Last time, as we both know, you escaped via an air duct. An air duct similar to that one. See it?"

Her gaze followed his pointing finger to a rectangular aperture in the ceiling.

"But that option's foreclosed in this instance," Cray added sadly. "I've told the staff to check the vent cover daily for any sign of tampering. Last time, as you recall, you spent many nights loosening the screws by hand. Such a slow, tedious undertaking. What patience and determination you showed. Admirable, really. But not to be repeated, Kaylie. We're more vigilant now. At the first indication that you've been at work on the vent, you'll be in a straitjacket—or strapped to the bed. Do you understand me?"

Kaylie nodded. She knew it was true. She'd seen the orderlies check the vent cover with a flashlight every morning since she'd been unstrapped from the bed.

"So you can't get out that way. As for the door, it's always locked, of course. And there's no window. No exit, then. Or so it appears. Still, there is one thing a clever girl could do to free herself from this predicament. Surely I don't need to spell it out for you."

Did he expect her to solve this riddle unaided? She tried to reason her way to an answer, if there was one. Vent, door, window . . . another way . . .

"Oh, but I forgot." Cray grinned at her with cruel solicitude. "Your brain's sick, isn't it? Then I guess I'll have to do your thinking for you. Well, consider."

He leaned forward, propping himself on the bed with an outstretched arm.

"We've had no escapes from the institute since you were our guest. But we have had one almost equally unfortunate incident."

Kaylie waited.

"The patient in question was a young man who found a most creative way to release himself from his torment. It involved a bedsheet, like this one here." Cray snagged a fold of the rubber sheet between two fingers. "And that vent I mentioned. The vent cover, with its metal grillwork, is quite securely fastened to the ceiling, and just high enough above the floor that if a person were to stand on the commode and loop one end of the sheet through the grille bars, then take the other end, take it and tie it in a slipknot around her neck . . . her slender, fragile neck . . ."

Kaylie understood.

This was the gift Cray offered her. It wasn't enough that he had put her in this room, ravaged her life, made her a pariah and a fugitive. No, he wanted to finish the task of demolition he had begun—to finish it not by his own hand, but by hers.

Anger cleared her mind for the moment, and she saw why Cray had allowed the nurses to unstrap her from the bed, the wheelchair. He needed her ambulatory, at liberty within the cell, so that no artificial restraint would prevent her from taking her own life.

"You fucker," Kaylie snarled, fury cresting in her like a hot, boiling wave.

"No need for indelicacy." Cray smiled. "I'm merely passing along a harmless anecdote—"

With a rush of hatred she sprang at him.

Her hands came up fast, fingers hooking into claws, taking him by surprise, and she caught him in the cheek and raked four deep grooves in his skin.

Cray shouted, a hoarse, inarticulate sound.

He had shouted in the desert when she sprayed him with ice to save her life. She'd hurt him then, wanted to inflict a new and worse hurt now.

She swiped at him again, but missed, and then he swung her around, pitching her sideways off the bed onto the hard shock of the floor.

She struggled to rise, couldn't, because already he was on top of her, straddling her hips as she lay prostrate.

Over her groan of panic she heard commotion in the hall, the nurse shouting, "Dr. Cray, are you all right?"

"I'm fine!" Cray snapped. "No problem, Dana." He struggled to catch his breath, then added in a softer voice, "No problem at all."

He released Kaylie and stood. She rolled onto her side, staring up at him. He was huge. He was everything evil in the world.

"Very well then, Kaylie." He had recovered his composure. She saw him grope in his pocket for a handkerchief, then wipe the threads of blood from his cheek. "You haven't lost the will to fight, I see. Or the will to live. You're strong. Stronger than I'd expected. But your strength won't help you. You'll die tonight."

"I won't," she whispered. "I'm not going to do it."

"Oh, I believe you, Kaylie. But that merely means I'll have to do it for you."

She pushed herself half-upright and studied him, taking his measure.

"You can't," she said finally, working hard to string words together, enough words to make her point. "There are . . . people around. They'll see."

"They'll see nothing. Leave the details to me. I've got it all worked out. In all honesty, I was hoping you'd oblige me by proving more compliant. But I was prepared for your intransigence. I'm always prepared, Kaylie, for any eventuality. Surely you've discovered that by now."

She was tired, suddenly. She couldn't fight him, couldn't bear to listen to him anymore.

"Go away," she murmured.

"Yes. I think I will. Enough therapy for one day. But I'll be back."

Cray moved toward the door, walking slowly, gracefully, in his liquid, leonine way. He was a stalking animal; why could no one see it except her? Why was the whole world blind?

At the door he stopped, favoring her with his insolent gaze. "You won't have to wait long, Kaylie. When night falls, I'll make my move. Some things are best done in the dark."

She found her voice. "It's not going to work. You can't get away with it."

"You know I can. And I will."

He left her, shutting the door. She heard the thunk of

the pneumatic bolt, a sound as final as the dropping of a casket lid.

He hadn't lied. She knew that.

Tonight, sometime after the dinner hour, when the patients were safe in their cells and the room lights had been dimmed, he would be back, and he would take her life.

48

"You'll say I'm crazy."

Paul Brookings smiled. "What else is new?" The smile faded as he saw the look on Shepherd's face. "Sit down, Roy. Talk to me."

Shepherd didn't sit. He was restless, and he needed movement, action. He paced Brookings' office, while outside, the late afternoon traffic crawled past on Stone Avenue. Five o'clock, the start of rush hour.

"It has to do with Kaylie McMillan," he said.

He expected the same reaction he'd gotten from Alvarez. Gentle ribbing, and a reminder that he had higher priorities. It had been his certainty that he would make a fool of himself that had kept him out of the lieutenant's office for hours, fighting the urge to discuss the problem, until finally he'd had no choice.

But Brookings didn't challenge him. He said only, "What about her?"

"It's not my case, right?"

"Is that a rhetorical question?"

"I guess so."

"Well, I've never been much for rhetoric, so why don't you just tell me what's on your mind, and why I ought to doubt your sanity."

The lieutenant said it lightly, with just the right blend of humor and understanding, and Shepherd knew he had underestimated the man.

He shouldn't have. He should have remembered how Paul Brookings had been there for him during the hellish days when Ginnie was hospitalized, and the still worse months after her death.

At the hospital Brookings had visited Shepherd and Ginnie every day. Twice he had stayed up nearly all night with Shepherd, the two of them sitting together in an alcove near a noisy freight elevator, Shepherd talking aimlessly, the lieutenant doing the work of listening.

The morning Ginnie died, Shepherd had called Brookings, waking him in the dawn twilight. Brookings had handled most of the details—paperwork, funeral arrangements—while Shepherd drifted in a mist of grief.

Later, there had been fishing trips, long walks, dinners at Brookings' house where Paul's wife, Chloris, served homemade, multicourse meals and soft music played.

Brookings had nursed Shepherd through the hardest part of his life. Of course he was the right person, the only person, for Shepherd to turn to now.

"Okay," Shepherd said. "Here it is. I talked to Chuck Wheelihan over in Graham County a few hours ago. He told me some things that got me thinking. I don't know why, really. It's nothing specific. But I can't seem to let it go."

"Not sure I follow you. The woman's under arrest. As I understand it, no one's ever disputed the fact that she killed her husband."

"No."

"And she accused her psychiatrist of being the White Mountains Killer. So she's clearly delusional. Right?"

Shepherd hesitated, and Brookings pursed his lips.

"Oh," the lieutenant said. "You think maybe she's *not* delusional."

"I don't know if I'd go that far." Shepherd felt himself backing away from his suspicions, which seemed so obscure, so insubstantial, now that they were on the verge of being stated aloud. "I don't know what to think," he added lamely.

Brookings was quiet for a moment. He played with a stapler on his desk. On the street below, a car's horn squalled briefly.

"This isn't like you, Roy," Brookings said finally. "When a case is cleared, you let it go. What's different now?"

"It just feels incomplete. But hell, you're right. I'm probably just getting carried away."

"I didn't say that."

"Forget it, okay? Forget I was even here."

He took a step toward the door. Brookings stopped him with a command. "Hold on."

Shepherd turned to look at him. The lieutenant clicked the stapler again, then raised his head to meet Shepherd's gaze.

"It's Ginnie," Brookings said softly, "isn't it?"

"What's she got to do with this?"

"A lot, I think. Maybe everything. You can't bring her back, Roy."

Shepherd stiffened. "I'm fairly certain I already knew that."

"Too late to save her. You wish you could. So you try to save the next one. You try to get all the crazies off the street."

"I don't really see where this is going."

"Sure you do. It's why you went after the McMillan woman so hard. Above and beyond the call of duty. You needed to put her away, because she was another Tim Fries. Another lighted fuse."

"All right. So what?"

"Now you're having second thoughts. But you don't want to admit it. You don't want to help her in any way. Helping her feels like a betrayal. Like you're letting Ginnie die all over again."

Shepherd didn't answer.

"It's not a betrayal, Roy."

"I don't know. Maybe it is."

"No. Take a look at this woman, Kaylie McMillan. Who is she, really? She's been on the run for years. Got no money, no home. Scared all the time. Looking for help. Maybe she's a psycho. Probably she is. Or maybe not. Either way, there's one thing about her we can say for sure."

"What?"

"She's exactly the kind of person your wife would have wanted to help."

Shepherd nodded slowly. He thought of Ginnie in her study, working on her Internet project to aid the homeless. He thought of her in the health clinic, welcoming the people of the street.

"That's true," he said, his voice low.

"It's only a betrayal if you don't help her. So go. Do whatever you have to do."

"I need to talk to Kaylie's father-in-law. He seems to think she shouldn't be locked up."

"Sounds like a conversation worth having. Just don't break any speed limits to get there."

"I won't." Shepherd felt lighter suddenly. "Thanks, Paul. Thanks."

"Just doing my job."

"I don't know if this kind of thing is part of the job description. Maybe you should've been a shrink."

"And give up a civil service salary? I don't think so. Now get going. Traffic's already getting bad out there."

Shepherd was at the door when Brookings added in a quieter voice, "And, Roy?"

He turned.

The lieutenant studied him, calm wisdom on his face.

"Caring about this woman," he said, "this Kaylie—that's not a betrayal, either."

There was nothing Shepherd could say to this. He left without a word.

49

The director's residence at the Hawk Ridge Institute predated the rest of the complex. It had been a farmhouse once, surrounded by fields of barley. The orchard beside the house had provided oranges and lemons, which the farmer's wife had put up as preserves in a small, tidy fruit cellar.

It was in this cellar that Cray now kept his trophies.

The stone walls were crowded with faces, all of them female, all beautiful in their various ways, and all embedded in rectangles of solid plastic, protected from decomposition.

Cray had developed the method of preservation himself, inspired by the phenomenon of insects in amber. He purchased thermosetting polyester resin—liquid plastic—from a biological supply outfit on the East Coast. When blended with a peroxide catalyst, the resin would gel into a hard, transparent mass.

He kept each victim's face preserved in a jar of formalin, like any wet specimen, until he was ready to make a permanent mount. A ceramic mold, lightly lubricated with kerosene, was used to contain the plastic. Cray put down a bottom layer of liquid resin and let it harden, then cleaned the face under running water, dried it, and centered it carefully in the mold. Then he filled the mold with plastic, pouring it on like syrup until the face was entirely covered.

Over a week's time, the plastic would polymerize at room temperature, sealing the face inside. Decay could not touch it. Its beauty was saved forever.

Finally the mold was removed—an easy task owing to the lubricant he'd applied and the slight, natural shrinkage of the resin as it set—and his prize was ready for display.

A woman's face, afloat in a crystalline block of plastic, a thing of eerie beauty.

Cray had become an expert in this technique over the years, as his collection grew. There were fourteen faces now. Every one of them, even those harvested a decade earlier, remained as fresh and vibrant as young life.

Cray stood admiring them now, in the sharp light of a ceiling bulb. He was still in his business suit, having descended to the cellar immediately upon arriving home from the office. There would be time to change clothes soon enough. First he needed a few moments with his trove of lovelies.

"Sweet," Cray whispered, scanning the eyeless faces, the smooth skin and parted lips. "Sweet."

He had known each victim's name when he acquired her, but such details were quick to fade from his memory. Now only Sharon Andrews remained real to him as a distinct person, and even her identity was gradually losing its sharp outlines in his mind. Soon he would know her only as the latest one, the blonde. He would recall nothing of her name or place of business. Already he had all but forgotten the news accounts that told of a young son she'd left behind.

But the hunt itself he would remember. His liberation from the ordinary, his mad steeplechase under the moon.

Those memories would not fade. Not ever. The first hunt, twelve years ago, remained as vivid in his thoughts as the most recent.

But on the first hunt, he had not hunted alone.

Justin had been with him. Leading him.

His guide. His mentor, in some ways. Most of all, his partner and soul mate, the only human being who had ever understood Cray, and the only human being Cray had loved.

Justin had loved him too. They had shared something—no, it was not sexual—something of the spirit, or if that word was too anachronistic for a new millennium, then something instinctual, a common inheritance in the blood.

Whatever satisfaction Justin had found in his brief marriage to Kaylie, it could not compare with what he and Cray had known together, on the one night when they ran free as wolves, chasing their prey through the White Mountains until they brought her down.

They had made a perfect team. Justin was a natural hunter, cruel and patient and starved for blood. A natural sociopath as well—Cray knew the type. The combination of an outdoorsman's skills and a killer's instincts had made Justin McMillan the ideal partner for John Cray—Cray, who had never killed anything other than the schnauzer, Shoe, which he'd strangled and secretly buried in the woods.

Except for that one incident, Cray's nearest encounter with death had been the dissection of corpses in medical school. But he had come to realize that he would have to widen his horizons if he were ever to grasp the full reality of his essential nature. Observation and analysis were useful within limits, but some things must be experienced firsthand.

Aware of the need to take this next step in his evolution, he had sought out Justin, befriended him, and persuaded the younger man that they could do great things together.

And so one night they'd gone cruising, venturing miles afield, until Cray spotted a female hitchhiker on a dark highway.

There's one.

Cray still remembered the tremor of exhilaration in his voice, and how he'd leaned forward in the passenger seat of Justin's pickup truck to point to the girl on the shoulder of the road. A girl disheveled, forlorn in the night, and utterly alone.

Justin had slowed the truck. *You're sure?* he asked, the question coming slowly but without the least quaver of fear.

Cray nodded. *She's perfect. She'll never be missed.*

The girl, still a teenager, had been wary of the two men who'd stopped for her. But preferring their company to the nocturnal desolation of the highway, she'd accepted the ride.

Later, when she realized her mistake, she had put up a fight, scratching and pummeling until Cray subdued her with an ampoule of sedative.

She awoke in the White Mountains, beyond the reach of help. The moon was high and nearly full, the ridgeline shiny in the light.

Cray hadn't made any sort of speech to her. On later occasions it would become his practice to inform the victim fully of the lethal sport that was about to be played, but on that first night he and Justin had exchanged no words with the girl, had not even acknowledged her confused questions and pleas.

They had merely shoved her out of the truck and watched her land sprawling in the brush, and then Justin had raised his rifle and fired a single shot into the air.

The rifle dipped, targeting the girl. No speeches were necessary. She understood.

And she ran.

By silent agreement Cray and Justin lingered near the truck for fifteen minutes, allowing the girl a head start. Then Justin said, *Let's go.*

Simple words. But packed tight with meaning, as richly crammed with all the potentialities of an unknown future as a bridegroom's utterance of *I do.*

What had followed was the greatest experience of Cray's life. He had always been staid, aloof, safely cerebral in his habits and predispositions. Even murder had come to him largely as an act of intellectual daring, the last link in a chain of propositions carried to their logical terminus.

But that night with Justin, the two of them racing in pursuit of the girl, Justin advancing with practiced confidence, Cray slower and less sure, stumbling on loose rocks, snagging his trouser legs on thorny brush, gasping to keep up—that night, when he and Justin hunted in tandem, a team of human predators, hot for blood, hungry for the kill—that night was Cray's awakening.

He remembered the chase as a dream of fury and

need, and high-pitched animal howling that was around him and above and below and inside him too, howling that was his own, because in his extremity of excitement he could not contain the instinctive impulse to bay the moon.

Later, Cray marveled at the changes that had come over him, the inexplicable madness that had consumed and redefined him. He could not understand it, but he knew it was real, and he knew there was no going back.

He had unleashed something in himself that would not be caged or killed. From his Apollonian torpor he had emerged into a Dionysiac frenzy, shedding inhibition, yielding to instinct, mad as a Bacchal reveler in the high hills of ancient Macedonia, wild as a lion. He returned from the hunt like Zarathustra descending from the mountaintop, like Rousseau's unspoiled savage. The mummy wrappings of intellect and culture had been peeled away, and there was only the predatory ape, living for the thrill of hot flesh and crunched bone.

When the time had come to kill the girl, Justin had let Cray do it. *Go ahead, Doc,* he'd said in his calm way. *She's yours.*

Cray had never heard an offer so tender. And then Justin had handed over his knife, and Cray, his hand trembling only slightly, had cut the girl's pale throat.

He had not meant to take her face. His first trophy was a product of pure accident. In cutting his victim's throat, he loosened the flap of skin over her skull, and remembering an autopsy he had witnessed, he had simply lifted the skin flap, peeling the face from its substructure of bone.

Justin had laughed in rare delight. *Man, that's a beauty,* he'd said. *You could hang that on the damn wall next to a four-point buck.*

Cray had given Justin this prize. It was only right that the younger man should keep the trophy, after Cray had been honored with the kill.

A generous gesture, but in retrospect—calamitous. Had Cray kept the trophy, Kaylie never would have found it. Justin need not have died by her hand.

And Cray need not have mourned the man who meant most to him, the one man who had mattered.

Well, there was no point in pondering such things. The past was fixed and final. Justin was gone, but Cray, alone, had continued their work. And he used Justin's knife—the sharp knife in its leather sheath—a knife for hunting, and better still for flaying the quarry when caught.

If events had worked out differently, he would have used that knife on Kaylie. Now that option was foreclosed. Her face would not be added to his wall.

A disappointment, surely. But he could live without that particular trophy. It was her life he wanted most, and her life he meant to take.

He patted the vest pocket of his jacket, reassuring himself that its secret contents were still in place.

On his way back to the office after his session with Kaylie, Cray had stopped in the hospital's storeroom, a repository for all varieties of contraband collected from the patients. Amid the haphazard assemblage of junk, he had found an unopened pack of Marlboros and a Bic lighter.

Tonight he would have need of them.

Tonight—less than two hours from now—he would

toss a lighted cigarette into the shrubbery outside the main door of Ward B.

There had been no rain since August. The brush was tinder-dry, easily ignited.

Once the blaze was roaring, he would barge into the ward, feigning alarm. Nurse Cunningham and the orderly on duty would fetch fire extinguishers and put out the fire.

Meanwhile, he would check on the patients upset by the commotion. But only one patient concerned him, of course.

He would enter Kaylie's room at 7:30, roughly half an hour after her last scheduled injection, when the methylamphetamine would have peaked in her bloodstream, rendering her most vulnerable to attack.

Agitated and confused, she would be easy to overpower. All he need do was pin her down, then slide a needle into her arm and pump in four milligrams of lorazepam.

A strong sedative, used on patients undergoing surgery. It would put Kaylie to sleep instantly.

No more resistance after that.

He would lash one end of the bedsheet to Kaylie's neck, hoist her up, then run the other end through the grilled vent cover and tie it tight. . . .

And let her dangle as breath was choked off by the sliding knot.

A peaceful death, really. Quicker and easier than Walter's. She would be unconscious for the worst of it. She would know only a moment of struggle against Cray's superior strength, then the stab of the needle and a numbing plunge of vertigo, then nothing, ever again.

He wished he could make it harder on her. He wished he could see her suffer.

But the important thing was that she would be dead, and when Anson McMillan showed up with authorization to see his darling Kaylie, he would cast his eyes on nothing but a corpse.

McMillan might well suspect foul play, but his accusations would be dismissed as an old man's dementia. To the rest of the world it would be obvious that Kaylie had hanged herself in her cell. And because it was obvious, no detailed autopsy would be required and no toxicology tests would be done.

No one would ever find evidence of amphetamine poisoning or a massive dose of sedative administered immediately prior to death. No one who mattered would ever suspect a thing.

"You cost me a great deal, Kaylie," Cray whispered to the crowd of faces that were his silent audience. "More than you know. Now you'll pay the price."

50

In the hall, the squeak of rubber-soled shoes.

Kaylie knew that sound. The night nurse, whose name tag read CUNNINGHAM, had left her station and was coming this way.

"Talk to her," she murmured. "Make her understand."

It won't work, Justin said coldly. *Nobody'll listen to a sad little piece of shit like you.*

Kaylie ignored him. She had to get the nurse to listen. Cray had promised to be back after nightfall, and although she couldn't judge the time of day in her windowless room, she knew from the crawl of hunger in her belly that evening had drawn near.

She had no idea how he would gain entrance, what subterfuge he would use, no idea how he would end her life and how he expected to cover it up. But she knew he would find a way.

Since Cray's departure she had not moved from the floor. Now she struggled to her feet, dizzy with the effort, while the voices of Anson and Justin blended in a singsong mockery of her failing strength.

Weak as a baby. . . . She's always been weak. . . . Running scared, hiding like a mouse in one cubbyhole or another. . . . Weaklings never last, not in this world. . . .

She staggered under the deluge of insults. For a moment she could only sway on unsteady legs, the room blurring around her.

Then she saw the nurse pass by the plate-glass window in the door, and a sudden fear that she had missed her chance drove her across the room in two steps. She pounded the glass.

"Nurse! Nurse Cunningham! *Nurse!*"

The shoes stopped squeaking. A momentary silence. Then with surprising abruptness the small window filled with Nurse Cunningham's face, a face both stern and sad.

"Yes, Kaylie?" Spoken through the glass.

"I need to talk to you." That was good, it had come out fine, it had sounded calm and lucid.

"Go ahead."

"Can you open the door?"

"I'm afraid not." Hesitation. "I saw what you did to Dr. Cray. That was bad, Kaylie. You mustn't keep misbehaving like that."

Cray? What had she done to him? Oh, yes, scratched his cheek—a few lines of blood, quickly dabbed up with a handkerchief.

"I need your help," Kaylie whispered.

The nurse tapped her ear impatiently, and Kaylie realized the words had been inaudible through the glass.

She repeated herself more loudly. "I need your help."

"We all want to help you."

"No, that's not true. Dr. Cray doesn't want to help me. He wants to kill me."

"Oh, Kaylie." No trace of belief in the nurse's voice, only a tired pity.

"It's true. I know it sounds . . . I know you think I'm . . . But I'm not."

She had been in this situation before, she was sure of it—insisting she wasn't crazy, warning of the danger Cray posed, and hearing only patronizing solicitude. . . .

The 911 call. Yes. This was like that.

Time had passed, things had happened, but nothing ever changed.

No one listened. No one believed. No one cared. No one could be counted on. No one anywhere, ever.

"It's *true!*" she screamed in a rush of uncontainable frustration, and suddenly she was beating her fists on the glass and weeping. "It's *true,* why won't anybody help me, what's wrong with all you people, what's the *matter* with you?"

"That's enough!"

Nurse Cunningham barked the command, startling Kaylie into stillness.

"Now," the nurse added more gently, "just get hold of yourself. I know what the problem is, and I've taken steps to fix it."

Kaylie heard this without comprehension. "Steps?" she echoed blankly.

"It's the medicine you're taking. It doesn't seem to work at this dosage. But I've spoken with Dr. Cray, and he's agreed to consider lowering the dose, starting tomorrow. That should help you, Kaylie. If it doesn't, we'll try something else."

Kaylie lowered her head, worn out. "He was lying," she said softly, no longer caring if the nurse could hear. "He knows I'll be dead tomorrow."

"You won't be dead, Kaylie. You're just imagining things, that's all."

"Don't let him in my room."

"Kaylie—"

"That's all I'm asking." She looked through the window again, trying one last time to reach the nurse. "Just for tonight. Don't let him in my room."

"There's no reason Dr. Cray would be visiting your room tonight."

"But if he shows up—don't let him see me."

"He won't show up."

"Don't let him see me."

The nurse looked away, fatigue written in the puffy flesh under her eyes, the slack muscles of her face. "Dr. Cray is the director of the institute," she answered tonelessly. "If he needs to see you, Kaylie, of course I have to let him."

No hope then.

No chance.

Told you, Justin chortled, but Kaylie barely heard.

"All right," she mumbled, surrendering.

"I have to check on another patient. Okay?"

"Go ahead." The nurse began to move away, when Kaylie added for no reason, "After I'm dead, you'll know he did it."

Nurse Cunningham frowned sadly. "Kaylie, don't think that way. It doesn't help you to get better."

"After I'm dead," Kaylie repeated stubbornly, "you'll know. *He* did it. Remember that. Will you remember that, at least?"

"Dr. Cray would never hurt you, Kaylie. He would never hurt anyone."

Kaylie sagged. She pressed her face against the glass, feeling its cold kiss.

"You bitch," she whispered. "Stupid, stupid bitch."

"I'm sorry," Nurse Cunningham said from what seemed like a great distance.

Kaylie didn't respond.

"Your dinner will be here shortly," the nurse added, as if this would make everything better.

"Don't want dinner."

"You need to eat. You had no breakfast, no lunch."

"Not hungry," she said, though she was.

"I hate to see you starve yourself, Kaylie."

Cray was going to kill her, win his final victory, and all this prattling idiot could think about was food.

Last meal for the condemned, Justin said.

Don't turn it down, Anson advised. *If you're not hungry, girl—we are.*

Laughter from them both.

"Shut up," she said weakly.

The nurse assumed the comment was aimed at her. "Fine, then," she said stiffly. "If that's the way you want to be, we won't bring you any dinner. You'll be ready to eat by morning, I'll bet."

There would be no morning. But Kaylie knew it was pointless to say so.

The nurse lingered another moment, perhaps expecting Kaylie to reconsider, but Kaylie was silent, leaning disconsolately against the door.

"Sometimes," Nurse Cunningham said finally, "I wonder why I even try."

Her shoes squeaked again as she stalked off down the hall. Kaylie heard her go.

It was the sound of hope retreating . . . fading . . . gone.

The nurse would not stop Cray. No one would stop him.

You're dead, girl, Anson said, and Justin added, *As dead as me.*

They kept talking, saying awful things.

Kaylie turned away from the door and stumbled to the bed and fell on it, her fist jammed in her mouth, her whole body shaking as she contracted into a fetal curl.

This wasn't happening. None of it was real. It couldn't be. Cray and Nurse Cunningham and this room and the bed with rubber sheets and the steel toilet in the corner—all of it—this cramped and dismal universe she inhabited alone—it was a fake conjured by her mind, a cell that existed in imagination only, and if she concentrated hard enough, if she wished very hard, like a child wishing for a visit from Santa, then maybe it would all go away and she would be free.

But she knew she could never be free, not really. There was no exit from this nightmare, no escape from Cray . . . except the one he himself had pointed out.

She lifted her head, blinking at the harsh overhead bulb in its wire cage, and then slowly her gaze traveled to the air vent in the ceiling, the grille fastened to the frame.

For a long time she stared at it while a thought took shape, a thought floating in space, offered for her inspection and approval.

Kaylie sat very still, contemplating that thought.

For once the voices were gone. There was silence inside her and around her, the hurricane's serene eye, and in that calm place she was herself again, at least for the moment.

She saw her situation plainly.

And she knew that there was only one way out. One plan that could work. One chance, and one hope.

Strip the sheet from the bed, then tie a knot . . .

A slipknot.

With a trembling hand she touched the rubber sheet. It was smooth and cool between her thumb and forefinger.

How would it feel, wrapped around her neck and drawn taut as she dangled, dangled . . . ?

"No," she murmured, "I can't."

But she had to.

If she didn't, Cray would come, and he would kill her.

Could she give him that final victory? After everything he had done to her, could she allow him the obscene triumph of taking her life by his own hand?

This new thought of hers was the only alternative, her only choice.

If she dared to do it.

If she had the will.

The strength.

Time for you to go, Kaylie, said a voice that seemed oddly familiar, not at all threatening—a gentle, persuasive voice. It took her a moment to realize that it was her own.

Slowly she nodded.

"Yes," she whispered. "It's time for me to go."

All right, then. Do it.

Now—quickly—before the nurse returned for the day's last injection.

Kaylie rose from the bed with a sleepwalker's unselfconscious grace and, moving fast but with no sense of strain, began to strip the top sheet from the bed.

"Yes," she was saying in a quiet monotone. "Yes, it's time. It's time. It's time, at last, for me to go."

51

Shepherd found Anson McMillan in an unfenced desert lot at the rear of his house, an ax in his hands, logs of mesquite scattered on the ground.

The sun was low over the Pinaleno range, the sky burning with fever. Shepherd had expected to find Kaylie's father-in-law indoors, perhaps fixing a leisurely dinner or nursing a beer in a frosted glass—not splitting mesquite cords while his lank gray hair dripped with sweat.

He watched the ax rise, then drop in a gleaming arc to bisect another dark brown trunk. Then he took a step forward and lifted his hand in a wave.

"Mr. McMillan?"

The older man wrenched the ax head free of the wood before looking up with unhurried curiosity. His face was square and tan, bristling with a silver mat of beard. He stood for a moment, the ax half-raised like a weapon, and then he remembered courtesy and lowered it to his side.

"That's me," he said, his soft, growling baritone traveling easily across the few yards of prickly pear and agave that separated him from his visitor. "To what do I owe the pleasure?"

"I'm Detective Roy Shepherd, Tucson police."

"Tucson?" McMillan digested this. "You helped arrest her, didn't you?"

Shepherd almost asked how he knew, then recalled that the local paper had given the story extensive coverage. Though he had not granted any interviews, his name had been mentioned.

"I did," he answered. "Now I've come to talk with you about her."

McMillan let the ax fall. He wiped his hands on a flap of his denim shirt. "What for?" he asked.

"Undersheriff Wheelihan tells me you're concerned about Kaylie. I'd like to know why."

"It's a long way to come, just to chat about a girl who's already locked up. You city cops must have a lot of time on your hands."

Shepherd took this with a smile. "Could be. It looks like you're putting your time to good use, anyway. Laying up firewood for the winter?"

"Hell, no." McMillan surprised him by looking at the cut logs in disgust. "I hardly ever start a fire. Got good electric heat. I'm doing this"—his shoulders slumped—"just because I need to work it off somehow."

"Work what off?"

"The frustration. My damn lawyer says it'll be a couple of days before he gets me in to see her. A couple of days. . . . Somehow I think that might be too long."

"Too long for what?"

"I'm not even sure. It's just a feeling I have. A bad feeling. And dammit, there's nothing I can do."

"There's one thing."

"Yeah. I can talk to you. Right?"

"That's it."

"I've said it all before. Years ago. Said it to the sheriff and to every friend I've got and to any soul who'll listen."

"But you haven't said it to me."

McMillan squinted at him, taking Shepherd's measure. Slowly he nodded.

"Okay, Detective. Let's go sit on the porch and watch the sunset like a couple of old ladies, shall we? And I'll tell it all again. I'll explain to you why I care so much about the woman who shot my boy."

The porch was up high, offering a good view of the desert around the McMillan house—a ranch house with adobe walls, resting on an acre of unincorporated county land west of Safford.

Shepherd had obtained the address from a phone book—as he'd expected, there was only one Anson McMillan in Graham County—and had tracked down the one-lane rural route after only a few wrong turns.

On the porch McMillan offered him a root beer, which Shepherd accepted out of politeness, though he hated the beverage. He sipped a little, swallowed it without a grimace, and set down the bottle on a hardwood table that had been hewed by hand.

Anson's hand, surely. The man's thick fingers were callused and misshapen from a lifetime of serious labor.

"So," Shepherd said, letting silence complete the question.

McMillan stared at the sun now kissing the rim of the mountain range, its harsh theatrical light ruddy on his face.

"To understand Kaylie," he began finally, "you first have to know about Justin. And about the guns."

"Guns?"

"That's what did it, I think. Or at least, what brought it out in him."

"I don't follow you, Mr. McMillan."

"Hell, call me Anson."

"And I'm Roy."

"Okay, Roy. That root beer cold enough, by the way?"

"Perfect," Shepherd said. He hadn't touched the bottle after his first reluctant sip.

"I love a good root beer. Takes me back. Well, anyhow, the guns. Thing is, my wife, Regina—may she rest in peace—never permitted a single gun in this house. That was her ironclad rule, and I went along with it, which marked me as unusual among fellows in these parts. Most of them would sooner die than give up their guns, or at least that's what their bumper stickers say. Me, though—well, I just never cared for the damn things."

Shepherd, who had seen what a gun could do in the hands of a drunk or gangbanger or a child, nodded slowly.

"So Justin grew up playing softball and washing the neighbors' cars for pocket money, and he never had a rifle to his name. Never went hunting. None of that."

Hunting. The word stirred a small, furtive anxiety in the back of Shepherd's mind.

He hunts them, Kaylie had said to the 911 operator. *It's a sport for him. He lets them go, and he tracks them, hunts them down like animals.*

"Now, I don't want to mislead you, Roy. When I

speak of Justin's boyhood, I don't want you to think he was any sort of angel. Guns or not, he did get into trouble. He hot-wired cars, for one thing. Got himself a rap sheet by the age of fourteen for joyriding around."

"Did he?" Shepherd said softly.

McMillan showed him a sly look. "Yes, sir. You're thinking of Kaylie, aren't you? The way she hot-wired a truck after she busted out of the institute twelve years ago?"

"As a matter of fact, I was."

"She learned it from Justin. Must have. He was chock-full of these special talents." The man sighed, releasing a great billow of breath. "I don't mean to make light of it. Fact is, matters got pretty serious for a while. Justin set a fire in the high school gymnasium. Might've done some real damage if the gym teacher hadn't smelled smoke and doused the flames with a fire extinguisher."

"Why did Justin do that?"

A lift of McMillan's shoulders. "Why does a cat play with a ball of string? For the sheer pleasure of it, I expect."

"Were there other fires?"

"None that were linked to him. There were a few, though, that were never explained. The Gilfoyles lost their mobile home in one blaze. Justin swore he didn't do it. Me and Regina—we wanted to believe him."

Shepherd had read up on the behavioral development of psychopaths. Fire starting was often one of the earliest warning signs.

"This sort of thing went on for couple years," McMillan said quietly. "Then a miracle. Justin straightened out. He quit the joyriding, the shoplifting—yes, there'd been some of that, too. But not anymore. He was a normal kid suddenly. Better than normal. Outstanding. Folks started saying that Justin McMillan, after a spate of hell-raising, had turned out all right."

"What happened? Why did he change?"

"There was no reason. Certainly nothing we did for him. It appeared to be just what I said—a miracle." Anson stared at the far mountains, their humped backs red with the ebbing glow of the sunset. "But maybe there are no miracles. Maybe he never really changed at all. Maybe he just pushed it down deep—that part of him—and it took a while to burrow its way back to the surface."

He took a long swig of his root beer, and Shepherd, out of courtesy, made a pretense of swallowing another sip.

"Justin graduated from high school, moved out on his own. He got a good job clerking in the hardware store. He was going to night school to learn the computer trade. You know anything about computers, Roy?"

"Not much. My wife was the expert."

"Was? You divorced?"

"She died."

"Sorry to hear it. My Regina's gone too. I visit her grave once a week and on holidays. Never miss her birthday. You visit your wife?"

"Sometimes."

"We all lose what we love, don't we? In the old country they have a saying about it. In the end, they say, the world will break your heart."

Shepherd watched the sunset's afterglow. He was silent.

"Anyway, Justin was learning all about computers. He had a future, or so we all thought. Then to top it off, he started dating Kaylie Henderson, who was, I believe, just about the prettiest girl in town. She was the quiet type, sort of aloof, and people got the idea she was stuck up. They were wrong. She was shy, that's all, painfully shy. You couldn't blame her, after the life she'd had."

"What do you mean?"

"You don't know? She'd had it rough, Roy. Her mom and dad both died in a car wreck back when she was ten years old. After that she was raised by an uncle who hardly gave her the time of day. She learned to keep to herself. She still does. She's never told me—I mean, she never did tell me exactly what happened on the day Justin died."

Shepherd noted the slip. He was unsurprised. No doubt Anson McMillan had stayed in touch with Kaylie for years. After her escape from Hawk Ridge, she would have needed cash, a fair amount of cash, to obtain transportation and lodging and a false identity. Someone had to funnel the money to her. Since she had no family of her own to turn to, Anson and Regina would have been her only hope.

"Anyway," Anson went on, "Justin proposed to her after six months' courting. They got married, both of them nineteen. Rented a house not far from here. We helped out with the rent money. Things were fine."

He paused, perhaps savoring the last good memories he had.

Then quietly he added, "Not long after he wed Kaylie, Justin got some new friends. Guys he'd met at the hardware store. They persuaded him to buy a rifle and take up hunting."

"You and Regina didn't object?"

"Regina did. I held my tongue. The sport's not for me, it's true. I can't see what pleasure a man can take in blowing some dumb animal's brains out. But there are those who like it, and I've known plenty of them, and mostly they're fine. Mostly. There are a few, though, who maybe like it too much. Like it in an unhealthy way."

"Justin's friends were like that?"

"No, not at all. Far as I know, they were decent fellows. Couple of them were Justin's age, and the others were older. They all were married, raising families, holding down honest jobs. They could go in for their weekend adventures and come back Sunday night ready for the next day's nine-to-five."

"Then what was the problem?" Shepherd asked, already knowing the answer.

McMillan tossed back another gulp of root beer, and then the answer rushed out of him in a spill of words. "Problem was Justin himself. He got a taste of hunting wild game, and it was like he was a starving man who'd gotten hold of a bone. The more he gnawed at it, hungrier he got, till he couldn't ever get his fill. Justin took to hunting in a way that wasn't natural, or maybe it would be fairer to say—wasn't civilized. It was more than sport to him. It was something ugly, born of the same wildness that had made him start fires and heist the neighbors' jalopies. He'd pushed it down, covered it over, tried to stamp it out, but some things you can't hold down forever. They come out in a new disguise, and worse than before. Not wildness anymore. Sickness."

Shepherd let a moment pass. A fly traced lazy loops

around his head, drawn by the root beer's sugary scent. He brushed it away.

"Sickness is a strong word, Anson," he said quietly.

"Then you tell me what to call it when a man starts drinking blood."

Shepherd blinked. "Say that again."

"He'd heard some hocus-pocus nonsense about how you could absorb the strength and courage of the animal you killed by drinking its blood. Heart blood, the richest kind. He came back from the woods one night with a gutted bobcat slung over his shoulder and his mouth stained bright red. Kaylie told me that one."

"So Kaylie saw it? Not you?"

"She saw it, right. And she saw other things too. She told me. Sometimes she cried when she talked about it. Justin had put up gun racks in the garage, and he'd hide away in there, seated in a folding chair, polishing the goddamned things, babying them like they were living creatures, while all around him were relics of the animals he'd killed—antlers of a mule deer, skull of a bobcat, hide of a javelina. He had this tape of Indian chants, which he played on a cassette player, the volume so high it would make your ears bleed, Kaylie said. And sometimes at night he would sit there stark naked, with candles lit, and take blood he'd saved from the hunt, blood in jars, and smear it on himself like war paint. . . ."

A shudder moved through him and escaped his body as a sigh. He looked toward the bruised patch of sky where the sun had been, moisture bright in the corners of his eyes.

Shepherd shifted in his chair. "Did anyone else see all this? You or Regina or anybody at all?"

"No. No one else." Anson sighed. "I know what you're driving at, Roy."

Shepherd said it anyway. "It's possible Kaylie hallucinated these incidents, if her mind was already unbalanced."

"Sure. That's what the sheriff and his boys told me too, after Kaylie shot Justin and got arrested for it. They said it must be all in her mind, and to prove it they went into the house and searched the garage."

"And?"

"They found Justin's guns and trophies, but nothing more. No jars of blood, no cassette tapes of Indian chants, not even any candles."

"That seems to undermine Kaylie's story, doesn't it?"

"They thought so. I don't. The stuff disappeared, I don't know how. But if Kaylie saw it, then it was real. I can't explain its absence. Well, I can't explain why owls hoot, or what makes the desert smell of wood smoke after a summer rain. There's plenty I can't explain, but I know what I know. The problem was never with Kaylie. It was Justin, always."

"If you knew all this, why didn't you get help for him?"

"Psychiatric help? Personally, I've never bought into that headshrinking stuff, and I still don't. But Regina had a different view of things. She talked to a doctor, for all the good it did. You've met the gentleman. Dr. John Cray."

Shepherd sat very still.

"Cray?" he said quietly.

"The Hawk Ridge Institute is the only psychiatric hospital in the area. It was the logical place to go. Cray was the director even then. Regina had a meeting with him. She told him everything about Justin—the car theft, the fires, the shoplifting, and now this new strangeness in his life, the hunting. She hoped Justin could be treated as an outpatient, but she was prepared"—Anson hesitated, the words painful to utter—"she was prepared to have him committed."

"Did Kaylie know about that meeting?"

"No. We never told her. She had enough to deal with as it was. Anyway, nothing came of it. Cray promised he'd consider the case. But he never called us, and when Regina telephoned him, he was always out, or so his secretary said."

"Why would he give you the runaround?"

A shrug. "I always figured it was because Justin didn't have any insurance. Goddamned institute needs to maintain its profit margin, after all."

"You could have tried somewhere else. There must be a few psychiatrists in private practice around here, or a psychiatric ward in a local hospital. . . ."

"Regina talked about it. I believe she would have found somebody, in time. But there wasn't time. Justin died too soon. Less than two months after Regina's meeting with the good Dr. Cray, our boy was dead."

Twilight had passed by now. The sun was long gone, and even the mountains had vanished. There was only darkness.

"Do you know why Kaylie shot him?" Shepherd asked.

"I can only make a surmise. Way I figure, Justin got crazy and violent, and Kaylie had to kill him in self-defense. She ran away for no good reason—she was in shock, not thinking straight—a scared girl, nineteen years old, out of her mind with panic. The cops caught her, and after that she was the one at Hawk Ridge."

"Under Cray's care."

"Yes."

"He treated her personally."

"So I was told." Anson looked at him. "You find some significance in that?"

Shepherd didn't answer. He studied the dark.

"Roy?" Anson pressed. "Just what are you thinking?"

Shepherd thought for a moment longer, then asked, "Do you know how we arrested Kaylie?"

"The newspaper said she was on the grounds of the institute. I don't know why she would go there. It's one of the things I wanted to ask her, but they won't let me in to talk with her."

"She was stalking Cray."

"Stalking him?"

"Following him around. Trying to break into his house."

"That doesn't make any sense. Why would she do that?"

"She seemed to think he was guilty of a crime. She wanted to prove it."

"What crime?"

"Murder. A whole series of murders."

"She never said—I mean, she . . ."

"I know what you mean, Anson. She never told you anything about it, in all the years you kept in touch with her."

"You know I can't admit to that, Roy. Aiding and abetting, they call it." He looked away. "But if she'd had any suspicion of such a thing, she'd have told me."

"Not necessarily." Shepherd hesitated. "Not if she thought it would hurt you."

"Hurt me? How could anything Cray had done . . . ? Oh. I see. It's not Cray alone you're thinking of. It's Justin."

"Possibly."

"You think Cray got hooked up with Justin somehow? You think after he met with Regina, he sought out Justin on his own and struck up some kind of unholy partnership?"

"I don't know what to think."

"It doesn't add up, Roy. Whatever else you think of him, Cray's smart. He wouldn't need Justin's help for anything. If he meant to kill somebody, he could do it all alone. What could Justin tell him?"

"How to hunt," Shepherd said, the idea taking shape in his mind in the moment he uttered it aloud.

There was silence between them, just silence and the dark.

"Yes," Anson allowed at last. "Yes, my boy could've taught him that."

Shepherd rose from his chair. "What's the fastest way from here to Hawk Ridge?"

"Take High Creek Road east and hook up with Highway Two-sixty-six. That'll take you to One-ninety-one."

"I'll get going, then. Thanks for the root beer."

Shepherd headed for the porch steps. Anson's voice stopped him.

"Roy. You going to talk to Cray? Is that it?"

"Not Cray. Kaylie. She has a lot to tell me, I think. She tried more than once already. I'm afraid I didn't listen." Shepherd took the steps two at a time. "This time I will."

52

At seven o'clock, midway through her three-to-eleven shift, Nurse Dana Cunningham headed down the hallway of Ward B to give Kaylie McMillan her evening injection.

An orderly walked beside her. Cunningham never entered the room of any violent patient without backup. This was a lesson she'd learned years ago at a youth facility in Phoenix, when a kid had gouged her cheek with the pull-tab of a soda can. She still saw the small puckered scar every time she looked in a mirror.

She didn't mind the scar. It was helpful. It was a reminder.

"McMillan's a tiny little thing," she told the orderly, "but she killed a guy once—her husband, I think. So watch her."

The orderly just nodded. Not a talker.

Cunningham's rubber-soled shoes squeaked on the tile floor, but otherwise the ward was quiet. Most of the patients—those who were permitted free run of the hospital's common areas throughout waking hours—were still in the commissary finishing dinner, or in the day hall watching TV.

A few of the hard cases lingered in their rooms, but

they were so heavily sedated as to be barely sentient. Well, at least she'd persuaded Cray to consider lightening McMillan's dosage.

At the door to Kaylie McMillan's room, she paused and, as a standard precaution, looked through the plate-glass window before entering.

Kaylie was there.

Hanging.

Hanging from the grille of the air vent, Jesus, hanging with a rubber bedsheet around her neck. . . .

After I'm dead, you'll know he did it.

Kaylie's words, less than an hour earlier. Not mere paranoia. A confused confession of suicidal intent.

Cunningham snapped a glance at the orderly, who was staring past her at the sight framed in the window. "Call security," she said, not shouting, the words precise and calm. "Tell them we have a suicide attempt. *Go.*"

The orderly ran for the nurses' station.

Cunningham found the latch button, depressed it with her fist, heard the release of the steel door's pneumatic lock.

Then she was inside, pushing the plastic chair out of her way and running for Kaylie in the far corner, Kaylie who was suspended near the steel toilet she must have mounted to reach the ceiling, her body swinging slightly, blonde head lolling to one side, her back turned, left arm drooping, and Cunningham grabbed her. . . .

Get her down, get her down. Still a chance to save her if her neck wasn't broken—and if she hadn't been hanging for too long. . . .

The noose was knotted under Kaylie's chin. Cunningham turned Kaylie toward her, groping for the knot, and she had time to see that Kaylie's right elbow was crooked close to her chest, her hand wedged under the rubber noose to prevent asphyxiation, and her eyes—blue eyes, pretty eyes—were open wide.

Ambush.

This one word bloomed in Cunningham's mind, and then Kaylie's two legs came up together, bending at the knees, and with two slippered feet she kicked the nurse squarely in the face.

Dana Cunningham was a large woman, horse-strong, but the double kick caught her off balance, and she went down in a swirl of vertigo.

Kaylie cast off the noose and dropped to the floor.

Cunningham snatched blindly at Kaylie's ankle, seized hold, yanked the girl to one knee. Got her, she thought with a flash of triumph, before Kaylie spun sideways and hefted the plastic chair and slammed it down on Cunningham's head.

Pain dazzled her. She forgot Kaylie, forgot everything except the orderly's name. *"Eddie!"* she screamed as Kaylie scrambled past her, out the door.

The orderly was still on the phone with security when he heard a crash from the far end of the ward, then Cunningham's cry, and he knew there was worse trouble than a suicide.

"Got a situation here," he said into the phone. "Sounds like—oh, *shit.*"

He saw her sprinting along the hallway, straight at him—Kaylie McMillan in her blue cotton trousers and blouse.

Behind one of the locked doors, some other patient

started a furious rant, roused to excitement by the activity in the hall.

The chief security officer was saying something over the phone, but Eddie didn't care. He dropped the handset and sidestepped away from the desk into the middle of the corridor, blocking the exit.

"You're not going anywhere, lady."

He was sure he could take her. She was only, like, five foot four, hundred pounds, and the drugs she was on ought to make her sluggish, dopey.

Then he saw her face, and there was fever in her eyes, something feral and inhuman.

She ran straight at him. He tensed for a collision. He wished he wore glasses. If she went for his eyes—

At the last instant his nerve faltered just slightly, and he stepped to the side and tried to tackle her as she blew past. He got both arms around her waist, spinning her around, slamming her against a wall, then felt a hot blast of her breath on his face, and he was fumbling for her wrists, fighting to control her hands before she found a way to hurt him.

Worried about his eyes, he forgot his groin, until she reminded him with a sharp knee thrust that bent him double.

"Fuck," he coughed. "Fuck . . . bitch . . ."

He took a swipe at her face, catching her cheek, and suddenly her fist came at him, and with a grunt of rage she shattered Eddie's nose in a rush of bloody mucus.

Pain dropped him to his knees. He clutched his face, amazed at all the blood, humiliated and angry and too dazed to do anything about it.

Distantly he heard her mumbling a low, repetitive chant, urgent and monotonous.

"Time to go. Time to go. Time to go. . . ."

When he looked up, he saw her retrieve something from the desk—the keys, damn—she needed the keys to unlock the ward door, which was key-operated on both sides.

As she tried each key on the ring, he lurched to his feet.

She spun, wielding the keys as weapons, their sharp teeth protruding from between her knuckles.

He thought of his eyes. "You win," he whispered, backing off.

The next key she tested was the right one. The ward door opened, and she ran outside, slamming it behind her.

Somewhere the distressed patient was still shouting, his cries ululant and surreal.

"Eddie . . . ?"

That was Nurse Cunningham, emerging from Kaylie's room far down the hall, a glaze of red on her forehead.

"She's gone," Eddie said, finding it hard to talk while breathing through his mouth.

"Well, chase her."

"She took the keys."

Without the passkey he and Cunningham were locked in, and to be honest, Eddie was just as glad about that. He didn't want to tangle with the McMillan woman again. She'd been pumped up, more than just crazy. It was like—hell, like she was on speed or something.

Cunningham registered his statement, then slumped against a wall. "Call them."

Eddie still didn't react, until the nurse fairly screamed the order.

"Call security, you idiot!"

Security. Damn. He still had the chief officer on the phone.

Eddie stumbled to the desk, found the handset dangling from its cord, and spoke four words into the mouthpiece:

"There's been an escape."

53

Cray pulled on his black slacks and shirt, then smiled at himself in the bedroom mirror.

Black. His favorite color. Camouflage for a predator.

Camouflage that was unnecessary tonight, of course—but he felt the need to clothe himself in darkness.

It had been months since he'd taken Sharon Andrews from the parking lot outside the auto dealership. The deepest part of him, the elemental self that announced its presence only in the dark, was restless for blood sport.

What he'd done to Walter had sated his urges not at all. He needed a worthy victim. Kaylie. That was the prey his blood required. And he would have her. In mere minutes, she would trouble him no more, ever.

He checked his shirt pocket for the cigarettes, the lighter. The only other item he would need was a syringe filled with sedative. Then he would be ready for this special kill.

With his hair combed back, his heart beating fast and steady, he descended the stairs to the living room. Mozart played on the stereo system wired throughout the ground floor of his house. He found the music relaxing, and he preferred to be relaxed before the start of a nocturnal outing.

The piece now playing was the *Requiem*. It had been composed as a tribute to things spiritual—the majesty of God, the highest aspirations of the human heart. In Mozart's era, so long ago, such notions had not yet been rendered laughable and quaint. People had believed, back then. They had yearned.

Cray knew better. He was a man of the new millennium. He believed in nothing but brute facts, measurable, reducible to numbers. He yearned for nothing high, great, or noble. He knew that Mozart's gift had been no more than the excited firing of neurons, his moments of highest passion merely a surge of stress hormones—adrenaline, noradrenaline, cortisol—triggered by electrical overstimulation of the brain. Cray himself could duplicate this neurological phenomenon quite easily, in the operating room adjacent to the anteroom of Ward B, where he sometimes performed electroconvulsive therapy on the most recalcitrant patients. By passing a hundred joules of voltage through a patient's two cerebral hemispheres, he could produce a storm of excitation equal to anything Mozart had experienced.

But he could not produce the *Requiem*. This stray thought, irritatingly provocative, teased him as he went into the den and turned off the stereo.

The house was silent, Mozart's hymn muted.

Cray was leaving the den when the phone rang.

"Yes?" he answered, hoping it was nothing important, impatient to get going.

"Sir, it's Blysdale." Bob Blysdale was the Institute's chief security officer, and he sounded nervous. "Got a problem. The new patient, the forensic case—McMillan."

Cray stiffened. Kaylie.

Was it possible she'd accepted his advice? Taken her own life? Part of him would be almost sorry if she had. Although it would simplify matters a great deal, he would prefer to take care of her personally.

"What about her?" Cray asked, proper concern in his voice.

"She broke out."

Cray heard this, but it made no sense. It was some sort of unintelligible message in another language, or a joke, or insanity.

"What?" he breathed.

"She ambushed the RN and a tech. Got out into the yard. She's on the loose right now."

On the loose.

Kaylie, on the loose.

The only successful escapee in his tenure as director of Hawk Ridge, and now again she was out, she was uncaged—and his plan—the fire, the fake suicide—it was all spoiled now.

She'd cheated him, the bitch.

He held his voice steady. "When did this happen?"

"Couple minutes ago, is all."

Then she hadn't had time to go far.

She could be caught.

Cray's anger vanished, replaced by a sudden warmth of good feeling. Every crisis, as the cliché had it, could be seen to represent an opportunity.

"I'll meet you and your men outside the administration building," Cray said coolly. "In five minutes."

"Ten-four. And, sir? Should I call the sheriff?"

"Not yet. We'll handle this on our own."

"She's a felon, sir. I think procedure—"

"On our own, Bob."

He slammed down the phone, then ran to the foyer closet. With all the repair work that had been done on his Lexus in the last week, he had felt it prudent not to keep his satchel in the vehicle's storage compartment. It was stowed instead in the back of the closet, behind an empty suitcase.

He hefted the satchel and swung it in one easy motion onto the sofa by the front window, then rummaged in it for his flashlight—a mini-flash with a red filter to preserve his night vision. He pocketed it, then searched further until he found his knife.

Justin's knife, originally. But Cray's, for the past twelve years.

The leather sheath, blood-spotted and worn with use, was as familiar to his touch as a lover's hand.

He slipped the sheath inside his jacket. There was nothing else in the satchel he could use. His burglar's tools were of no value in this situation, and his gun, the Glock 9mm, had no silencer. He couldn't risk firing a shot. The noise would travel for miles in the stillness of the desert foothills.

That was all right. He wouldn't need a bullet for Kaylie. Only the knife's keen blade.

He left the house at a run. Crossing the hospital grounds, passing the cemetery where Walter had been laid to rest a few hours earlier, Cray reflected that Kaylie would have been better off had she committed suicide, as he'd suggested.

A slipknot, a short jump, an instant's pain. Her death would have been quick that way.

Not now.

54

Bob Blysdale and four security officers in khaki uniforms were assembling before the entrance to the administration building when Cray arrived. He had sprinted the full distance from his house to the meeting place, four hundred yards, but he was not the least bit winded.

He was, in point of fact, invigorated.

"How did she get through the exterior door?" he asked Blysdale.

"Stole a set of keys."

"Then she has access to every building on these grounds."

"Sure. But you don't think she'll hang around, do you? I figure she'll try to find a way out."

"Quite likely. But how?" Cray was thinking aloud. "Last time she just climbed the fence."

She couldn't do that now. After Kaylie's escape twelve years ago, the perimeter fence had been topped with spear points and razor wire.

"She could try one of the gates," an officer named Collins suggested.

"Main gate's guarded," Blysdale said, cocking a thumb at the gatehouse, where the silhouette of a guard was visible in a lighted rectangle of glass.

"But not the gate at my driveway," Cray said. "It's how she got in the other night. It may be how she tries to get out."

"I'll send a man there, have him stand post."

"And the others should fan out, search the perimeter. She may be looking for gaps in the fence." There weren't any, but she wouldn't know that.

"All right, Dr. Cray." Blysdale sent Collins to watch the driveway, and then he and the rest of his men scattered to the four points of the compass.

Cray watched them go. The various assignments ought to keep them busy. But none of them would find Kaylie. That was his job, and his alone.

He was the hunter. She was his prey.

Running again, past the administration building, to the side door of Ward B, the exit Kaylie had taken.

He switched on the mini-flash, beaming a dim red cone of light at the ground. The grass had been trampled by too many shoes. Some of the guards might have rushed to this spot in the first frantic moments after the reported escape.

He moved farther from the door, into virgin ground. Here the grass was stiff and smooth. He detected no tracks, no spoor.

He drifted away from the building, not in a straight line but in a wide semicircle. Standard technique. When unable to pick up a trail, circle ahead in the hope of intercepting the tracks.

Cray walked in silence, his toes pointed forward to feel their way, each step taken with the ball of his foot only. He kept to a fast stride, arms swinging loosely, gaze sweeping the grass. Looking not for shoe prints alone, but for less obvious signs as well: scattered twigs, crushed leaves, clots of dirt kicked up by racing feet.

Justin had taught him all this. Justin had taught him so much in their brief partnership.

There.

A puddle of standing water, residue of the sprinkler system, which soaked the lawns each morning in the predawn dark. At the edge of the puddle, the partial impression of a shoe heel.

But was it Kaylie's? Or a false lead, a print left hours earlier by some wandering patient or groundskeeper?

Cray knelt, examined blades of grass flattened by the footstep. Bent but not broken, even now springing back. The track was recent.

It was hers.

Cray felt a twitch brush the corners of his mouth. He required an instant to identify it as a smile.

He stood. Looked ahead, following the direction of the print.

The wide expanse of the lawn was interrupted here and there by eucalyptus trees, some growing close together, others majestic in solitude. Small thickets of mesquite and purple sage glimmered in the starlight.

Cray let thought leave him, summoning instinct in its place.

A fleeing animal tends to take the easiest route, cutting through the widest spaces between the trees, avoiding thickets of underbrush that would impede progress. The hunter, seeing the lie of the land as his prey would see it, could sometimes deduce his quarry's line of advance.

The most direct and least obstructed path would have taken Kaylie McMillan on a zigzag run between a ragged colonnade of trees, bypassing any snarls of ground cover.

Cray followed this route, running hard, not bothering to look for other tracks. He knew that a hunted animal would normally proceed as far as possible along its original avenue of escape.

He stopped only when he reached a denser thicket of ground cover bordering a duck pond. In the scatter of bird droppings along the muddy shore, he found more shoe prints.

She had turned here. Turned south.

That was odd. The nearest stretch of perimeter fencing lay to the east. He would have expected her to head for the fence in search of a way out.

Instead she had veered in a different direction—back toward the buildings of the institute.

The last place she would want to go, or so it seemed. The administration building and the two active wards were staffed twenty-four hours a day.

But the other building, Ward C, the abandoned ward . . .

A person could hide in there. A person who had stolen a full set of keys, as Kaylie had. And she knew the building. It was where she been incarcerated during her first stay at Hawk Ridge.

Had she planned to conceal herself in the abandoned ward from the start? Or had she panicked after escaping, when she realized the guards would be called immediately and she would have no chance to find a way out of the hospital compound?

The answer didn't matter. In either case, she was in the old ward, hunkered down, a huddle of fear.

Easy prey.

Grinning fiercely, heart thumping with a familiar savage joy, Cray started running again.

55

The guard at the gatehouse took a long look at Shepherd's badge before handing back his I.D. holder. "You here about the McMillan woman?" he asked.

Shepherd leaned out the window of his idling sedan. "How'd you know?"

The answer came with a shrug. "She's the only escapee we've got at the moment."

It took Shepherd a moment to absorb this. "She escaped? Tonight?"

Another shrug. "Thought you knew. You said you were here about her."

"I want to ask her some questions."

"Our guys'll have to find her first. She busted out. Pretty hard case, that one—though you wouldn't think it to look at her."

"How long ago did this happen?"

"Ten minutes, is all."

If he couldn't talk to Kaylie, he would do the next best thing. "Where's Dr. Cray?"

"That, I don't know. In his residence, I'd guess. Want me to ring him up for you?"

Shepherd preferred not to give Cray any advance

notice of his arrival. "That's all right. Can I drive to his house from here?"

"Sure. Go straight to the parking lot, hook left on the maintenance road, and when you're past the utility shed make a hard right."

"Thanks."

The gate opened, and Shepherd pulled through, then followed the directions, driving fast but not recklessly, his thoughts racing.

During the drive from Anson McMillan's house, he'd had time to piece together a possible scenario, still hypothetical, quite conceivably all wrong.

But suppose . . . just suppose . . .

Suppose Cray was a killer, as Kaylie believed. Killers might be born or made—Shepherd had no opinion about that—but however they got started, there was always one critical moment in their development, the moment of transition from fantasy and speculation and preparation to the deed itself.

Now just suppose Cray had needed help with that step.

Shepherd could picture him as he'd been twelve years ago, a much younger man, a man who'd passed his time in classrooms and seminars, a man with soft hands.

A murderer in embryo. Evolving by degrees toward the final, fatal commitment.

How had he started along that path? With a man like Cray, his progress would have begun as an intellectual proposition. At least this was how he would have rationalized and justified any strange new emotions that invaded the cool sanctuary of his self-control.

We are animals at heart. The self is mere window dress-

ing. A mask, a false front. We hear about "mind over matter." It would be more true to say that the mind doesn't matter.

Cray had said that to Shepherd. The idea obsessed him. He'd written a book on it.

Shepherd had slept through most of his mandatory Philosophy 101 course in college. He was no expert in the subject. But he knew that Cray's viewpoint was grounded in a deep aversion to humanity, an aversion that could easily translate into contempt or hatred.

What a man hated, he might wish to destroy. But being soft and cloistered, he would not know how.

And then into his office comes Justin's mother, telling him of this son of hers, with his guns and his blood lust and his sick obsessions and his skills at tracking game.

The man Cray needs. The partner he has been seeking—seeking perhaps unconsciously, as the last missing piece of himself.

So Cray goes to Justin McMillan, feels him out. There are ways for a clever, manipulative man to gain the trust of someone younger and inexperienced.

He proposes an arrangement. They will hunt together. Justin will teach him to stalk and kill. And Cray—Cray will procure a more interesting quarry than any bobcat or mule deer.

Cray has the intellect, the talent to plan a crime and execute it without leaving clues. Justin has the practical experience at killing. Each completes the other.

And so they hunt. Twelve years ago . . .

In his investigation of the White Mountains case, Shepherd had compiled a list of possible abductees and other missing persons throughout southeastern

Arizona over the past fifteen years. There had been no fewer than four disappearances in the early spring of 1987, the proper time frame.

It was unlikely that Cray and Justin were responsible for all four cases. But perhaps for one. Just one.

And if Kaylie had found out? If she had learned that her husband had killed a woman, skinned her face as a trophy?

If she tried to go to the police, and Justin attacked her, and she shot him, then went into shock afterward, mute, helpless, entrusted to a doctor's care . . . ?

Cray's care.

Only a scenario, a sketch of what might have happened. All of it could be wrong. But if it was true, then an unforgivable injustice had been done to Kaylie McMillan.

And Shepherd, though unwitting, had played his own role in that injustice, and bore his own measure of guilt.

Cray's house appeared in the headlights. Shepherd braked the sedan and got out. At the front door he leaned his fist on the buzzer.

"The doc's not in."

Shepherd turned, saw a guard in khaki approaching from the shadowy foliage near the gate.

"Hey," the guard added, "I know you. You're the cop from Tucson."

"Right."

"I saw you here the night you collared her. My name's Collins. I always wanted to be a cop."

"Roy Shepherd."

"Yeah, I know. That was nice work, what you did."

We'll see how nice it was, Shepherd thought grimly.

"Any idea where Dr. Cray might be?" he asked Collins.

"Oh, probably out helping to look for McMillan." The guard shrugged. "I get stuck playing sentry at a goddamned driveway. Waste of time. She won't come here."

"No?"

"She'll try to go over the fence, like she did last time. But she won't make it. Security's tighter than it was way back when. At least that's what the older guys tell me."

Shepherd figured that he himself would qualify as an older guy in Collins' estimation. The guard must be all of twenty-two. "So you've been standing post for the last few minutes?"

"Yeah. No action. Maybe you can find Cray out in the yard. I can radio the boss and ask him about it."

Shepherd didn't want to give Cray any warning. "That's not necessary." He turned back toward his car.

"It's no problem," Collins said, eager to help. "I was going to do it anyway. I think Dr. Cray forgot something of his, which he might want."

Shepherd looked at him. "What did he forget?"

"His black bag. His medical kit, you know. He left it on the sofa. He'll need it if he has to subdue McMillan with a sedative."

"You were inside the house?"

"No, saw it through the window. Shouldn't have been peeking in, but . . ."

"Which window?"

"Living room. Right there."

Shepherd stepped to the bay window near the front door and looked in.

The sofa lay adjacent to the window, the black bag

clearly visible. It had been left open, the drawstring clasp untied.

He had seen Cray's medical kit on the night of Kaylie's arrest. This wasn't it. This was . . .

A bag. Kaylie's voice on tape came back to him. *A satchel. . . . It's got all his stuff, the stuff he uses to break into places and kidnap women.*

Shepherd's heart quickened. "You have a key to this house?"

"Dr. Cray's residence? No way. Nobody ever goes in there."

"Until now," Shepherd said, and with a thrust of his elbow he punched through a three-foot pane of the bay window, then swept the glass shards clear of the frame with his jacket sleeve.

"Hey, Roy—I mean, Detective—I mean . . ." Panic jumped in the guard's voice. "I mean, what the hell are you fucking *doing*?"

"I'm taking a look at what's inside that bag."

Shepherd climbed through the window, onto the couch, then grabbed the satchel and dumped its contents on a teakwood coffee table.

Duct tape, a glass cutter, a suction cup, locksmith tools, a Glock pistol with a spare magazine. . . .

It was true, then—what Kaylie had said. All true.

"Roy." Collins, at the window. "I gotta radio my boss about this. I'll lose my damn job—"

"I thought you didn't like this job. I thought you wanted to be a cop."

"Well . . . yeah."

"Then get in here. I need you to find a phone and make a call." Shepherd found Chuck Wheelihan's name in his address book and read off the undersheriff's home phone number. "Say I need some backup fast. All the patrol units they've got. But no lights and siren. They come in quietly. Okay?"

"Shit, Detective, what is going on?"

"Just do it."

Shepherd left the living room while Collins was still scrambling through the window.

The house was large. He had no time to do a thorough inspection. But he had to check out the obvious places.

Kaylie had told him to search the house, had insisted Cray kept his trophies inside. She'd been right about the rest of it. Maybe about this part too.

He made a quick circuit of the ground floor—den, bathroom, kitchen. The freezer held no surprises.

Garage? The Lexus was parked in there. He found some tools in a cabinet, cans of paint and other innocuous items on the shelves.

He stepped back into the alcove that led to the garage, then noticed another door. He opened it. Stairs descended into the dark.

A cellar.

Shepherd knew then. He knew even before he found the wall switch just inside the doorway and switched on the single, unshaded ceiling bulb.

I steal their faces.

Mitch's voice floated back to him, Mitch with his warehouse gallery of photo cutouts.

Shepherd walked halfway down the cellar stairs, looking at the walls, concrete walls streaked with mildew, and on the walls a series of unframed plastic blocks, transparent and smooth.

In each block, a woman's face.

Cray had preserved his trophies in plastic, sealed away from air and germs. Eyeless faces. Open mouths. Ragged edges where the blade had sliced through the tender flesh of their chins and foreheads.

The blade. . . .

There had been no knife in the satchel.

Cray had taken it.

He'd left the gun, because an unsilenced firearm was useless to him on the institute's grounds. But the knife he had carried with him when he left the house.

He needed it. He was hunting her.

Shepherd had turned to climb the stairs when Collins appeared in the doorway. "I talked to him. You didn't tell me I was calling the goddamned undersheriff. This better be—"

Then he saw the things in the cellar, and he blinked.

"They're not real," he whispered, "are they?"

"Cray's been busy." Shepherd reached the top of the stairs. "He still is."

He guided Collins away from the cellar door and shook him gently to get his attention. "Here's what you need to do now," Shepherd said. "Find your boss, the chief security officer. What's his name?"

He didn't care about the man's name. He just wanted the kid to start thinking again, to unfreeze his mind.

"Blysdale," Collins said after a moment.

"Good, Blysdale. Track him down. Tell him what's going on."

"I can hail him on the radio."

Shepherd had already thought of this—and had remembered how the satchel Kaylie left for the police had vanished before the squad car got there.

Cray had retrieved it. He could have found it only by monitoring police cross talk, beating the patrol unit to its destination.

"No," he said, "I don't want you on the air. Cray may be listening in. We can't afford to tip him off. Got it?"

"Think so." Collins nodded, then said more firmly, "Sure I do."

Shepherd patted his shoulder. "You'll be fine."

He moved away, toward the door at the rear of the kitchen, which led outside.

"What about you?" Collins called after him. "What are you going to do?"

Shepherd opened the door on the night, then looked back.

"I'll find Cray," he said, "and make up for a bad mistake I made . . . if I still can."

56

Ward C, the abandoned ward of the Hawk Ridge Institute, was a one-story building in the shape of an L, with a brick exterior and a flat roof and not a single window, barred or otherwise. Access was afforded by doors on the north and east sides.

When it had been in use, Ward C had been known variously as the barred ward, the violent ward, the forensic ward, the disturbed ward. The hard cases had been interred there. Kaylie McMillan, murderess, had been one of them.

She was here again, not a prisoner now, only a hunted animal, crouching in a tight cluster of fear on the tile floor of the corridor, precisely at the midpoint of the building, the bend in the L.

There was no light in the ward. She hugged herself in the utter dark.

Her garments had been scratched and torn by brambles and cactus spines. She was dirty, rank with sweat. Her hair lay pasted to her scalp in a dense mat. Nausea bubbled in her gut. Her teeth chattered softly, though she was not cold.

Perhaps she had intended to come to this place. Perhaps it had been her plan to hide here. Equally likely, she had come only because she sought shelter, temporary concealment, with no strategy, no longer range in view.

Whatever she had done, she'd had no conscious reason for it. Her last instance of rational planning had been the moment when she'd heard the squeak of rubber-soled shoes in the hallway outside her cell and had known the nurse was coming. Then she had slipped her head into the noose she'd so carefully prepared, wedging her hand in also to relieve the deadly pressure on her throat.

Everything that had happened since had been instinct, reflex, the blind impulse to survive. No thoughts. No identity. Only terror, panic, the brutal slamming of her heart against her ribs.

She had been a person once. A fugitive concocting aliases. Justin's widow. Anson's daughter-in-law. She had been someone real, an individual, all quirks and insecurities and self-doubts and loneliness and proud perseverance and determination.

All of that was gone now, just gone. Where the woman named Kaylie McMillan had been, there was only this dirty, exhausted, tattered, desperate thing, kneeling on cold tiles, hunched with fear, drawing shallow breaths that could not feed her lungs.

The voices, at least, had left her. Confusion and conflict had been banished. She had no alternatives to debate, no decisions to reach. She existed purely in and for the moment, without a yesterday or a tomorrow.

She would stay here, crouched like this, waiting like this, for as long as she had to, an hour or a week or a lifetime. She would never move, ever, until her heart stopped racketing in her chest and she felt safe.

From the end of the corridor, thirty yards from where she knelt, came a rasp of metal.

She looked up, her eyes straining in darkness.

There it was again—the noise—low but audible.

She knew that noise.

A sharper tremor passed through her, and a new squeeze of fear cramped her belly.

Hinges.

The rusty hinges of the exterior door, the north door, the door she'd unlocked with a key from the ring of keys she'd stolen.

Hinges creaking now as that door opened for a second time.

Panic impelled her upright, and she retreated around the bend in the corridor, and then she was running to the door on the east side, the only other exit.

A hard carom off a wall, and with a gasp she came up short against the steel door, yanking furiously at the handle before remembering that all the doors in the hospital wards were locked on both sides, and a key was required to enter or exit.

She had keys, they were in her left hand, and she fumbled with them, jamming one after another into the keyhole until she found the key that fit, then twisting her wrist clockwise.

The bolt, strangely loose, seemed to yield immediately, as if it had never been secured at all.

She tugged the handle again, pulling the door inward. Still it would not open.

Stuck.

Somehow the door was stuck, wouldn't open, and she was trapped in here, no way out.

* * *

Cray stepped out of the night into the north corridor of Ward C, then clicked on his flashlight. The red-filtered beam wavered over the tile floor and concrete walls, reaching halfway down the hall.

She was not within sight. But her tracks were. The prints of muddy shoes, tracing an irregular, panicky path away from the door.

He breathed in, out. There was a calmness in him, the strange calm before the gale.

He had her. She could not escape.

True, she had a passkey that would unlock the east door. But the bolt on that door had been broken years ago, and rather than bothering to replace it, Cray had merely ordered the door padlocked.

Padlocked from outside.

The door could not be opened from within, a fact Kaylie no doubt had discovered by now.

She could double back and run straight into him. Or hide at the farthest end of the east corridor and wait for his arrival.

Or she could scream. Scream for help.

He would like that. He had never heard her scream.

No one would answer her cries, if there were any. Screams were common on the grounds of the institute. The staff had long ago learned to ignore such distractions.

Cray turned and shut the north door behind him, then carefully locked it with his passkey.

Then he pivoted to face the corridor again and advanced, guided by a beam of red, into the beckoning dark.

* * *

Kaylie stumbled away from the door that would not open, her hands slapping blindly at the side wall in search of an escape route, finding the door to the last cell in the row, not a good place to hide, but the only place left.

The press of a button released the pneumatic lock. The door swung wide, and she slipped into the room, then shut the door and looked for a latch on this side, but there was none, because in rooms like this, patients were locked in. They could not lock others out.

In the mesh window of the door, a faint red light appeared.

Flashlight. Still far away, but growing brighter.

Cray.

He had turned the corner, rounding the bend in the L, and he was closing in.

Cray aimed his flashlight down the east hallway, alert for any blur of movement.

Nothing.

He scanned the floor. Her tracks, increasingly faint as the dirt was pounded off her shoes, disappeared a few yards away.

She must have run to the exit and found it locked. After that, she would have backtracked. But how far?

No way to tell. The only certainty was that she was hidden . . . and close.

Rows of closed doors lined both sides of the corridor. Rooms where patients had been domiciled—stalls for cattle, pens for sheep.

Kaylie had been kept in one of these rooms, many years ago.

It was right for her to die here.

He would take her face, peel it from the subcutaneous tissue that wrapped her skull, and in the flashlight's red glow he would display it to her, the bleeding mask—her own face, disembodied, the last thing she would see.

Later—tomorrow night, perhaps—he would bury her in the woods. She would never be found. Another successful escape, or so the world would think.

But first he had to find her.

Behind which door was his prize?

He moved to the nearest one, thumbed the button, aimed the flash inside.

Empty.

To the door on the opposite side. Same procedure. Same result.

There were twenty more doors. He would open them one by one. The task would not take long.

His sense of calm receded. A new force grew in him, wild and strong. A keening exultation.

He had known it before. On the hunt with Justin, and later, hunting alone. He had known it each time he tracked his prey in the sallow moonlight.

It was an inner heat, an excitement of the blood, a sudden rush of pure stimulation that sharpened his sight and hearing, even his olfactory sense.

He was a predator. And he knew in this moment—a transient thought, lost before it could be captured—but for one moment only, he knew that on those nights when he stripped bare the mask, the first mask he cast off was his own.

John Cray was nothing and nowhere. There was only the driving heartbeat, the itch of need, the flash and eddy of unfiltered sensation, and the knife, sharp as teeth, the knife and the urge to use it as he opened the next door and the next.

He lifted his head, and losing himself entirely, he bayed at shadows, a wolf under the moon.

Kaylie heard the noise, echoing on stone, on tile.

A coyote's howl. But not a coyote, of course.

Him.

Some answering panic rose in her own throat, and she nearly let loose a fatal scream that would draw him instantly to this room.

But that was what he wanted, wasn't it?

Not just her death.

Madness.

I strip away the mask, Cray had told her in the desert. *A human being is an onion, layer upon layer. . . . Peel the onion, strip off the mask, and what's left is the naked essence. What's left is what is real.*

First he took his victim's mind and spirit, and then, only then, would he take her life.

She understood all this, saw it clearly, and with a snap of altered perspective she came back to herself—not entirely, but enough.

She knew who she was. She was Kaylie McMillan. Not a hunted animal. She was a person. She mattered. She couldn't give up yet.

That howl again. Closer.

Cray must be searching each room in turn.

This room was last in line. Even so, he would not take long to reach it.

Kaylie backed away from the door, retreating into a corner, putting distance between herself and Cray.

She had keys. Sharp. She could fight him. Go for his face, his eyes. She—

Her hip banged against cold steel.

A commode, still embedded in the floor—invisible in the dark, its shape apparent only to her touch.

She'd stood on a commode like this on several nights many years ago, fumbling at the grille over the air vent, straining to loosen the screws that held it in place, with nothing but a strip of torn elastic from her mattress cover to improve her grip on the small, devilishly slippery screw heads. . . .

The job had taken hours, nights.

But now—

Keys in her hand.

A key could turn a screw.

Nearby, a steel door clanged. Cray was at least halfway down the hall.

She stepped onto the commode bowl's lidless rim, reaching blindly for the vent cover in the ceiling. Her fingers touched the grille, velvety with dust. Four screws secured the cover to the ceiling. She found the first of them and struggled to insert a key into the notch in the screw head.

The key was too big. Wouldn't fit.

Another door clanged, closer.

She tried another key, thinner than the last.

It fit. She wrenched her wrist clockwise, and the screw turned, loosening.

From the hall, a wild baying and another slam of steel.

The screw unwound another few turns and dropped into the dark.

Three left.

Not enough time.

She found the second screw and worked it free.

Glanced back.

Red glow in the mesh window of the cell door.

His flashlight, very near.

Another door swung open and crashed shut. She felt the vibrations through the stone wall as she fumbled for the third screw.

He was perhaps two doors away. Coming fast, too fast.

The third screw was caked in dust, hard to discover by feel alone, but she found it and jammed the key into the notch.

It wouldn't yield. It was implanted too tightly in the frame.

The door directly across from this room creaked open.

Cray would look in here next.

She gave up on the third screw, found the fourth.

It was loosely set in its hole, easily dislodged with a few turns of the key. She let it fall.

The door across the corridor banged shut.

She threw away the keys, and with both hands she reached overhead and grabbed hold of the grillwork, tugging with her full strength, and the vent cover, fastened by just one screw, shuddered and pulled free of the ceiling.

It clattered on the floor.

Red light in the room.

Cray, beaming his flash through the mesh window.

She didn't look back, not even when she heard the thunk of a pneumatic bolt retracting and knew the door had opened.

Into the vent, scrabbling, clawing for purchase on

the dusty metal, her legs swinging as she hoisted herself up and bellied in—grunt of exertion and blind panic—she was in the duct, prone in the horizontal shaft, but her legs still hung out the opening, and she squirmed forward, grabbing at the smooth metal sides of the passageway, pulling herself all the way in, and there was pain, pain in her leg, like biting teeth—knife—Cray's knife slashing her, too late, because with a final effort she hauled herself completely into the shaft and then she was plunging ahead.

She'd made it.

But not for long.

The duct trembled, groaning with new weight.

Cray, lifting himself into the hole.

Following.

Red glare behind her. The flashlight.

She shouldn't look back, shouldn't look back, but she did, and there he was, scrambling in pursuit, the flashlight in one hand, knife in the other.

She heard his fast, hysterical breathing, or maybe it was her own.

Forward. Go.

There was nothing for her then but a smeared impression of her elbows and knees in furious motion. Speed and panic and pure darkness ahead, red death behind.

She'd done this before—crawled like this, through this ventilation duct—crawled when she escaped from Hawk Ridge. Only then no monster had been chasing her, and she had crawled slowly, silently, afraid of being heard. Crawled to the midpoint of the ward, the bend in the L, where a vertical shaft intercepted this duct and rose a few feet to an opening in the roof.

Ahead she saw a faint fall of starlight, the roof exit, her one way out, her last chance.

Yards away.

Too far.

Cray was closing fast, and she wouldn't get there.

She kept going, terror drumming in her chest. She was all fear now, nothing but fear, as Cray was nothing but hunger.

He grabbed her ankle.

With a gasp of panic she shook loose. Drove herself forward, pawing at the shaft, her hands gummy with old dust, the light from the rooftop opening still too far away.

Behind her, Cray sped up.

He had her scent in his nostrils now, the flavor of a fresh kill tingling in his mouth, and with feral quickness he came on fast, chuffing hard, the flashlight abandoned, the knife bared like teeth, and Kaylie almost in range for the final, lethal pounce.

She crawled for the light, the exit, and then the light was gone, blotted out—she didn't understand how, and there was no time to think about it, because she heard Cray snarl, a low indrawn sound packed full of menace, the sound a dog would make in the instant before it leaped, and she knew he was tensing for the kill.

Directly ahead, something dropped into the shaft.

A human figure.

Twisting toward her—a man—and in his hand, a gun which rose for a shot he could not try, because Kaylie blocked the target.

"Take it!" he shouted, and he pitched the gun at her, a handgun, sliding along the shaft.

A gun that was just an illusion, like the man himself, a mirage out of nowhere.

Cray sprang.

The pistol completed its slide, spinning into Kaylie's grasp, and remarkably it was real—as tangible and solid as the gun that had killed Justin many years ago—and with the gun in both hands she twisted onto her back, face to face with Cray as he fell on her, and she fired one shot directly into his heart.

Cray shuddered all over. Kaylie looked up into his eyes in the dim ambient light, eyes that widened with sudden intelligence, the shocked awareness that somehow, impossibly, she had beaten him.

Then she saw darkness filling those eyes, a flood of darkness, extinguishing the light, and Cray saw it too, she knew he did. He saw the dark tide that was fast flowing in to wash him away, and for the first time he was frightened by the dark, afraid like a child, afraid and alone.

She saw all this, in the moment when their gazes locked for the last time, and then the last living part of him was devoured by the dark, and everything was gone from his eyes, forever.

Cray sagged, a limp, dead thing, the knife in his hand as harmless as a toy.

Kaylie let go of the gun. It clattered in the vent with a hollow sound.

She made no further movement. She couldn't feel anything, couldn't think.

"Kaylie?"

A familiar voice. She'd heard it before, but when? Oh, yes. On the night of her arrest.

It was Detective Shepherd's voice. He was the man

who'd materialized out of nothingness and saved her life.

She had no idea how he'd gotten here, no strength to ask. Later she would make him tell.

Later.

"Kaylie? You all right?"

He had crawled to her. Blinking, she looked at him.

"I'm fine," she said, as if it were a summer day and she had merely responded to a casual pleasantry. "Just fine."

He released a long-held breath. "Thank God."

"Cray's dead."

"I know. Let's get out of here."

"Cray's dead," she repeated for no reason.

"There's an exit to the roof." Shepherd took her hand, gently coaxing her forward, away from the dead sprawl of John Cray. "Come on."

She eased free of Cray's loose, boneless limbs. "I know about the exit," she whispered. "I used it to escape from this place once before. But . . . not really."

Abruptly she lifted her head, searching for Shepherd's gaze in the faint light, wishing to make eye contact, feeling suddenly that it was very important for him to understand about the years of running, the scared-rabbit hiding, the night dreams and daytime fears.

"I never *really* escaped," Kaylie said quietly.

Shepherd tightened his grip on her hand. "This time you did."

Epilogue

"How did you find me?" Kaylie asked.

It was ten days after the events at Hawk Ridge, and she was sitting in an armchair by the window of her hospital room, a book in her hands.

Shepherd stopped just inside the doorway. "No hello? That's the first thing you say to me?"

"Hello comes later. I have to know."

"Well, at the sign-in desk the nurse told me you were in Room Three-twenty-two."

"I meant that night, when I was in the air duct with Cray. You showed up and saved me. How?"

He smiled, circling the bed to approach her. The day was clear, the view through the window green and bright. He had not expected the grounds of Graham County's medical center to be so nicely landscaped.

"You mean nobody's told you in all this time?" he said, teasing her by withholding a reply.

"Nobody seems to know. I was in too much of a daze to ask you that night. The stuff Cray was giving me . . ." She put down the book and hugged herself. "I was half out of my mind."

"A thousand milligrams of methylamphetamine a

day would make anybody crazy." The smile slipped off his face. "How's your treatment coming?"

"I've gotten over the addiction. The withdrawal symptoms weren't too pleasant. But I can't really complain." She spread her arms to take in the room, with its sterile bedding and gleaming countertops, its private bath. "This place is a lot nicer than my previous accommodations—and I'm including the motels I used to stay in, not just Hawk Ridge."

"You have the room all to yourself."

"The institute's paying for it." She raised a mischievous eyebrow. "They'll be paying for quite a few things. That lawyer Anson hired is pretty darn good." Then she frowned. "You still haven't answered my question."

"First I'd like an answer to one of mine." He took a small manila envelope from the inside pocket of his jacket. "I want you to look at this." He unclasped the envelope and removed a photograph, then hesitated. "It may upset you."

"After all that's happened to me recently, I'm past being upset."

Even so, her hands trembled slightly as she studied the photo during a long, thoughtful silence.

"It's her," she said finally. "The one in the garage, twelve years ago."

"We thought it was. She's the only victim who disappeared in the right time frame. This is her yearbook photo, senior year."

"Who was she?"

"Rebecca Morgan. Age nineteen when she was reported missing. She was never found. She got into a fight with her boyfriend and went out to the highway to thumb a ride home."

"And Justin picked her up. Justin . . . and Cray."

"They must have."

Kaylie nodded slowly. "Nineteen. My age at the time. I wonder if Justin would've gotten around to hunting me before long."

Shepherd didn't answer.

"When I saw her," Kaylie went on softly, "she was only a face. Like a mask. A rubber mask. That's what I thought it was, at first, until I touched it, felt the texture. . . . Justin had preserved her with some sort of tanning oil, and pressed her between two plywood planks, like a dry leaf pressed in a book."

"Cray used a different method later on," Shepherd said, but she didn't seem to hear, and he knew she was not in this room, but in the garage of the house she'd shared with her young husband, the garage with its secrets, its insanity.

"I went in there," she whispered, "because Justin was always ordering me to stay out, mind my own business. I knew he was hiding something, and finally I couldn't stand it anymore. But I never imagined—until I found that . . . trophy . . ."

"And then he found you."

Her eyes closed briefly in confirmation. "He'd gone out that night, in his camouflage fatigues. Normally when he went hunting, he didn't return for hours, even days. I thought it was safe to poke around. But that time he came back only a few minutes after he'd left. He'd forgotten something, I guess. He walked right in on me—while I was holding it in my hands—that girl, Rebecca Morgan—her face in my hands—"

Shepherd stepped beside the chair and touched her shoulder gently. She managed a weak, faltering smile.

"I guess you were right," she said. "I guess I am still capable of getting upset. It's just that I've dreamed about it so often in the years since. Nightmares, awful ones. And seeing her picture now just brings it all back."

"I'm sorry. But we needed to confirm that last detail."

"I'll be okay." She remembered the photo she was holding, and handed it back without another look. "Anyway, I'm glad to know her name. For all these years she's been a mystery to me. She didn't live in Safford, did she?"

"Miles away. A whole different county. Justin and Cray must have been cruising far from home when they gave her a lift."

"That's why I never heard about her disappearance. If she'd been local, I would have known. As it was, I only knew she was some stranger Justin had murdered, and he'd kept part of her—kept it the way he kept the antlers and hides of other things he'd killed. And later . . . later I began to think he hadn't acted alone."

"Because the evidence vanished. There was nothing in the garage when the police searched the house."

"It was all gone. The girl's face, and the jars of blood, the tapes with Indian chanting on them—everything. So nobody ever believed a word I said. They didn't even listen." She shook her head. "If I'd been thinking clearly, I would have taken some of it as proof, gone straight to the police. But I couldn't think at all. After I shot him . . ."

The words trailed off, and for a moment Shepherd thought she wouldn't speak again, but then she lifted her head, determined to finish the story.

"I had no choice about it. He had backed me up against the garage wall, and he was closing in, and his eyes—I've never seen eyes like that, so wild and dangerous, tiger's eyes." She stared into some far distance, and Shepherd knew she was seeing those eyes now. "All I could do was grab a pistol off the gun rack. He always kept them loaded. I squeezed the trigger once, and it was so loud, the noise, and there was blood, a lot of blood, spraying me, my hands, all red. . . ."

Her fingers interlaced, her wrists twisting.

"After that, I lost it. I just went away somewhere, and whatever I did, I was only going through the motions. When they found me in the desert, I was on my knees, crying, and I couldn't say a word."

"You were in shock, Kaylie. That's all."

"I thought I was insane. And when I heard all the evidence was gone, I thought maybe I'd imagined the whole thing—that maybe there never had been any woman's face, that Justin hadn't tried to kill me, that all of it was in my mind, and I'd killed him, murdered him, for no reason at all. . . ." She took a breath, then added, "And Cray, of course—my therapist—Cray did his best to convince me that I was crazy. He told me I was a hopeless case, and there would never be a cure."

"When did you start to suspect him as Justin's accomplice?"

"Only later, after I'd escaped from Hawk Ridge. I

asked myself if there was any way the evidence could have really existed and then vanished. There was only one answer. Justin had a partner—whoever he was meeting that night. And when Justin didn't show up, his partner came to our house, found him dead, and cleaned out the garage so the police would find nothing incriminating."

"You still didn't know it was Cray."

"No. I was never sure. Even after I read about Sharon Andrews—how she was found in the river, found without a face—even then, I didn't know if Cray had been Justin's accomplice, or if it was someone else, or if I really was deluding myself about the whole thing. But I knew Cray *might* be the one. Because at Hawk Ridge he'd hated me so much. And why would he hate me, unless I'd killed someone who mattered to him? He's a loner—a lone wolf—but with Justin he found someone who understood him. Justin must have been the only person who ever meant anything to Cray. The one person he loved."

Shepherd realized he was still holding the photograph. He took a last look at Rebecca Morgan, smiling into the abyss of her future, and then he slipped the photo back into the envelope and fastened its clasp.

"Well," he said, "that wraps it up, I think. Case closed, after twelve years."

"I guess so. I guess. . . ." Then Kaylie lifted her head, playful annoyance furrowing her brow. "*Hey*. You're still holding out on me. The air shaft—remember?"

Shepherd shrugged. "It's getting late. You can wait another few days, can't you?"

"Tell me, or I'll get violent. I'm good at it. Ask that poor nurse I ambushed at Hawk Ridge."

He smiled, giving in. "It's less of a miracle than it might have seemed. See, I was looking for you. I knew Cray was on the hunt. Then I heard the noises he was making inside the abandoned ward. Animal cries, but it was no animal. I couldn't unlock the doors, didn't have any keys, but I remembered Cray telling me how you'd gotten out years ago through an air shaft. I figured I could get in the same way. I climbed to the roof, dropped into the vent—and saw you coming, with Cray right behind." He shrugged. "That's it."

She nodded, absorbing this. "Thanks," she said after a moment. "I just wanted to know."

Shepherd could hear fatigue in her voice, and he knew he ought to depart, but he lingered, reluctant to leave her.

"They letting you out of here soon?" he asked.

"Couple days."

"Then what?"

"I'll stay with Anson for a while. Don't know what I'll do afterward. I have to get used to thinking of a long-term future, not just living moment to moment, on the run."

"You'll handle it."

"Oh, sure." She hesitated. "I've been thinking I might try to find a way to help other people like me. People on the street, with nowhere to turn." A shrug. "I don't know how. But it's what I'd like to do."

Shepherd thought of his wife's computer, untouched for two years. Her project. A way to help people on the street.

"I might have an idea about that," he said slowly.

"Do you?"

"I don't know if you'd be interested. We can talk about it some other time. When you're feeling all better."

Still he didn't go, and suddenly he knew why. There was something he had to say, something she deserved to hear.

"I should have listened to you, Kaylie. That night when I put you under arrest, you told me to look in Cray's house. You told me."

"You thought I was a psycho."

"That's not an excuse."

Unexpectedly she smiled at him, a light and easy smile, girlish on her freckled face. "Roy, you're the first person, other than Anson, who ever *did* listen to me in all this time. Not to mention that you saved my life. So don't be too rough on yourself."

"I'll try not to be. And . . . thanks."

"Anson feels the same way, incidentally. He wants to have you over for dinner once I'm staying with him."

"I'd like that. I, uh, I'd like to see you again—if it's all right."

"Of course you can. You've got an idea for my future, remember? I want to hear it." Her smile widened. "I need all the help I can get."

Shepherd suddenly felt young, younger than he had since Ginnie's death. The world was new again, a burden lifted.

"Well," he said, "I'd better move along. You can get back to your book. What are you reading, anyway?"

He took a step closer to the table where the slim hardcover volume lay, and he read the title.

The Mask of Self.

Cray's book.

"I asked Anson to bring it to me," Kaylie said.

Shepherd stared at the book as if it were a spider. His voice was low and puzzled. "Why?"

"I wanted to understand Cray. I thought this might help."

"Has it?"

"Yes. I think so." She picked up the book and flipped idly through the pages. "Everything we ought to revere in people, he saw as an illusion. When you think that way, you shut off the best parts of yourself, and all that's left is the animal inside."

"He would say that's all there is."

"And look where it got him." The book thumped on the table, released from her hand. "We have to believe there's more to us than just instincts and chemicals. Even if we can't prove it, even if it's not even true, we can't live any other way."

The afternoon sun was golden on the desert when Shepherd drove back to Tucson. He let the highway flow under him, the Pinaleno range passing to the north, then dropping back as shadows lengthened.

Dusk would arrive soon, and the desert would stir with the prowling of the sly and hungry things that waited for the close of day. They were all around him, even now. They were always there, and always waiting. Sharon Andrews had fallen to one of their number, as had Rebecca Morgan and the rest.

Ginnie too. Shepherd tightened his grip on the wheel, thinking of Timothy Fries with his rusty knife and his insanity.

His wife had fallen in the same kind of fight, victim of the same darkness.

Instincts and chemicals. If Cray was right, if that was all Ginnie had been—all any of them had been—then life was only accident and pain, and the predators had won already, and would always win.

But perhaps there was something more. Something not to be lost, even in the dark. Something a knife's blade couldn't take.

We have to believe, Kaylie had said.

We have to believe.